W9-CLB-875

A STITCH IN TIME

For information on how to purchase Pocket Books in bulk at special quantity discounts, please contact: Attention: Corporate Sales Department, Simon & Schuster, 1230 Avenue of the Americas, 9th floor, New York, NY 10020.

For information on how individual consumers can place orders, please write to Mail Order Department, Simon & Schuster Inc., 100 Front Street, Riverside, NJ 08075.

For orders other than by individual consumers, Pocket Books grants a discount on the purchase of **10 or more** copies of single titles for special markets or premium use. For further details, please write to the Vice President of Special Markets, Pocket Books, 1230 Avenue of the Americas, 9th Floor, New York, NY 10020-1586.

For information on how individual consumers can place orders, please write to Mail Order Department, Simon & Schuster Inc., 100 Front Street, Riverside, NJ 08075.

A STITCH IN TIME

Andrew J. Robinson

POCKET BOOKS

New York London Toronto Sydney Singapore

The sale of this book without its cover is unauthorized. If you purchased this book without a cover, you should be aware that it was reported to the publisher as "unsold and destroyed." Neither the author nor the publisher has received payment for the sale of this "stripped book."

This book is a work of fiction. Names, characters, places and incidents are products of the author's imagination or are used fictitiously. Any resemblance to actual events or locales or persons, living or dead, is entirely coincidental.

An *Original* Publication of POCKET BOOKS

POCKET BOOKS, a division of Simon & Schuster Inc.
1230 Avenue of the Americas, New York, NY 10020

Copyright © 2000 by Paramount Pictures. All Rights Reserved.

STAR TREK is a Registered Trademark of
Paramount Pictures.

A VIACOM COMPANY

This book is published by Pocket Books, a division of
Simon & Schuster Inc., under exclusive license from
Paramount Pictures.

All rights reserved, including the right to reproduce
this book or portions thereof in any form whatsoever.
For information address Pocket Books, 1230 Avenue
of the Americas, New York, NY 10020

ISBN: 0-671-03885-0

First Pocket Books printing May 2000

10 9 8 7 6 5 4 3 2 1

POCKET and colophon are registered trademarks of
Simon & Schuster Inc.

Maps by Alan Kobayshi

Printed in the U.S.A.

To Irene, my life's partner.
Your nurture, encouragement, and unconditional love
make it all possible.

RAMAKLAN ROCK REDOUBT

North Flank   South Flank

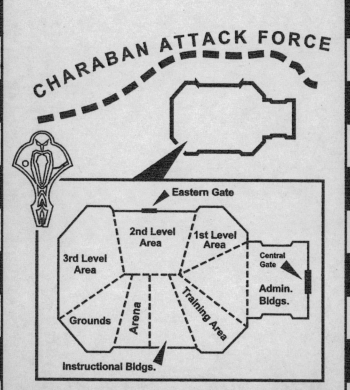

CHARABAN ATTACK FORCE

Eastern Gate

2nd Level Area

1st Level Area

3rd Level Area

Central Gate

Admin. Bldgs.

Grounds

Arena

Training Area

Instructional Bldgs.

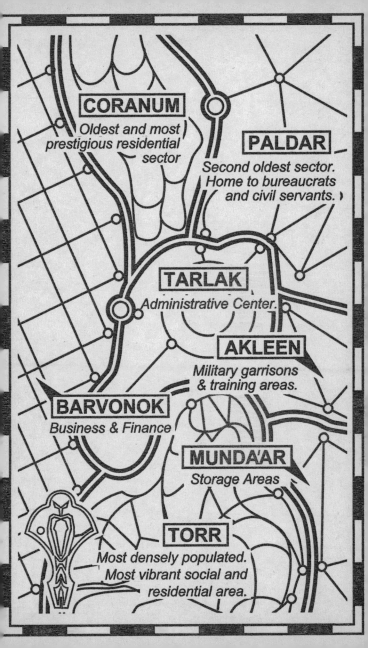

PROLOGUE

*"Of all the stories you told me, which
ones were true and which ones weren't?"*

"My dear Doctor, they're all true. . . ."

"Even the lies?"

"Especially the lies."

My dear Doctor:

Forgive my delay in responding to your kind communications. I wanted to give this modest chronicle I've enclosed a modicum of organization and update it before I sent it on to you. Thank you for your concern. I have thought of you often since our last meeting, and I am pleased to hear that your life on Deep Space 9 remains challenging and productive. Considering all the changes that have taken place I would have expected nothing less. And I'm certainly not surprised that your research proposals have been accepted. You're a brilliant young scientist—even if you are genetically enhanced. As for my life here . . .

It's the dust.

I can live with the rubble. I can live with the survivors who move like holographic phantoms and spend every waking hour scavenging for whatever will keep them alive. I can even live with the stench of the corpses that litter the broken streets, waiting in grotesque poses to be transported to mass graves.

But it's the dust that suffocates me and challenges my sanity. It clogs my nose, blurs my sight; my mouth is filled with a chalky paste that food and drink (scarce commodities) only thicken. We exist in a penumbral world where every shape and sound is blurred and muffled by this restless cloud of dust that refuses to settle and chokes my every breath.

Yes, Doctor, I have returned home. The only house I have ever known has been reduced to rubble. Fortunately, the little outbuilding in the back where Tolan stored his landscaping implements is still standing, and I've been able to clear a path to it and make a small place for myself inside. Indeed, as I write this, I am sitting here, the door open to make the space feel larger. It's an ironic view I command: the dust and rubble of the home of Enabran Tain, the man who attempted to destroy the Founders' homeworld.

The Founders have indeed exacted a Cardassian justice.

And then there's the added irony of my own homecoming, Doctor, and finding nothing but Tolan's tools and shed; an irony I think you will fully appreciate when you finish reading this recollection. Yes—I'm afraid you weren't expecting this response to your kind inquiry; it goes a bit further than "Greetings from Cardassia—Wish you were here." It seems I'm arrogant enough to believe this collection of reminiscences is something that may actually interest you.

I began writing it when I was first exiled to Terok Nor/Deep Space 9. It was an episodic and desultory effort chronicling my life on the station. Then last year, Captain Sisko invited me to join the initial invasion of Cardassian space—"the Battle for the Chin'toka System" as our Klingon friends trumpeted—an event I wasn't sure I'd survive. My fondest wish at that time, as you well know, was to free my homeland from Dominion tyranny. Because of this uncertainty over whether or not I'd survive, I found myself devoting more time and energy to this journal with the following result. And now, here I am, a survivor in a "liberated" Cardassia, a Cardassia haunted by the souls of the countless billions slaughtered, who have taken the collective form of this dust cloud that constantly swirls and shrieks across this wasteland, vainly searching for a peaceful place to rest. It's almost as if my homecoming was accomplished at their expense.

PART I

"You've come a long way from the naive young man I met five years ago. You've become distrustful and suspicious. It suits you."

"I had a good teacher."

■

To: Dr. Julian Bashir
Chief Medical Officer
Deep Space 9

Entry:

How odd you humans are. Or is it just the Starfleet people? Captain Sisko has just invited me to join the invasion—for which I am eternally grateful. The opportunity to liberate my homeland renews and animates my sluggish spirit. But the good captain makes no mention of the fact that this invasion is now possible because of the incident with the Romulans. I am simply to report to his office at "oh-nine hundred hours" with ideas as to where the Dominion defense perimeter might be vulnerable. Oh, our dealings with each other are nothing less than proper ("Mr. Garak," "Captain Sisko"), but what's so odd is that he pretends the incident never happened. And you and I both know how deeply affected he was by the whole business. Only when we exchange direct looks do I perceive a flicker of . . . what? Anger? Betrayal? Violation?

Odd people.

Humans seem to walk through life's infinite variety of

relationships and situations taking them all at face value. They rarely look behind the façade or the mask, where real intentions—the truth of our motives—live. And the fact is, more often than not they deny that they have any mask at all. These humans (and I do exclude you, Doctor—I will come to that shortly) believe that what they present to the world and, conversely, what the world presents to them, is the truth. It's this belief that makes them dangerous.

In Cardassian society, we are taught from an early age to mask all feelings and thoughts, to deflect all outside perception and observation. The objective of this education is to create a citizen who can work within the group to accomplish a group goal established by the leader, and at the same time work in such a way that none of the other members of the group knows what he or she is doing. As long as the goal is accomplished, it's nobody's business how you went about your work.

So why Captain Sisko is so upset with me because I accomplished the goal (which he established!) of getting Romulus into the war against the Dominion baffles me. And it's not because of the few lives that were sacrificed. Federation expansion has taken a toll in countless life-forms—about most of which they are blissfully unaware. The moment you step into a garden and begin to cultivate and prune, you become a killer. Perhaps the captain was upset because he had hesitated to do what was necessary to insure the integrity of *his* garden. Sentimentality is another trait that makes humans dangerous.

But why am I writing this to you, instead of waxing philosophical over one of our lunches? I see that overly polite smile, your "Get to the point, Garak" mask. Patience, dear Doctor. First, let me explain why I can exempt you from this human bondage to appearance and sentiment. Long before it was revealed that you were genetically "enhanced," I recognized in you an intelligence, a capacity for understanding that I found lacking in other humans. As much as the subject irritates you, you have not been so much genetically enhanced as "arranged." The people who did this to you had specific reasons, which you have long since outgrown. And having assimilated these changes you've accommodated yourself to this "arrangement" according to the demands of your life. For me, this means that in a sense you are more Cardassian than human. Which is why I am able to share this document with you . . . and why I sat down to lunch with you in the first place.

Before you cringe with horror at the thought of being a Cardassian, let me give you an example. Human memory is selective and linear. Simply put, a human remembers the best of times in progressive order, beginning with earliest childhood. The rosy memories are only challenged by nightmares. A Cardassian remembers everything on every level all the time. For us, past and present are not neatly separated. We live with everything in the moment—including the nightmares. And so do you. To a human this would be chaotic, unbearable. For us it's just the way it is.

This is one reason why I am addressing this recollection to you. Fate lines are converging, like memories to a dying man. I *need* to write this, Doctor, and you're the only person on this station who will understand. The invasion of Cardassia is momentous. Many will

9

die. If I don't survive, I want you to deliver copies of this to some people I will name at the end.

There's another reason. I know that we have grown apart and that's as it should be. We learn what we can from certain people, then we move on after we've taken what we need. When we learn nothing new about ourselves in a relationship that's when the relationship is over. Or it's over the moment when we're *afraid* to learn something new about ourselves. But what I have been learning about myself . . . whatever it was inside me that was sparked and challenged when I first met you . . . is deeply connected to this story. I'm an unfinished man, Doctor, like a suit of clothes hanging on a display rack waiting for the final touches that may never come; I need to tell this story to make a peace with those parts of me that were left unfinished. A healing. Indulge me, if you will; I need you as a witness. A stitch in time. . . .

2

Entry:

When I was at the age of emergence, I was sent to the Bamarren Institute for State Intelligence to begin my education as a security operative. This kind of education is usually reserved for children of the current ruling elite, but sometimes a child from the service ranks is identified as promising. I was one of those children.

My father was a maintenance foreman in charge of the grounds, monuments, and memorials of the Tarlak Sector, a majestic and ghostly place that commemorates the heroes of the Cardassian state. My mother was house-keeper to Enabran Tain, the man who owned the house we lived in, who worked at the Obsidian Order, the mysterious agency responsible for "state security." We lived in the basement apartment of "Uncle" Enabran's house, and my parents proudly identified themselves as servants of Cardassian public ritual and cleanliness.

It was always assumed that I would become apprenticed to my father. Many of my earliest memories are of preparing for and cleaning up after state funerals and dedication ceremonies. I was a serious little boy, assiduously carrying out my duties and responsibilities. I had to. Father was much older than Mother, and he never said much, but what he did say was always clear and to the point. Anyone who worked for him understood that if he had to repeat himself you would very quickly be demoted to maintaining the city's sewers.

Mother not only maintained Tain's house but also worked with him at the Obsidian Order. He was particular about who cooked and cleaned for him, and depended upon Mother for all his personal needs. I was never sure what it was he did; I just assumed he was important enough to afford a house and a servant. The Obsidian Order was housed in those days underneath the Assembly building, and it was years before I even knew where the entrance was. As a child I would go to the Tarlak Sector with Father, and while he supervised his crews I'd play by myself amid the black-and-white angularity of the monuments, imagining myself a great gul or legate giving the funeral oration for a fallen comrade. There was nothing about the Obsidian Order that inspired or excited my childish fantasies. Nothing but silence and mystery.

But Tain at home was anything but mysterious. It was not unusual for Uncle Enabran to appear and take me away on some excursion that involved a long walk through a section of the city. During these walks he'd test my awareness, and challenge me to describe a house or a person we'd just passed. If I hadn't been paying attention and couldn't remember the details, the walk was over and we'd silently return home under the oppressive weight of his disapproval. He also seemed to know how I was performing at school, and if he wasn't satisfied with my progress or behavior he'd punish me. I was a hard worker but I had a mischievous streak, and I enjoyed getting others involved in questionable activities and arranging it so they were found out and took the blame. On those rare occasions when I was caught, Tain would somehow find out and punish me—not for my misdeed, but for having been caught. And after he discovered my fear of small, dark spaces, his favorite punishment became keeping me in one until I had convinced him that I had analyzed and fully understood how my mischievous scheme had gone wrong. I found it odd that Mother and Father never had anything to say about these punishments.

One day, shortly after the emergent ceremony at school where I was acknowledged as a man, I came home ready to assist Father at the dedication of the Boltar War Memorial. I was surprised to find my parents at home with a stranger. They were never at home at this time of day, and we rarely entertained guests. They were very private people, and even discouraged me from bringing any of my schoolmates home. Both were clearly ill at ease with this man whom they introduced to me as an official from Institute Placement.

At first I thought I was in trouble, and my face must have reflected this fear because Father attempted to reassure me with a forced smile. But the uncharacteristic falsity of his behavior and his barely concealed agitation only made the situation worse. I had never seen him like this. Mother's face was a mask; it revealed nothing. She spoke as if I needed to clean off the day's work before we ate.

"Elim, it seems you have a sponsor. You are going to be placed at a prestigious institute. You leave today."

Just like that. Any kind of response was beyond me—I had no idea what this meant. I stood there, looking at the three of them looking at me and expecting some kind of reaction on my part.

"The Bamarren Institute," Father added, as if this was the vital and missing piece that would enlighten me. Oh I knew about the institutes. What student didn't? I knew that each student needed a sponsor, someone high up in the government or military who would recommend the student and guarantee his or her performance. And I knew that I had reached the age when students were moved on to their next educational level, the level that would determine their working lives. But those school-mates of mine who had been identified and assigned to an institute had known well in advance that they were going. And who the sponsor was. When I began to ask who mine was, Father cut me off.

"That's not your business, Elim. Your business is to get cleaned up and ready to go."

"His business is to serve Cardassia and the Empire in thought, word, and deed," intoned the official. "Your childhood is over, Elim Garak."

I was stunned. I wanted to ask more, I wanted to ask about the dedication ceremony that afternoon, but I didn't dare. Father had that look when one of the workers didn't get it right the first time. But what had *I* done wrong? Mother, as if reading my mind, suddenly turned to me.

"This is a great honor, Elim!" she said with a passion that startled me and belied her mask. I felt that it was anything but.

It was a long time before I learned the truth about my "sponsor."

3

You will be pleased to hear, Doctor, that I have volunteered to work with an emergency med unit in the City. Whenever people are found alive in the ruins, we are called in to administer aid and make sure that they can be moved to a medical facility. It's a miracle how some have survived for days, even weeks, buried under tonnes of collapsed buildings. Just yesterday, searchers detected life signs in the middle of rubble at least four stories high. When we managed to reach the survivors, we found a dead mother with her baby—who was still alive. Dr. Parmak, the unit leader, worked furiously to stabilize the little girl, and when she was evacuated by the transport unit he broke down. He's a very good man, this Dr. Parmak; he reminds me of an older version of you, Doctor. But what is again ironic is that Dr. Parmak was once marginally involved in an illegal political group, and when he was arrested, guess who was responsible for his interrogation? The man is anything but a coward, but his sensitivity is such that all I had to do was stare at him for four hours and he told us everything he knew. He claims that even today he has a hard time looking me in the eyes. I have asked his forgiveness, and he has been kind enough to give it. I hope the new Cardassia will have more people like him.

This morning I went to the Tarlak Sector and attended the memorial service for Legate Damar, and the dedication of a simple marker to his memory. When Kira and I were first assigned to work with Damar's resistance group, I had every intention of killing him at the first opportunity in revenge for his murder of Ziyal. But as we worked together, I came to understand that he was a true product of Cardassian militarism and devoutly believed in his duty. When Ziyal "betrayed" her father, Dukat, and chose to remain on the station, Damar saw that his superior officer was becoming unhinged and believed it was his duty to kill her. But Garak, you'll say, there's *no* excuse for killing a defenseless woman. And there isn't . . . unless you've been brought up in our system.

I also came to admire Damar's idealism, which led him to renounce his allegiance to the Dominion. If he had one weakness it was his propensity for long-winded speeches. But given the fact that none of us are perfect, the man would have made a fine leader.

As I stood at the memorial service, I thought about all the grand affairs I had witnessed here when I was a boy. None of our famed heroes and statesmen has ever had such a humble service—and none of them, from Tret Akleen on, deserved more than Corat Damar.

I also thought about this Cardassian sense of duty and

how it is largely responsible for bringing those of us who are left to these current circumstances. I asked Dr. Parmak how an entire people can come under the sway of this duty and blindly give allegiance to a state that goes mad and murders its own children.

"Poisonous pedagogy, Elim," he replied. "We believe what we are taught."

4

Entry:

The Bamarren Institute is located in the highlands adjacent to the Mekar Wilderness, a hot and arid area with sublimely beautiful rock formations and an endless network of subterranean caverns. At first the landscape was foreign, even threatening to my city mind and body. The seemingly endless skies and empty vistas—empty, that is, of man-made incursions—made me anxious.

The Institute itself also made me anxious. Every waking moment was planned and accounted for. The Cardassian educational system is dedicated to the ideal that each generation needs a coterie of leadership, an elite in every segment of society. Artists, soldiers, politicians, scholars, and business and tradespeople all have appropriate Institutes where they are sent at the age of emergence. At that point, he or she is "identified" and assigned to live and study apart from family and home for nine years.

The course of study is divided into three progressive levels; every three years, one either advances from one level to the next or returns to serve society in a necessary but relatively humble position. If a person makes it through and completes the Third Level, he or she is then placed in the ruling vanguard of that segment.

My first day set the tone for my new life. After the orientation for the incoming students at which the First Prefect, the head of the Institute, likened us to the "missing pieces of the mosaic of Cardassian civilization," the adults handed us over to upper-level students who promptly separated us according to gender, stripped us of all personal possessions, gave us our scratchy, drab uniforms (Swamp green and black; is it any wonder I ended up a tailor?), and assigned us to living quarters consisting of ten narrow beds each connected to a private compartment for our few belongings, and an adjoining tiled room for hygiene. For the next three years, with the exception of our instructional docents, we rarely came into contact with adults. My childhood was indeed over.

I was assigned to the Lubak Group, Level One, and my numerical designation was Ten. From that moment I was no longer Elim Garak but Ten Lubak, and we were sternly warned never to refer to ourselves or to each other by anything other than this number/group designation. We were the "missing pieces"—and in order to find our place in the mosaic of civilized society, we had to be broken down and reconstructed from the bottom up.

"Ten Lubak!"

And the person who began this restructuring process was our section leader, One Tarnal, a physically powerful Third Level individual with a thick neck and close-set eyes.

"Y-yes?"

"Yes, section leader!"

I was instructed to go to the stockroom and bring back implements for cleaning the hygiene chamber. After he gave me directions, he told me that I could take as many of my section mates as I wished to accompany me. I was somewhat confused by the offer, but I thought it was a test of my self-reliance and replied that I could handle the errand by myself.

"Then go!"

After wandering through what seemed like a labyrinthine maze, in which I saw other new students on similar errands, I finally found the stockroom. The door opened, and a student my age came stumbling out with cleaning equipment, looking very untidy. He gave me a quick and fearful glance before he disappeared down the corridor. He should be punished for his appearance, I thought.

"Next!" A distinctive and gruff voice shouted from within. I entered and was surprised by the enveloping darkness.

"Hello . . . ?" I hesitated, afraid of stumbling into something.

"Did you come alone?" The Gruff Voice asked.

"Yes, I came for the . . ." Before I could finish, a hand grabbed me by the hair and the lights went on. Facing me were three older students, perhaps Level Two.

"Why did you come alone?" The Gruff Voice was behind me, along with the owner of the hand that held my head facing front. When I tried to turn, the hand painfully tightened its grip.

"I thought that . . ."

"You thought only of yourself. You didn't think of the group. From now on you are going to learn *never* to think of yourself apart from the group."

At which point I was punched and kicked several times. I tried to resist, to fight back, but there were too many of them. I went down on my knees, trying to catch the breath that was knocked out of me. Clearly overpowered, I refused to cry and I refused to concede defeat. I would die before I did either.

"Enough!" the Gruff Voice called out. One of my attackers pulled me up and another handed me two buckets filled with cleaning solutions and implements.

"Take them and go back to your section. And remember, Ten Lubak, this is what happens when you separate from your group. All individuals are hunted and punished. By yourself you're pudding. We're going to be watching you."

I was pushed toward the door and the lights went out. The door opened, and as I stumbled through with the buckets I nearly bumped into another student who was waiting to go in. We looked at each other and I recognized the disapproval on his face. I thought of warning him, but something told me to return to my section. I hurried past him and heard the Gruff Voice call out, "Next!"

5

Entry:

"Tell me, Mr. Garak," Captain Sisko said, as he intently studied a viewscreen diagramming the Cardassian Union. "Where do you think the Cardassian defense perimeter is most vulnerable?"

I laughed. How do you explain to an alien that's the one place where Cardassians are not vulnerable? The good captain gave me one of his bemused stares.

"The likelihood of any exploitable weakness," I replied, "would be in the chain of command between the Founders' orders and the execution of these orders by the Vorta and their drug-addicted Jem'Hadar soldiers. If it's a perimeter put in place by the Cardassians, it won't be vulnerable."

The Captain gave me a skeptical look. "That's a very confident assessment."

"Captain, Cardassians come into this life with an awareness of their protected perimeters—what the doctor calls our 'reptilian brain dominance'—and die defending them."

The Captain nodded and turned back to the diagram. I almost added that, in between, we perfect this awareness at places like the Bamarren Institute.

6

Entry:

Males and females of the First and Second Levels were kept separate at Bamarren. While we shared certain docents and outside training areas, each group had its own living quarters and facilities. It was explained to us that until we became disciplined in our relations with the "complementary gender" we would make better progress this way. When I asked One Tarnal how we would learn this discipline without interaction between the sexes, he blinked and mumbled something about "distractions." When I asked what that meant I was told that I had a loose mouth and given five days of hygiene-chamber maintenance as punishment.

"You don't know enough to ask so many questions."

I started to ask him how could I learn without asking questions when he pulled out his murking stick (so named because they are used to beat "murks"—that's what First Level students are called) and gave me a whack on the leg and told me to get to the storeroom for cleaning implements. When the pain passed through me, I looked around for group "support." You can be sure that this time I wanted to be accompanied by as many of my mates as possible. There were five students in the room, but when I made my request four of them gave excuses ranging from barely plausible to outright suspicious. Three Lubak, the biggest in our section and the one I most wanted to go with me said, "The section leader's right. You talk too much."

Unfortunately, the only student left was quiet Eight Lubak, who kept completely to himself. He agreed to accompany me and quickly moved to the door. He was short and slender, and his dark eyes and long lashes made him look younger than the rest of us. He was almost too delicate for a Cardassian. I was not encouraged . . . but I had no choice. I went through the door, unconsciously imitating the Gruff Voice from my previous experience.

"All I need is an extra pair of eyes. Just keep them open, and let's get the job done!" Eight said nothing and followed me out.

The trip to the storeroom was uneventful, and we received our supplies without incident. On the way back, however, we noticed that an intersection of two corridors was much darker than before. Eight, who was walking behind, touched my shoulder.

"I think we forgot something," he said with uncharacteristic loudness. He motioned for me to follow him. We backtracked to the previous intersection, made a right turn and continued down another corridor until we came to a third intersection. He stopped and took the cleaning implements from me and carefully put them down. He chose one that was attached to a pole and handed it to me. He took a shorter implement, looked around the corner down the darkened corridor and quickly moved to the other side. I started to follow him, but he made it clear that I should stay where I was and wait. All during this, Eight was quiet and controlled—and as sure of himself as if he'd done this many times. How did he know where he was going? How did he . . . ?

We heard footsteps coming down the corridor from the direction Eight had anticipated. He held up two fingers indicating how many people. We kept out of sight on either side of the corridor as they approached. His face was dark, intense with concentration; his brow ridges, which were unusually pronounced, cast shadows over his eyes. My heart began to pound when I realized what Eight was planning. These were certain to be older students, but he expressed no hesitation, no doubt.

Just as the two unsuspecting students passed, the one closest to me caught sight of me, but it was too late. We were on them, and we both knew exactly what to do. First we disarmed them of their murking sticks with blows to their hands and arms. Then we laid into them with such ferocity that they fled down the corridor.

"I'll show you who's pudding!" I started to follow.

"No!" Again the strength of his voice shocked me. I stopped, and before I could ask why, we heard a high-pitched whistle screech out the emergency signal for immediate assistance we had just learned in a field-training class. We grabbed our implements and ran as fast as we could all the way back to our section.

We burst through the door, flushed and out of breath. Most of the group was present and wanted to know what had happened. In my excitement I started to tell the story when Eight dropped a pail with implements and grabbed my attention. He looked sharply at me.

"W-what?" I stammered.

I followed his nod to the door where One Tarnal was giving me a hard look. Eight moved to his sleeping area and quietly busied himself in his private compartment. I immediately shut up, gathered the implements and took them into the hygiene chamber.

Shortly after, when we were alone, I asked Eight how he knew about the corridors. He didn't answer. He turned away and picked up his orientation chip and punched a code. I was about to comment on his rudeness when he turned back and handed it to me. It was a diagram of the rooms and corridors on the storeroom floor. We had all been given the schematics of the Bamarren spaces. I assumed that no one paid any attention to them.

I didn't know then if I could ever call Eight a friend. Something about him was strange and impenetrable. But it didn't matter. At least I knew there was one person in my section I could trust. How I had misjudged him. It was obvious that Eight had what Cardassians call a ferocious spirit—and that I could learn a great deal from him.

* * *

Much of the focus of Cardassian education, especially during the early years, consists of exhausting and merciless physical training. The training area on Deep Space 9 always amused me. People struggling by themselves with weights and machines in front of a mirror. The results seem more about strengthening the appearance of the body rather than the fiber of the character.

Our training centers on trials of one person's skill matched against the skill of another. But where Klingons regard physical combat as the primary test of mastery, we *begin* at that level and then progress to the subtler methods of confrontation. There are enough levels of expertise for two lifetimes, but a student has to master each one before moving on to the next. It was during these trials that we came to know each other.

We assembled in the burning sands of the "Pit," where each day we had long "eye, hand, and foot" sessions. The Pit was the most feared training area at Bamarren; it truly took the measure of each student. These initial sessions were the fundamental underpinnings of all subsequent training. Basically, the concept was to teach the eyes, the hands, and the feet to operate independently, in order to function in countless combinations called "strategems" controlled by the brain. The strategems ranged from simple fight combinations of kicks and punches to complicated dances that resembled religious trance.

Calyx, our martial docent, was a gnarled old man with one glass eye. It was rumored that he was an infantry gul who'd been demoted because he'd refused the privilege of executive status and had put himself in danger along with his men. It was after his demotion that he dedicated himself to mastering the strategems. Of course we called him Calyx behind his back, since that was the name of the whirling muscular beast-of-many-appendages in our childhood stories. Like the fabled Calyx, our docent was capable of blinding displays of fighting prowess, yet at rest he was about as remarkable as a rock.

On the first day in the Pit, we stood in formation for what seemed like hours while he simply stared at us. I was drenched in my fluids, nauseated by the baking sun. Six Lubak fainted, and when Five made a move to tend to him Calyx spit in his face. As with humans, this is a humiliating, demeaning gesture. We were stunned.

"Step forward, Five." His voice was jarringly gentle and a half-smile replaced the blank mask. Five just stared at him, the spittle dripping from his face with the sweat. He behaved as if the docent had spoken an alien tongue. The mixed signals had confused us all.

"Stand in front of me," Calyx motioned. Five was compact, and his trained, athletic body moved carefully in anticipation of a trick. He stopped in front of Calyx, whose half-smile revealed broken and missing teeth.

"I want you to get me off of my place without losing yours," Calyx explained. Five seemed transfixed by the half-smile; I wasn't sure he'd understood the request. I wasn't sure *I'd* understood. We remained in formation while they stood facing each other. This standoff lasted forever. Five wavered, but he held his position, never taking his eyes off Calyx. My entire body was by now screaming in pain.

The Pit was in the far corner, away from the other training areas. Each was cut off by a barrier, so you couldn't really see what was going on in adjoining areas. Voices and sounds would drift in and out of awareness. My mind wandered. I was sure that I heard sounds of the women students gusting with the winds. Suddenly mother materialized . . . she looked like she was apologizing. I wanted to tell her how much I missed her, but her image dissolved and . . . Father took her place. I knew he was telling me something very important, but I was growing dizzy and afraid that I'd join Six on the ground . . . his words were carried away by the winds. Father faded, and gradually I became aware of a figure entering from the right side of my peripheral vision. He was dressed in the student black and green, moving slowly across . . . No! *She* was dressed . . . in the classic long skirts. This was against the rules. What was she doing here? She glided into full view and stood between Calyx and Five. The dry Mekar winds billowed her skirts and whipped her purple-black hair, obscuring her face. Did anyone else see her? I wanted to look around, to have my vision corroborated, but I couldn't take my eyes off her. She stopped and returned my look. Her hair whipped behind her, exposing her unguarded eyes. She said something . . . but again I couldn't hear the words. I moved to her. She was radiant . . . I was drawn to her. . . . Everything else fell into shadow, as if I were moving through a tunnel. . . .

"Where are you going, Ten? You're losing your place." It was the Gruff Voice from the storeroom. My female vision reacted to the voice and looked in the direction from where it came. I followed her look, and just as I began to discern the outline of another person—tall, graceful, an emerging negative image of a picture—I experienced an icy, painful spasm that pulled me back to the Pit. It was as if my heart had been crushed in a strong grip. I staggered and nearly fell.

"You look lost, Ten." I turned to the voice, which now was familiar and no longer gruff. It was Calyx, and I was standing in front of him. What happened to Five? I wanted to look. I wanted to look for the young woman. For the Gruff Voice. But I didn't dare take my eyes away from Calyx.

"Did you see them or hear them?" he asked. I hesitated, wondering how he knew.

"Both," I replied.

"Did you recognize them?"

"My . . . parents. Not the other two." Someone behind me started to laugh, but Calyx stopped him with a look.

"The other two. Is that when you lost your place?" I nodded. His questions were softly asked, almost kindly. I don't know why I wasn't surprised that he knew. Instead, I was grateful; it told me I wasn't going mad.

"You have your work cut out, Ten."

I nodded again as if some part of me understood what he meant.

"Are you up to this? Can you learn to hold your place?"

I just stared back at him not knowing how to respond. Softly he blew two acrid breaths into my eyes and, blinded, I stumbled back.

"Can you even *find* a space to hold?" he asked.

I came back to my sweating body and felt totally exhausted and beaten. We were dismissed, and I watched everyone move away. I had no idea of what had just happened to me. My work was cut out, Calyx had told me: I had to find my space and hold it. How do I even begin?

7

And how do we even begin to rebuild a world that doesn't exist anymore? A world that exists in my mind with the same arid bitterness as the dust in my mouth. I have never lived with despair, Doctor, the way I live with it now. It's almost like a phantom companion that shadows me and casts doubt on whatever I do.

"Why save him?" it asks, as we remove a young boy from the rubble of a school. "You're only keeping him alive for a future of privation and chaos. Wouldn't it be more satisfying to join the burial unit?"

I want to scream at this phantom, to shut it up. Once I turned around suddenly and raised my hand to strike it. When I realized it wasn't there, it was too late. Everyone in the unit was looking at me; I'm sure I must have looked like a madman. Dr. Parmak tried to send me home, but I refused—alone it's even worse. He offered me a relaxant, and I put it in my pocket.

"Later," I said. "It'll make me drowsy now." And we continued to dig for more children.

When I returned to my shed, a rare rain was falling. I was chilled to the bone. I found the last of my *rokassa* juice and settled in front of the open door. I removed the pill Dr. Parmak had given me and I swallowed it with a gulp of juice. I watched the rain mix with the hazy dust and turn everything into a muddy swamp. As my muscles relaxed, figures began to emerge from the haze and take shape. They stood there—indistinct, silent—turned toward me as if awaiting my instructions or decision. There was nothing threatening about them; indeed, they were only the outlines of childlike bodies, standing patiently. My despair was finally in abeyance, and I experienced a relaxation I hadn't known for a long time. I began to think that they were my old Bamarren schoolmates, and I wanted to speak to them, to welcome them back into my life. Yes, I thought, relief from the horror. I must get more of these pills from Parmak. As I tried to put faces on the shadowy children, they began to approach me. They became more distinct as they moved through the rain and haze. Can you believe it, Doctor? They weren't my schoolmates; they were the Cardassian orphans from the Resettlement Center on Bajor we once visited. The orphans left after the Cardassian occupation forces withdrew. The same young girl was their leader and her lips formed the same question.

Have you come to take us home?

I jumped up. I felt the shed closing in, threatening to swallow me. I ran out into the rain and gloom.

"There is no home anymore! Can't you see that? Look around you! It's gone!" I screamed at them and fell to my knees in the sodden waste. They continued to stare back with that same look of fragile trust that I would somehow relieve them of their fear and bring them home. I couldn't look at them anymore and dropped down into the muck. My despair was no longer just a voice; it was this monstrous world the evil had created, and it surrounded and overwhelmed me.

I don't know how long I remained curled up in the mud. I felt myself being lifted and half carried, half dragged back into my shed. It was Dr. Parmak. He cleaned and changed me as best he could. He prepared a cup of Tarkalean tea, which made me think of you, Doctor. How ironic, another doctor pulls old Elim out of the muck of his despair, but this time he's a Cardassian. Parmak offered me another pill, but I declined.

"I'm afraid they don't react well with me," I explained.

"I understand," he said.

I wondered—did he? Did he understand that I have to live with this brutal reality—live in it!—without hope of a cheap escape? Just as I learned to live on Deep Space 9 without the wire that anesthetized my pain. The same harsh lesson. I'm sure he did. After all, he has to live here, too. And he's a doctor. A Cardassian doctor.

Perhaps there's hope for us yet.

8

Entry:

All the lessons at Bamarren were harsh. Like my father, no one wanted to repeat an order or instruction. If they did, you paid the painful price. If you had to relearn a lesson it was made doubly difficult. Consequences always escalated. Like every other group the ten of us traveled in a tight and disciplined pack; we covered each other's backs and punished stragglers who jeopardized our safety. We learned very quickly that group integrity was paramount, individual effort an alternative only when there was no group solution.

The lessons I came to look forward to in Level One took place in the actual Mekar Wilderness. At irregular intervals we were taken out to desolate areas and, depending on the exercise, were assigned to hunt as a group or evade capture as an individual. If it was the group hunting exercise, we were told that a certain number of individual enemies were operating somewhere in our part of the Wilderness, and that our task was to track them down and take them into custody. We were given no supplies, no navigational instruments, and no information as to their location. If we returned without having captured all of them our mission was considered a failure. Needless to say, all failure at Bamarren had serious consequences.

We were quite successful at the group exercise. Since we had no idea in which direction to begin our hunt, we used an elaborate system of whistle calls and signals as we radiated out from a central base. When one individual was located, only those hunters in that particular quadrant were assigned to apprehend him. The others continued the search in their respective quadrants, and we all reported back to the center, with or without our prey. There was only one instance when the length of the hunt far exceeded our supplies such that by the time we returned to Bamarren we were all dangerously dehydrated and exhausted. Six (the student who fainted in the Pit) had the hardest reaction to this exercise. He was studious, and excelled in a classroom situation, but while he wasn't as slight of build as Eight he didn't have the latter's stamina. For a while he was near death, and spent nearly two months in recuperative care. It was to his credit that he returned to the group.

We learned about each other through this training. One of the things that quickly became apparent in the Pit, the classroom, and the Wilderness was that our initial numerical designations were not truly indicative of ability. The numbers assigned to us were presumably based upon our previous school performance record. But just as important and rarely mentioned were our family and class status. Eight also came from a "service" family background, and it was soon clear to everyone that he should have been designated One Lubak, a fact not lost on the actual holder of that designation who, judging from his behavior and speech, came from the highest echelons of our society. Nine, however, came from an important political family but was as dim as a moonless night. Three wasn't much brighter, but his physical size and strength—as well as his family's connection to power—gave him a higher place.

The patterns of political alliance within the group had about them the inevitability of iron filings on a magnet. To keep the low-born but gifted Eight in his place, One immediately recruited Three and Nine. Not only were they of the same class, but One could mentally dominate them. Two went along with this group, but his political adeptness enabled him to remain on good terms with everyone. Four also went along with this group, but the only thing that captured his interest was finding a way to make contact with the women. This preoccupation—and his well-developed shoulder ridges—made him seem older than the rest of us. Five was an athlete who also did well in class. I could see that he was attracted to Eight. As indeed I was. Seven seemed to be the youngest and most unformed of the group. He was another "service murk," and his allegiance went to whatever person he'd spoken to last. Six, when he wasn't recuperating, preferred his books and kept his distance. He wanted desperately to succeed at Bamarren, but he was vexed by his physical limitations. We all knew that these allegiances and predilections existed under the surface of our everyday interactions, but we also knew that the dominant mask we were required to wear was one of unity. Especially in the Wilderness.

My first exercise as the hunted individual was not successful. Four, Eight, and I were taken to separate desolate areas, as all the hunted students are, and set loose with the lone instruction that we make it back to Bamarren without being detected by any of the hunting groups. We carried nothing but the clothes we were wearing.

Once I was left to my own resources I despaired. This was not the city. The landscape was unyielding and harsh; it held no clues that I could read as to what direction the Institute was in or how far. I wandered about in the searing heat, doing everything in my power to be captured. I was in terrible agony. Of course, it took no time at all for the Furtan Group to accommodate me. Four was captured, but only after a much longer hunt, and Eight successfully returned to Bamarren without being detected. I was judged an abysmal failure and assigned to solitary detention, as an example of what happens to lackluster effort and to think about how I could change for the better.

But it was in the Pit and my work with Calyx that I suffered the most. My dreaming made me "an air man."

"You have no grip, no focus. How can you find your strength if you can't hold your place? Living in your dreams is like living in exile."

His critique cut to the heart. It was only my determination to somehow find my place in Bamarren—in the group, in myself—that kept me from total despair. But I was very close to giving in.

After a particularly brutal session in the Pit, when Three pinned me face down in the sand and nearly broke my neck, I lingered in the training area to be alone and deal with another bitter defeat. The worst thing about it was that it was self-inflicted. I wasn't as strong as Three, but I was much smarter and my instincts were truer and faster. However, there was always one point during a strategem where I would panic and lose control. It would happen the same way every time: A difficult move under pressure against strong physical resistance from an opponent . . . and something would snap. A painful blow might set it off, a whispered insult, perhaps just a thought or a feeling of hopelessness, and I would suddenly lose control and lash out like a madman. I became suffused with a raging, crimson anger that poured out from some black hole somewhere deep inside me. At first I appeared ferocious, and my opponent would back off. But it was Eight, of course, who efficiently exposed my lack of strategic control and the utter impotence of such behavior. Without Eight, Three would never have gotten past my berserker appearance.

As I sat on a bench and went over the moves that had led to my latest failure, I heard a female voice in the adjoining area. The voice was saying something about what constitutes a crime in a covert assignment. I heard no voice in reply, and I thought I was having another one of my visions. I started to leave before it took over—this was the last thing I wanted. But the sweetness of the voice stopped me. It had a piping and melodic lilt, firm and confident. And there was a soothing quality as it spoke of dry legal definitions. It acted as a balm for my bruises and bitterness. I began to feel such longings. It was like hearing music that you love when you least expect it. How I missed Mother, and working with Father in the flower beds. How I longed for home. I dropped my guard and surrendered to the voice. The tears I was determined never to shed accompanied choking waves of shame and relief, sadness and joy. I finally was able to admit to myself how unhappy I was.

I had lost track of the voice. When I was able to exercise some control I began to pull myself together before someone saw me. I used my dirty tunic to wipe my eyes, looked around . . . and there she was. The young woman from my vision in the Pit. Except that I knew from her look of concern that this was not a vision.

"Are you hurt?" she asked.

I wanted to hide, I wanted to say yes. I just looked at her. How could her eyes be both so clear and so unfathomably black?

"Thank you," I managed.

"For what?" She was confused, concerned, but I could see the hint of amusement in her look.

"I . . . you have a . . . pleasant voice." Pleasant! I think I actually cringed. But she laughed at this. She had such a delighted look on her face.

"Then was it something I said?" she asked.

"What?" I had no idea what she meant.

"If my voice didn't make you cry it must have been my speech," she continued to laugh. "I don't blame you. The establishment of the Habburitic Code and its relevance to covert intelligence missions is enough to make the angels weep."

"What are angels?"

"A human religious tradition. You get all that in Second Level. It's a lot more fun than Foundations of Cardassian Law. Are you alright?"

"Yes . . . uh, I'm . . ." I shook my head, embarrassed.

"Homesick, I know. This can be such a cruel place.

But you know the secret, don't you?" She asked this with exaggerated confidentiality, looking around as if there might be spies. I was still getting used to her manner, and I looked around as well in case there really were.

"No . . . I don't think so."

"Your sense of humor. Without it you're lost."

I wasn't sure I understood.

"You strike me as being very serious and ambitious. That's fine, most of the students are," she patiently explained. "But it's pretty funny around here."

"I don't know." I was dubious to say the least.

"No, really. You study with Calyx, don't you?"

"Yes," I glumly answered.

"I know. The Pit wasn't my favorite place either, but look at his eyes when he's instructing or when he watches the others. There's a glint. He's enjoying himself. What's your name?"

"Ten Lubak."

"No, your real name."

"But we're not supposed to . . ." I stammered, truly shocked.

"I'm not going to tell anyone. My name is Palandine. What's yours?"

"Elim." It barely came out of my mouth.

"Our secret. Agreed?" Faced with her smile I would have agreed to anything.

"Agreed." Suddenly she was running off.

"I have to deliver this silly thing for next class. Remember, it's all funny. Think about it . . . Elim." She whispered my name, laughed, and disappeared behind the barrier. I didn't even say good-bye. I didn't even know what her proper designation was. I looked around and saw the Pit. I tried to see what was funny about it, but my mind wasn't yet ready for this concept. I wasn't even sure that I had this mysterious sense of humor. Suddenly I felt angry. How dare she? She broke two rules that could get us both in serious trouble. And like a fool I'd told her my name. The use of our real names was a serious transgression. From the beginning it's drummed into us that the less security operatives know about each other in any given unit, the less they can divulge if they fall into enemy hands. I felt like I'd given up a precious secret to someone I didn't even know. Someone who seemed almost frivolous. There's nothing "funny" about Bamarren. As I walked off, I considered telling someone about this encounter. But how would they interpret my part in it? And what about the secrecy agreement I had made with Palandine? I didn't know what to do . . . but I did feel much better.

9

Entry:

"Doctor Bashir is with Chief O'Brien. He should return at fifteen hundred hours. Unless it's an emergency."

I assured Nurse Jabara that it wasn't, nodded my thanks, and walked back out to the Promenade. I stood there for a moment, trying to deny that I was upset. This was the umpteenth time I had come to invite the doctor to lunch, only to find that he was already engaged with the Chief. Playing darts. Building models of old wars. Battling ancient enemies in ancient flying machines in some holographic fantasy. Or the latest diversion, listening to the insipid "lounge" music at Vic Fontaine's. Child's games. That's it, I decided, if he wants to have lunch he can damn well ask me.

A Bajoran lout nearly knocked me into the perfume display and continued on his way without so much as a glance back. I controlled my temper and followed him. The Promenade was crowded, and I quietly negotiated the crowd until I made my way directly behind him. I slipped my left foot between his two legs, hooked his right ankle and pushed him hard in the small of his sweaty back with my left hand. He went down like a demolished building, taking two or three innocent pedestrians with him, and I peeled off to Quark's bar. As I entered I could hear a fight erupting. My action served a double purpose; not only had the lout been dealt with, but Quark's now emptied out as the fight escalated. Louts and buffoons—and we're going to war to save them from the Dominion. Bajorans find it difficult to believe they can ever be on the winning side; more and more they seem to prefer the dark side. I wonder if the Kai's actions on the Promenade haven't brought the entire society closer to the abyss.

I sat down at the end of the bar instead of going to my usual place on the second level. I wasn't sure how long I wanted to stay; I just had to get out of the crowd and a grip on my feelings. I was in a dangerous mood. Ever since that ridiculous holosuite program, I thought. The spy game. Well of course it's a game. It's all a game. But it's not a holosuite program. And yet, the moment Julian wounded me with his ridiculous weapon, everything changed. I thought it was a magnificent moment. He showed me that he had the spine to play the game as it ought to be played. But why then did he back off? Why couldn't he go beyond that moment? Why did our relationship end?

"Garak!"

Odo's voice was sharp enough to pull me out of my musings. He was standing next to me, with that mask of detached hauteur he wore when he'd decided you were the culprit. A mask upon a mask.

"Constable. What a pleasure. Have you had lunch yet?" I asked. He just looked at me. "Yes yes, I know, you don't eat lunch—but join me anyway." I gestured to the stool next to me. He didn't move.

"Someone witnessed you creating a situation in the Promenade," he said.

"A situation? Really? I so rarely create anything these days. What with the impending invasion. . . ."

"Did you attack a Bajoran by the name of Londar Parva?" Odo's sternness could be impermeable.

"I assure you, I am not in the habit of attacking people I don't know in public places. We got our feet tangled in the crush, and he went down—just as, moments before, I nearly wiped out the scent display when he ignored the fact that I was standing in his path. I trust he's not hurt."

"I expect more from you, Garak," Odo lectured. "We're all under a great deal of strain."

"As am I, Constable. Please, sit down at least. I feel like a schoolboy being disciplined by the docent."

Odo sighed and awkwardly perched on the barstool next to mine. I waved off the approaching Ferengi barkeep, no doubt another "relative" of Quark's working for slave wages.

"I can't stay long. I have to finish dealing with this . . ."

". . . situation," I finished. "You're very fortunate, Odo."

"How so?" he asked.

"These people have come to trust you. They rely upon you. You've made a real connection here."

Odo merely grunted. I was careful not to mention Major Kira, knowing how reserved he was on the subject.

"Do you still want to go home?" I asked.

The question startled Odo, and for a moment the mask of official reserve dropped from his face. This was the first time I had brought up the subject since his admission to me during the "interrogation" in the Romulan warbird and Tain's ill-fated attempt to destroy the Founders' homeworld.

"I . . . can't say," he replied ambiguously.

"Well, I can. There's certainly nothing here to keep me."

"I never told you how sorry I was about Ziyal's death." Odo could be quite sensitive in such matters.

"You did, actually," I nodded. "But thank you."

"Still, you and Dr. Bashir have created a strong bond."

"Not really," I answered quickly. "I'm afraid that what I have to offer has run its course. It's certainly no match for darts." I heard the bitterness of my tone, and so did Odo. We sat in silence for a moment.

"I understand you'll be involved in the invasion. You must be pleased." Odo steered us away from the heaviness that had descended.

"Yes," I replied, grateful for the change of subject.

"It's very gratifying to know that I can be of some use to the effort."

Odo was about to say something when he saw Quark approaching. He rose abruptly from the bar.

"I have to get back to work," he stated.

"When do you want to schedule your consultation?" I asked. Odo—no doubt influenced by his budding relationship with the Major—was about to branch out sartorially. But it occurred to me that Quark was the last person he wanted to know about it.

"We'll talk," he replied, nodding to Quark as he briskly marched back to the Promenade.

"What's his hurry?" Quark asked.

"He has a 'situation' out on the Prom

"A big fight. Sorry I missed it. W about?"

"The usual," I replied. "People rush

10

Entry:

My solitary confinement was agony. The only way I got through it was to rethink all my attitudes about the Pit and the Wilderness and to focus on how I could make my strategems more effective. Just as I had learned to do when Uncle Enabran locked me in that suffocating closet. Was this the universal torture for failure, I wondered? I also thought of Palandine, constantly replaying our meeting in my mind. I felt more able to keep my despair at a distance, which in turn allowed me to breathe.

When I returned, even the sessions in the Pit weren't quite so disastrous. I did, however, notice the twinkle in Calyx's eyes when he was teaching, and that somehow helped ease my fear.

The next time I was assigned to evade capture in the Wilderness I decided to wait until darkness before I made any effort to find my way back. I was left on the edge of a long, narrow rock formation that sloped down to the southern part of the Mekar, where it was said that the last of the *honge* still lived. The *honge* were nocturnal flying predators whose medium size belied their strength and ferocity. Their swooping attacks were known to kill and carry off large canids. They lived in subterranean nests during the day, and as I burrowed into an escarpment that offered a depression large enough to conceal me until night I was trembling at the prospect of meeting one. The vision of wild *honge,* the intense heat, and my growing claustrophobic discomfort filled me with a choking anxiety. Not only would I fail again—I'd probably die horribly.

I stayed absolutely still, counting my breaths. Just as I began to stem the rising panic, I noticed a movement in the earth in front of me. My first thought was the *honge,* and my heart thumped against my chest as if it wanted to flee my body. But the movement was more like the wind stirring the loose sandy soil. I was able to discern that it was being caused by a colony of desert *regnars,* reptilian creatures that are rarely encountered—and for good reason. They blend in with their surroundings with such transforming facility, that only by remaining still for so long was I able to detect them. They knew I was there, I'm sure, and they were attempting to move away from me. But they never panicked. They only made their moves when the wind or the shifting shadows masked their progress.

I was totally absorbed and fascinated by these creatures. They moved in silent concert, fanning out multidirectionally so that the surface of the sand would just look as if a slight wind were rearranging the grains. It was the most elegant choreography. I observed how changes of color tone rippled across their skin as they moved between light and shadow, rock and soil. I counted five of them. They moved toward a deeper recess, which most likely led to a safe retreat. Somehow, I knew intuitively that they were my answer to this incredibly difficult situation.

I also knew that in the dying light I would soon lose them forever—which felt the same as losing my last hope. I moved my right hand very slowly toward the closest *regnar,* amazed that I was able to maintain a steady control. With a sudden move I was even more amazed that I was able to grab hold of it, careful not to do it any harm. With my left hand I took the sun cover from my hat, filled it with the sandy soil, and placed the *regnar* inside. Before I closed it up, I noticed that although the creature had eyes, they didn't focus. This beautiful, magnificently adaptable creation of the Wilderness was blind, and yet it had more sensory awareness than any technology we could ever imagine or invent. I closed the sun cover and placed the *regnar* in a safe pocket where it would not be crushed. I apologized to the others for disrupting their family; I explained that I had great need of this creature. Not only was Mila (as I eventually called him) the answer to my current problem, he was as important as any of the docents at Bamarren, with the possible exception of Calyx.

When night came, I emerged from my lair. I was fortunate that none of the three moons were shining. Quietly, carefully (the hunting parties had already fanned out across the Wilderness), I stood and allowed my cramped muscles to expand in the desert night. The Taluvian Constellations were pulsing their complicated rhythmic patterns—indicating, according to Docent Rilon, an advanced intelligence that astrophysicists were still attempting to decode. After hours spent buried alive in the suffocating heat and dust, the freshness, the clarity of the smells and sounds and feel of the night air against my skin was overwhelming. I was a new person, no longer intimidated by the task at hand. Unlike the last time, I had preparation and an ally.

Thanks to Calyx and the recent work in the Pit I was finally learning how to sense an opponent's energy, to anticipate his attack and choose or change a stratagem in the moment. Everything gives off energy signals, he told us, and these signals were organized according to the electromagnetic field that undergirds all creation. The same is true with our intentions: they, too, are organized along these energy lines.

"If you train your awareness to be sympathetic, to tune into the interdependence of energies, then you can anticipate your opponent." Calyx told us that anticipation was just the beginning, and that as we grew stronger we would be able to "foresense," by which he meant that we would be able to know who our opponents were before they appeared. Calyx then gave me one of his long looks, which included the unsettling twinkle.

As I stood in the darkness of the Wilderness, I first made certain that no one was near. Satisfied that I was not being observed by my hunters, I then used the Prime

Taluvian Constellation to orient myself directionally. Once I determined the direction of Bamarren, the hard work began. Between the rock formations lay great expanses of flat desert. During the day anything that moved in that expanse was exposed to the naked eye from a great distance. Plus the midday heat severely punished anyone foolish enough to be traveling out in the open. The Mekar sun was a challenge even to heat-tolerant Cardassians. I had to cover as much distance at night and find rock cover by sunrise. Of course the hunters knew this, and while one had to be careful traveling at night, the real danger was not finding an undetectable niche during the day. And then there was my greatest fear: the more effective the hiding place, the worse my claustrophobia would flare. My earlier confidence began to ebb. I felt a slight movement from the pocket where Mila was. Whether or not that was one of Calyx's signals, I knew that I had to be on my way.

I made good progress that night and early the next morning. Toward dawn I felt the presence of a night probe and flattened myself on the ground just before its faint beam knifed over me. I judged the direction it came from and adjusted accordingly when it felt safe to continue. I had sensed the signal before it appeared. That was a good sign.

There was still perhaps an hour before light, when I encountered what looked liked the dark outline of a badly constructed outbuilding. It was a tall rock formation that narrowed at the top. I was debating with myself whether to continue in the hope that I would find another formation before light when I heard the barely audible but unmistakable whistled signal and response of a hunting party. I scurried into the first opening I saw, a cranny that appeared to offer enough invisibility in the predawn darkness. I entered and curled very quietly against the dead end. Above me was a slight overhang, and to my left the rock was depressed just enough for me to conceal most of my torso. My legs, however, no matter how tightly I pulled them against me, were visible to anyone standing outside and looking into the cranny. I also knew that the sun rose on the other side of the rock, and that this position would become untenable when it crossed over to my side and exposed me. Either I would be easily spotted or, if I weren't, baked to death.

As the sun came up, the otherworldly beauty of the Wilderness was gradually revealed by each succeeding gradation of light. I was deeply moved by the presence of so much color in what had initially looked like a dead world to me. Beginning with a cold pale gray, the dawn flowed through a range of blues and into the softest rose and pink and then to a hot red that soon gave way to the merciless bleached bone-white of midday. I was able to see how much territory I had covered the previous night.

Unfortunately, the hunting party I had overheard decided to use this rock formation as a base during the day, and sent out brief search expeditions in shifts. There were three of them, and they had found shelter in a place above the cranny and to my right. As I listened to their boring and desultory conversation I realized, ironically, they were part of the Furtan group who had captured me in my last pathetic attempt. Judging from their voices, they were fairly close. I prayed, not only that they would stay where they were, but that before the sun shifted to my side they would move on, so I could look for a less exposed haven.

The morning wore on, and the hunters made no sign

of moving. I became increasingly concerned; the sun was getting higher, and the overhanging ledge was now my last source of shade. At one point I took Mila out of his wrapping to check on his condition. At least that's what I told myself. I was afraid that if I was honest and admitted that the real reason was to solicit help from a *regnar,* the slide into total insanity would be swift and sure. I was getting desperate. Just then one of the hunters decided to have a last look around before settling in for the blistering afternoon. As he detached from the group, I could hear that he was coming my way.

Holding Mila to the side I scrunched myself into the space as tightly as I could and dug my feet into the sand. I didn't know what else to do. I looked at Mila, who was absolutely still. As he sensed my attention his coloration subtly adjusted to the exact color tones of his immediate area. I heard the crunch-crunch of approaching steps and closed my eyes in a childish attempt to disappear. All I could hear was my heart beating like a drum, and I was afraid that if it didn't give me away my ragged breathing would. I tried to hold my breath, but that only made each heartbeat more furious. I began to panic, and again looked to Mila, who was now barely visible. How did he remain so still, so self-possessed? I studied him as if my life depended on it; it was then that I noticed that his flanks moved ever so slowly as they filled with air, and slowly as they released. Then there was a long moment of no movement at all before the cycle began again. I surrendered to the same rhythm, and the pounding of my heart began to subside.

The steps came to a stop just outside my cranny. I continued to breathe with Mila. Silence. I could now hear the hunter's breath struggling with the heat, and feel his directed energy as he inspected the opening. He must have been looking directly at me. I knew that somehow I had to depress my energy, avoid locking into his focus. Like Mila. Think of Mila. Blending from one moment into another. Moving at the edge of shade and light. Transforming with shifting hues as light changes angle and moves across surface. My focus flattened; my energy, slowed by the rhythm of my breathing, seeped out around me and was absorbed by the surrounding surfaces. I surrendered Elim Garak—Ten Lubak—all identity—to the sand and rocks. And all the while I felt clear, calm . . . and guided.

After what seemed like forever the hunter moved away. I remained in this suspension, this utter peace, until I became aware that the sun had lowered and was exposing me to its full force. I knew that I wouldn't last long, and that a move had to be made. My calmness, however, prevailed, and I knew what to do. I placed Mila on the ground in front of me and waited. His coloration again subtly adjusted to the change. Wherever he went I would follow, even into the depth of the rock formation if necessary. He moved to the opening. After a few more moves I painfully unwound myself, got as close to the burning sand as was possible and followed. Every time Mila made a soundless scurry I went with him. The ground heat was suffocating and my hands were screaming. It was a shock to experience my body again. We moved to the left, away from the hunters, who had obviously found shade. We stayed close to the rock and out of their sightline. I began to anticipate Mila's moves, and for a while we moved as one. How ridiculous this must have looked, a grown man scurrying after a *regnar* in the sand. But how liberating to discover resources and a teacher beyond the limits of conventional wisdom and pedagogy.

Three more members of the Furtan group were on the other side of the rock formation, but Mila had found a hidden depression that required some quiet digging to get into, and we avoided detection. We settled in and re-sealed the opening with sand and loose rocks. After an indeterminate period, the Furtan hunters left. As we waited for nightfall I fell into a deep sleep. My dreams were a jumbled mess of images and actions, at the center of which Palandine was laughing at something or some-one I couldn't see. At one point I was awakened by the sounds and voices of another group. They were probing our immediate area. I was confident that we were secure.

"Take out your grapples and probe the higher opening, Three! If this murk is not caught, everyone shares the punishment."

My heart jumped into my throat. It was the Gruff Voice. It took me a while to calm myself. But by then the group had passed. What murk? Me? Have all the oth-ers been captured? Surely not Eight. I couldn't believe that was possible. I poked through an opening when I was certain it was safe. The last gray streaks of light were fading on the horizon. By the time I tucked Mila safely away it was time to continue. I reoriented myself, chose the direction and set off. I was determined not to be captured—especially not by the Gruff Voice.

It was a long, nerve-wracking night. The beams of night probes were constantly criss-crossing the darkness. We eluded two other groups, including the Tarnal. I could hear our section leader, One Tarnal, urging on the others with the same threats of punishment. Were there this many hunting groups the last time? And were they as advanced as the Tarnal? Since I'd been captured so quickly I couldn't know. And I refused to allow these questions to interfere with the task at hand. I walked, I ran, I crawled, I curled up into a ball, I dug myself into the sand; I did whatever was necessary. On one occasion, passing hunters should have detected me. I was amazed when they passed within feet of my crouched and curled body. Perhaps they thought I was a rock. Mila's lessons were making the difference.

Just before dawn I strolled up to the Central Gate. The two sentries were shocked and speechless.

"Ten Lubak returning from the field," I announced. A tall and graceful figure quickly emerged from the darkness behind the sentries and into the harsh floodlight.

"There's nothing to smile about, murk."

My blood froze. It was him. Unfortunately, my self-satisfied smile also froze. So much for my newly discovered power to adjust to changing circumstances.

"Pleased with yourself, aren't you?" the Gruff Voice asked. "Were you also pleased after your great victory in the storeroom corridor?" Obviously he knew it had been Eight and me, and it wasn't a forgotten incident. I continued to smile.

"We'll see about that . . . and about your idiotic smile. Get back to your section!"

"Yes . . . uh . . ." I didn't know how to address him.

"One Charaban, murk!" He wheeled away back into the darkness.

"Charaban?" I weakly repeated as I watched him leave. *The* dominant Level Two group. "They were assigned to this hunt?" I asked the two sentries.

"All Level Twos were assigned. It happens once a year. How did you elude them?" The younger sentry was violating all protocol and rank distinction with the question.

"That's enough, Six!" the other sentry snapped. "You heard One Charaban, murk. Get back to your section." He pushed me in the direction of the gate.

As I walked among the buildings just beginning to come alive with dawn activity, I tried to piece together what had happened. The Gruff Voice was the leader of the Charaban, which meant he was the leader of male Levels One and Two. Small wonder he was not pleased with me. The failure of a Bamarren elite cadre to capture all the murks would not polish their reputation, and it certainly wouldn't help One Charaban's quest for the ultimate leadership position in Level Three. While I understood that I would have to watch my step with One Charaban, I also acknowledged that I had never been in a manlier or more attractive presence. It was like encountering an ideal that I'd only dreamed about. As I walked back to my section and accepted the congratulations of my mates, I was baffled not so much by the appearance of this new and commanding person in my life as by my recognition of his strong connection to me. But what connection? Did it have anything to do with the vision I'd had that first day in the Pit with Calyx?

From that point on, no one at Bamarren ever captured me again. And it was not for lack of trying. I became a bit of a legend. Other students constantly asked me about my evasive techniques. When I wasn't forthcoming, they grudgingly agreed that giving up this information would make me vulnerable in future hunts. I maintained, with a certain amount of truth, that with docents like Calyx such information was accessible to all Bamarren students. Of course I couldn't tell them the truth. How could I? Then I would have to tell them about Mila. Pets were strictly forbidden, and anyone caught with one was punished, and the pet destroyed. How could they accept that Mila taught me the lessons that had enabled me to crawl out of the Wilderness undetected?

And how do you explain those lessons? I struggled to explain them to myself: cultivating stillness and silence; relying less on sight, sound, and physical touch and developing the finer senses to gather intelligence. So much of what we see and hear is not the truth of any given situation; sometimes it's necessary to close the eyes and be still, to extend our awareness *beyond* what we've been conditioned to believe is our field of sensory operation. Only then can we learn the patience to trust that *all* the information that we need will come to us. This is some of the wisdom of the *regnar*. The wisdom that helped me hold my place for the first time. And for better or worse, it was this wisdom that set the unexpected course of my life.

■

Entry:
The other day, the Doctor, Odo, and I were at the Replimat having lunch, an event that Odo, after our conversation, had taken it upon himself to organize. The station grows more tense each day the invasion is put off. The fabric of community interaction is wearing thin, and flaring tempers are no longer confined to Quark's. Indeed, after my "situation," the Promenade witnessed several such incidents. Each day we look for

signs that might indicate who will be assigned where, for what duty, and when. Each day we're disappointed, and the tension is further bloated with rumors that range from the plausible to the wildly fantastic. As the casualty figures mount, some of us attempt to keep the prevailing sense of doom at arm's length with what the Doctor calls "gallows humor."

"The one I heard this morning was about you, Garak." It was clear from Odo's expression that he'd been looking forward to this moment. "I was warned that not only were you a changeling, but that the reason you spent so much time in the Replimat was that you had found a way to slowly poison us all."

"I'm sure the Replimat is quite capable of doing that without my help." I was only half-joking.

"That must be the same person who came to me and accused you of sewing a deadly toxin into his shirt," the doctor said.

"Yes, I remember him. He didn't want to pay for the shirt." And I did remember him—another Bajoran who thought he could alleviate his troubles by targeting the Cardassian tailor.

"When I did an analysis of the shirt," the Doctor went on, "I found nothing but traces of his own bodily fluids."

"Which were toxic only to the people in his immediate presence," I added just before a fight broke out in the food line. Two Romulans had decided that waiting in line was beneath their dignity, and the others were vigorously disagreeing. Odo did not appreciate the interruption and gave our new allies a blunt lesson in station etiquette. They left with sneering disdain. With friends like that. . . .

Odo sat down and gave me a look.

"It was Captain Sisko's idea to get the Romulans involved, Odo. Not mine," I answered the look.

"Humph," was his only reply.

"But what about you, Doctor?" I asked, returning to the business at hand. "It seems there's a movement afoot to have you replace Captain Sisko." The doctor winced.

"Is this true?" Odo asked. We both looked to the doctor for confirmation. He sighed.

"There's a group of . . . genetically enhanced people who feel that one of their own should be guiding the station during this emergency, and they've petitioned the Federation Council, but it's Jack and his group, and no one takes them . . ." Exasperated, he broke off. "Garak, how did you hear about this?"

"My clientele talk and I listen." This was also true: an idiot savant who wears his presumed genetic superiority like a badge of privilege walked into my shop and never stopped talking. Of course I encouraged him, and by the time he left I had heard all about some organized attempt to elevate Dr. Bashir to the leadership position. I could see that the doctor was upset that I'd divulged this information. Clearly this genetic business was not his favorite topic of conversation.

"Is this something we should keep an eye on?" Odo asked, studying us carefully.

"No, not at all," the Doctor assured him. "It's just Jack's people. This was nearly a year ago, and I'm afraid they have too much time on their hands—like some other people I know." He pointedly looked away from me as Odo continued to study us, trying to decode the undercurrent of this last exchange between us. No wonder he was such a capable security operative. Odo registered every change in tone and temperature and tracked the change down to its cause.

"Tell me something, Garak." It was clear that he had found an opening for one of those deferred questions he kept on a prioritized list somewhere in his changeling head. He was still a basically shy and tactful person, especially when it came to other people's business, but lately he'd become more openly inquisitive. I wondered if it was Major Kira's influence.

"Certainly, Constable," I replied.

"If Cardassia remains within the Dominion sphere, would you stay on the station?"

"Judging from the sartorial styles," I gestured to the crowded room, "I'd say a good tailor is a necessity." I smiled, not believing for a moment that I'd survive an aborted invasion of Cardassia or that there would still *be* a Deep Space 9 if we failed. This must be the lunch where we deal with uncomfortable subjects.

"But if Cardassia is liberated from Dominion control . . ." Odo went on.

"*When* Cardassia is liberated," I interrupted.

"Would you return?"

"Would you return to the Great Link?" Odo reacted with sharp annoyance to the question. It wasn't a fair one, because although we were both exiles, we were in very different circumstances. With the humanoid shape he was still learning to live with, and his deepening relationship with Major Kira, Odo was discovering a new mode of existence, a new link. He had an alternative, however difficult the choice. I didn't.

"Yes, I know. You can't say." I was sorry I had asked again. It was a question he was obviously struggling with.

"Would you return to the same Cardassia?" the doctor asked.

"What do you mean 'same'?" But I knew perfectly well what he meant.

"To a Cardassia containing the political and social elements that made the current situation possible."

"My dear Doctor, that's also the Cardassia that made *me* possible." I half-hoped my joke would end this conversation . . . but I knew better.

"Yes, certainly, but given its totalitarian bent, do you really believe that the previous regime served its people? Liberation might allow for a new government that would ensure the freedom and well-being of its citizens, one that was based upon democratic principles."

I made no reply. We've had our clashes on the subject of Earth-style democracy during previous lunches. Dr. Bashir was of the opinion that the Cardassian political system allowed too many competing groups, especially the military Central Command and the Obsidian Order, to function in secret and above the will of the people. No one was surprised when the Detapa Council, the ruling civilian authority, overthrew the Central Command; and very few people, certainly, mourned the demise of the Obsidian Order. But while I didn't disagree entirely with the Doctor's analysis, I found it somewhat simplistic. One cannot understand a political "system" detached from its societal context. I also found his eagerness to promote these political remedies somewhat condescending, but I knew the good Doctor was on a mission, and I was determined to show good manners and let him make his case.

"With your background and experience, Garak, I'm certain that you could serve as a liaison between a new Cardassian government and the Federation." The Doctor paused and waited for a response. None was forthcoming. "I once suggested that you visit Earth as a member of the Cardassian government-in-exile. . . ."

Laughter erupted from my mouth; I truly couldn't stop it. "Forgive me, Doctor, but the people who call themselves our government-in-exile wouldn't have me to lunch—and I wouldn't let them clean my shoes."

"But you see," the Doctor exclaimed, "that's just the problem. Each group has its own agenda. You're all so busy finding reasons to dislike each other that you don't have the will or the energy to find common ground. You're so dedicated to your . . ."

"Reptilian mind-set," I prompted.

"Well . . . yes."

I laughed again, but inside I was beginning to lose patience with the analysis.

"You are, Garak. Democratic principles, on the other hand, are about adjusting boundaries, negotiating these differences . . . finding some kind of consensus."

"Your common ground." No one could accuse me of not listening, especially to the key phrases.

"Yes. Because without common ground there's nothing left except the kind of selfish interest that eventually leads to anarchy. Don't you see? That's why the Dominion found Cardassia to be easy pickings."

I looked over at Odo. He was nodding in appreciative agreement, as if he'd learned something new and interesting. Indeed, there were several people at adjoining tables who were hanging on to the Doctor's passionate words, as if he'd been anointed not just leader of the station but the savior of the Alpha Quadrant. Of course they loved his analysis of the evil Cardassian empire.

"That's why I urge you to go to Earth and experience, firsthand, a democracy that has evolved and united so many disparate groups . . ."

I had had enough. "First of all, Doctor, I don't quite know what you mean by 'democratic principles.' Are you referring to the appalling lack of discipline and self-control I've observed on this station? The exaltation of individual freedom above the welfare of the group? The fact that the 'first among equals' in democratic society seem to get preference and privilege?"

"Go back to Cardassia!" someone shouted from a table.

"Dominion spy!" cried another.

"That's enough!" commanded Odo. He wasn't going to let this get out of control.

"That's another principle, is it not, Doctor?" I gestured to the crowd. "Free expression of one's opinion?"

"Yes, it is, Garak."

"Educate me, Doctor, please. I'm obviously in the dark about these principles. What about the shabby manner in which certain acts of public service are ignored because they don't measure up to ethical Federation standards? Is that also a principle? Whereas lying, cheating, and stealing seem to be encouraged and amply rewarded as long they keep the wheels of commerce turning and bring in a profit. You see, my friend, I'm somewhat confused. One man's democratic principle seems to be another man's political and social nightmare!"

My voice had risen to an uncharacteristic pitch. It was still ringing in my ears as the Doctor stared at me as if he were studying a baffling microbe. I, too, was baffled. I had no idea where this outburst came from. I know that a distance has widened between us during the past year or so and I know that the holosuite program incident and the revelations of his genetic enhancement are the symptoms of this distance rather than the cause. It's only natural—we're very different people. I also know that he had only the best intentions in suggesting that I use the Federation model in order to influence the future of Cardassia. Misguided, yes, and somewhat patronizing and arrogant, but hardly sufficient to elicit this embarrassing and public loss of control.

I mumbled some sad excuse which the good Doctor and Odo were kind enough not to challenge and left the Replimat to return to my shop. As I passed Quark's I caught his eye and we nodded. Why I included him in my outburst also puzzled me; I rather admire his industry and resourcefulness. I especially admire the way he consistently bends Federation rules so that they work for him.

Back in the shop I shut the doors and tried to work on an outfit I had started to cut and to come up with some designs for Odo. That brown uniform of his is so drab, I was pleased when he decided to take my advice about something more stylish.

What is going on with me? Surely it's not about Captain Sisko ignoring my contribution to the Romulan solution. I know better; the reward for work well done is the work itself. I've been included in the invasion of Cardassian space, regardless of how limited its ambition and scope or when it takes place; the rest of it—recognition, medals, monuments—is truly not important to me. What *is* important is that I feel that I am necessary, that I function with all my faculties in the service of a greater cause. And while I wait for this invasion, is making Odo more attractive to Major Kira a greater cause?

I threw down my sketches. I didn't want to stay in the shop with these colliding thoughts. But as I was about to leave, I was stopped in my tracks.

I knew what it was: Odo's question. What will I do if Cardassia remained in Dominion control? Where would I go? The Doctor's interruption prevented me from answering, but truly I have no answer. I don't know where I'd go. Much more troubling to me, however, is another question. Will I have a home if Cardassia is liberated?

12

Entry:

As I progressed through my First Level at Bamarren, I acquired a reputation as a resourceful and serious student. Not only had I broken all previous records for evasion of capture in the wilderness, but I had also excelled in my studies. The only member of my group who performed as well in all areas was the taciturn Eight.

I had no real friends to speak of, and told myself that

loneliness was the price I had to pay for success. I considered the games and behavior of my mates to be childish, and that any unnecessary interaction would only distract me from my work. The truth, of course, was that I didn't know how to forge those kinds of bonds. I wanted to be closer to Eight, and to a lesser degree Five, who besides being one of the great Pit strategists Bamarren ever had was fair in all his dealings. The rest, to one degree or another, I found to be jealous and manipulative. As I began to progress rapidly after my success in the Wilderness, One and his allies obviously felt threatened and maneuvered as a unit to cut me out of the unity we were supposed to be creating as a group. They did the same to Eight. Because this was directly counter to our training goals, they had to be clever and subtle about their methods. They had a harder time with Five, because he wasn't as aloof as Eight and I. We made their job easier for them, Eight with his silence and me with Mila.

Inspired by my guide Mila, I would experiment at withdrawing my presence when I had to remain in the same room with people I didn't like. Of course I couldn't change my coloring like a *regnar*, but with constant practice I was learning to change the nexus of thought, feeling, and perception that defines my presence in space. If I am sitting on a rock, I surrender to the vibratory rate of that rock, using the techniques I began learning in the Wilderness. The more successful I became, the more I was able to keep the other students at a comfortable distance—especially the ones so involved with their own agendas, they were not paying the attention they should have.

When I smuggled Mila into my section, I made a

Entry:

After my success in the Wilderness, I briefly encountered Palandine a few times after our initial meeting. The one time we could have spoken together (again in the training area near the Pit) I made an excuse and hurried off. That such meetings were against the rules was how I justified my abrupt behavior. As a Level Two student she should be more responsible. I didn't know what she wanted from me, but I found her presence threatening and disorienting.

Docent Rilon gave me permission to do some research at the Archival Center on wormhole phenomena. First Level students were not allowed in the Center without special dispensation, but I had proven myself a serious student, and became one of Rilon's favorites. When I entered my permission chip at the entrance, I was instructed by a disembodied voice:

"Attend to your business in section three, row eight, monitor five. You have two units of time."

The door opened and I entered. I proceeded to my designated area and punched in my request for specific information as to the spatial conditions that alert us to wormhole activity. I prepared my recording chip for notes and settled in for a quiet and pleasurable investigation of one of my favorite subjects, the wormhole funnel that connects the here-and-now to seeming infinity. The mystery always fascinated me, and those people who dedicated their lives to its exploration were among my heroes.

There was Joran Kine, who had camped outside the Prime Moon Wormhole in an old *Galor*-class shuttle and waited for the next turbulent opening. He believed that he had decoded a cyclical regularity and that the next opening would give him time to enter the wormhole, move through to the other side, do some exploration, perhaps collect some samples, and return before it closed. It was like saying that you could come back from death. Everyone thought he was on an insane suicide mission. They didn't believe he could succeed. And when he did and he reported his findings, the scientific community didn't want to believe him. His description of the journey thrills me even today. But when others tried to use his cyclical calculations and were lost, Kine was discredited; he eventually died in disgrace.

"Elim."

I heard my name, and thought it was coming from the Barzan Wormhole I was studying.

"Elim!"

This time I turned around—and there was Palandine, sitting next to me.

"You must be very special if they let you in here," she said without irony.

I looked around to see who else was in our row.

"There's nobody here. I waited until you were alone. Why are you avoiding me?"

The directness of the question stopped me. I didn't know how to respond.

"Did I insult you? You were positively rude to me the last time we met."

"I'm not . . . comfortable . . . calling me Elim. Nobody does that," I struggled to explain.

"How much time do you have left?" she asked. I looked at the screen.

"Less than half a unit."

"Come with me," she said as if it were a simple request.

"I can't."

"Why not? Who's the docent who gave you permission?" she asked.

"Rilon."

"Ah, yes," she said with recognition. "And of course you're serious enough to be his prize student." Now the irony was creeping into her tone. "Whatever you have it's going to be enough for your report. Come on, I want to show you something."

I didn't know what to do. My body was twitching with discomfort.

"You're still not having fun, are you, Elim?"

"No, I'm not. Especially with you bothering me. Will you leave me alone. And stop calling me Elim. I'm Ten Lubak!"

She just looked at me as if seeing someone she didn't expect. I could see that I had hurt her.

"I'm sorry . . . Ten Lubak. I won't bother you again." All the brightness, the airy ease was now shaded with genuine disappointment, almost sadness. She smiled with her mouth only and walked away.

Why? I asked myself. Why?! For the life of me I could not understand why it was important to her that I respond. Why should she—so beautiful, so alive—be disappointed if I didn't return her . . . what? What did she want from me? Friendship? Why me?

I was in turmoil. Her grace and manner, the way she tilted her head and half smiled when she listened, as if everything amused her . . . it was like a forbidden dream of the unattainable. The attraction was painful because I instinctively knew that while my life would be simpler and more controllable without her, it would also be as drab as my Bamarren uniform.

I knew I wasn't going back to the wormhole today. I withdrew my chip, got up, and followed without thinking in the direction she had taken. There were several rows in the area separated by barriers. I was quickly lost, and began to panic that I wouldn't find her. I was now operating on some emotional level that no amount of rational thought could stop. Where was she? I turned a corner and nearly ran her down.

"I'm sorry." My nervous energy and anxiety left me short of breath. "I don't mean to be unfriendly. I just don't know why you . . . I mean, I'm not very . . . I'm trying my best to get along here and follow the rules and be . . . and you . . . confuse me." Her head was tilting and her whole face began to form that maddening smile.

"I'm just a murk!" I nearly shouted. She was delighted and began to laugh.

"Are you making fun of me?" It was at that moment, when I asked the question, that I realized just how afraid I was of being the object of her ridicule. She stopped laughing and for the first time she was speechless. Something behind me, however, caught her attention and her expression instantly changed.

"No, you're *not* supposed to be here, murk. You're obviously lost. Follow me!" The change was stunning. She brushed by me, and I indeed followed. Then I saw the reason for her change. Approaching us was a Third Level intern. At this last Level you were no longer called a student.

"Good day to you, sir." She bowed her head slightly as he stopped in front of us. He nodded to her and looked at me.

"Who's this?" he asked as if I was a specimen.

"A murk who's lost, sir." Her personality was totally submerged.

"Your permission chip," the intern demanded. I held it out to him, but he never took his eyes off mine. I began to sweat.

"Who's your docent?"

"Rilon . . . sir."

"This is not the technical section. Why are you here?" His eyes were tightly locked into mine. There was no wobble room with this intern; he knew his business.

"I thought I was going out the way I came in. I'm sorry, sir."

"Sorry for what?" he asked.

"For my loss of direction."

"Yes," he agreed. "You need more work in the Wilderness. Who's your superior?"

"One Tarnal, sir." If he ever finds out that the Wilderness is the one place I *don't* need work. . . .

He turned to Palandine. "One Ketay."

"Sir!" she responded with vigor. I was not as familiar with the female Levels, but Ketay struck me as familiar.

"See that his section leader is informed of his need for Wilderness experience."

"I will, sir."

"And make sure he leaves the Center now."

"I will, sir." Palandine bowed her head again and motioned me to follow her. He was still looking at me like a specimen, but now one with a bad smell. I followed as we made our way back to the entrance, entered our chips, and left the building. We continued along a walkway that led behind the Archival Center.

"I'll take you another time," she said, looking straight ahead. I assumed she was talking about whatever it was she wanted to show me.

"Elim."

"Yes?"

"Call me Palandine."

I hesitated.

"Elim, when I first met you I knew that you could become a good friend. Don't ask me why, that's my business. Unless you're a total idiot you don't go about making friends by ridiculing them . . . unless they ask for it," she added with a sidelong glance. "Am I clear?"

"Yes."

"Yes, what?"

"Yes . . . Palandine."

She stopped and pointed to the pathway on the right with a gesture I thought slightly larger than necessary. "You go that way, murk." She winked at me and took the left pathway. I watched her departure until I looked back and saw that the intern was watching us from a window in the Center. I turned and headed back to the First Level Study Center feeling that if I had dared, I could have flown there.

Ketay! It came to me just at the moment Eight kicked out my right leg, spun me around, and sent me sprawling into the Pit sand after a motionless standoff that had lasted well into darkness. Six had fainted, Three had fallen asleep twice and Seven's hallucinations had been severe enough for Calyx to intervene. As I rose, spitting grains of sand from my mouth, I was not so much embarrassed by my lapse as I was excited by my realization that Ketay was the elite female Level Two group, and

Palandine's designation as One put her on an equal footing with One Charaban.

"Do some of your best daydreaming here, eh, Ten?" Calyx wryly observed. Eight had the look of someone who'd been given an unexpected gift. This had been a grueling session for everyone, and there was much relief that it was over. But even with my lapse this was probably my best showing in the Pit, considering the advanced strategem and the quality of my opponent. Nobody outlasted Eight. Whatever I had found in the Wilderness, he had found in the Pit.

"Even one thought that takes you out of the moment is fatal here, Ten. There is no recovery, no second chance." Calyx concluded his critique and walked away. Class was over. There were no beginnings and ends for him—only the continuum.

I was always the last one to leave the Pit. I told myself it was because I was slower than the others, but the truth was that ever since my first encounter with Palandine here I secretly hoped to see her again—especially after our last meeting. This time, however, Eight uncharacteristically lagged behind with me. What was even more unusual was that he apparently wanted to talk.

"You were good today," he said.

"Thank you." I was genuinely grateful for his approval.

"Did you see him?" he asked.

"Who?" I looked around.

"One Charaban was watching our strategem. He left at the end."

"Charaban watching *us?* How do you know it was him?" This made me nervous. The last time we met at the Central Gate he told me he'd be watching me.

"It was him." His confidence dispelled all doubt.

"But why?" I asked.

"I don't know. But I think we should be careful." I nodded in agreement. We stood in silence for an awkward moment. "Are you going back to the section?" he asked.

"No . . . uh . . . I'm going to stay here awhile and . . . do some forms," I managed to say. Eight remained for a few more minutes. I had the feeling that he wanted to say something more to me. Suddenly he turned and disappeared behind a barrier. The air was filled with whatever went unsaid. He was as shy as anyone I had ever known.

As I waited to see if Palandine would come, I was true to my word and worked the kick-spin forms that Eight had danced through while I stumbled. Just as I decided that she wasn't coming and prepared to leave, I heard approaching steps. I turned in their direction expectantly and found myself face to face with One Charaban. I immediately tuned into my Pit focus, with the altogether different expectation of self-defense. Charaban saw this and began to laugh. His reaction completely disarmed me. Was this the same person?

"Don't worry, Ten. I left my murking stick back in the storeroom." Only his gruff voice revealed it was indeed the same person; everything else about him had changed. His tall, wiry body was relaxed, and his smile seemed genuine. I began to relax as well, and then I reminded myself that as a One designate he was most likely a skilled Pit warrior. I maintained my focus.

"And I only came to watch, not to engage," he said, accurately reading my adjustment. "You and your mate put on a fine exhibition. That's a difficult strategem. Calyx must think highly of you both."

"Eight said that you were watching us."

"He noticed—and you didn't?" he asked with his smile.

"Nobody is stronger than Eight in the Pit," I admitted.

"Nobody? That's quite a claim."

"Nobody in our group and probably in the First Level," I boasted for Eight.

"Is that because he can beat you?" Charaban exposed my boast. There was truth in his question. "Well, I certainly want to speak to him as well . . . when the right time comes. Please, Ten, walk with me. I have a proposal." I stood there, mystified by his offer. His smile widened and he motioned me to follow.

Charaban led the way toward the Bamarren Grounds, which were hidden by perimeter barriers. Inside was another world, planted and maintained like the public grounds at home. I could almost see Father's work here, and the reminder stabbed at my carefully defended homesickness. Walkways led through soft ground cover and flowering bushes that reached up and met above our heads. It was my first time inside—First Level students aren't allowed except in the company of upper students—and I was amazed by its softness and serenity, especially in the darkness, punctuated by glowing lamps spaced along the way. It was dramatic relief from the prevailing Bamarren harshness. Charaban stopped at a bench and invited me to sit. In this setting I couldn't help but relax, but at the same time my mind was trying to work out the meaning of his invitation.

"Do you know about the Competition?" Charaban had read me correctly again.

"The simulated battle at the end of term," I managed.

"Simulated in that no one is killed, but it can get

rough," he said. "And the one coming up will be rougher than most because we have an unusual leadership succession this time. Has anyone spoken to you about this?" he asked.

"No." I waited for Charaban to explain why anyone would, but his mind was following its own logic. He looked at me as if he were appraising an inanimate object for its value.

"You've impressed a number of people here. My second, who's the strongest hunter in our Level, wouldn't believe that you got past him that night. He insists that you didn't abide by the rules," he challenged. I understood that this was another way of asking how I had eluded capture. When I didn't respond, Charaban laughed with that same disarming grace.

"I didn't expect you to answer . . . and you shouldn't. Not yet. This brings you power and opportunity. Like the one I'm about to offer. Just tell me one thing: have you told anyone about your methods?" he asked with his easy smile.

I was about to respond when something told me not to. It was the voice that Calyx had been urging me to listen for. The voice that can be heard only when fear and fantasy are not in control of the moment. When I didn't answer I could see that Charaban was surprised. This time he didn't laugh; he merely nodded.

"Yes. You're not a murk anymore, are you? But not answering the question tells me what I need to know." His expression had changed; he had determined my value.

Light footsteps and female voices suddenly intruded. I realized in the moment of their interruption how intense this exchange with Charaban had been. When I widened my focus I was shocked to see Palandine and a friend emerge from the darkness. She never looked at me. They nodded to Charaban, he nodded back and they disappeared as a desert wind moved noisily through the foliage. A fleeting incongruity. The whole evening was like a dream.

"Hard, isn't it, Ten?" Charaban broke in. "To be treated like you don't exist. Of course she treats everyone like that, not just murks." He was looking in the direction the two females went as if he still could see them. Was he referring to Palandine? He turned back to me, all business.

"I've challenged Third Level leadership to a Competition earlier than usual, on the grounds that they are inferior. I refer especially to the interns of the Ramaklan Group. It's my prerogative as leader of the Charaban. Bamarren is neither inspired nor unified by their example, and I am urging a succession by trial." It was clear from the ease with which this was stated that Charaban was politically astute and organized. And ambitious. I felt that I had been allowed to enter an inner sanctum and been made privy to a revolutionary decision.

"In order to mount a successful challenge, I need the best team I can assemble. Being Third Levels they have the advantage. Not only does One Ramaklan have the obedience of the most proven interns, but in the Competition itself they are simply required to defend their position, and nothing more. As challengers, we have to devise an attacking strategy that will prove the worth of our accusation of inferiority. This is not a simple matter, Ten." Charaban engaged me as if I didn't understand.

"I don't think any challenging leader has ever asked a First Level student to accept a planning position . . . and certainly not one with a Ten designation," he added with a tinge of condescension.

"I am responsible for my work, not for my designation," I hotly reminded him. He had touched a sensitive place, and he knew it.

"Nevertheless, you're a Ten and until you prove yourself otherwise you'll always remain a Ten. And I'm not talking about excelling in class or eluding capture, no matter how brilliantly, or settling for second best in the Pit. I'm talking about planning and executing group action that ends in nothing less than total victory, the Cardassian ideal of excellence this school was built upon!"

The air around us rang with the passionate challenge. Charaban was right; he was offering me an opportunity—and I knew it.

"What do you want me to do?" I was trembling as if my body were chilled.

"More than anything, Ten, I want you to banish failure. There's no longer any room for it in your life. Agreed?" Charaban offered his hand. I grabbed it like a drowning man. I'm sure he felt me struggle to control my shaking body.

"Agreed." I was also thrilled. Other than in combat this was the first time I had physically come into contact with another student. We stood for a long moment in the bowered and darkened pathway holding each other's hand. Aside from Palandine and Eight, this was the only other person I was able to look directly in the eyes. Charaban broke the contact.

"I'll communicate with you through Nine Lubak about our planning sessions," he said. I was surprised. Why Nine?

"He's my cousin." Charaban again read me.

"Nine?!" I was incredulous. "But he's . . ." I caught myself before I finished.

"He's . . . a true Nine," Charaban replied with a diplomatic smile. "But he can carry a message, and in war we have to use every soldier according to his strength. We'd better get back. I'll have you excused from the evening assembly."

It wasn't until Charaban mentioned the assembly I had missed that I realized how late it was. We made our way to the entrance, and he parted without a word. Once I was alone I felt like I could breathe again. I began to doubt this agreement. This Charaban had a powerful presence, but how did I know he was telling me the truth? This could be some kind of test . . . a trap. After all, this was the person who had had me beaten in the storeroom. As I stumbled through the darkness on the edge of the training area I was in a daze. Yes, I wanted to prove that I was not a Ten, and Charaban knew that. What student doesn't want to make his mark? But my doubts only increased.

"Elim," the voice whispered. I was so wrapped in my competing thoughts that I didn't see Palandine standing at the edge of the pathway. In the darkness she was more like the apparition I first saw.

"You have the strangest friends." I strained to see her face, but I could hear the amused irony in her voice. "It's not every evening we find Barkan Lokar strolling with a murk through the Grounds."

"Lokar? My father buried the Legate, Turat Lokar," I said without thinking.

"Did your father kill him?" Palandine joked. But I didn't laugh. The Lokars were a legendary family, and the old man's funeral was the largest I had ever seen.

76

"Barkan is the grandson and the shining light of our generation. So what's he doing with you, Elim?" There was a grating quality to her irony.

"I . . . should get back. It's late." I started to leave.

"It's the Competition, isn't it?" Palandine's question stopped me.

"How did you know?" Again I wasn't thinking, only reacting. I winced at how my training evaporated in her presence.

"Elim, it's my business to know. That's why I'm here. That's why you're here."

"I think I know why I'm here, One Ketay." There was an energy building up in my stomach that was making me nauseous. I wanted to end this conversation. Palandine looked at me for a long moment with her half-smile, which observed everything and revealed nothing.

"It's a great privilege to be recruited by Barkan. He's as talented as he is ambitious. He'll most likely get what he wants—he usually does," she added with a tone of familiarity.

"I don't even know if I'm going to do this Competition," I admitted.

"Really?" She was mildly surprised. She moved closer to me. Her face, softened by the darkness, was now visible. "Why?" she asked tenderly. "What are you afraid of?"

"Who said I was afraid?" But as soon as she asked the question I knew that I was.

"Elim, why do you think we have these ridges?" She stroked the scalloped cords of cartilage and bone that ran along her neck and down her shoulders with a delicacy that stopped my breath. The energy had turned into molten liquid that was now flowing into my groin. The rest of the world was swallowed by complete darkness and I was back inside the tunnel.

"Because . . . we do," I replied stupidly.

"Because we need them. Not to support a weak spine as some aliens assume, but because we're a warrior race and we evolved these ridges as a defense against predators. But if we relied solely on these ridges to protect us in battle, we'd be no better than Klingons. That's why we're here, Elim—to develop our minds . . . and our hearts." She splayed her long, tapered fingers across her breast. For the second time tonight I was spellbound by another's passion. In very different ways, Charaban and Palandine held me in their orbit, like powerful suns. "To be a great warrior is to be a great strategist, and Barkan is offering an opportunity."

Again that word. But here in this tunnel, with the rest of the world cut off, opportunity had a different meaning. I was learning something new about myself—an emerging desire for power, but a power that had less to do with mastery over others than it did with connecting *to* them. The way I felt the connection to Charaban . . . and especially to Palandine.

"You seem to know Charaban," I said.

"I know that he can help you achieve your goals here. The fact that he's expressed interest in you . . ." She smiled and shook her head. "Usually he walks around here as if he breathes the air of a higher plane."

"He said the same thing about you."

"Really? What?" She laughed with that sudden delight.

"That you treat people like they don't exist," I managed to remember.

"Really?" she repeated. "Well, it will do him some

good. An oversized head is not attractive on a man."

The night horn signaling return to quarters blew in the distance like an ancient call. The walls of the tunnel dissolved; I had reentered a different world.

"Goodnight, Elim. I know you'll make the choice that's right for you." She ran off. It took me several moments before I could put movement back into my body. When I did, I realized that for the second time in my life I could fly.

14

Entry:

Still no word about the impending invasion. I didn't want to return to the shop after lunch so I lingered at my Replimat table, strategically placed opposite the airlock doors to watch the comings and goings of the station. There wasn't much activity, mainly Klingons coming from or going to the war front. I soon grew bored and decided to move to my other observation post, the second level of Quark's.

When I entered, I was surprised to see Rom serving the lugubrious and lumpen Morn at the bar. A spirited dabo game involving several Klingons and a serious-looking dabo girl I hadn't seen before caught my attention. If Quark had been present he'd be giving her one of his congeniality lectures. I truly sympathize with the young woman; if I had to spend all day with these drunken dolts. . . .

"Can I help you, Garak?" Rom asked.

"What brings you back to Quark's? Don't tell me you miss being abused by your brother."

"N-no," he replied blushing. "He's away on business and I agreed to look after things while he's gone."

"Ah, how kind of you," I nodded. "If I could have some *kanar* upstairs."

"Certainly," Rom replied. I smiled at Morn and moved past the dabo game, which was heating up. The new dabo girl, however, maintained an appealing coolness and calm.

My favorite table was occupied, as were most of the tables on this level. I was evidently not the only one taking a break from work. Finally, I found one from where I could observe the first level as well as the upper Promenade. Rom soon appeared with a small container of *kanar*. He was wearing an outfit I had made for him.

"H-here you are, Garak. I hope you enjoy it." Ever the gracious host.

"Thank you, Rom. And please, try not to let your collar lie there like a dead *targ*." I adjusted the offending fabric, and Rom sweetly tolerated my fussing.

Rom returned downstairs, and I realized as I took a sip of my drink that I was in a dangerous mood. Drinking in the middle of the day. The Doctor would be quite disappointed with me. When I'm unable to immerse myself in work my mind becomes occupied by an invading army of thoughts intent upon conquering all equilibrium and peace. *Kanar* is a valuable if unreliable weapon I employ against this army. The pills the Doctor gives me are a poor substitute.

Ever since the Romulan business and Captain Sisko's near breakdown (outside of the Doctor, whom I told shortly after the incident, no one knows about this, but one recognizes the symptoms), I've been obsessed with memories of Bamarren. Somehow, in the convoluted recesses of my mind, my years there are related to my exile on this floating prison. Yet no two places could be more dissimilar.

The Klingon commotion from the dabo table momentarily distracted me. I took another sip of the bittersweet liquid.

Three Lubak was right—I did think I was smarter than anyone else. And at the same time, I hadn't felt that I belonged at the Institute. I'd been an outsider with no pedigree, and there were those students who'd never let me forget it. One Lubak and his inbred clan. But I had been just as taken with the quest for power at Bamarren as anyone else, and determined that I would make my mark in the Competition. I laughed to myself, and a few heads turned. I nodded and smiled back. Another drunk talking to himself.

A scream cut through my thoughts and the bar. I looked down and saw Rom flying over a table and Morn scurrying out. There was only one Klingon left in the bar, a giant who had the terrified dabo girl by the arm. Without thinking, I threw the container of kanar down and it crashed at the giant's feet. He looked up, and I immediately knew two things about him: he was inebriated beyond reason and he was one of their shock troopers, a callused veteran of hand-to-hand combat. I took a deep breath; as dolts go he was quite impressive. My spirits were suddenly and immeasurably lifted.

"You spoonhead!" he growled at me. I hated that word.

"And you . . . a great warrior who brings down dabo girls with a single blow." He looked at me trying to decide if I had insulted or complimented him.

"P'tak!" I shouted, "I mean that you're the biggest coward in the Klingon Empire." He released the dabo girl, and as he moved to the narrow stairway I thought that he was also the biggest Klingon in the Empire.

I looked for my advantage. This was not an equal match, and my gigantic friend was in the full flush of a berserker blood lust. I sighed. I'm too old for this, I thought. I needed to slow him down and find better ground than this. As his head appeared coming up the narrow circular stairwell I charged, grabbed hold of the stanchion, swung my body around, and kicked the side of his head with both feet. This just made him angrier. I made for the upper Promenade—and wondered if Calyx might be enjoying this spectacle from wherever he was. The giant's roar caught the attention of the people on the upper Promenade, one of whom was Chief O'Brien, who emerged from an alcove where he had been doing some repair work on a panel.

"Garak, what have you got yourself into now?" he asked as I approached.

"Get security, Chief, and tell them to prepare the biggest cell they have . . . or a smaller coffin for me," I said as I moved into the alcove and squeezed through the opening where the panel had been. I had an idea. I could hear the Chief behind me try to reason with the berserker, who just pushed him aside.

I came out into a Jeffries tube. I wasn't sure which direction to take, but I had to choose quickly. My pursuer was struggling with the small passage, but he was not going to be deterred.

"Go left, Garak," the Chief kindly directed, "and take the third opening on your right!" I think he understood my plan. The massive Klingon followed me as I crouch-ran up the tube. One, two, three openings. Could I fit in? No time to debate. I squeezed in on my belly and shimmied forward. The giant grabbed hold of my left foot and started pulling me back. I strained against his vise-like grip . . . and my boot came off in his hand. I managed to shimmy beyond his reach and thankfully out the other end and into a larger parallel Jeffries tube.

I turned back to see if the Klingon was foolish enough to follow. It was such an obvious trap. His anguished roar answered me. Somehow he had managed to squeeze himself far enough into the passage to get thoroughly stuck. He couldn't go forward or back. And I recognized the look on his face. He was suffering from a claustrophobic attack. The more he struggled, the worse it got.

"Don't move, it'll only get worse," I warned him. His look was a mixture of wanting to kill me and desperately needing my help.

"Don't move!" He calmed down. "Keep breathing, deeply. Deeply. That's right."

"Help me," he croaked. I was touched by the giant's childlike surrender. I knew the feeling well.

"I will," I replied and immediately wondered why I had agreed. I'm getting soft, I thought. However, I needed to find someone who could help me help him.

"Don't leave me!" His voice was on the edge of panic. The tables had indeed turned.

"I won't. But you must promise me that you'll behave once you're extricated." His eyes flashed with impotent anger. I decided that I might as well get something for my trouble. "I'm not going to help you unless you promise me that you'll behave like a gentleman."

"I promise." Claustrophobic anguish won out over Klingon pride.

"And you must promise me one more thing." I wasn't finished.

"What?"

"That you'll never call me or any member of my race a spoonhead again."

"But you *are* a spoonhead," he reasoned. The request was incomprehensible to him.

"I'm warning you, unless you make a solemn warrior's promise, I will desert you."

"I promise." The poor creature was nearly in tears. I almost felt sorry for him.

The day after the incident, Odo called me in to take my statement. As I approached his office, the giant, accompanied by two security people, was coming out. He stopped when he saw me, and I braced myself for trouble, as did the two guards. Instead, he solemnly thanked me for staying with him until O'Brien and Odo arrived.

"I wouldn't have expected that from a . . . Cardassian—you see, I haven't forgotten my promise," he assured me. They moved off, and I must admit that I was quite taken aback. Evidently there is honor among dolts.

Odo was his usual thorough self. After my version of the incident, he reckoned that since the damage was minimal and the Klingon was returning to the front the case could be closed.

"What about the dabo girl?" I inquired.

"She's not pressing charges."

"How magnanimous of her."

"Magnanimity has nothing to do with it. Quark won't let her," Odo said with disgust.

"Ah—let me guess: Bad for business."

"Yes. But she seems quite interested in seeing you to express her gratitude," Odo said with no irony.

"Well, that's not necessary."

"As you wish. Her name is Tir Remara." The name rang a bell.

I was about to leave when Odo asked about the designs for his "new" sartorial look. I could see that he was masking his concern, so I assured him that the sketches were some of my finest creations, and would be ready within the week. He grunted his thanks and I stepped out onto the Promenade. Love does make fools of us all.

15

Entry:

The days of preparation for the Competition were exhilarating. They started when Nine approached me as I sat alone in our quarters reading the first part of Cylon Pareg's *Eternal Stranger*, a saga spanning several generations of a Cardassian family during the early and middle Union. Spellbound by its magic, I tried to avoid the interruption until I saw the expression of demented awe on Nine's face as he stood waiting. I then understood why he was there.

"Charaban One says that the first meeting . . ."

"Should you be telling me this here, Nine?" I interrupted. Perhaps he could carry a message, but he didn't know how to deliver it. At that moment Eight appeared and paused in the doorway to register Nine and me before going to his area. Nine was nonplussed; he didn't know what to do. I put my padd back in my compartment, stroked Mila—who was visible only to me—and quickly walked out. After a confused moment, Nine followed.

When he caught up with me in the corridor he tried to continue with the message, but I motioned him to be silent. His almost total lack of awareness astounded me; he must indeed come from an important family to have lasted this long at Bamarren. The subtleties of security training were evidently eluding him. We were well into the common ground triangulated by the three First Level buildings when I stopped and faced him.

"Was this necessary?" Nine asked. Judging from his offended air, any kind of security was beneath him.

"What's your message, Nine?" I smiled at him. I wanted to slap his pinched, inbred face, but I doubt that would have furthered my cause. He liked me even less, especially in the present situation.

"Charaban One. . . ." It stuck in his throat. Why was I, a low-born Ten with no connections, on the receiving end of this message? I waited and continued to smile.

"Yes, Nine?" He grimaced as if he swallowed something bitter.

"The first meeting is tonight, after your tutorial.

You're to report to the Palaestra for cleanup duty. The assignment has been filed with One Tarnal, who will meet you there." Nine was now back to his officious self. "This is extremely confidential, Ten!" he ended with a final attempt to maintain his superiority.

"I assume Eight is excepted," I replied.

"What?" He had no idea what I meant. Eight had walked into our quarters and seen the two of us, and was at this very moment putting together a scenario that would be very close to the truth.

"Of course not! No one must know. The fate of Bamarren depends on these plans," he intoned. A young man whose received wisdom consists of the scraps others have thrown away.

"Thank you, Nine," I replied graciously. I know he wanted desperately to ask me why I was being involved in his cousin's mission. He certainly didn't dare ask Charaban. And it was beneath his dignity to ask me. He swallowed again, an even more bitter taste, and marched off to a life of diminishing returns. It was just as well Eight was alerted. One of my goals was to get him involved before he was recruited by Ramaklan.

When I arrived at the Palaestra after a computer-systems tutorial at which I was severely criticized for my wandering attention, Second and Third Level agonistics—the advanced training phase after the Pit—were just finishing. One Tarnal met me in the main atrium and led me to the custodial office, where I was given implements and instructed to work until I had cleaned the twelve studios and two hygiene chambers in the building.

"Another murk was supposed to assist you, but he's

been reassigned, and nobody's taken his place. Don't dawdle or sleep, and be out of here by the morning classes. Now get going!" As I walked away I heard the custodian ask Tarnal what it was I had done to deserve this punishment.

"Nobody told me. But I know he's got a mouth on him," Tarnal replied.

I was well into my fifth room, and convinced that Charaban had set me up and that I *was* being punished, when a person I didn't know suddenly appeared in the doorway. He looked around to make sure I was alone.

"Follow me," he said, satisfied that I was. His body had a low and powerful center of gravity, and his eyes sliced into me when they made contact. There was no denying him. I dropped what I was doing and obeyed. Without a word, he led me down three subterranean levels and into a conference room that featured a large monitor at one end. Charaban and an immensely overweight student were waiting. The latter's formlessness was a contrast to the compactness of my guide.

"Is this the murk?" the heavy one asked.

"You don't recognize him, do you?" Charaban replied with his smile.

"He's filthy," the heavy one observed with a contemptuous look.

"I've been cleaning half the night!" I was indignant. The work was bad enough without the insult.

"I didn't ask for your opinion, murk!" the fat student snapped. The sharp-eyed one just studied me, which added to my disorientation.

"A murk who got by you twice," Charaban needled. He was enjoying himself at the fat one's expense and I was the instrument. "I don't think that ever happened to you before." Charaban turned to me. "He still doesn't believe it happened."

The other snorted in disgust, and his jowls shuddered in agreement. I wondered how someone that heavy could endure the physical regimen at Bamarren. He truly was the exception to the reigning student ideal of lean and muscular.

"We'd better get started," Sharp Eyes quietly suggested.

"This is Ten Lubak," Charaban abruptly announced to the others. "Ten, this is One Drabar," indicating Sharp Eyes, "and this is Two Charaban, who was eager to finally meet you." Two snorted and shuddered again. One Drabar moved to a control panel and entered a code. An image appeared on the monitor that was part topographical map and part diagram.

"There are spies operating everywhere, and we know who most of them are. The best ones we don't know, of course." Charaban was not smiling when he looked at me. "You'll be approached by Ramaklan if you haven't been already." He paused and the three of them looked at me. I now understood One Drabar's function.

"No. No one but One Charaban has talked to me about the Competition," I directly addressed Drabar. He held my look with his probing eyes and then turned back to Charaban, who computed his look before he continued.

"Ramaklan will. Expect it, Ten," Charaban ordered. It was impressive how he could move with warp speed between smiling charm and steely command. I nodded in response. He referred to the monitor.

"The rock formation at the center is the one Gramarg successfully defended two Competitions ago. Tarnal couldn't touch them. It doesn't look like much of a challenge . . . until you actually get out there. The exposure, the slope of the terrain . . . it all works for the defender. Considering the stakes of this Competition, Ramaklan is well advised to defend here." He pointed to the redoubt an obvious stronghold for the defenders. "It's a real challenge." Charaban fell silent, and the four of us studied the graphic.

This was a part of the Wilderness I was not familiar with. Charaban was right; at first sight it didn't look formidable. But as the coordinates revolved dimensionally and we perceived the gradual and insidious angle of the rising slope that led to the formation, we understood that the shape of the high ground allowed for no blind spots. There were 360 degrees of unobstructed exposure for the defenders.

"Any ideas? Observations?" Charaban asked.

"Ramaklan bastards!" Two Charaban muttered. "Look at that!" His stubby finger traced a circle in the air. "They can see everything around them. They won't need that many men scanning terrain from inside. So of course they'll commit the better part of their troops to the flanks coming out of either side of the rock formation to intercept any attempts to get behind them."

"Which can work to our advantage," Drabar said.

"How?" Charaban asked.

"If a small force *can* get behind their position, they'll encounter less resistance in a surprise attack," Drabar replied, never taking his eyes off the diagram.

"But how do we get behind their position?" Charaban asked.

"Outflank them. It's the only way," Two Charaban maintained.

"Both sides?" Charaban pressed. His fat second paused, not sure.

"Yes," he finally replied.

"Then what's left for the main frontal attack if we commit enough troops for both sides?" Charaban didn't wait for an answer. "No, Drabar's right. It has to be a small flanking force that surprises from behind and executes a holding action while the main force engages frontally." Charaban was sure of that much. "How do we get behind, Drabar?" He wanted an answer.

"I don't know yet," Drabar replied.

"Ten?" Charaban's eyes were almost angry, as if to ask what I was doing in the same room with them. All charm and politesse were gone. I was startled; it was the same look he'd given me at the Central Gate when I airily announced my success.

"There's something I don't understand," I began carefully. "Why can't a small force position itself behind the enemy *before* they array their flanking positions?"

"Because, murk, they are allowed to establish their position before we can begin our attack!" Two Charaban threw an exasperated look to his superior.

"They can dig in, Ten," Drabar explained, "and then we have from dusk to dusk of the following day to dislodge their position . . ."

". . . and take their place!" Charaban punctuated.

"Why are we dancing around, One?" his second wanted to know. "You invited the murk for a reason, and it wasn't to ask stupid questions." They all looked at me: Two Charaban with an impatient sneer, Drabar like I was another graphic on the monitor, and One with a questioning smile that wondered if I knew that this was the right moment to grab my opportunity. The image of Palandine stroking her ridges appeared.

"I'm here because I know how to get past their flanks and behind the rock formation," I said with a confidence that was part bravado.

"Really? Well, mates, I'm glad to have been present for the second coming of Gul Minok," the fat Charaban bellowed with utter contempt. Gul Minok was a legendary hero of the early Union. I bit down and held my ground.

"Do we know the status of the moons that night?" I asked.

"What do you think, Ten?" Charaban returned the question, not unkindly.

"If it was their choice of time as well as place, all three will be at full strength," I answered. He nodded in agreement. I was now on surer footing.

"But it's not that important," Drabar interjected. "In a Competition all the night probes are coming from one source—the defended area—and they're trained on the expected direction of the attack. Night is not the advantage one would expect."

"But still enough of an advantage for the major part of an attack to take place," Two stated.

"And the advantage grows proportionally to the skill level of the flanking force in operating with stealth," Charaban added, looking at me.

I knew what he wanted. It didn't take genius for someone to figure out that my success in the Wilderness depended on my ability to diminish my presence. But to give him what he wanted meant that I would have to teach others the skill. What would I be left with? Would I not surrender the source of my power?

And what would I receive in return? The image of Palandine helped me to remember what I had learned that night: that I was being offered the opportunity of a greater power. Charaban watched me. I was at the edge of my experience, and the only way I was going to expand the frontier was to act.

"The difficulty is finding students who can execute the necessary maneuver," I said, answering Charaban's look.

"What?" This was too much of a leap in logic for fat Charaban. "What maneuver?" Drabar didn't understand either, but that only increased his attention.

"*Stealth,* Two Charaban. Did you leave the room or is it getting too late for you?" Charaban was sharp with his second. He turned back to me. "It's even more difficult than that. Whoever you use can only come from your group. And as you decide how many you will need, remember that once inside the rock formation you will have to throw up an effective resistance to create the diversion we need." Charaban was pushing me now.

"With phasers we should be . . ."

"No phasers inside the rocks," Charaban interrupted. "Only outside. Once you get in it's hand-to-hand combat." Charaban pushed me even harder. "What's your plan, Ten?"

"Six men. Two groups of three." I was sweating with the effort to visualize the operation as I studied the diagram.

"Yes?" Charaban urged.

"I lead one group along the southern flank, which is the more difficult one. One Lubak will lead the . . ."

"No," corrected Charaban. "You can't use One."

"Why not?" I asked.

"Because he will resent your leadership. He already

regards you as a threat. One must never know what you're doing."

"That means I can't use any of his allies." I was worried as to how I was going to assemble a team with what was left of the group.

"Unless they find greater opportunity with you." Two Charaban's tone was almost civil.

Opportunity. Of course. Ambition. The power is with the leader others are willing to follow because he promises them an advantage they lack. I began to see what the exchange was.

"Who leads the other team?" Charaban wasn't finished.

"Eight." Logically the best choice, once I got beyond my obligation to One Lubak.

"And if he's the Pit warrior you claim he is then he should work with the others." Charaban remembered my assessment and challenged its truth.

"It's crucial that the members of your group perform well in the combat phase," added Drabar.

Besides Eight and myself there was Five . . . and Three. I detested Three. Plus he was an ally of One. But his massive strength was matched by his ferocity. Charaban knew that I was struggling with choice.

"Whoever they are, Ten, just make sure that Ramaklan hasn't already recruited them. Our task is difficult enough; betrayal would make it nearly impossible," he warned.

"And betrayal means that the leader has failed to earn the trust of his men," fat Charaban added to the warning.

When I had finished cleaning the last room and replaced the implements, the first colors of dawn were stretching across the desert and lighting my way back to the First Level compound. I was exhausted from the long night's test. I had made my first alliance, and was now part of a cohort looking to seize political power by an act of force. I felt stripped and exposed. The boy who had played among the stately monuments in the Tarlak Sector and pretended to heroism and great deeds had been left behind. Now that I was faced with the hard work of actual leadership, the fear of failure—the very thing Charaban told me there was no room for—had assumed new dimensions. Find your allies, I heard Calyx say, and work from there.

That morning Eight and I were assigned to a construction unit repairing an old barrier on the western perimeter. I told him I needed to talk without other ears, and we managed to work ourselves away from the rest of the team. He knew about the Competition, and he knew that the Ramaklan and the Charaban were recruiting. It happened that he had an appointment to meet with a Ramaklan recruiter that evening.

"But I knew I'd be contacted by you," he said as a simple matter of fact.

"How?" I asked.

"Charaban warned me." Eight studied my confused reaction. "He didn't tell you we spoke?"

"No." Anger replaced confusion, but we had to continue our work of identifying weak sections of wall and marking them for repair. And I had to continue assembling my team. "What did he say?"

"He asked me to be involved. When he told me you were committed I agreed." Again, simply stated. We scraped the wall to cover our conversation.

"Thank you," I said with relief. Eight was the difference between success and the abyss; especially with the others. Eight was respected by everyone, even Three. One despised him, but he harmed Eight at the expense of his own leadership stature.

"He said you were leading our team, and that you would make the assignments. That's quite an honor." In his quiet way Eight was impressed.

I described our mission and what I wanted from him. He would take Five and Three to penetrate the northern flank while I led Two and Four on the southern. I explained my choices, based on the restrictions Charaban had given me.

"Don't take Two," Eight said.

"Why?" I asked.

"He can't be trusted—especially if One is not involved. They're family." How did everybody except me have this personal information? "If Two agrees, chances are he's a Ramaklan spy."

"Who's left?" I was certain there was no one.

"Seven," he replied.

"He's too raw. His ridges have barely emerged. We need fighters," I protested.

"He has great heart, and he's loyal. I'll make sure he's ready to fight," Eight assured me. "I'll take him on my team and you take Three. *That*'ll be the challenge. If you can get Three past their flank undetected. . . ."

The signal to stop working interrupted Eight, but I knew what he meant. Stealth requires the kind of sustained patience that's almost totally missing in Three. If there's no room for failure, then there must be a solution to every problem. I wanted very much to believe that that indeed was so.

Entry:

During the period leading to the Competition, my only respite from the preparations was when Palandine and I managed to spend some time together. Besides the training area, we would meet in the secluded study nooks of the Archival Center and in sections of the Grounds she knew would be safe. Tonight we were in an enclosure of the Grounds that was made impenetrable by the thick surrounding foliage. This was the place she had wanted to show me before we were interrupted by the intern at the Center.

Our conversations covered all the areas that were forbidden—names, personalities, family backgrounds, and most important, the true power structure of Bamarren. The Institute was a microcosm of Cardassian society, and the adults—prefects, docents, and custodians—controlled from a distance. The idea was that students would become more effective citizens of the greater culture if they learned how to administer the microcosm themselves. There was a constant striving upwards at Bamarren, just as there was in the greater society, and at the highest levels that striving was transmuted into imperial expansion. The students of Bamarren were the future guardians of Cardassian security; we would become the eyes and ears of the military, the diplomats and the politicians. In these meetings Palandine was teaching me how to use my eyes and ears in a manner that complemented the teachings of Calyx and Mila.

"And you have to use that wonderful smile of yours more often, Elim."

"What's that got to do with listening?" That was the subject, and Palandine had typically made a jump in logic I couldn't follow. She also forgot that I was a Cardassian male and smiling was not one of our strong features.

"If they feel comfortable with you, people will tell you stories about themselves that will reveal their deepest secrets."

"But what if the stories aren't true?" I challenged. "I could smile till my cheeks hurt, and you could tell me any kind of story you wanted—and what would I know about you except what you invented?"

"You would know, if you were truly listening, the kind of story I use to define myself," she asserted.

"But it's not the truth!" I maintained.

"Why not? Because it's not what *you* believe? Or it doesn't fit a definition of the truth that someone taught you? Look at people, Elim." Palandine gestured as if the enclosure were filled with people. "Observe them. The way they walk and talk, the way they hold themselves and eat their meals. That's what they believe about themselves. Is it the 'truth'? Are they really that way? I don't know. Perhaps it *is* a lie. But what people lie about the most are themselves, and these lies become the stories they believe and want to tell you."

"As long as I'm smiling," I mumbled. This conversation had started when I complained that others—especially Palandine—seemed to have information that was inaccessible to me. It progressed into one of our heated discussions relating intelligence gathering to the nature of truth itself.

"Truth, as we've learned to define it, is not only overrated," she went on with a controlled passion, "it's designed to keep people in the dark."

This last statement stopped me.

"You mean the way we've been taught?" I asked.

"Of course."

"What about our government?"

"They tell us the stories that we need to know in order to be good citizens," she replied carefully.

"They don't tell us the truth, is what you're saying," I concluded.

"There you go again. They tell us *their* truth, Elim, and we are here to learn how to listen." Palandine paused and gave me one of her looks that went to the back of my head and made me shiver. "You're so serious, Elim, so glum that even before you open your mouth you're telling a story. But the nonverbal stories are the most dangerous, because they can be interpreted any number of ways. You have to smile, because you have power. If you listen to people with the look you have on your face right now, they'll suspect that you'll disapprove or criticize or—even worse—laugh at their stories. And there's nothing worse than being ridiculed. You know that."

And I did. Perhaps that was why I was so resistant to the idea of smiling. It made me feel vulnerable to others, the way I had with Charaban that night at the Central Gate.

"Let the ones without power scowl and make fierce faces. You smile. It's an invitation to connect with another person. And once the invitation is accepted, relax and listen . . . you'll come to know as much as you'll ever need to about that person," she said with a smile that I greedily accepted.

* * *

Palandine also introduced me to poetry, particularly the work of Maran Bry, who was notorious for being critical of the Bajoran occupation.

> Ghosted light, colored by the gas and
>   dust of the Corillion Nebula
> Dances in my dreams and descends
>   like a shimmering wave
> Where it fills the space between sleep and waking
> And clothes my loneliness with your naked birth.

She opened her eyes and the light from the Blind Moon, the third and weakest in our system, reflected the excitement she felt in his poetry. At that moment I could have died and gone to the Hall of Memories if I'd been able to take this moment with me.

"Yes, 'Solar Winds,' " a voice said behind me, so soft as to be almost unrecognizable. "I also enjoy his 'Paean to Kunderah.'

> The price they paid in blood is returned
>   by your healing kiss,
> My matriarch, keeper of the mysteries and companion
> To those heroes who stood between us
>   and eternal night.

It was Charaban; and as stunning as his sudden presence was the choice of poem. "Kunderah" unfavorably contrasts the celebrated victory against the Klingons with the Bajoran Occupation. He stood there, watching us with a bemused expression, framed by the narrow opening of fendle leaves that connected the pathway to our green and muffled enclosure. With his easy grace and smile, it was as if he'd always been here.

"I didn't know you liked Maran Bry, Barkan." Palandine behaved as if she expected him.

"You never asked . . . Palandine," he replied, amused by this use of their names. "And what kind of example are we setting for Elim Garak?" This was the first time I had heard my full name since I had left home, and it suddenly made me feel self-conscious. I stood up awkwardly.

"No, no, please," Charaban motioned me back down. "I didn't mean to disrupt your . . . poetry reading."

Palandine's laugh was more delighted than ever. " 'No, no,' said the Mogrund, 'I didn't mean to take the bad children to the subterranean city,' " she said with Mogrund ferocity.

"I hope you're not comparing me to the Mogrund," Charaban said with mock outrage.

"Well, I suppose you're a little better looking than that," Palandine allowed. (The Mogrund was a spiky lump with several frightening red eyes.)

"Unless there are some wrongs here I need to right." Charaban imitated the creature's voice—which was easier for him since his own voice was already halfway there. I knew they were enjoying the banter but I felt caught in the middle, and vulnerable. According to the rules, I was in a place I did not belong, with a female student, indulging in "personal excesses." But if the two of them were concerned, they certainly didn't show it.

"I never would have guessed the two of you shared a love of poetry," Charaban said with genuine surprise.

"Who exposed us?" Palandine asked.

"Drabar. I asked him to do a security check on Ten Lubak. You're not a Ramaklan spy, are you, One Ketay?" he asked with the same lack of concern. Her answer was another laugh and a provocative look that challenged any and all assumptions he dared make about her. I jumped up.

"I swear," I began, trying to overcome a very dry mouth. "I've told her nothing of our plans, One Charaban, and she has never asked." It was true; we talked about everything except our work.

"Why not? Aren't they worth talking about?" he asked with a serious face. I had no idea how to respond.

"You're confusing him, Barkan. That's not very nice."

"My apologies. Believe me, Ten, I would have been surprised if you had."

"But Drabar thought he had," she said.

"No, actually, it was Two Charaban," he replied.

"So this 'security check' is now common knowledge," she wryly observed. I had the same thought.

"This is as far as it goes," he assured her. Palandine nodded in response, giving him a last careful look. Charaban smiled back with an openness that seemed to answer her concern. He sat down on a rock, gave me a look that was more a reappraisal, and then looked away. In the ensuing silence, each of us became involved with our own private thoughts. In the corner where she sat cross-legged, Palandine studied her exquisitely shaped hands. Now, with the three of us, the dynamic in the enclosure had changed, and we were all adjusting. I no longer had Palandine to myself—but surprisingly, I didn't mind, in fact I was pleased that Charaban was here. His stillness, like everything else about him, had grace and strength. I sneaked another look in his direction and marveled that this was the same person I had first encountered in the storeroom. He returned my look, and in the next few moments a bond grew between us that I had never thought possible. The whooshing flap of a night bird pulled our attention up to the section of glimmering sky that was visible.

"I love the Blind Moon," Charaban said softly.

"Why is it called that?" I asked, deeply relieved by the mysterious change that had come over us.

"It's the time for lovers' assignations," Palandine answered. "The moon will give them enough light to meet, but not so much for them to be discovered."

"So if you and Elim were true lovers I wouldn't have been able to find you," Charaban teased.

"That's right, Barkan," she said with a direct look. I shifted position in the ensuing silence and tried to hide my disappointment with Palandine's reply, but at the same time, the pleasure I felt in the company of these two people kept growing.

"See?" Palandine suddenly addressed me. "You *can* do it."

"What?" I was startled by her delighted burst.

"Smile. Look at that, Barkan. Wouldn't you tell someone with that smile everything he wanted to know?" she demanded.

"The first time I met him—well, the second . . ." he corrected himself, "he had a smile that I wanted to wipe off his face." He was referring to that early morning in front of the Central Gate.

"But it wasn't *that* smile," Palandine insisted.

"No," he conceded. "Definitely not that one." And the truth was that I could feel this smile throughout my entire body.

We settled into another silence that lasted until the Blind Moon disappeared behind the foliage. I was certain at the time that for each of us this silent gathering was a precious respite from the relentless strivings of Bamarren ambition. There were other such gatherings, but this was the one that I will take with me to the Hall of Memories. If I could have stopped time . . .

17

Entry:

Today I thought I'd have lunch at the recently re-opened Klingon establishment in honor of my new friend from the Jeffries tube, who turns out to be a nephew of General Martok. As I made my way through the Promenade—which gets more congested every day—I thought of the dabo girl, Tir Remara, and wondered why her name was so familiar. Odo said she wanted to see me to express her gratitude, and I laughed at the irony: a Bajoran wanting to thank a Cardassian. On a sudden impulse, I redirected myself to Quark's.

When I entered the bar, Quark smirked at me. "The savior of dabo girls. You know, Garak, you used to have a wonderful reputation as someone who minded his own business. What happened? Was it a bad brand of *kanar*?"

"No worse than usual," I smiled. A master of compassion, our friend Quark. But judging from the large and loud group of Klingons present, he needn't have worried about a drop in business.

Remara saw me, and we made eye contact. She finished paying out latinum from the last spin of the wheel, motioned to another girl to take over the table, and approached me. Quark was not pleased.

"Make it fast, Remara. The Klingons are here for you—not Byla." Quark stayed as if to monitor our conversation, but Remara just looked at him with a level, clear expression. He blinked.

"You heard me." And he moved away. When she turned those clear, gray eyes to me, I immediately understood why so many people wanted to play dabo when she was spinning the wheel.

"Thank you. For yesterday," she said simply.

"Well, I . . . I don't think. . . ." I was astounded—I couldn't get a clear sentence out of my mouth. But she knew what I was going to say.

"He was very drunk and he was going to hurt me. He's not a bad man, but he's the type who's dangerous past a certain point."

I could only nod in agreement. She was older than I had originally thought, and clearly more intelligent than the usual dabo girl. Girl. She was as much of a girl as I was a boy. Other than Leeta, this was the first dabo woman I had ever seen. I'm sure her popularity among the Klingons must be immense, otherwise Quark would never allow such intelligence and maturity to spin the wheel. As I stood there, I totally forgot that she was wearing that silly skimpy outfit. Her poise, the directness of her gaze . . . I also forgot that she was a Bajoran.

"I have to return to work, but I'd like to talk with you. We had a mutual friend. I'm done after the second shift—is that too late for you?"

"N-no. No, not at all." My lips were betraying me. I sounded like Rom. "Shall I meet you here?"

"No. The observation lounge on the second level."

As she went back to the table I noticed Major Kira sitting in the corner. She was giving me the same look she had used whenever I had been in the company of Ziyal. Because of those hard, impenetrable eyes, I can only imagine what she thought of this exchange. I nodded and . . . smiled.

It was late, and there were few people on the second level. As I waited in the observation lounge it came to me why Remara's name was familiar—she'd been a friend of Ziyal. I remembered now Ziyal saying that Remara was some kind of teacher on Bajor, and that she occasionally worked as a dabo girl to support her family. When she'd made enough latinum she'd return to her life on Bajor. Quark put up with this arrangement because her statuesque beauty attracted many people—not just Klingons, and not just men—to the dabo table. Even those who never played.

"Thank you for coming." Her voice came from behind me. I jumped up from my chair, surprised. She was standing there in a tasteful but modest frock. Without her dabo-girl shoes we stood eye to eye. Her face was scrubbed clean of the makeup and her hair was unpinned, falling below her shoulders. It was somewhat darker now, and I wondered if she lightened it somehow when she was working. There was also a distance in her look which, coupled with her directness, created an odd dynamic. The distance challenged you to work yourself closer—if you had the courage.

"You surprised me," I said, reminding myself to

breathe. "I expected you to come from the other direction."

"I wanted to get out of my child's costume. I hope you're not disappointed."

"Please," I laughed. "I'm relieved. To be truthful, I'm not terribly comfortable around those outfits."

"Really? Are they too revealing for you?" she asked.

"Not at all. The design puts my teeth on edge." It was her turn to laugh.

"Amazing, isn't it? People seem to love the way they look."

"I don't think it's the way the costume looks that they love," I offered.

"Well," she smiled modestly, "I'm not complaining. It keeps the dabo wheel spinning."

"Which pleases Quark to no end," I added.

"Indeed." She took one of the chairs, and I sat in one across from her.

"Elim, isn't it?"

"Yes. Elim Garak."

"Ziyal spoke well of you. She was particularly grateful for your kindness. This always intrigued me."

"Why?" I asked, knowing full well what was coming.

"You're a Cardassian."

"There's nothing I can do about that, I'm afraid." We looked at each other for a long moment, and the distance felt even greater. I wondered if anyone had ever made the crossing.

"I think Ziyal once mentioned that you were a teacher." I shifted the focus onto her.

"In a manner of speaking. I'm a counselor. When

I'm not being a dabo girl, of course. My work here is to counsel people out of their latinum."

"And on Bajor?" I asked.

"I counsel people out of their nightmares from the Occupation," she said, without any inflection.

"Ah," I replied, with as genial a smile as I could muster.

"And you're a tailor."

"I am."

"Have you always been a tailor?"

"Has anyone always been anything?"

"Were you trained as one?"

"In a manner of speaking. For that and other things."

"Like?"

"I worked as a gardener for a period," I replied. She was unapologetic about her questions. Either she had a great appetite for information about other people . . . or something else was going on.

"I love to garden," she said.

"Really? You're very fortunate then. Bajor has a salubrious climate for growing things."

"Oh. So you've been to Bajor?" she asked.

"No. Not really."

" 'Not really'?" she repeated with a bemused look.

"I stopped over . . . once. On the way here actually. Just long enough to transfer to a shuttle. But your climate is well known."

"In Cardassia," she added.

"Yes. Among other places, I'm sure." A game was in full operation now, and I felt excited and challenged to find out just what the game was.

"What's your favorite plant?" she asked.

"The Edosian orchid," I replied without thinking.

"Yes," she nodded. "It has an extraordinary blossom."

"Have you grown them?" I asked.

"No, I'm afraid I don't have the patience."

"It's not so much patience, I think, as it is the willingness to live with their mystery."

"How do you mean?" She was a genuinely curious person.

"They're deceptive. They appear to be rather common at first, but if they're treated well . . . if you watch for the clues carefully . . . they'll almost tell you how to grow them."

"Ah, but I was never under the impression that they were common." Her smile was deeply engaging, and I felt somehow that the distance had narrowed. We had come to an understanding.

"But I must get some sleep. The dabo tables spin early tomorrow and I'm on a shuttle back to Bajor in the evening."

We rose. She held her hand out to me. It's an unaccustomed gesture for me, but I took it. Her grip was warm and firm; my senses were alert.

"When you return, I hope you'll visit my shop. I'd be happy to serve you in any way," I said.

"That's very kind. Thank you, Elim." A familiar, pleasant sensation went through me when she said my name. "And I, too, would be pleased to serve you however I could." She squeezed my hand slightly and left the way she came. The understanding, I thought as I watched her graceful strength move away, was that this was only the beginning of the game.

Entry:

A strong wind blew just before sunset and I hoped that it would continue; it would make our task of getting past the Ramaklan flanks much easier. But as soon as the sun dipped below the horizon behind us the wind stopped, and the darkening Wilderness was preserved in a resounding stillness. I took a deep breath.

"Lubak!" Charaban growled with his gruffest voice. I stepped forward from the mass of our troops who were standing in formation in front of the Eastern Gate, and marched up to Charaban who was flanked by Drabar and fat Charaban. It always amazed me how he was able to transform himself and become whatever person the situation—the context—demanded he be. I wondered if Charaban was part *regnar.*

"We'll wait for your signal, Lubak, but if there's any indication that your teams have been exposed, we'll attack. In that case you must do whatever is necessary to prevent their flanks from collapsing in on us. Understood?"

"Yes, One Charaban!" I replied.

"Position your men and begin," he ordered.

I nodded to Eight, and he stepped forward with his team, Five and Seven. I could see that Seven was wide-eyed with tension, but Eight had assured me that he was ready to fight. Five appeared as solid as ever. Eight gave me a last look before he led his team to the north and disappeared in the gathering darkness. I motioned to Three and Four, and they stepped forward from the ranks. Four looked typically bored, but Three surprised me with his apparent calm. He had been a difficult student during the training sessions, and I was anxious about his performance.

"For the Empire!" Charaban growled.

"Victory!" we roared in answer.

As the main troops deployed, I led my team south to a predetermined rock formation. These were the last rocks we would have as cover until we met the enemy. Before us was the exposed desert slope that led to the enemy position. We had been instructed to wait here until the first assault probe was launched. This probe consisted of a small team that would be sent right up the middle of the slope and straight toward the enemy redoubt. The purpose of the probe was to draw enemy fire, during which we would hopefully get an idea of how their defenses were aligned and then begin our own advance during the brief engagement. The probe, of course, was a purely tactical move and had no chance of success. We scanned the now moon-saturated darkness as we waited for our moment.

"Last equipment check," I whispered.

"Ready," Four replied after a moment.

"Three?" Did he hear me?

"What?" he snapped.

"Equipment check!"

"Yes, I'm ready! How many times are you going to ask?" Three hated the fact that I was in charge, and during the training he had grudgingly taken instruction when he realized that mastery of my stealth techniques was absolutely necessary for success. He wasn't bright, but he was ambitious, and he was hoping for a number One designation at the next evaluation.

Response to the probe should have happened already;

it was being launched as we moved out. I could only guess that the enemy—aware of the tactic—was allowing the probe to penetrate as deeply as possible until it nearly reached the redoubt, at which point it could be intercepted without the flanks ever revealing themselves. The probe had been Two Charaban's idea, and when I'd brought up this lack of enemy response as a possibility he'd dismissed it.

"What's going on?" Four demanded, with more concern in his voice than I'd ever heard. He was a clever operator, very observant; he gauged the temperature of any given situation and acted accordingly. He wasn't as accomplished as Charaban in this regard, and you never knew where his true loyalty was, but he always took care of himself.

"Nothing's going on that's going to help us," I replied, concerned that we were losing precious time. "Let's go."

"We're supposed to wait for the engagement," Three resisted.

"Let's go—that's an order!" I was the leader, Charaban had told me during the last planning session, and I must never allow a challenge to compromise my position. "Triangulate. I'm in front, Four rear right, Three rear left." I wanted to keep Three as far away from the enemy flank as possible, since he was the biggest and least adept at stealth.

We began the slow crawl. I immediately flattened and spread my consciousness, feeling my breathing respond accordingly: movement only on a long outgoing breath, complete stillness on the intake. The three of us had to be synchronized, and I could feel Four adapt beautifully to my pattern. Three struggled, as I knew he would at the beginning, but with Four and me holding the pattern he was able to settle in. We moved as one.

We heard the response to the probe, and as I had anticipated it revealed nothing about the flanks—at least on our southern side. I had no idea how they would angle the flank out from the central defensive position, and this meant we had to proceed with extreme vigilance from the beginning. My only concern was not with the moonlight—even with the ghostly illumination we could blend in well enough—but with the total lack of wind, unusual for the Mekar. Four and I made almost no sound, but Three's bulk made enough of a dragging sound in the sand to warrant concern.

Then I heard a sound coming from the darkness in front of us: I had forgotten that the lack of wind could also work to our advantage. It couldn't be their flank, it was too soon. And why were they moving? We stopped and listened as the sound, a slow and muffled crunching, came closer and extended from right to left. The flank was moving toward us! I could make out the shadowy outlines of enemy soldiers, evenly spaced and moving with precise coordination in order to minimize all sound. It appeared that the flank was executing a hinging maneuver that would sweep its southern side. If the northern flank was doing the same maneuver, then both flanks, connected to the central redoubt, could conceivably meet in the middle. But this kind of pincer movement could leave them exposed to being outflanked, unless—

They were almost on top of us. This was our first test. I prayed that Three and Four were focused, and that. . . . An enemy foot came down next to my head; the other foot brushed my side pack. I could hear Three's breathing turn ragged, but thankfully the passing crunch, crunch, crunch was dominant. They passed . . . and I waited to see if there was any activity from the north that would indicate exposure of the other team. Nothing but the receding crunch, crunch, crunch. Three's breathing began to settle, and we moved ahead.

Time becomes meaningless working with this kind of concentration; only objects and events mark progress. But I knew our coordination was strong and sustained. This had been my concern from the beginning of training. It's one thing to work by oneself, it's another to get a unit to work as one. But when it happens, the mystery is how the flattened and spread energy of each is transformed into the energy field that sustains and propels all.

At one point we encountered a much thinner and fixed line of sentinels who were guarding against any outflanking Charaban maneuver. By then we were so well coordinated that there wasn't a ripple of anxiety in our unified field as we passed them. Just as I was beginning to hope that perhaps we would have a clear path to the redoubt, again I heard the faint crunch, crunch, crunch from behind us. The hinge was swinging both ways.

We stopped, and returning anxiety dissolved our unity. As we waited, I could feel the night chill creeping into my body and creating a tremulous reaction. The more I tried to resist, the more I trembled. I was now afraid that my cooling body would betray me to the approaching soldiers, who were just behind us. I was planning how I would respond to being discovered when the soft crunching sound stopped. We waited, in a long silence broken only by the distant cry of a night *honge* hunting for prey. My trembling became worse. No matter how I tried to employ my technique, my body was too chilled to respond. I wondered if Three and Four were also struggling; I had lost contact with them.

Suddenly the crunching sound began again. I put my hand on my phaser. I was on the verge of jumping up and taking out as many of the enemy as I could. But now the sound was receding. We must have gone beyond the limit of the flank's hinging arc. Yes, they were moving back in the other direction. That meant we now had a clear path to a position behind the redoubt from which we could stage our attack. If only Eight's group had also eluded their flank.

We moved ahead at a faster pace. I wasn't sure how much time we had before light, but I knew it wasn't much. The Ramaklan had positioned their defenses so that the sun would rise in the eyes of Charaban's attacking force. We had to time our diversionary action so that they would have the same problem when they faced us. If they were blinded by the first rays of sunlight hitting them at eye level, that would wipe out some of their advantage. Once again the three of us moved as one, and I began to feel more confident. I speeded our pace until I sensed that we were close to the redoubt. I stopped, took out my night vision lens, and there it was—the distinctive outcropping of rock that faced our side. We had calculated correctly, and there wasn't much more distance to travel. Judging from the faint ghosting of light on the horizon line, there also wasn't much time before we became visible. We started our final move around to the rear of the rock. The ghosting light was also creeping toward the redoubt, and the slight movement of a solar wind began to stir the air around us. I was aware that the success of the mission now depended on how well we were able to work with the elements. Or I thought I was aware.

Just as I was looking for Eight's group and a place to stop, a faint and sudden shadow accompanied by a whooshing sound and slap of air flew by my head. My heart leaped into my mouth; I thought we were being attacked. And we were, but not by the Ramaklan. I looked up, and a swad of *honge* were taking advantage of the faint light to do some hunting—we must have looked like well-fed sand worms. I could now make out the outlines of Three and Four.

"Cover your heads and stay still," I whispered. "They'll pass." I pulled my sun cover down and curled up. I felt a sharp, painful stab on my shoulder, but I didn't react. I wanted them to pass without drawing the attention of the enemy.

"Get away! Get away from me!" Three was on his feet, screaming at the attacking *honge* who were screaming in response. His huge form was now the focus of their attention, as he waved his phaser and tried to take aim. He stumbled over Four.

"Get down, Three! We'll be spotted!" I whispered hoarsely, but I knew it was too late.

"Who's there?" a Ramaklan soldier called out from the rock.

"What are we going to do? They know we're here!" Four's eyes were enormous. Three was still doing his grotesque dance to ward off the *honge*, who were cutting and slashing from all directions. The predators obviously had drawn blood and were going for more. The light was growing stronger; we had to take some action.

"Declare yourself or we'll fire," the same Remaklan voice demanded.

"Cover me," I told Four.

"What are you going to do?" he asked.

"Just keep the *honge* off me!" I jumped up. "It's all right! We've got him!" I announced. "It's a single Charaban probe! We've got him!" I could barely make out figures above the rock line. I fired my phaser at a *honge* slashing toward my face. It went down. Four hit another. Three let out a horrible scream. I was desperately looking for Eight's team.

"Who are you?" another voice asked from the rock.

"One Lubak!" I lied. "Ramaklan flank. The Charaban probe was attacked by *honge*." The *honge* had been driven off by the phaser fire, and Three was now eerily silent. He turned to me, and the right side of his face was covered in blood. When I looked closer I could see that the eye socket was empty. He was in shock, and totally disoriented. I aimed my phaser and stunned him into unconsciousness.

"What are you doing, Ten?" Four cried out.

"He's under control!" I yelled to the rock.

"Bring him in!" the second voice ordered. I wondered if this was One Ramaklan.

"We're coming!" I answered. I started to lift Three, but his dead weight was impossible. "Help me, Four."

"You're not going to bring him to them?" He was incredulous.

"No, *we* are. Now help me!" I ordered. Four hesitated. "We have no choice. We use him as cover to get there and then begin our attack. That's our assignment. Now help me or you're on report!"

Four got up, looked around fearfully for any remaining *honge* and then helped me lift the huge body. It was then he saw Three's right eye was missing. He nearly lost his hold.

"Steady, Four!"

"His eye!"

"We're coming," I yelled. "Let's go," I said to the horrified Four. As we struggled to the rock, trying to keep the body in front of us—to mask our Charaban-green uniforms as opposed to the Ramaklan black—I detected movement to my right. *Let it be Eight,* I thought.

"As soon as we get close enough, we have to force our way inside before they can use their phasers. Use Three as a shield." I was almost breathless with effort, and Four could only grunt in response.

Just as we approached the rock, I could see that three or four Ramaklan soldiers were massed at an opening, waiting for us. About twenty paces away, sunlight suddenly beamed straight past us and lit up their bodies and faces as the sun came over the horizon behind us. The timing couldn't have been better.

"Steady, Four. On my signal," I whispered with what little breath I had left. We came closer; there were four of them, very distinct in their identifying black vests, shielding their eyes and training their phasers on us.

"Stop," one of them said. We were five paces away. "Put the body down," he instructed.

"Of course," I replied. "Don't let go," I whispered to Four. I began to stumble toward them as if I had lost my balance.

"Stop!" the voice repeated.

"I'm sorry. I lost my footing," I apologized. We were two paces away.

"Wait! He's not . . ." one of them began to say.

"Now!" I cried, and using Three as a barrier, Four and I pushed through the opening and knocked at least two of them over before they could use their phasers. We were inside—and the fight had begun in earnest.

"Here they come!" I heard someone yell, and in the chaos that followed I couldn't be sure if he meant us, Eight's team, or the main force. All I know is that Four and I immediately moved into a shifting tandem strategem, and we fought like we were possessed by the spirit and strength of many. The advantage of surprise was ours. Fear and pumping fluids fueled us. It became a blur of action and reaction, parry and blow, shift and stand, attack and defend; there was no space in between, no moment of thought or pause. I was hit several times, but I felt nothing. At one point, I saw Seven fighting like a screech crake and I fought even harder, encouraged by his ferocity of heart, which I had doubted.

"Over here, Ten!" I followed the call for help without hesitation. I had lost Four, but by now the main force had joined the fray, and the fighting was scattered over the entire area. It was fat Charaban being pummeled by three Ramaklan soldiers. He was doing his best and moving with surprising agility, but to no avail. I grabbed one and threw him off, but before I could turn back I was picked up from behind like I was a baby and tossed hard against a rock face. The air was crushed out of me, and I was on my hands and knees desperately trying to draw it back in, but before I could fat Charaban was thrown on top of me, and I began to suffocate. This was my worst fear. Besides the memory of Tain's punishment, I was tortured by nightmares in which I was buried alive. A red, insane surge of energy came from somewhere inside me, and with a scream I threw Two Charaban off me, grabbed the closest Ramaklan—who was twice my size and was probably the one who'd thrown me against the rock—and used every skill I had learned in the Pit to punish him for bringing me face-to-face with my nightmare death. The expression on the big Ramaklan was one of shock and incomprehension as I hit and kicked and elbowed and gouged. The action had become suspended in another reality. Everything else dropped away as this student became the focus for all my rage and fear. Suddenly I felt hands all over my body and I was pulled away.

"That's enough, Ten!" I heard a familiar voice say.

"No, it's not enough!" I didn't recognize my voice; I thought someone else had spoken for me. It wasn't until the hands had gotten control of me that my anger began to subside and I came back from wherever I had gone. The faces of the people holding me back began to look familiar. The first one I saw was Eight.

"Didn't you hear the signal? We've won." He was looking at me with real concern. My face felt wet, and I wondered where the moisture had come from. I wanted to ask him—I wanted to ask him what had happened. I knew, looking in Eight's eyes, that he would always tell me truth. But I didn't ask. I felt ashamed.

"It's over, Lubak!" This time I recognized Charaban. "It's over." Or I thought I recognized him. This was yet another Charaban, but this one was a slightly distorted image of the original. It's a mask, I thought. Then I remembered what had happened to me underneath Two Charaban's massive bulk, trying to draw breath. And I realized that the moisture on my face was my tears.

"Get up, Lubak," he said with a hearty and somewhat wooden jocularity. It's a new mask; it didn't have his usual grace. "We're heroes." He turned to the gathering crowd. "We've broken all records for the Competition!" he announced. "Victory!" He thrust his fist to the sky.

"Victory!" the crowd repeated.

"For the Empire!" Charaban thrust again.

"Victory!" They responded even louder. It was astounding. The mask was softening and integrating into the rest of Charaban. As he interacted with the crowd of students, as he accepted their adulation and fealty, I could see that he was taking ownership of this new persona with increasing confidence. Could anyone else see this? I looked around. I was surrounded by masks. I looked at Eight. His mask was stoic, but his eyes were always there, constant. Did he see what I saw? Palandine would laugh at such a question. How could he, I answered myself—he has his own eyes. I struggled to my feet, with Eight's help. My body felt broken beyond repair.

"Breathe. Don't stop breathing—no matter how much it hurts," Eight instructed. I tried to follow his directive, and gasped as the air turned into broken glass as it entered my lungs. I desperately wanted to share in the joy of victory I saw on the faces surrounding me, but the moment was so mixed with physical pain—and with another, more complicated feeling. I didn't like what had happened to me when fat Charaban's body had nearly swallowed me—being overcome by the fear of never drawing breath again. I was also disturbed by what I saw in Charaban's face, and somehow, vaguely, the two were related. I tried to shake off these feelings and thoughts and join in the celebration. And with Eight's help, I was able to pull myself back into this moment of triumph.

19

Entry:

There was an almost surreal quality to Bamarren the next day. The Institute looked like a clean and orderly outpost harboring the sick, wounded, and disfigured from some horrific war. With the help of a cane, I walked with a painful, crouching limp; my right leg and back were just short of being broken. Others were not so fortunate. The infirmaries were overflowing with serious cases like Three, who had lost his eye, and worse. Those races who accuse Cardassians of being nothing better than mindless predators would rest their case if they saw the elite of our youth on the morning after the Competition.

At a special assembly in the outdoor arena, the Bamarren students gathered as Charaban and One Ramaklan stood on the sunken stage waiting for us. I sat with Eight and the other Lubaks, and we dedicated our lives and loyalty to the Empire in a rousing version of "Cardassia Forever." Unity was the stated theme of the rally, but the actual business was the transference of power from Ramaklan to Charaban, a ritual that was performed by the opposing factions after every Competition to legitimize the new order.

With a brittle dignity, Ramaklan handed the Bamarren Saber, the symbol of student leadership, to One Charaban, who graciously accepted it. In his speech, he praised the Ramaklan side for their "courageous and well-planned opposition" and we all cheered, knowing that never in the history of the Competition had a side capitulated so quickly. As I watched him speak, I tried to remember that moment the day before when I had clearly seen him assume the mask of leadership. What was it I saw in that moment that continued to nag at me? Could I even trust what I saw, given the state I was in? But his mastery was so complete now, his speech and carriage so elegant and reassuring, that I let the memory of that moment go and joined the others in acceptance and adulation.

I scanned the audience from my vantage point, looking for Palandine. This was one of the few occasions when males and females were brought together. The females had their own Competition and leadership structure, but we all participated in any major group ritual. I finally located her sitting down near the front. She was strongly focused on the ritual transfer and on Charaban. I understood that she'd soon be preparing for her own Competition, and that whatever transpired here today would have special meaning for her.

And then it happened. The irony, of course, was that I had gotten past my mixed feelings of yesterday and was basking in the glow of our victory. I even enjoyed the aches and pain of my body as evidence of my participation. I accepted Charaban's patronage and leadership, and was prepared to serve as a member of his council. At one of our last planning sessions, Charaban had told me that after we'd won the Competition he was going to ask me to join the council as his Second Level liaison, a prestigious position that would consolidate my own base of power. I was about to become a member of the inner circle of Bamarren leadership.

As Charaban introduced each member of his council, with his title and a brief description of his duties—Two Charaban would coordinate and organize the council agenda, Drabar would oversee all school training programs—I was becoming increasingly intoxicated with a nervous excitement. As a young boy playing in the Tarlak Sector, my dreams and fantasies had been fueled by a desire for this kind of recognition. I grabbed hold of my cane, determined not to stumble as I made my way down to the front.

". . . and last, for the important position of Second Level liaison, which requires someone who is able to represent his entire Level in such a way as to assure their voice in all policy matters. . . ."

All First and Second Level business would funnel through me before it reached the council. The power of the position was self-evident. I positioned my good leg, so that I could rise without wobbling. Eight, anticipating that I would be called, was ready to assist if necessary.

". . . Nine Lubak!"

I started to rise, expecting a correction. I had heard the words, but my body was programmed to go. Eight, however, grabbed my elbow and prevented me from making an even bigger fool of myself. Nine Lubak? But there was no correction. Nine, sitting almost directly in front of me, rose to the cheers and applause that rightfully belonged to me. Nine Lubak!? I had a violent urge to vomit. Eight turned to me. I thought he was going to instruct me to breathe again, but he knew better. I retreated inside and put on a neutral mask. At the end of the ceremony we rose and chanted the Ten Obligations and ended with—

"Victory!"

"For the Empire!"

—three times. Eight, I knew, wanted to speak, but I

remained behind the mask and hobbled off. I didn't want to speak to anyone . . . and I didn't, for days following the ceremony. I simply disappeared.

20

Entry:

The truth is that I have come to enjoy tailoring. The problems of measuring, choosing a fabric and design suitable to the person and the occasion, cutting and putting the pieces together in a comfortable and attractive fit can keep my mind away from those realities over which I have no control. And the more difficult the problem, the more peace of mind I am able to maintain. Designing something for Odo, for example, is a unique challenge. He appeared in my shop one day and began to inspect the mounted displays as if there were hidden messages in the designs and arrangements. When I asked if there was something I could help him with, he replied that he was looking for some "ideas."

"Changing style, are we?" Odo shrugged, trying to appear unattached to such frivolous concerns. But I knew what this was all about—it was only a matter of time before he decided to make himself more attractive to Kira. Yet as I tried to elicit the specific details of what he wanted, he became shy and reticent—almost irritable.

"Something that's not so . . . baggy," he said as he impatiently gestured to his drab constable uniform. I could understand his concern. Major Kira's tightly wrapped figure made us all look baggy.

I looked up from Odo's designs, stretched, and felt a twinge of stiffness in my lower back. I had lost track of time, and decided that a short walk would relieve the tension that had accumulated from holding the same physical position for so long. As I came through the doors I nearly ran into Dr. Bashir.

"Doctor. What an unexpected surprise." And it was . . . for both of us.

"Hallo . . . Garak. . . ." I realized that his breeziness was a cover for the awkwardness of this chance encounter. Was he passing by? Coming in? Standing here debating with himself?

"Can I offer you some tea?" I asked, perversely ignoring his discomfort.

"I don't want to be a bother. I'm sure you're busy," he gently demurred.

"No bother. Your timing's impeccable, as always. I was just taking a break. It's that time of day, isn't it?"

Bashir smiled and accepted the invitation. I led the way back into the shop, and while I coaxed two teas—one red leaf and one Earl Grey—from my ancient replicator in the back, the doctor strolled about as if he were genuinely interested in the various sartorial displays. He was clearly ill at ease, and I wondered how the gulf between us had widened to such an extent. I was determined to narrow it.

"Who was this Earl Grey person?" I asked, as I cleared a space for us at the counter and positioned two stools.

"I don't really know. Probably a rich man in our

nineteenth century who came up with this blend," he speculated.

"More money than taste," I replied. The smell of the tea always put my teeth on edge.

Even with his discomfort, Bashir's laugh had an ease and charm that reminded me of someone else. We remained silent as we sipped our respective teas. Sounds from the Promenade drifted in.

"I understand that you were quite the knight in shining armor the other day," he said, breaking the silence, obviously referring to my escapade with the Klingon giant.

"Please, Doctor, it's an incident best forgotten by everyone," I replied.

"Why? You behaved honorably not only toward the dabo girl, but with the Klingon soldier as well. Staying with him like that when he was suffering was well beyond the call of duty," the Doctor said sincerely. "Are you embarrassed by what you did?"

"I'm embarrassed by the attention it's brought me. Please, let's say no more about it," I requested. The Doctor shook his head and went back to his tea. We drifted into another silence.

"What I *am* embarrassed about," I said too loudly, "is my lack of control at our last luncheon. It was inexcusable."

"It's one of the reasons I stopped by today. I hadn't seen you since and I wanted to make sure you were all right," he said.

"That's very kind of you, Doctor. I'm fine." This took me by surprise. Perhaps this was not such a chance encounter after all. He *was* kind—perhaps the kindest person I've ever known. His courtesy, his consideration, indeed, his willingness to put himself at risk for people he didn't even know often astonished me. But I found his present concern about my welfare grating. I renewed my determination to rise above my irritation.

"You seemed quite upset when you left," he began, knowing full well how crotchety (as he put it) I could become at these ministrations of his. "Have you been taking those pills?"

"No . . . well, yes, but I don't think they're doing much." After the incident when the Doctor removed the cranial implant and saved my life I had terrible headaches. They have lessened considerably, but during moments of stress my head can sometimes feel like it's coming apart.

"You should have told me," the Doctor admonished in that parental tone he took with his disobedient patients. "I'll reconfigure the formula and have some new pills for you tomorrow."

"That's very kind of you, Doctor," I repeated, attempting to control my growing impatience.

"What is it, Garak? What's going on?" he asked with the disarming directness of his profession.

"Other than waiting for this invasion to take place? I'll be an old man when the Federation finally gets organized. Is it really necessary to get everyone's input? Romulans and Klingons need to be *told* what to do, not consulted or persuaded!" The expression on Bashir's face told me that I was working myself up again. "As you can see, my patience is being strained."

"Are you afraid of what you'll find there when the invasion happens?" he asked.

"Perhaps of what I *won't* find there," I replied. He nodded. Silence returned as we sipped our cooling teas. Even if I had wanted, how could I even begin to explain to him?

"Quark has a new, rather interesting holosuite program," he said, changing the subject—or so I thought.

"Let me guess. It has to do with some epic battle pitting the beleaguered British against some Cardassian-type implacable foe," I needled.

"No, no," Bashir laughed. "I'm afraid now's not the time for that. Reality has overwhelmed fantasy. No, the new program enables one to revisit his past. To pick a time, a pivotal incident."

"For what purpose?" If I wasn't sure, my returning irritation alerted me to where this was going. I knew I had to be careful.

"With a minimum of programming—time, place, key people—you can recreate a scene where you feel something happened that . . ." Bashir paused, looking for the word.

". . . that was negative, injurious, a wrong choice," I prompted.

"Yes," he conceded.

"So you can change it," I added.

"Well, not *actually*, of course . . . but psychologically, physiologically. . . ." He also was treading very carefully. I took a deep breath.

"And you think this is something I should do?" I asked bluntly.

"Honestly? Yes, I do," he replied, relieved that it was finally said.

"I see." The tea was cold now, but I kept sipping. "But you wouldn't need a program like that, would you, Doctor?"

"Oh, I don't know. I have moments in my past. . . ."

"No," I interrupted. "I mean that with your enhanced genetic capacity you are able to revise your personal history just by sitting in a room and rethinking those 'moments' from your past."

Bashir said nothing. With a faint smile, he looked down into the mug of tea he was holding between his hands, as if trying to keep it warm.

A Bolian client came down the steps outside the door and was about to enter the shop, but for some reason he stopped at the threshold. He looked at us, turned, and went back the way he came.

"I'm keeping you from your business." Bashir stood up. "I won't take up any more of your time."

"I'm pleased you stopped by." I was about to escort him to the door.

"No, you're not," he said quietly.

"Excuse me?"

"Garak, I come from a culture that has perfected the 'stiff upper lip,' " he explained with the same faint smile.

"What does that mean?" It was a genuine question; there was a change in his attitude.

"It means that we never complain, never admit to our feelings, never ask for help. It's just not done," Bashir explained. "And those people who 'lack character' and insist on airing their needs—especially in public—are subject to ridicule . . . and worse. Does this sound familiar?"

"Perhaps," I replied softly.

"But I'm also a doctor, Garak. And I know which group of people suffers the most. I really won't take up any more of your time." He extended his hand, which he rarely did, and I took it. "Thank you for the tea." He turned and went out the door.

I stood there for a long moment, deeply upset. I felt trapped within myself, knowing what I had to do to get out but unable even to begin. Yes, Doctor, it does sound familiar. But as to the question of which group suffers the most. . . .

21

Entry:

At the end of three years, a review process was customary, to determine whether or not a student would progress to the next Level and if so, with what designation. It was a nerve-racking time for all of us. If you didn't progress, you were sent back home in disgrace. And if you did, you were given your position in the group commensurate with your evaluated performance of the past three years.

After Charaban's betrayal I became as withdrawn and solitary as I had been when I first came to the Institute. I tried to spend time with Palandine, but it never quite worked out; between her regular duties and the recruitment and planning for the female Competition, she had little time for anything else. But there was something else, a distance that had crept between us that I didn't understand. I felt ashamed, that somehow I had failed and it was my fault, but I found it difficult to discuss. This was probably the loneliest I had ever been.

On my way to the review hearing I felt conflicted. The lonely, betrayed part of me desperately wanted to go home and happily follow in Father's work. I hadn't seen my family in three years. And yet was it possible, after what I'd experienced here at Bamarren—the taste for success and recognition and, yes, power that I'd developed—to spend the rest of my life cleaning up after parades and tending gardens? The childish fantasies had been replaced by real accomplishment and real friendship. No—I wanted to stay.

And the moment that I came to this decision I realized that I wanted to achieve two goals: to beat Charaban in the next Competition and to win Palandine's love. The conflict dissolved, and I knew why I wanted to be here. All I had to worry about now was my designation. I was certain that I would progress, but to achieve these goals I needed a high place in my group. I began as number Ten because I came from the lower orders of society. To remain at Ten would mean that I had made little or no impression—which I didn't for a moment believe would happen. It was clear to everyone that family and social standing count at the beginning, but after that advancement was solely dependent upon performance. Even Charaban's betrayal could be overcome.

By the time I arrived at the Prefecture I was ready for my hearing. I walked into the anteroom, where other students—including my section mates—waited in varying degrees of anxiety. One Lubak was pale; it was almost certain that he would be demoted. Nine wore a sneering smile and looked at me from his superior height. Ever since he was made Second Level liaison he truly believed it was because of merit. He couldn't even deliver a message. I smiled back. Three had been sent home; his disability made him unfit for further education. Two fidgeted, preparing, I'm sure, a complicated presentation designed to tell the review panel exactly what he thought they'd want to hear. Why he never went to the political Institute I'll never know. Four was his relaxed self. He had nothing to fear; he would move through Bamarren from beginning to end on a straight line. He always knew how to take care of himself. Five would no doubt move up; he was an asset in every area, and except for Eight the most decent one in the group. Six had long since gone home. He wanted to succeed so badly, but his body couldn't withstand the constant assault of the training. I'm sure he found an academic situation. Seven was amazingly calm. Ever since the Competition he was a new person. Even his ridges looked stronger. He was sure to advance. Eight was the only person who deserved number One as much as I did—maybe more. My solitary behavior was not always in service to the group. Eight and I exchanged encouraging looks. The support of my one constant friend was all I wanted. I sat there and shut out everything else.

"Ten Lubak!" I jumped up and One Tarnal, our section leader, ushered me into the Lower Prefect's office. Going in numerical order, I was the last one of my group to go in. I was surprised when Tarnal didn't come inside with me. And when my eyes had adjusted to the darker room, I was even more surprised to see only two people, the First Prefect and someone in civilian mufti standing with his back turned toward me pouring a drink. Where were the student evaluators? The Lower Prefect? Why would the First Prefect involve himself in a First Level evaluation? And who was . . . ?

"Hello, Elim." The stranger turned and it was Enabran Tain!

"Ten Lubak." The Prefect motioned me to the chair, but I couldn't move. The two men just looked at me. All my preparation for the evaluation flew out of my head, and I felt as exposed as I had my first time in the Wilderness.

"Ten Lubak," the Prefect repeated.

"Yes, Prefect," was all I could manage. What was Tain doing here?

"Sit down," he instructed. I obeyed. Tain passed an information chip to the Prefect, who consulted it. During the ensuing silence I stole a glance to Tain, who was wearing his avuncular smile. What do I call him, I wondered. Certainly not Uncle Enabran.

"What do you think you've learned here?" the Prefect finally asked. It wasn't so much his question as his attitude that threw me off balance. The question I had expected; his air of boredom, as if the day was one student too long, I hadn't.

"I . . ." He wasn't even looking at me. Tain, however, continued to smile and wait patiently for my answer. Somehow his presence, disorienting as it was, encouraged me, and I found myself directing my answers to him.

"I've learned that appearances deceive and that the purity of my thinking creates a sure path to the truth," I replied.

"So," Tain began, "you believe all this to be a lie?" He gestured to the room.

"It's deceptive."

"Why?" he asked.

"Because our thinking is impure. . . ." I still didn't know how to address him.

"Is that all? The purity of one's thinking?" he pursued.

"'There are the hidden intentions of others.'"

"How are they hidden?"

"By what they say they are. How they present themselves. But pure thinking is trained to penetrate these guiles and come into direct contact with the true intention." My confidence was returning, and I was able to maintain a strong contact with Tain. Ordinarily it would be considered extremely disrespectful to look at an elder like this, but behind his genial demeanor was a serious challenge. It was like the game we had played when he'd tested the keenness of my observation on the street.

"How is pure thinking able to penetrate the appearance?" Tain's smile was now gone. I hesitated.

"How, Elim?" The questions became sharper.

"Initially by watching the direction of the eye movement when the interrogee answers, the frequency or absence of blinking; the intonation of the voice, the inflection—was it flat? Overstated? Were the answers glib, prepared? The breathing. . . ."

"Yes yes," Tain pushed me beyond the basics. "What else?"

"If the person can't hold his space."

"Space? Explain."

"If the energy field around him loses its shape and dissipates, then he has no defense against my probe and I can penetrate to his essential core." As I held Tain's look, I realized that I was locked into *his* energy field. We were two Pit warriors engaged in a strategem.

"Who am I, Elim?"

I didn't hesitate. "Someone I must never let out of my awareness." This was the first time I was not terrified by his steady and unblinking eyes, which revealed nothing but my own reflection. After a moment he nodded and broke eye contact.

"And what do you think has been your most serious lapse of discipline, Ten Lubak?" the Prefect asked in his disinterested tone. Or was it rather an uninflected way of asking questions that would reveal nothing. I began to answer that there were certain classes where I had given in to the boredom and did nothing to motivate my interest.

"And what about your *regnar*, Elim?"

The breath flew out of me. I looked at Tain with naked amazement.

"Mila. Is that his name?"

In an instant, my carefully constructed mask for this meeting was ripped away, and I experienced a fear I had never felt before. I realized then that Tain knew more about me than I had ever imagined. The Prefect now looked at me for the first time.

"Ah, I see," Tain continued when I couldn't. "You think that you're the only one who can 'disappear.' A big mistake, Elim." He watched as I started to breathe again.

"Is there a lesson here, do you think?" he asked gently.

"If you've mastered a tool or technique. . . ." I began, but I needed more air, and my tongue was thick and dry. They both waited patiently while I swallowed and breathed. ". . . Then there are others who have done the same before you," I managed to get out. Calyx first taught me this lesson.

"That's right, Elim," he said as if he were addressing a child. "Whatever your mind conceives or imagines already exists in the world. It doesn't make the thought or conception any less valuable; it just means that this technique you've discovered must be used carefully, and with the understanding that if you use it against other people, it can also be used against you."

With a clarity I'd never had, I heard what he was really saying to me. Charaban had deceived me by masking his true intentions, hiding them behind a friendship he'd never meant to extend beyond the Competition. I had taken it for granted that because he befriended me he had no hidden intentions. I felt a rush of shame. What a fool he had made of me. And then a disturbing thought attacked me: was Palandine doing the same? I knew what Charaban had wanted from me—but what did *she* want?

"Then you know about One Charaban and One Ketay." I looked at them both.

"So you *have* learned this lesson. I'm impressed, Elim." Tain turned to the Prefect. "I think this will suffice." The Prefect nodded and turned the chip off.

"You will be leaving Bamarren," the Prefect said to me.

I just stared at him. It was clear that this was the end of the review—and I had expected to receive my new designation.

"Leaving?"

"Today. The shuttle will meet you in front of the Central Gate before the Assembly," the Prefect explained.

"But . . . this is . . ." It was a stunning blow, but I refused to submit. "This is unfair, Prefect. Yes, I admit . . . I broke rules. But I have done good work . . . in the Pit . . . ask Calyx! In the Wilderness! Charaban's victory was. . . ."

"He probably would have won, but nowhere near as

impressively as he did with your contribution. We know all this, Elim, even with his negative recommendation," Tain added with his half-smile. I wasn't surprised by this last piece of information, but it sharpened the bitter taste in my mouth.

"You're being assigned to another school," the Prefect informed me.

"What kind of school?" I asked as my heart sank into the floor.

"You'll discover that when you get there," the Prefect answered. "Today you will return home. You will tell your parents only that you are awaiting reassignment. In the meantime, you will work with your father until the orders come. I advise you to make your preparations."

I automatically stood up, but I couldn't leave. There was so much that was unsaid, unresolved.

"What is it, Garak?" the Prefect asked, using my name. Just like that . . . I was no longer a student.

"If I had stayed. . . ." I began.

"But you didn't, Elim," Tain interrupted. "Pure thinking doesn't include 'what might have been if.' "

I snapped to, inclined my head and started for the door.

"Mila," Tain's voice stopped me. "A woman's name for a male *regnar?*"

I just stood there, looking at them both. Did the Prefect know my connection to Tain? Did he know that my parents lived in his house, and that my mother was his servant?

"No matter." He gave me a last smile, and I left the office. The waiting room was filled again with other nervous students who were studying me intently, trying to discern my fate. I drew myself up and made the choice to expand my presence. I looked them each in the eye. I am number One, no matter what might have been, and from now on I'm going to make my presence count.

22

My shed has become somewhat more bearable, but the clutter and confinement of the interior space requires that I leave the door open. To keep myself busy when I'm not working with the med unit, Doctor, I am engaged in a project I must tell you about. It baffles me. Perhaps you can tell me if I'm losing my mind altogether.

Tain's house, as I mentioned, is rubble. One day I began moving some of the debris and arranging it into a pile. Since there was too much debris for just one pile I arranged another. And then another. Until after hours of work I had carefully assembled several piles of debris in varying shapes and forms. I continued to create these piles and arrange them for two, maybe three weeks, not knowing what I was trying to accomplish. But the work was satisfying, Doctor—it felt good. And each day, when it became too dark to work, I would survey my creations, and I never felt prouder of anything I had ever done in my life. I don't know where the shapes came from, and I certainly couldn't explain their significance; but somehow they held me in their power.

After several weeks I asked Parmak what he thought this was all about. He'd stop by intermittently and check on my progress at various stages, but he always kept his own counsel. On this day, he moved through the piles (there were dozens by now) and studied them from all vantage points. A very careful man. Finally, after what seemed like an age, he stopped in front of the pile that was the largest and held the central, dominant position. He turned to me with the strangest expression on his face— and looked me directly in the eyes for the first time.

"I think this is your own archeological dig, Elim. You are unearthing the artifacts of a previous civilization—a civilization that will never return—and arranging them into a memorial for that civilization and its dead. This is your own personal Tarlak Sector. You're clearing the way for us to move on. Thank you, Elim. This is an honor for me."

Parmak then chanted a section of the Cardassian burial ritual. He mentioned the names of several friends and relatives, and as he chanted, the cumulative emotional power of his voice was almost unbearable. I, too, had a list of the dead that long, and whispered their names as he chanted. Parmak then took his right hand, ripped open a finger on a sharp piece of metal, and allowed the blood to drip on this central "monument."

"Thank you," he repeated, and walked away, his finger still dripping blood.

But what baffles me, Doctor, is that I attach no meaning to what I'm doing here. I'm just doing it because I need to. And to be truthful, I don't see this as a memorial at all. On the contrary—if I could, I'd singlehandedly rebuild this city myself, piece by piece. I stood here watching Parmak's blood dry on this pile of rubble, engulfed by a feeling of loss and utter mystification as to what these piles mean.

Just assure me that I'm not going mad, Doctor.

Entry:

I knew where Palandine was in the training area, and I waited behind a barrier for her class to come to an end. She was speaking with a classmate when I made my presence known. Her mate was somewhat shocked that a male student would behave in such a brazen manner, but Palandine gestured that she would deal with me and sent the mate on her way.

"So what did you use me for?" I asked.

"What do we ever use each other for?" she replied without hesitation.

"Answering a question with a question is an old trick, Palandine."

"No trick. I needed a friend."

"And you don't need a friend now." I hated the tone that was creeping into my voice.

"It's complicated, Elim."

I was afraid to ask why.

"What did you use *me* for?" she asked.

The question truly baffled me. I only wanted her love. Was that using her? I would gladly have given mine in return. I would give anything . . . and I still would.

"I'm leaving Bamarren," I said. "Today."

"Why?" It was her turn to be baffled.

"They didn't say. I was just told that I was being sent to another school." As I said it, my heart began to sink again.

"Then you're not being sent home?" she asked, genuinely not understanding.

"Only until I am reassigned."

"Reassigned?" She thought for a moment. "Elim, are you sure it's a school where you're going?"

"That's what the First Prefect told me."

"The First Prefect?" I began to sense her concern.

"What do you think it is?" I asked.

"I don't know. I've heard of a student being asked to leave—it happens often. But never 'reassigned.' Who else was at your hearing?"

Simultaneously, I realized that I should not be telling her any of this—and Charaban appeared. He stood behind Palandine. She saw my change of focus and turned. She shook her head.

"Not now, Barkan," she told him.

"What better time? This is the opportunity, so we take it," he explained to her. I didn't know what they were talking about, but I strongly felt the need to be prepared for anything. Especially when Charaban spoke of taking an opportunity.

"Hello, Lubak. Is it still Ten or are you number One?" he inquired.

"My name is Elim Garak," I replied.

"Yes, I know that," he laughed. "But is it you or is it Eight Lubak that I have to keep my eye on now?" It was the appearance of warmth that made his charm so attractive. A part of me wanted to tell him everything, to challenge the duplicity of his negative evaluation, but the clarity I found in the Lower Prefect's office was still with me. Looking at him, I was reminded how Palandine had taught me to smile when I asked questions.

"You have to watch both of us, Barkan."

"Yes, One and Two. Of course. But who makes the final decisions? Whose thinking do I pit mine against?" he challenged. He assumed that he had some kind of advantage and he pressed it. I saw three openings for attack. He saw my stance and prudently covered the openings.

"I think it's you, Elim." He countered with another stance.

"He's leaving Bamarren today," Palandine told him. She was also telling him something else. Charaban maintained his stance and never took his eyes off me, but his expression changed.

"Why?" If anything, he was even more surprised than Palandine. Even with his treachery, he hadn't believed that my dismissal from Bamarren was a possibility. This told me that he had had little or nothing to do with my change of fortune. His entire attitude toward me changed. I was no longer an opponent to be engaged and probed for weakness, but a baffling specimen of some lower order. Assuming I had been rejected and sent home, he stepped out of the stratagem.

That's *his* weakness, I thought, and said nothing to counter his assumption. After a long moment, when he understood that I was not going to be forthcoming with any details, he moved on.

"So it's Eight," he said, dismissing me from his world.

"I don't think you understand, Barkan. . . ." Palandine began to say.

"It's not necessary that he understand," I dismissed him from *my* world. "If you don't mind, I'd like to have a few moments alone with Palandine before I go." This seemed to amuse him, and he looked at Palandine, who nodded back.

"Certainly," he said, with a smile that showed how gracious he could be. "Good-bye . . . Elim Garak. Perhaps we'll meet someday in the Tarlak Sector." I understood the kind of circumstances under which he imagined such a meeting would take place—Elim the maintenance worker setting up the dais for a triumphant hero of the Empire. But it was my fault; I had told him everything he wanted to know about my life. All you have to do is smile when you ask. I answered him with a smile of my own.

"Perhaps you should tell him," he said to Palandine. They held a look before he turned and left. I wanted to ask what, but I waited for her.

"We're to be enjoined after the Third Level Culmination," she finally said.

And it all became clear. Of course. Palandine and Barkan had been connected all along. How else could his sudden appearances be explained? She was a vital part of the recruiting process.

"I wanted to tell you. Especially as I got to know you and . . . like you. I'm sorry, Elim."

I was surprisingly calm. I felt nothing.

"It was important that we win the Competition," she said.

"We," I smiled.

"Yes. We. Our lifelines are going to be enjoined, Elim; we're partners, and our success can only be ensured by our working together."

"So he told you to recruit me for the Competition," I said.

"No. That was my idea. When I first met you I knew."

"Knew what?"

"That you were . . ." She hesitated, carefully maintaining a distance. ". . . Different."

"Well . . . I suppose I should be honored." I was working very hard to maintain my own distance.

"I wanted to tell you. But when I realized . . . I didn't want to hurt you," she said with a gentleness that rankled me.

"I'm not hurt. Neither one of you can hurt me. I wish you a successful . . . partnership." I didn't want to stay any longer; my numbness was beginning to dissolve, and I couldn't trust myself to control whatever was emerging. I made an awkward bow—a pathetic attempt to be proper—and started to leave.

"Please, Elim." She stopped me. "I meant it when I said I needed a friend. I could talk to you. I'll always consider you my friend."

"And Barkan? Is he also my friend? Should I accept the way he treated me—used me—as friendship?" The numbness was gone, which only made the pain of losing her much worse.

"Barkan is ambitious. I wanted you on the council, but he felt that it would only give you an advantage when you—inevitably—challenged him for the leadership. He *could* be your friend someday, Elim." I laughed, too loudly, and she flared in response. "You're so naïve. You still don't know what this is all about, do you?"

"I wonder if you're not the one. . . ." I stopped. I was afraid that once I started to relate the details of his treachery I wouldn't be able to contain the rage that was spreading to every part of my body like a deadly disease.

"I love him, Elim. And I'm also ambitious. I want what he wants. You'll understand this when you find someone to share your. . . ."

"I have to go." I shut myself off like a closing wormhole. "Good-bye, Palandine." I turned and left. I am number One, I kept reminding myself.

* * *

Eight, who was now designated the number One of Lubak, helped me clean my area. We said very little. When everything was done, I stood in front of my compartment.

"Let me show you something," I said. He moved next to me. I took Mila from her sandy home. At first he didn't see her, but when I brought my hand close he reacted.

"So that's what it was," he said as Mila's skin rippled and changed coloration to find a suitable disguise. "We knew you had something in there, but after what you did to Three nobody was going to try to find out again."

"He's the reason I succeeded in the Wilderness," I said.

"And in the Competition," Eight added. He understood what I meant.

"You can beat Charaban." I lowered my voice to a fierce whisper.

"We'll see." Eight replied.

"No, you can. Because you have the very quality that goes right to his weakness. I had to have Mila to learn how to cover my thinking, but even then I walked into his traps. You won't, and he'll be forced to make assumptions about you—and they'll be wrong." We watched Mila ripple and change. "My name is Elim Garak. I don't know where I'm being sent, but I hope you'll remember me as your friend."

"When I was told today that I was One Lubak, I was honored . . . and afraid that I'd lose you as a friend. Thank you. My name is Pythas Lok."

Neither one of us ever took our eyes off Mila, who was still trying to blend into his surroundings.

* * *

I had just enough time to complete my last mission at Bamarren. I returned to the Mekar Wilderness with Mila and to the rock formation that was his original home. I found the escarpment where I had hidden myself that first day, and put Mila on the ground in front of the opening. He stood poised and still, various shades of desert playing across his skin. Something powerful was stirring deep inside me, and I began to shake. Mila snapped his head to the side, the way he does when he senses light or heat change. Convulsive waves pushed up from my center and tears filled my eyes, blinding me. I had absolutely no control over what was happening to me. By the time the convulsions subsided and my eyes cleared, Mila had disappeared into the rock-and-sand home he came from.

As I hiked back to the Institute, I had the thought that maybe somebody was doing the same thing for me and bringing me back home.

PART II

"Truth is in the eye of the beholder, Doctor. I never tell the truth because I don't believe there is such a thing . . ."

"You're not going to tell me."

"But you don't need me to tell you, Doctor . . . if you'll just notice the details. They're scattered like crumbs . . ."

I

Entry:

I'm afraid that the "invasion" was not all I had hoped for. The Dominion's grip on Cardassia is as tight as ever, and it's going to require another, greater concerted effort on the part of the Federation and its allies to loosen that grip. The most significant change is that the wormhole is closed . . . and so is my shop.

And Jadzia is gone. The station is a sadder and grayer place without her. I'm surprised at how keenly I feel her absence. Even though I know that her symbiont has been "joined" with another person . . . well, it's not the same, is it? Indeed, knowing that Jadzia's personality is somehow contained along with several others within this other person, I wonder how I would react if we were ever to meet. It would take some preparation on my part. Trills are such a unique race.

But are they? We all—to some degree—contain the memories, traits, fragments of those personalities that came before us. Indeed, perhaps we are even "joined" on a deeper, more spiritual level. The first Hebitians believed this. Each generation is not only succeeded by the next, it is subsumed by it, so that the past is always present and actively involved in creating the future. So in a sense there is no past and future; there is only the present. And I must say that Jadzia's spark and vibrancy reflected this immediacy.

Which is why we were all drawn to her—like moths to a flame.

I must say, however, that Commander Worf's manner of mourning has completely baffled me. Entombing himself in that ludicrous holosuite program with Vic and his incomprehensible human gibberish . . . those maudlin songs. . . . The doctor has reminded me that these are personal choices, and it's not for us to judge how one chooses to mourn. Quite so. Who can even begin to understand another's grief?

"Do you judge people by the clothes they ask you to make?" the doctor asked once. I bit back my response, but the point was well taken. Besides, I'm not making anyone clothes these days. I now spend my time decoding Cardassian military transmissions, some of which are prototypes of codes I created for the Order. Ironic . . . and disturbing. Odo has been charged with the task of gathering the intercepted transmissions and bringing them to me. One day I asked if he wasn't ever disturbed by the fact that he was at war with his own people. Did he feel a sense of betrayal? As far as he's concerned, the Founders conducting this war are betraying everything the Great Link stands for, and therefore they must be defeated. I nodded and agreed . . . but I'm still disturbed.

And I hate this work! I'd much rather be sewing.

"What does Tir Remara want with you?" Colonel Kira demanded, ignoring my offer of tea. Immediately an entire picture formed in my head of the scenario her abrupt question suggested: Tir Remara—a spy, perhaps even a changeling, preying upon a lonely Cardassian who was working for the Federation and engaged in top-secret work.

"She wants to have my children," I replied with a serious look.

"You can't be serious," she managed.

"I'm not. Now do you want this tea or not?"

"No . . . thank you," she allowed. It was so difficult for her to muster even a sliver of civility with a member of my race.

"Remara and I are friends. Not terribly close. We get together occasionally. We're curious about each other." I sipped at my tea. Kira watched me with a cold expression, waiting for me to continue.

"We found we had a mutual friend, and we have come to . . . enjoy each other's company."

"What mutual friend?" Kira was puzzled; who or what would a Bajoran and a Cardassian have in common?

"Ziyal," I replied.

Kira nodded. "Yes, of course." The mention of her former protégé's name reminded her of what we held in common: a great affection for Ziyal.

"Why are you asking, Colonel?"

"Because Remara has been making inquiries about you, Garak."

"Really?"

"And if you are friends, I don't know why she wouldn't be asking you directly."

"Yes." My mind was racing. "My thoughts as well. Unless, of course . . ."

"What?" Kira asked.

"She's planning to write a book about me."

Kira didn't think that was humorous. "Watch her,

Garak. And be careful what you tell her." She left as abruptly as she entered. I smiled at the irony of being told to watch my mouth. What was going on here? Was it Kira's concern about a possible breach of security? A friendship between a Bajoran and a Cardassian? And if Remara wasn't writing a book, what did she want this information for?

2

Entry:

"Careful, Elim. These plants have delicate tendrils. Lower them slowly, so they find the holes."

I took the Edosian orchid from Father and slowly lowered the pale, dangling feelers over the prepared soil. These orchids were his favorite flowers, and somehow he was able to make them grow in this section of the Tarlak Grounds.

"Just hold the plant for a moment directly above—the tendrils will align themselves." His voice was almost a whisper. "Now watch closely."

As if they had eyes, the tendrils swayed until they found the openings Father had dug and paused above them.

"Now lower the plant slowly." I did. When the root ball had settled in the depression, Father immediately filled in the sides with his special mixture, which he claimed was the secret. People would come from distant places to see the Grounds and especially the miracle of Father's orchids, which had no logical reason to exist in this climate. When someone asked how he was able to grow them in an outside environment, he'd gauge how serious the questioner was and answer accordingly. To those few he judged to be sufficiently patient, he gave a soil sample and some instructions; to the rest he'd smile and say that Tarlak had a secret ideal quality. And it did—but only because Father had made it that way with his care and unlimited patience.

The Grounds was Father's passion, and when I returned from Bamarren I worked as his assistant while waiting for my next placement. At first it felt odd to be working at these simple and mindless tasks. But I began to notice that Father was now talking to me more, telling me about the various plants and shrubs and flowers. We spent very little time among the monuments and tombs. Gradually, I began to accept the change and even to enjoy the pace of this work. This was probably Father's intention.

When I first arrived home, Mother and Father accepted the fact that I was no longer a boy. They looked older to me, especially Father, and the changes I had undergone at Bamarren had created a distance between us that we all found awkward.

During this period I never saw Tain. Once I asked Mother how he was, and she replied that as far as she knew he was fine. I occasionally heard footsteps above us and wondered when he'd come back into my life—a question tinged with some anxiety—but Mother and Father never mentioned him, and I went about my own business.

I spent very little time at home. I found a training area nearby where I practiced my sets of martial forms. I was determined not to lose the fine edge of my conditioning.

Occasionally, I would be challenged by someone, usually an ex-soldier or martial student, but they were never strong or accomplished enough to give me a true match. In a short time I found myself conducting an informal class, where I taught a variegated group the rudimentary forms. These classes were far more valuable than fighting outmatched opponents.

Otherwise, I reverted to a solitary existence, waiting for my life to find new purpose and constantly wondering what my friends . . . and enemies . . . were doing at Bamarren. I had ideas about the coming Competition that I wished I could communicate to Pythas, ideas that would ensure Barkan's humiliation. And there were feelings I had no words for that I wished I could make known to Palandine.

"That's who he is now, Tolan. He's a man." I heard mother's voice as I approached the opened door to our housing unit after a training session.

"He's hard, Mila," Father said.

"He has to be," she replied.

"But to the point where he's unreachable?" Father asked. "Where nothing penetrates? How can he express even his basic needs if he's trapped inside a shell?"

"It's better this way, Tolan. I know what's in store for him," Mother interrupted. There was a momentary silence.

"More Bamarren," Father said, almost to himself. There was another silence indicating the discussion was over. I decided to take a walk.

The next day, Father and I were weeding and pruning across from the children's area where mothers and caretakers bring children to play. The adults talked among themselves, worked, or read while the children's voices created a constant background of musical chatter. We had been working quietly and steadily, but I knew Father wanted to speak. I didn't know why he hesitated.

"Elim, have we ever spoken about the first Hebitians?" Father broke the silence with a question so strange it almost made me laugh.

"No," I carefully answered.

"What do you know about them?"

"They were . . . the first peoples . . . before the climatic change." Our school histories never spent much time talking about the Hebitians. "They had primitive solar technologies. When the rain forests and grasslands were taken over by the deserts, they died off. They couldn't adapt."

"That's what you were taught." Father barely shook his head. "That's not what happened, Elim."

I said nothing. We continued to work as I listened to the children's voices punctuated by the clipping and raking and digging.

"The only thing that was primitive about the Hebitians is the way we've treated them in the historical record." I stopped working and looked around. This was the first time I had ever heard him challenge received orthodoxy, and my first concern was that no one was listening. Father noticed this and smiled.

"I see your Bamarren education has taken hold. Fertile ground for young minds." Slowly and painfully, I thought, he raised himself to his full height, stretched, and picked up his bag.

"Let's have some tea." He laughed because he knew that the tea he drank, which was brewed from the roots of some shrub, had made me gag the first—and only—

time I'd tried it. I had a separate container of the common *choban* variety. We took our containers and settled in a shady place that faced the playing children.

"Look at them. With young minds you can plant anything and it grows into ideas and beliefs." We watched one child begin to explore beyond the play area until she was intercepted by the caretaker who, judging by her gestures, was explaining why the toddler mustn't stray.

"The first Hebitians had an advanced culture that was sophisticated on every level, Elim. Yes, it was solar-based, but they were able to support themselves, and this is what most of the planet looked like." He waved his tea container to indicate the Grounds. The idea was almost too outlandish for me. Soft and green places are rare on Cardassia.

"It's hard to imagine, isn't it? We live in constant struggle with the land. We've become as hard and dry. . . ." Father trailed off and sipped his tea. I thought of my favorite place at Bamarren, and almost told Father about it—but how could I describe the enclosure without speaking of her?

"What were they like?" I asked, giving my full attention to him.

"Do you remember, Elim, when I took you to the Hebitian remains outside Lakarian City?"

"Yes." I was just a boy then, and we had walked around the crumbling walls and piles of stone and pulverized tile. I had enjoyed the trip more for its novelty than for anything else, but I remembered one carving on the side of a wall. It was of a winged creature with a Cardassian face that was turned toward a sun disc. Extending down from the creature's body were several tentacles that divided just before entering the bodies of people who were standing on a globe and looking up to the creature. The tentacles went through the people and into the globe itself. I told this to Father and he laughed.

"You remember that?"

"And you said that it should be preserved before it eroded." I remembered his indignation.

"I did. When I went to my superior and suggested that what was left of the entire city be preserved, he told me that it had already been taken care of. What was salvageable was sold to Romulan art dealers, who in turn placed the pieces in various museums and collections throughout the quadrant. All that's left now is dust." Father was silent again.

"What were they like?" he muttered, repeating my question. "They valued the soul, Elim. They were organized—they had to be, they had determined enemies—but their energy wasn't devoted to the conquest of others, to accumulating resources they couldn't produce themselves. They were able to support themselves, and this self-sufficiency allowed them to nurture and celebrate their group soul with art and culture."

"Who were their enemies?" I asked, fascinated and somewhat uneasy with what Father was saying.

"We were."

The paradox stopped me. "But . . . how is that possible? We . . . we are descended from those people." I remembered that Calyx had called me an "air man" and wondered if I didn't get it from Father. Mother often complained that he didn't have a grasp of what she called our "power-driven reality," and he would reply that his reality was driven by the same power that grew his plants and shrubs. These arguments always left the house feeling divided and cold.

"I know this is hard for you to understand, Elim. Our racial policies forbid enjoining with subjected peoples. The Hebitians were the envy of the surrounding planets, what we now call the Cardassian Union. As long as their planet, this one we call Cardassia Prime, was healthy and self-sufficient, they were able to withstand any attempts at conquest. But when the climate began to change and resources dwindled, the 'group soul' weakened. People lost their faith in the old ways . . . disease killed millions . . . it was just a matter of time. The ones who were left surrendered to the invaders, who brought their organization based on military conquest and expansion and blended with them. We come from both these peoples."

Father fell silent again. A howling child caught our attention. I was grateful for the distraction from Father's very different version of our past. I'd been taught that the first Hebitians were a primitive people and had died off in the climatic catastrophe; that the survivors had built a new civilization that became superior in all ways.

"I love this place, Elim. And it means a great deal to me that we're able to spend this time with each other working here." Father smiled and put his hand on my shoulder. He rarely touched me, and the contact embarrassed me . . . and sent a warm feeling through my body. I felt like one of his plants. He kept his hand on my shoulder and stared at me with an intensity that made me afraid of what he was going to say next.

But he said nothing. We finished work and packed our things in silence. The silence continued throughout the trip home on the public transport. Just before we entered the house, Father stopped and looked at me.

"I want to show you something, Elim."

He led me into his private chamber, where he kept everything from cuttings to work records. He put his bag down and unlocked a huge compartment. After a moment of moving things I couldn't see, he pulled out something that looked like a face that was made from stone-like material. He held it out to me. It was the same creature's face as on the carved mural I had remembered earlier.

"What is it?" I asked.

"It's a recitation mask. Hebitian poets wore it at festivals that celebrated Oralius."

"Was he . . . their leader?" I asked.

"In a spiritual sense."

My confusion must have been apparent, because Father nodded his understanding. "I know this is difficult. Oralius was not a corporeal being, Elim, he didn't live as we do. He was a presence, a spiritual entity that guided people toward the higher ideals they were encouraged to live by." Father was working hard to describe something for which I had absolutely no reference point.

"How did this 'encourage' them?" I asked.

"At the festival, the poet would put the mask on before he'd recite. In this way, he was no longer Elim or Tolan or any of 'us.' He was a conduit . . . a connector who with the help of his poetry brought the higher power of Oralius down to those of us who were there . . . who wanted this . . ." Father searched for the word.

"Encouragement? "I ventured.

"Yes." Father was pleased with my interest.

"Was this your . . . 'power,' which makes the plants and flowers grow?"

Father's face broke into a beaming smile, and I thought he was going to grab me. He had never looked at me like this, and I felt somehow proud that my question had gotten such a reaction. Suddenly he looked past me, and his expression—so open and so animated with the attempt to explain what essentially was unexplainable—became as unreadable as that disembodied mask.

Mother was at the door. I don't know how long she had been there, but she was not pleased.

"Oh, Tolan," was all she said.

"Get cleaned up, Elim," Father said. I was aware of a strong forcefield that I had been caught in the middle of many times before. It always made me feel helpless, and this time was no exception. I gladly complied. As I was about to leave the room, however, I saw Mother's eyes as she looked at Father. Intimate was not a word I would ever have used to describe their relationship—efficient or collaborative, perhaps—but I had never seen how much distance actually existed between them until this very moment.

I hurried past Mother and out of the room.

3

Entry:

"Is it too hot for you?" I asked.

"It's hot." Remara tentatively arranged her long body along the surface of the smooth rock. "But I think it's bearable."

Remara had asked several times if she could join me in the holosuite program I frequented, but I had never taken her seriously. I was convinced that only Cardassians could bear the heat of the rocks. Finally I agreed, but I was prepared to end the program immediately, anticipating that she'd change her mind after the first blast. But somehow she not only survived it but managed to find a position on her rock that looked almost comfortable. I must confess that her lithe body pressed against the rock presented a vision of feminine sensuality that added to my enjoyment.

"You used to come here with Ziyal, didn't you?"

"We both enjoyed the experience. It was like a haven from the storm."

"Yes, it must have been difficult." Remara shifted her body, and I could see that she was perspiring profusely. Her skin began to meld with the rock.

"What was difficult?" I asked.

"Your relationship with her father. It must have affected you and Ziyal," she replied.

"She knew who he was," I said.

"Did she know who you were?"

"Of course," I smiled. "A plain and simple tailor who craved a friend to sit with on the rocks." Remara smiled back, but she was not to be deterred.

"Did Ziyal know that you had played a part in the death of her grandfather?" Her smile was even more radiant because of the effects of the heat. The longer she endured, the more beautiful she became.

"I'm glad to see the heat agrees with you, my dear. I had no idea that Bajorans had this kind of tolerance."

"We're very fond of our solar baths," she said, shifting again to another graceful position. "Did she hold his death against you?"

"If she did, she never shared it with me."

"Weren't you at all curious to know?"

"Not nearly as curious as you are about me. When Colonel Kira asked me why you were making inquiries, I joked that perhaps you were writing a book. Perhaps it's not a joke. You're very well informed."

"Nerys asked you that, did she?"

"And she found it curious that you wouldn't address these questions to me directly."

"I'm not surprised." Now she was fully reclined on the rock with her face up. It was getting difficult to breathe. How ironic if I were the one to call off the program because of the heat. "Nerys and I have had our difficulties in the past," she said, her voice seeming to come from a great distance. Her eyes were closed, and she was totally integrated with the rock

"Oh?"

"We knew each other on Bajor."

"Really? Were you in the Resistance as well?" I watched her raise her right leg and flex her foot, which made the lean muscles along her thigh ripple. I forced myself to breathe deeply. Perhaps it was the heat, but even with the distance between us her physical presence was crowding and overpowering me.

At one point Kira and I became quite close," she said dreamily. I wondered if she were about to fall asleep.

"And now you're not."

"Our lives took very different paths. No," she finally answered, "I didn't join the Resistance." Remara opened her eyes, sat up, and gave one last serious stretch. "You know, Elim, I think I've reached the limit of my tolerance."

And not a moment too soon, I thought. In one easy motion, she slid off the rock and led the way to the exit. I lingered for a moment, to savor her movement and wondered how an artist could capture the exquisite harmony of her physique. I also wondered how a man could continue his relationship with her knowing full well the danger involved. The major's question echoed in my head: What *does* she want from you, Elim?

4

Entry:

The next morning I was surprised to find that Father had left for work without me.

"You're coming with me this morning," were Mother's first words. When I began to ask where we were going she cut me off.

"You'll find out," was all she would say. I quickly ate something while she waited. Neither of us spoke; the heaviness in the room said everything.

Out in the street I followed as she set a brisk pace. She was a sturdy, compact woman with prematurely graying hair and strong features that were now leading the way. She was always very patient with me, but I was under the impression that she had something of weight and consequence on her mind that discouraged everything but essential interaction. As we moved through the busy, crowded streets I was struck by the way she appeared to be unaffected by the activity surrounding her. On a Cardassian street there is a lot of jostling and bumping and competing for lane space, but Mother set a fixed course and everyone moved out of her path. She behaved—and appeared—as if she were utterly isolated.

"You're going to work today, son." She remained true to her course and didn't look at me when she spoke.

"I've been going to work every day," I responded, out of a childish loyalty to Father.

"That's *not* your work," she stated. "You're a man now, and you're being given a great opportunity. I want you to behave like a man and submit to the path that's opening up before you."

"Have I ever opposed your wishes, Mother?" I probably imagined the slight crack of a smile on her face. My name as a child was "Sleg" after the *sleg corgan,* a huge crawling beast that in certain seasons would barely move at all. I was oddly diffident about what this path would be. Perhaps this was a defense against this new "opportunity"—a word I now associated with betrayal.

"I've been told that you showed aptitude at the Institute," she continued. "I've also been told that you had lapses . . . of a sentimental nature."

I said nothing. For some reason it made me uncomfortable to think that she knew about Palandine.

"Your father has ideas I don't agree with . . . that are best left unexpressed. I advise you to forget them. They'll only make your work more difficult." She stopped and looked at me for the first time. "Understand, Elim—you are being given the opportunity to move above the service class."

I recoiled from both the word I mistrusted and the implication that the work Mother and Father did was low and demeaning.

"I was taught that the service class was an irreplaceable piece of the Cardassian mosaic," I replied with crude irony.

"Listen to me!" she said with a passion that startled

me. "You are my son and you are a Cardassian. Not a Hebitian. Look around you!" she commanded. I did. We were in the great public area which is surrounded by the buildings that house the power of the Union. "Hebitians did not build this. Cardassians did. Your father and I serve and maintain, but we do not influence or guide the destiny of the Union. You could. That's why you must submit right now! Do you understand me, Elim? Once we walk through that door," she indicated the one that led to the subterranean levels of the Assembly building—to the Obsidian Order—"you must submit to your fate."

Mother's eyes were burning with an intensity that communicated a care and passion that was every bit the equal of Father's. I nodded dumbly. She took a deep breath and composed herself. Unconsciously, she smoothed my hair and tugged at my tunic.

"You're a good boy . . . Sleg." This time the smile was real. She led the way and we entered the building. What I understood was that I had no choice. Father, I'm sure, understood that—which was probably why he was gone this morning. The rest was a mystery.

And the mystery deepened when the man who greeted us was Enabran Tain.

"A pleasure to see you again, Elim. Thank you, Mila." He dismissed Mother, who left without returning my look, and fixed me with that long and disconcerting smile of his. Did his eyes ever blink? "Sit down."

I obeyed. Submit, Mother told me. And don't ask to what. I tried to orient myself: the room was small and cluttered. My first impression of Tain in these circumstances, reinforced by his portly figure and shapeless clothing, was that he was not an important person. But I now knew better than to trust any first impression, especially one calculated by Tain.

"Everyone has an opinion, Elim,"

"Excuse me?" Had I missed the beginning of this conversation?

"Was Bamarren the right place for you?" he asked.

"I. . . ." Listen to him and answer truthfully, a voice said. "Yes. I would have liked to complete the course."

"You and the First Prefect. He was not happy losing you." Tain studied me in silence. Listen, the voice reminded me. Don't turn away. Breathe. It's Calyx, I thought. Instead of a sandy pit, it's a dusty office.

"If you ask ten people, you'll get ten opinions. Would you like to hear mine?" Tain asked politely.

"Yes. . . ." I still didn't know what to call him.

"We get what we need, Elim. We listen to everyone's opinion, but in the end we get what we need. What do you need?"

"I never . . . asked myself."

"Most people don't. They're led by instinct to satisfy the basics. What they don't realize is that if you *don't* ask, other people will answer for you, and then you never discover who you are."

"Is that what you're doing? Answering for me?" The anger in my voice surprised me.

Tain smiled. "You learned what you needed from Bamarren. If you had stayed longer you would have developed . . . habits . . . useful for other organizations. We're different, you see? I'm not even sure the First Prefect understands."

"But what am I here for?" I now felt bolder.

"You're here to find out who you are. And to create your own story."

"Story?"

"Your history. Up to this point you've been defined by other people's needs. Mila's. Tolan's. Your docent's."

"Yours?" I asked. Tain laughed.

"Perhaps. But here you have the opportunity to change all that."

Opportunity. The word clung to me like my shadow. Tain touched his comm panel. "Limor, please come in."

"The Obsidian Order?" I asked.

"What do you know about us?"

"Nothing."

"That's a good start."

"What will I do?"

"To begin with, you'll learn how to gather and process simple information." As Tain said this, a tall, wiry man of indeterminate age entered the office quietly. Tain rose to meet him.

"And Limor Prang will get you started. This is Elim Garak, our newest junior probe," Tain said to Limor, whose facial expression appeared permanently set to reveal nothing. Tain turned back to me; the smile was gone. "You will no longer live at home. Visits to your family will be limited to holidays and name days. You are never to say anything to anyone about your work other than your designation as a research analyst in the Hall of Records. When you see your mother, she is 'Mila' and you are to treat her like any other service worker." He held my look to see how I would react to the last order. "You will receive all information and assignments from Limor. Thank you."

Tain returned to his desk and Limor started to lead me out. We were dismissed. Just like that, my life had changed again. Tain noticed my hesitation.

"You have a question, Elim?"

I had nothing but questions. "I . . . don't know what to call you now," I managed.

The smile returned. "My name is Enabran Tain. Have you forgotten?"

"No . . . Enabran."

In all my life I had never met a man who communicated so much with so few words as Limor Prang. Everything about him was as lean and spare as his body. He always looked like he was obscured by a shadow. In the brightest room one had to look twice to see that he was there. I thought that I was good at erasing my presence, but Limor made me look like a clumsy exhibitionist.

At the end of our first session Limor gave me my personal comm chip. "This has your schedule and data. It will answer all questions. Run the first program before you leave the building." I looked down at the chip, which was smaller than the tip of my thumb, and when I looked back up Limor was gone. I sat down in the only chair and activated the chip.

"Elim Garak: code name, *regnar;* grade, junior probationist. Place chip in right ear," the recorded voice instructed. I did, and the orientation program explained that communication is run once and not repeated. This is where the mnemonic training at Bamarren would be invaluable. I was given the location of my living quarters and the time and place of my first cell meeting. I was instructed where and when my training would begin. The program then rattled off a number of codes that would serve me in a variety of situations, from adjusting time and place coordinates to describing degrees of danger.

By the time the program finished, my head was throbbing with the effort to hold on to this plethora of vital data.

5

As I moved building debris and arranged them into piles of different shapes and sizes, I came to realize that the ground floor of Tain's house had been constructed strongly enough to withstand the destructive blast and hold the weight of the collapsed material. This left the basement undamaged. It was now just a question of clearing a way to the opening that led to the basement. But I hesitated: I knew what I would find down there, Doctor.

Most people, when I began this work, assumed that I was going to rebuild the house. After all, that was going on all around me. Cardassians are nothing if not industrious, and from the dust and rubble another, though more primitive, city was emerging. Each time the rudimentary shape of a house began to take shape, the morale of the sector was raised as well. At first people were confused by my efforts. Many assumed that I was unhinged and needed to do something, anything, to stay busy. Some even offered helpful advice about rebuilding, but when they realized that I wasn't receptive they left me alone. After a while, as the shapes formed, they became curious, and their attitude changed. Many, like Doctor Parmak, were respectful, even reverent. One evening I came back from work and encountered a small group that had surrounded one of the constructed piles close to the walkway. As Parmak had done, they were calling out names in the traditional chant for the dead.

It was at that moment that I decided that not only was I not going to open up the basement, I was not going to rebuild the house of Enabran Tain. Instead I constructed the largest and most ambitious formation of material where the center of the house—Tain's study—had formerly been located. This was my memorial to Mila, who remained entombed in the basement. If the people need a place to mourn their dead, to mourn a way of life that will never return, then I offer the home of Enabran Tain, the man most responsible for provoking this destruction. Parmak is right: otherwise, how can we ever move ahead?

6

Entry:

The first cell meeting took place in an empty, cold warehouse in the Munda'ar Sector that was almost entirely comprised of storage facilities for the foodstuffs and other goods that kept the city alive. I walked into the echoing, cavernous space, and saw that no one was there. I placed the comm chip in my right ear and was directed to a hidden ladder that took me down into a dark room, where ten chairs were arranged in a semicircle facing one chair isolated in a pool of light. Two of the chairs were empty, and it wasn't until I took one that I noticed Limor Prang in the chair facing us. The eight people who preceded me sat quietly in the shadow at the edge of the pool. Even though no one was encouraged to make contact we tried, sneaking surreptitious looks at each other, until we were interrupted by the last person descending the ladder. By then my eyes had adjusted, and when I stole a glance at the latecomer taking the last chair, I was struck by the familiarity of his face. I knew him—probably from Bamarren—but couldn't precisely place how.

"Don't ever be late again." It was stated quietly, but everyone in the room got the message.

It was a short meeting. This was a new cell—Limor said little and made sure that we introduced ourselves with code names only. The person who was eluding my memory was called Maladek. Limor told us to put the names together with the faces and voices as best we could. This would be the only meeting like this our cell would ever have. If we saw each other again it would be "on assignment." The clear implication was that we had better remember each other, even though we were given no opportunity to go beyond the faintest of first impressions.

Before we left, I took another look at Maladek, and a shock of recognition traveled through my body when he returned my look. It was at that moment that I remembered: at Bamarren he was One Ramaklan, the student leader who'd been humiliated in the Competition. His look, however, revealed nothing. We left one by one in the order we had arrived ("Never in a group," we were warned) and as I made my way to the ladder, Maladek/Ramaklan avoided my last look. Perhaps it was just an uncanny resemblance.

I decided to walk to the Torr Sector, where my new

living quarters were located, and requested directions from the comm chip. It was a beautiful night, and the sight of the Taluvian Constellations pulsing their secret messages made me think of the Mekar Wilderness and a simpler time. Perhaps if I could decode the pulses, I thought, I could begin to unravel the mystery that was engulfing my life. I slowed my pace, as I thought about Father and Mother and the path that was leading me to my new home. I felt oddly disconnected, almost as if I were walking next to and observing this person, Elim Garak, who was playing out a fateline that demanded his submission, and over which he had no control.

A group of people pulled me back into myself. How unusual for this time of night, and how clumsily they tried to appear inconspicuous, as if ignoring each other would be interpreted that they were several strangers who happened to be on the street at the same time. I fully appreciated why Limor warned us against such group behavior. And yet, as I studied these people, they expressed no guilt or shame in what they were doing. Indeed, there was a connectedness to them that any amount of pretending couldn't hide—and which almost made me follow as they entered this one building. Grudgingly, however, I admitted that I had better "submit" to my fate, and I continued in my direction at a quickened pace.

It was a modest dwelling in an old residential area. The comm chip gave me the entrance code and instructed me to a side door that led down to a clean, stark basement. Another basement, but much smaller than home. I wondered if I'd ever live at ground level or higher in the City. The few belongings I owned had been transferred from Tain's house, and were piled neatly on my pallet. It took me very little time to arrange them and acquaint myself with the room and its few amenities. When there was nothing left to do I decided to go to sleep. But I couldn't. From upstairs there came the faint sound of someone moving about. It wasn't Tain. But how could I be sure? He seemed to be everywhere else in my life. I thought of Father and wondered when I'd see him again. Would I ever have the chance to plant Edosian orchids with him again? The question was swallowed by the thick darkness of my new home.

The most horrible images of littered corpses and mass destruction crowded my mind's eye; my senses filled with the smells . . . the feelings. . . . I knew I couldn't take much more. Faces of everyone I knew—my parents, the people I cared most about at Bamarren—distorted and frozen in their final agonies, as the sounds of a final cataclysm rose to a shrieking pitch and suffocated all breath and hope.

And then nothing. In every direction. Surrounded by a deadened void; alone. The silence of the end of days. Nothing resounded; everything had been absorbed beyond grief and sorrow. My breathing began to clutch. The void was shrinking; the dense and darkened silence was closing in. I couldn't swallow. End it. End it now!

"That's enough," Limor's voice said, and simultaneously the room returned. He was intently studying my reaction as I struggled to return my breath to normal.

"You have to raise your threshold."

"But I didn't say anything." I was too defensive, and we both knew it. He was right; my fear made me identify with the images. I couldn't maintain the distance to remove myself from the pain. He just looked at me, and I knew I was on the verge. How would I ever survive even a moderately challenging interrogation?

"We'll continue to work on it," was all he said.

"I've . . . never gotten this far before. The third level seems to require certain adjustments. . . ." I knew I had failed—and I didn't want to let it go.

"There are ways, Elim," Limor said as he removed the device from the base of my skull. I rubbed the sensitive area in the back of my neck where the filament had been connected.

"That's enough for today." Limor took the "enhancer" and left the room. I pondered my failure, the first during my orientation training as a junior probe.

The enhancer is a chip-size modulator designed to be used for difficult interrogations—a "tool of last resort" Limor called it, which meant that it was used only when standard techniques of sensory destabilization were insufficient. The enhancer is dangerous, because clumsy modulation can unravel a subject to the point of incoherence and insanity, even death. Once attached, it targets the oldest area of the brain, the primal nexus, which contains the master plan of our physical creation and evolution. All recovery from injury or illness depends upon the integrity of this plan. The nexus is also the storehouse for our deepest anxieties regarding death and annihilation. The enhancer attacks the sophisticated nexus defense system with neutrinos that mimic stimuli sent by the new brain requesting information for healing and repair. As the barriers are broken down by the neutrinos, the images of this stored anxiety are released like poison into the new brain and "enhanced" until the whole person is destabilized—or worse. No one knows the fear any one person can live with, and in the hands of a fool or a brute the enhancer is merely a form of torture, rather than a means of intelligence gathering.

Limor had seen my deepest fear surface; I wondered if it would affect my future with the Order. So by the time I had moved through the various methods of interrogation and assassination, assuming identities and learning codes and complicated technological devices, I was eager to take on an assignment and prove myself in the field. It was with a good deal of relief that I received the order to attend my first operations preparatory meeting.

7

Entry:

All I could think about was Tzenketh, and the image of those walls collapsing in all around me. Reading, or sewing, or moving my display clothing (optimistic about the shop someday opening again), I'd feel the walls slowly moving in. I'd look up—and they were perfectly normal. I was relieved that it was time for lunch, so that I could spend some time away from the shop and these codes. Tzenketh was the rendezvous point where—years before—I was supposed to meet my Bajoran contact. It was only after the explosion went off that I realized I had been betrayed. I don't know how long I was buried alive in the rubble before I was dug out by my support unit. It was several weeks before I could function again. Ever since then, the image of the collapsing walls would flash in my mind's eye when I was under stress. I cursed these Cardassian military codes. I knew how desperately the Federation needed them decoded, but every time I worked on them the walls began to move in. And they weren't even that cleverly done! The codes we created at the Order were far more sophisticated.

As I walked along the Promenade to the Infirmary, I let go of Tzenketh and wondered why the Doctor had extended an invitation to lunch. In the past I wouldn't have thought twice about it, but it had been so long since we'd had one of our lunches that I felt somewhat apprehensive. Our relationship had changed irrevocably, and it was foolish to pretend that even a simple lunch would be unaffected.

"Hallo, Garak." He was waiting at the entrance. "I hope you don't mind, but I had something prepared for us and thought we could take lunch in my office."

"No—that sounds fine." I was taken back by the suggestion, since we had never dined in his office before. I followed as he led the way to the cluttered space he usually reserved for private consultations. When I saw that the table was set for three, my system went on full alert.

"Are we expecting someone else, Doctor?" I asked.

"Well, uh, yes . . . or rather, Odo was going to try to make it, but he may be held up." The doctor was almost too casual as he busied himself serving the prepared dishes. "He said we should start without him." He uncovered my food: *tojal* in *yamok* sauce, one of my favorite Cardassian dishes. Now I was certain something was up.

"Where did you find this, Doctor?" I didn't have the heart to tell him *tojal* is a breakfast dish.

"Oddly enough, the chef at the Klingon restaurant

fancies himself an intergalactic gourmet. However, I'm afraid the concept of chips still eludes him," the doctor said as he held up a long, greasy strip of what he called fried potato.

"What's the occasion, Doctor? You didn't have to go to all this trouble. You're a busy man."

"I just thought it'd be pleasant if we had some privacy today," he said, avoiding a direct look.

"Oh. For any particular reason?" I asked as I began to eat.

"Well, I . . . uh . . . actually was planning to talk about this after lunch." I could see that the doctor was out of his element. Perhaps he was disconcerted that we had to conduct this lunch without a third party.

"Talk about what, Doctor?" I put down my utensils and gave him my full attention.

"Well, I was hoping that Odo would join us." The Doctor looked toward the door with a look that corroborated my suspicion. He suddenly nodded.

"Yes, quite right. We should do this before; we'll digest better." He suddenly jumped up. "I have some *rokassa* juice . . . tea?"

"What is it?" My insistence pulled him back down.

"You know how important those codes are to us. I don't have to tell you what that information means."

"No one knows better than I," I said.

"Of course not. And I respect that for whatever reason you're . . . unable to continue to break them down for us."

"Yes?" I prompted.

"You see, this is so difficult, Garak. I know what a private person you are, and how you detest people meddling in your affairs. . . ."

"Ironic for a spy, isn't it?"

"No, everyone has a right to their privacy, but . . . circumstances being what they are. . . ."

"Captain Sisko would like it very much if I could somehow continue."

"Yes." With help, the doctor had finally gotten it out.

"Nothing would give me greater pleasure. But tell me, Doctor, how am I to do this?" I asked. "The moment I *see* those scrambled characters, my throat tightens, and then when I start working on them. . . ." I shrugged. How could I explain the unexplainable?

"But you see, perhaps it's something that I can help you address."

"Your holosuite program. The one that allows me to visit the traumas of my childhood."

"I hesitate to suggest this, remembering how you reacted the last time . . . but, yes, I feel it could make a difference," the Doctor gamely admitted.

"Oh, Doctor," I sighed. "We're so different. Perhaps someday I'll be able to express to you just how different we are." I pushed my food away, and took a deep breath to calm the rising anxiety. "All of my so-called childhood traumas are right here in this room with me, at this moment."

"Yes, of course they are," the Doctor readily agreed.

"But they're not hidden. They've happened, they've had their effect, and all of it is incorporated into who I am."

"I know this," the Doctor assured me.

"No, you don't. Because you're operating from a psychological model that is human. Would you use a human model as your guide if you needed to perform a delicate surgical procedure on me?"

"Of course I wouldn't."

"And you've proven that. Not knowing Cardassian biochemistry, you went to the Arawath Colony to get the appropriate data from Tain himself in order to remove the wire from my brain. Why should this be any different?" The question hung in the air. The Doctor had no answer, and I could see by his expression that he was genuinely embarrassed by the situation.

"Please, Doctor, I understand why you're asking this. But the stress, the anxiety, the fear a Cardassian experiences is about what *hasn't* happened. We've already processed the past; it's what's in front of us that's worrisome."

"And you don't think that what's in front of us has any connection to what's past?" he asked.

"Of course it does, but not in the causal manner you're suggesting. One model does not fit all, however admirable that model may be." I smiled and gestured to the Doctor; but he wasn't in the mood for a compliment.

"I'm not trained in this field, Garak, and I'm not going to send us off on a fool's errand—but I ask you as a friend to help us. However you can. This information could save countless lives."

"Help you by helping myself, you mean."

"However you can."

"You have my word, Doctor. I will do whatever I possibly can."

"I've never doubted that, Garak."

I nodded, looking at the third setting. "Tell me, Doctor, why did you invite Odo today?"

"I thought since you were working together on this project. . . ." His voice trailed off. We just looked at each other. "I think I was afraid to do this by myself," he finally admitted.

"I appreciate your honesty, Doctor. Please assure the captain that I will pick up more codes from Odo today."

"Thank you, Garak." The doctor seemed enormously relieved. He gestured to our food. "I'm afraid it's all gone cold. Why don't we just go to the Replimat after all?"

"Excellent suggestion," I eagerly agreed. The room was rapidly becoming much too confining. As we walked back out onto the Promenade, I wondered what it was about my future that was suffocating me. And how could I overcome it? Even as I thought this, I had to force myself to breathe.

8

Entry:

As I walked to the Diplomatic Service building, which was not far from the Hall of Records, I went over my cover information. I was to identify myself as Alardig Ra'orn, the youngest son of Krai, the newly appointed consul to the Cardassian Embassy on Tohvun III where the off-and-on Federation-Cardassian peace talks were on again. I had to be extremely careful (I was warned) with the military personnel who guarded the diplomatic compound. The military had their own security/intelligence apparatus, which did its best to discredit the Obsidian Order whenever possible. The military distrusted the Order and its seemingly autonomous position in the power structure. The fact that the Detapa Council chose the Order rather than the military for its Tohvun undercover operations only exacerbated the rivalry. There were instances of joint operations between the two, but they were rare and only happened when the Council twisted arms.

"All right, pass through," the glinn grudgingly allowed when my security code cleared. I smiled my thanks (this was completely ignored), and as I made my way to the appointed conference room I understood why the so-called rivalry was one-sided. The military mind doesn't lend itself to subtle and creative obfuscation.

The first person I saw when I entered the room was Maladek. He returned my look with a bored expression, and turned back to his comm chip. He was punctual for this meeting. Limor explained that Maladek was my older brother "Begom," and another member of our cell, Oonal, was "Krai," my father. As I studied the three of us, we did indeed look like a family.

The purpose of the peace talks was to determine a settlement of the often violent Cardassian-Federation border dispute that centered around several planets, Dorvan V being the most important. During these talks a truce had been declared. The assignment, as far as I was involved, was disappointing. Oonal was the experienced operative, and he was charged with the sole responsibility of working with his contacts on the Federation negotiating side. As probes, Maladek and I were there to give credibility to Oonal's cover, and beyond that simply to observe and learn.

"Learn your stories, follow orders, and serve Cardassia," Limor had admonished the two "brothers."

* * *

Tohvun III is a pleasant if somewhat damp and cold planet on the Federation frontier. It's mainly an outpost for traders and those tourists interested in trekking the forested slopes of Mandara, an enormous volcano that's been inactive for two centuries. The Cardassian Embassy compound, a bare-bones operation, consists of a main administration building and several attached residences, which were built as temporary shelters and over time became permanent.

Maladek and I were assigned adjoining residences; because of the shoddy construction, each of us could hear everything the other was doing or saying. The circumstances made me self-conscious, and I tried to live quietly, but Maladek thrashed about as if he was unaware or just didn't care. Odd behavior even for a novice security operative. His attitude toward me was guarded, but proper; neither one of us talked about anything unrelated to our work—least of all Bamarren. Even with the recognition that had passed between us at the first meeting, I was uncertain if he remembered me and, if he did, whether he knew of my contribution to the outcome of the Competition. This uncertainty kept me off-balance.

We were invited to all the social functions, and the reception at the Federation Embassy on the eve of the talks afforded me my first contact with humans. Before this evening, I had only seen them once from a distance, many years before when a delegation of Federation officials had attended the Tarlak funeral of Councilor Erud, who had been a leading proponent of a peaceful solution to the frontier wars, and whose name was invoked several times during the evening. Maladek seemed to be familiar with human ways, and when he expressed the strong judgment that they were a stupid race, I assumed that he knew what he was talking about.

"Look at the Vulcan," he directed me to a tall man with sad eyes. "They haven't the spine of a sandworm, but at least they're intelligent. They can grasp the complexities of a given political situation. I just hope Oonal is equal to the challenge," he said as he changed his focus to our "father," who was speaking with a short, graying Human.

"You mean Krai," I corrected. We were strictly instructed to use our story names.

Maladek looked at me with the expression he usually reserved for humans. "I think I'll try to have an intelligent conversation tonight." He moved off in the direction of the Vulcan, who was now standing alone. He does remember me, I thought, and he knows the role I played in the Competition. I decided at that moment that I had to watch him as much as the enemy.

"Hello." I'd been so focused on Maladek that I hadn't heard anyone approach. Standing next to me was a young human whose hair was as white as mine was black. I just stared at him. I'd never been this close to one of them.

"My name is Hans Jordt," he said carefully, not sure if I was on another communication level.

"My name is Alardig Ra'orn," I finally was able to reply. His insignia indicated that he held the rank of lieutenant, junior grade. He was solidly built, for a human, and his eyes were a shade of pale blue I'd never seen before.

"Forgive my ignorance," Hans began, "but what sports do Cardassians play?"

"Sports?" The question was so odd that I thought we might indeed be on different levels.

"Games. Contests." Hans attempted to be helpful, but it only got worse. I suspected this was obviously a clumsy attempt to cover a deeper intent.

"Perhaps I should explain," he bravely continued, in the face of my utter incomprehension. "A few of us are attempting to organize a game of football. Have you heard of it? Some people call it soccer."

"I've heard of it, but I'm afraid I wouldn't be of much help. Cardassians don't play."

"Ah—then perhaps you'd like to learn. We could play among ourselves, I suppose," he indicated the other humans in the room. "But I thought it might be interesting to get the other groups involved."

Hans looked at me with such intense, blue-eyed openness that it was difficult to maintain any kind of distance. He was a junior member of the Federation delegation, and certainly an intelligence probe. But that wasn't the problem—I welcomed this contact—it was the football. We don't play sports, at least not the team sports that Federation people have been trying to popularize throughout the quadrant. I could accept boxing and wrestling, which were primitive forms of pit competition, but basketball was mindless monotony and games like cricket and baseball were completely incomprehensible.

"I'd be pleased to participate," I replied, "but how could I possibly contribute? I know nothing about the game." As much as I wanted to establish contact with these people, I certainly didn't want to make a fool of myself.

"Yes, of course," Hans nodded in agreement. "But there is one position that does not require skill so much as athletic ability." He then gave me a lengthy and rather boring description of the game: defenders, midfielders, strikers working together to push a ball they were not allowed to touch with their hands or arms into an opponent's goal. Hans suggested that I participate as a goalkeeper.

"You see, all you would have to do is prevent your opponent from putting the ball into your goal."

"And I can't use my hands?" I asked.

"No, the goalkeeper can use any part of his body," Hans replied with the widest grin I have ever seen on a face. Children and their games, I thought. I had no idea of what I was getting into, but I agreed to defend one of the goals. It was at least a concept I understood.

After the reception, as I was laying out what I was going to wear for the next day's football match, I could hear Maladek in his residence. He was talking as he moved about. His voice was too soft for me to tell if he was talking to himself, into a recording device, or to someone else. I realized that I had lost track of him after I'd made contact with Hans, and I didn't see him for the rest of the evening. At one point, he laughed—a loud bark, really—and what sounded like a bottle crashed against the wall. There was a long silence punctuated intermittently by a sound I could only describe as a painful moan. A strange person, I thought as I fell into a disturbed sleep.

"Cut off his angle, Alardig!" I heard Hans instruct me as the "striker" broke through the defense with skillful control of the ball. I was all that was left between him and the goal. It was happening with the speed of a dream. The striker—a short, wraithlike Starfleet officer they called Mahmoud—feinted to my left, and my inexperience followed him. Just as my weight committed, he easily cut back to my right and kicked the ball into the back of the goal net. Ah yes, I thought, I understand now. That won't happen again.

And it didn't. For the remainder of the match I calculated distance, angle, and speed in such a way that Mahmoud's goal was their last. Hans was quite impressed with what he called my "uncanny anticipation," and suggested that I should pursue the game and introduce it to Cardassians. I smiled and imagined what would happen to this game if we adopted it. If they give "yellow cards" as warnings for slight infractions, and expel a player for the hard bump, kick, or trip, then a group of Cardassians would be gone in a matter of minutes. Even in today's game, there were complaints about the vigor of my defense, and I was trying to be "sporting" (to use the Federation expression). In our "games" you win by eliminating your opponents—or at the least severely limiting their ability to compete.

Still, it was quite instructive, especially during the time (which was most of the match) when the action was away from me and I was able just to observe. There is undoubtedly a skill to the game, and most people play to win (indeed, humans are capable of being every bit as aggressive as Cardassians), but they exhibited such a childlike joy and enthusiasm as they played that I came to understand another meaning of the word "game." What was more puzzling, however, was watching those people who played the game for no other reason than to . . . just play. If they or one of their teammates made a mistake, if the opposition scored . . . they didn't seem to mind. Some even laughed it off. And at the end, every one actually shook hands and congratulated each other.

They're not stupid—Maladek has dangerously underestimated them. But there's something we don't understand about these humans that limits our effectiveness in dealing with them.

There was quite a crowd for the match, which was due more to the fact that, other than hiking or turbogliding or attending Embassy functions, there wasn't much to do on Tohvun III. At the beginning I noticed Maladek watching with the tall Vulcan. Hans told me that he had tried to get Maladek as the other goalkeeper. I wasn't surprised that he'd refused; it was clear to me that he found his time better spent with the Vulcan, who was also a nonplayer. When we came back from the interval, the two of them had disappeared.

"Thank you, Alardig," Hans said to me at the reception for the players. "I can't get over how well you controlled your goal."

"Perhaps Cardassians have the ideal temperament for the position," I half joked. "Too bad you didn't get Begom for the other goal."

"Then we might not have won," Hans laughed. "But tell me, is he not feeling well?"

"Begom?" I asked.

"Yes. I only ask because he seemed perturbed when I approached him about the match."

"He's always perturbed," I said without thinking. At that moment I understood two things: I didn't like Maladek, and I had made a huge mistake. Hans was looking at me with his open face, so seemingly free of guile or ulterior intent. I immediately covered my misstep with a laugh and desperately tried to think of something that would mitigate my remark. But the laugh was artificial and the longer Hans stood there—smiling at me!—the more I felt the fool. Of course. Far from being stupid, these people know exactly what they're doing. Hans also knew what he was doing when he asked me to goalkeep. It was clear that they had more information about me than I had about them.

And Maladek knew all this as well.

The thought struck me as I made my way to the service compound, where I was to meet Limor. He was posing as an Embassy employee, although I hadn't seen him since I'd arrived. I sent him a message that I wanted a meeting as soon as possible, and he directed me to the groundskeeping building. I didn't know what else to do. As a junior probe I had limits, but what were they? How much do I respond to Hans's obvious interest in me? And what do I do about my increasing uneasiness concerning Maladek? A shadow moved, and Limor was next to me.

"Come with me," he said. Where had he come from? I followed as he quickly led me behind the building, through a back door, and into a small room I took to be the groundskeeper's office.

"What is it?" We stood in the darkness.

"It's Maladek. It's also the Starfleet junior officer, Hans Jordt. It's also . . . me." I struggled to organize my thoughts. I knew somehow there was a coherence, but I didn't have enough information to put it together for myself. Limor watched me, waiting patiently. I decided to start at the beginning. I told him about Bamarren and the Competition and how I was "certain that Maladek remembers not only who I am, but the part I played in his defeat." I told him about Maladek's contact with the Vulcan, his behavior with me and the sounds that were coming from his room. And I told him about Hans, the football match, and my unthinking reply to his interest in Maladek's well being.

"I know something is going on, Limor. But I'm missing something. Perhaps if I had more information. . . ."

"You're here to observe and to learn," Limor reminded me. "Information comes if your assignment expands. Otherwise, continue." He nodded dismissal and I started to leave.

"You can hear Maladek. He can't hear you." I stood at the door, letting this sink in. "And breathe once before you answer any questions."

As I walked back to the residence I understood that my assignment had expanded. I also understood that this expansion had been anticipated when I'd been given my residence. Very little is left to chance in this work. Even the lack of preparation for dealing with humans, which had so irritated me (and had made me think that Limor had been remiss) served a valuable purpose. Hans Jordt would not have shown such interest, I'm sure, if I had behaved in a "prepared" manner. The skill, I realized, was to assimilate these lessons without losing my innocence.

When I entered the residence, I immediately placed a chair next to the wall that connected to Maladek's. He was in there, restlessly moving about and muttering. I could only try to imagine the state of mind that impelled anyone to behave with such agitation. Not satisfied with my listening post, I tested various parts of the wall for better hearing. Not only did I find a slight indentation that allowed me to hear perfectly, but it also contained a cleverly disguised eyepiece that gave me a wide-angle view of Maladek's room. Why hadn't they told me about this to begin with? Because, my voice patiently explained, any expansion also depends upon information I uncover myself. Another piece of the mosaic.

Maladek was moving about the room as if he were being chased by fire. His muttering came in scattered bursts, and there were times when I was convinced other people were in the room with him. I could only make out the occasional word, and only then if it was repeated, like "yadik," which is what a young child calls his or her father. There was much about betrayal and someone called the "betrayer." As he harangued the room, he helped himself liberally from a bottle of *crinox*, a strong drink fermented from local berries. It was a pathetic sight, and one I never would have guessed from the self-contained superiority of his public face.

I watched him until he drank himself into a stupor and fell asleep in his clothes. The closest thing I could liken his behavior to was a man defending himself desperately before a chief archon who had judged him guilty. But even more disturbing was the impression that this presumption of guilt was driving him mad.

That night, my dreams reflected just how disturbed I was. Somehow I was barely hanging on to a steep ledge high up on a huge rock formation that dominated the Mekar Wilderness. In front of me was the flat summit and safety, behind me was a sheer drop into the jagged outcropping of the formation and certain death. A figure was on the summit offering me a rope to hold onto. The sun was behind the figure and I couldn't make out who it was. I kept repeating, "Who are you?" But the person wouldn't answer. I refused to take the rope until he did answer, but the surface was slippery and it was getting increasingly difficult to keep my footing. Finally, I had no choice and grabbed a rope. The person maintained the tension on the rope as I carefully climbed up. I stopped to take a breath and calm my anxiety.

"It's an opportunity, Elim," the voice said.

I looked up, and it was Barkan.

"It's an opportunity," he repeated and threw his end of the rope over the edge behind me.

I sat up on my pallet, bathed in sweat. I instinctively knew it was late, and that I had to hurry to get dressed and meet Hans at the main entrance. I had agreed to go on a hike with him up the Mandara volcano. I hoped that my dream had no connection to the day's activity. As I was leaving the residence, I looked toward the eyepiece in the wall; something in me didn't want to know what was happening on the other side. But it was my work, and I couldn't pretend otherwise. It was also in my interest to know, especially if the dream (as I suspected) was connected in some way to Maladek. I looked—but the room was empty.

"I've been told that this way has the greatest views," Hans said as he set a vigorous pace up the trail. It was clear that he was an experienced climber, and I followed, taking special care negotiating the broken lava rock and twisting roots. The density of the planet's atmosphere and the chilling dampness made the climb more taxing than I had expected. Finally we came to a clearing that afforded a view of the Mandara Valley rising up to a volcanic range of mountains, which floated above a bluish mist. Thankfully, there was direct sunshine that warmed the rocks we sat upon and helped to dispel the forest chill.

"This reminds me of my part of Earth," Hans said as we gazed out over the valley. He explained that everyone in his family loved to climb and hike. "If we manage to come to an agreement, many people from Earth would come here to vacation. I assume Cardassians would also visit Tohvum and Dorvan if there were peace between our peoples, no?"

"We tend to stay within the limits of our Union."

"Except where resources are involved," Hans said cheerfully, watching carefully for my reaction.

"What would you have us do? Cardassia is not a rich place like Earth. We have to live." I was equally cheerful in my reply.

"Everyone has the right to live, Alardig. But does it have to be at the expense of others?"

"If that's the competition, so be it. Very often, Hans, the game is about survival."

"But surely there's another way of dealing with scarcity than forcibly occupying another homeland and reducing its people to the level of vassals and slaves." Hans continued to smile, and I wondered if he really believed these sentiments—or was this another example of Federation hypocrisy? These people reduced all political complexity to pious platitudes, while they constructed the greatest empire in the history of the Alpha Quadrant.

"Have I been brought to this beautiful place to be subjected to a critique of our Bajoran policy?"

Hans laughed and looked out to the distant mountains. As the sun moved behind some clouds a cold wind kicked up. When he turned back he was no longer smiling.

"Your brother is not well. I'm sure you know that."

I took a long breath and nodded. "He hasn't been well for a while." I wasn't sure where this was going, but it felt right.

"Then you're concerned about his welfare."

"We all are." The art is to thread and extend meaning, using as few words as possible.

"Is he getting the help he needs?" So concerned, so caring. I took another long breath.

"Well . . . it's difficult. In our culture. . . ." I shrugged.

"Is that why he came to us?"

"Yes," I answered immediately, instinctively feeling that any hesitation would alert him to my ignorance and subsequent scramble for footing. I looked Hans in the eyes and resisted being swallowed by their immeasurable blue depths. I shivered against the cold. Hans saw this; I couldn't pretend that it hadn't happened.

"He's not a traitor. But he needs help. I told him not to go to you, that we'd find a way. . . ." I trailed off, translating my ignorant isolation into that of someone caught between two powerful forces. Tears came to my eyes, and I marveled that I had absolutely no emotional attachment to them.

"We know he's not a traitor. When Saurik came to us and explained the situation, he made it clear that your brother had no other recourse." Yes, the Vulcan. Careful now. Another breath.

"That's true," I replied.

"What usually happens to people in your culture who suffer from a . . . mental imbalance?" Hans was now treading delicately; clearly, they needed my help with Maladek. I wondered if he had really gone to them, or if they had enticed him in some way. Or was this all a lie?

"We kill them." Something very sharp emerged from the blue depth of Hans's eyes, and for the first time I was afraid I had gone too far. But it was too late to back down; I had to rely on human prejudice.

"Cowardice and madness are unforgivable," I went on. "They reflect flaws in the Cardassian character that can never be redeemed." This was to a certain extent indeed true of cowardice; madness, however, was looked upon as a mysterious disease, and those who suffered were isolated and treated well. In any event, no one was killed unless the cowardice occurred in battle.

"My God," Hans breathed, confirming, I'm sure, his belief that we were capable of any kind of atrocity. I hated his self-righteous superiority, and calculated the several moves that would send him flying into the abyss. Instead I turned and sat down on a rock that still held warmth from the departed sun. I put my head in my hands to give him the impression of my utter vulnerability.

"So, Alardig. What do we do now?"

"Father had hoped that if he brought Begom on this trip—got him away from home and the pressures—but it's only gotten worse. Father can't even concentrate on his work. We never should have come here. I'm afraid. . . ." I stopped as if I'd gone too far.

"Of what?" he asked. I just shook my head.

"I understand," Hans said, thinking that he had me. There was a long silence. "We'll take care of Begom. You have my word. I think I know a way." I looked at him, full of gratitude.

"Thank you, Hans."

"But we will need your participation. I am going to set up a meeting as soon as possible."

"With Begom?" I asked, hiding my concern.

"No. With the people who are helping him."

"Anything I can do . . ." I assured him with heartfelt sincerity.

"I know. Well . . ." Hans looked around, smiling again. ". . . we'd better get back before we lose the light."

As we came down the trail, I wondered about Maladek and his illness, the people who were "helping" him, and the exact nature of my participation.

That night I reported to Limor, and he checked and double-checked every detail I had related with probing, specific questions. I assumed that it was because the situation had reached a critical point and he was concerned that a probe was in the middle. But the discomfiting thought did occur to me, as I patiently responded to his interrogation, that he was also scrutinizing my veracity. I was about to ask him if he doubted what I was reporting, when he preempted me.

"I may put you on the enhancer."

I said nothing. It was enough of a challenge just to return his look.

"How would you feel about that?" he asked.

"I would . . . submit, of course."

"Is there something you're not telling me, Elim?"

"No." I continued to hold his look and knew better than to ask him anything now; I would only appear defensive. I waited in the long silence, and refused to back down.

"Consult your comm chip. There is some information I want you to pass on to Hans Jordt when you see him next." I was dismissed.

Hans contacted me two days later, and we took another hike up the Mandara. Once again he set a grueling pace on a different, steeper trail. As I struggled to keep up, it occurred to me that breaking me down physically was certainly a part of his strategy. When we stopped to "admire the view" (Hans's sentimental expression), I didn't try to hide my exhaustion. I flopped down, panting heavily, and giving the not untrue impression that I couldn't go any further.

"Are you all right, Alardig?" Hans asked, barely showing any effects at all of the arduous hike. I nodded. He watched me as I "struggled" with my breathing. He took a small instrument from his pocket and waved it over me. I was warned by Limor to deactivate my comm chip, because Hans would check to see if I was recording the conversation. He was satisfied that I wasn't.

"We've found someone who can help Begom."

I nodded again, pretending that it was still too difficult for me to speak.

"But to give him the help he needs, we're going to need some information."

I waited for Hans to continue.

"He speaks of betrayal, and he mentions you."

"Me?" I didn't have to feign surprise.

"Yes. Why would he say that about his own brother?" Hans asked.

"I don't know." And I didn't know how to reply to this. "What else did he say about me?"

"He told us not to believe anything you tell us. According to him you're here to pass on misinformation regarding the Cardassian position, and you represent an intelligence agency that wants to scuttle these talks. He says that you're not even his brother."

I couldn't believe what I was hearing. What did Maladek think he could accomplish by telling them this? Was this his revenge for what happened at Bamarren? Or was this another example of having only the information I needed for the moment? I had no choice but to stay with my story. I didn't even try to hide my true confusion from Hans.

"Are you a spy?" he asked.

"No. And I really don't know what there is to spy about. The negotiating positions seem to be common knowledge. Troop withdrawals from the neutral zone. Unarmed observers on all planets in question to monitor the truce and withdrawal. Cardassian control of Dorvan V. These are the main points. What's left are the details." This was an accurate summation.

Hans thought for a moment. "You're well informed."

"I'm here to work with my father and learn. And I thought Begom was as well. Unless . . ."

"Unless what?" Hans asked.

"Unless he's playing a dangerous game. No one pretends that a settlement with the Federation has the unanimous support of the Central Command. There are elements in the military who'd like to see these talks fail. I'm just afraid that Begom may have gotten involved with them."

"So now you're accusing each other." Hans was skeptical.

"But why would he say such a thing about me?" I asked fervently. "He hasn't been well ever since he came back from Bamarren."

"And Bamarren is . . . ?"

"It's our state security school. He suffered a terrible humiliation there, and I know he wants to do something that will somehow erase the shame. I'm afraid he's involved in something that's way over his head. He's playing some kind of game with you, Hans, and I think he's trying to impress someone."

"Who?" Hans asked.

"Father," I said, as if finally understanding. "Father always expected that Begom would be the one who'd go to the diplomatic institute and follow in his steps. When Begom went to Bamarren, Father was hurt and turned to me. Ever since, he's been trying to prove to Father that he made the right choice, but after the fiasco at Bamarren. . . ." I nodded vigorously, kicking up dust as I paced our small clearing.

"I don't know what he's telling you, Hans, but if it's anything like what he's said about me, then be careful. He's angry and he's disturbed, and he's going to say whatever he feels he needs to to redeem his pride and honor. He's always been an adventurer, and this whole spy business—I'm certain—is just another game to him."

Hans didn't say anything. He looked out over his beloved rain forests receding to the distant string of volcanoes, and his face was a mask.

"What was the information you wanted from me?" I asked after a long silence. Hans grimaced as if to dispel an unpleasant thought.

"No, Alardig, I think you've told me what's necessary," he said with formal politeness.

"I hope it's of use in helping Begom."

"I think this is a family matter, don't you? Begom and his father need to sort things out."

"Ah, if only they could, Hans," I said with a sigh.

We traced our way back down the volcano. I never saw Hans Jordt again.

I reported to Limor that evening. As I gave him every word, gesture, and detail he never took his eyes off of mine. After I had finished, I sat in silence while he made some notes on a comm chip that seemed to come out of his hand. The silence deepened as he waited for what I guessed to be a reply to his notes. There were so many questions I wanted to ask, but by now I knew that I was only going to get the information I needed to proceed— and nothing more. I had no idea as to what Maladek was up to, and I was worried about my improvisation that afternoon with Hans. Limor looked up from the comm chip.

"You will return to Cardassia tomorrow morning. Stay in your quarters until someone comes for you, and be ready to leave immediately." Limor's tone was flatter than usual, and I was worried even more that somehow I had botched my assignment—whatever that assignment had been. I nodded and moved to the door.

"You did well," he said in the same flat tone. It was amazing how quickly and completely my spirits changed. "But tonight you are to leave your comm chip on, so I can hear everything in your room. Do you understand?" I wasn't sure if I did.

"Yes, of course," I assured him.

Limor just looked at me. "Stay on your toes, Elim. This assignment is not over."

The first thing I did when I returned to my room was to check the eyepiece, but Maladek wasn't in his room. I wondered if he would ever return. Had he gone over to the Federation? Had they murdered him? My imagination was attempting to fill in the missing pieces. What was this about? I packed my things to be ready in the morning, and sat in a chair fully clothed with my phaser concealed but accessible. I adjusted the comm chip so that Limor could monitor. What I was waiting for I wasn't quite sure, but I had an idea.

* * *

There were all kinds of eyes staring at me. Strange blue ones that studied me like a specimen. Soft brown ones that signaled regret. Hard red eyes that looked at me with unaccountable hatred. I opened my eyes, and the red eyes were still staring at me. They belonged to Maladek, bloodshot with an inner torment I had only witnessed through the eyepiece. I realized that I had fallen asleep. How long had he been in the room?

"Maladek—what?" I started to get up, but he pushed me back. I didn't resist, because I saw that he had a small phaser in his hand, and I was better off in the chair anyway because that's where my phaser was.

"When I saw you at the cell meeting I knew you were nothing but trouble. Just as before." His deadly tone sent my hand for the phaser, but I couldn't find it.

"Maladek, I have never meant you any ill. . . ."

"From the beginning. With Charaban. You were an instrumental part of my betrayal."

"What betrayal?" I asked. "It was the Competition, and it was my duty to fight you and try to win."

"But you weren't supposed to win!" he shouted, raising the hand with the phaser. I still couldn't find mine. It must have slipped deeper into the cushions.

"Of course we were. Winning is the obligation of any Cardassian." I didn't know what he was talking about. He laughed with that loud, unpleasant bark.

"You're good, aren't you? They sent me back. They said I wasn't stable enough to trust. They said I should work it out with my Father!" He laughed again. "If they only knew. What did you tell them?"

"Tell who?" I asked.

"Don't play with me again!" He raised the phaser and moved toward me. I wondered if Limor was hearing this.

"Twice is enough, Ten Lubak!" Another bark. "A Ten!" he said with spitting disgust. "You threw that body at us and I knew Charaban wasn't keeping his end of the bargain."

"What bargain?" I suddenly didn't care about the phaser.

"You don't know, do you?"

"No."

"It was supposed to end in a stalemate. Neither of us would win. That way, Charaban could still assume leadership, and my placement after culmination would have been higher than an Obsidian probe." He suddenly looked at me as if he was seeing another person.

"Why did you leave Bamarren?" he demanded.

"I was told to," I replied.

"Why?" He couldn't compute this. "You were one of the unit leaders. You should have advanced with the betrayer."

I said nothing. I was not about to explain my own betrayal. Maladek began to weep.

"What did you say to them? You said something about my father." Somehow I knew he wasn't talking about "Oonal."

"I told them that you were in over your head and that it was because you were trying to prove something to your father." His eyes were suddenly furious, and he grabbed my neck with his free hand and held the phaser up to my head.

"What do you know? What do you know about anything?" he screamed in my face.

I easily grabbed the wrist of his phaser hand and disarmed him and kicked him back onto the floor. I stood up and held the phaser so he could see it. I wasn't sure, but I thought I heard footsteps moving away from the door outside.

"What am I going to tell him? They're sending me back. You seem to know everything that's going on in my life. How do I tell him I've been disgraced again? What do I say?" The look on his face—the red eyes and contorted muscles—sent chills through me. He actually expected me to give him an answer.

"Just tell him . . . you did the best you could." The bark this time shocked me. It was loud and mocking and had a concussive effect. I backed up, fully expecting him to attack. Instead, he walked to the door, opened it and left. I didn't follow him; I was too stunned by the last grotesque image he'd presented. I went to the eyepiece, but he didn't return to his room. I didn't know what to do. Somehow the fiction, created in a moment of need, had become blended in with an awful reality, and I felt that once again I'd been the unwitting instrument of Maladek's abysmal failure.

"Come in, Elim." Tain had his uncle smile working today. I entered the office, which was more cluttered than ever. There was barely room for me to stand.

"We did very well on Tohvun."

"I hope my contribution. . . ."

"Yes, we were able to scuttle those misconceived talks. We complained that the Federation was more interested in harassing our embassy people than they were in bargaining in good faith."

I nodded. There were so many questions. How I had managed to function during that mission, when I never knew what it was about or what I was supposed to do, I'll never know. This was my first experience with Tain's working methods. For him it was all a puzzle, and we were the separate pieces he put together at his pleasure. I had to accept that the final result—destroying the talks—was the one he wanted. But there was one question I needed to ask. Maladek's final look haunted me still.

"What is it, Elim?" Tain asked.

"What happened to Maladek?"

"You didn't hear?" He seemed surprised. "A terrible thing really. He killed himself."

I didn't move a muscle. I felt my throat begin to constrict. Tain watched me.

"Very upsetting. It was the reason the talks were cancelled. We had no idea he was so unstable."

That was the word the Federation had used when they sent him back. And while I believed that Hans Jordt had decided that Maladek was too much of a liability, Tain's unblinking look made it clear to me that this was a far more complicated world than that of Bamarren and the Competition. For one thing, the penalty for losing could be final. For another, we can never be certain what purpose we are serving. At least Maladek didn't have to worry about what he would say to his father now.

9

The city is rising from its ashes. From reports coming in, it seems that cities and communities all over Cardassia are digging out and establishing a new life. But it's difficult, Doctor. We have so few natural resources (which dictated our expansionist policy to begin with), and our infrastructure has been ravaged. So the Cardassia that's emerging is splintered and primitive. And dangerous. Each sector is attempting to organize so that food distribution can proceed in an orderly manner. I must say that the Federation has been prompt and generous in its response. However, I don't know how many more of these "ready meals" I can stomach. Give me the Replimat any day.

One of the problems with the reorganization is the quality of person who is answering the call for political leadership. The previous leadership structure has been discredited; people are aware that the military was the most influential group, and their agenda was to keep the mechanism for conquest and expansion well oiled. As long as they brought back the spoils of this policy, they were able to hold on to their power. And while I think most people now understand that direct responsibility for our current circumstances has to be placed at the door of the military, there are still many who believe otherwise.

In our own sector, a man by the name of Korbath Mondrig is attempting to take political control by appealing to our fears. He maintains in public speeches that a return to our former glory is the only way we will be able to protect ourselves from our ancient enemies, who now see us as easy pickings. But what pickings? We have nothing left. However, people are believing his idiocy, and his organization is growing.

Another man from our sector, Alon Ghemor, the nephew of Tekeny Ghemor, the legate who believed that Colonel Kira was his daughter, is organizing based on the political belief that we have to rebuild a new society administered by civilian leadership, one that lives in what he calls "creative harmony" with the rest of the Quadrant. What's interesting is that I went to school with Ghemor. I saw him at a rally that was held here (yes, my little Tarlak has become a focal point for the sector). When he appeared I yelled, "Five Lubak!" He didn't recognize me at first, but then his eyes widened, and he answered, "Ten!" He seemed genuinely pleased to see me. Dr. Parmak, who's an ardent supporter of Ghemor and organized the rally, was quite impressed. It's encouraging to see that my old schoolmate has remained a decent man.

But this is our problem now (and I can see you ready to pounce, Doctor): What is our new mechanism of choice? A small group of Mondrig's supporters are attempting to intimidate people, but to engage them with organized opposition would be dangerous. We have several small armies battling each other to fill a power vacuum and end up deeper in the dust and rubble. But that's what Mondrig wants—a competition. He maintains that the coming inevitable conflict will "revitalize our defeated spirit, and a renewed warrior society will return us to our former glory." Dr. Parmak, however, is a believer in the democratic principles you and I have spent many hours arguing over (what is it about you doctors?). He and Ghemor want the people of the sector to be able to vote. It's a new concept for us, but everyone is so weary from the war and its devastation that it's a serious possibility.

Yes, I can picture you sitting with your feet up, gloating with that self-satisfied smile of Federation enlightenment. And perhaps you're right.

10

Entry:

As I approached the house the door opened. Mother had evidently been waiting for me. I paused at the door.

"Hello, Mother." It'd been years since I had said that. A great space had widened between us, and I'd had to call her Mila the few times I'd seen her at the Order. Standing in the doorway, she looked older and heavier.

"Come in, Elim." It was also years since I'd been inside this house. The same smell of cooking oil and disinfectant prevailed, and nothing appeared to have changed. Except that Father was ill. I followed Mother down the stairs to the basement with an increasing sense of foreboding.

"He's very weak, Elim. Don't tire him."

"How long has he been ill?" I asked. The situation was obviously more serious than I was led to believe.

"For some time." Mother was terse, uncommunicative. She stubbornly maintained the distance between us.

"Why didn't you call me earlier?" Anger was rising within me, and I had to keep a tight control.

"You're so rarely in the city, and when you are I know that Enabran needs you."

It was true. The only time I spent on Cardassia was what was necessary to prepare me for my next assignment; any time left was spent in further training that Tain insisted that I have. I had long since shed my probe status. Indeed, judging from the way I was treated, I was regarded as one of Tain's protégés (the "sons of Tain" they called us), and held to a rigorous standard. I was envied and feared, but returning to this house had revealed the true depths of my loneliness. Mother stopped before we entered Father's room. She wanted to tell me something.

"He's not himself. He's . . . medicated, and sometimes what he says doesn't make sense. It's important to leave before he gets to that point." I nodded and we entered.

The room was dark, and the smell of decay assaulted my senses. I started to gag and worked to fight back the fear that seized me. When my eyes adjusted, I barely recognized Father. He was the size of a child. His hair was completely white, his face skull-like. I couldn't tell if he was sleeping or dead. In either case, death was the dominant presence. I was speechless. This was a man whose body had been lean and hard, and who had worked every day with unflagging vitality.

"Elim is here, Tolan," Mother said. "He came to say hello."

Father opened his eyes, enormous and glittering dark pools that overwhelmed his gray shrunkenness. What life remained had collected in them. It took him a moment to focus on me, and then he smiled.

"Elim," he whispered.

"Hello, Father." My voice sounded loud and false.

"Look . . . Mila. He's a man," he said with wonder, as if the intervening years had been mere days.

"Well, isn't that what I'm supposed to be?" I tried to joke.

He started to pull himself up. "Help me, Mila."

"No, Tolan. Rest. Elim will be back when you're feeling stronger." Mother started to guide me out of the room.

"No!" The strength of his voice stopped us. "Help me sit up, and then leave."

Mother had a stricken look on her face. She looked at me. I didn't know what to say.

"Please, Tolan. You need to. . . ."

"I need to talk to Elim." He turned to me. "Help me sit up." His body was nearly weightless, and as I lifted him up and reset his bolster, I wondered what kept him from floating away.

"Now leave us, Mila," he commanded.

I thought Mother was going to cry. She gave one last pleading look, but realized that it was useless. She turned and left.

Alone with Father, I didn't know what to say. He motioned me to come closer. I knelt down on the floor so that my face was level with his.

"I'm dying, Elim." He could see the distress in my face as I tried to stammer something. "No, no, no. I'm old, and this is what's supposed to happen now."

"And all this time. . . ." I tried, but my voice choked off. "I'm sorry, Father."

"You have nothing to apologize for, Elim. I'm the one who's sorry."

"Please, Father. . . ."

"I'm not your father."

I studied his face to make sure that he wasn't drifting away. His eyes were clear and present; if anything, the glitter had intensified.

"Of course you are." I spoke to him as if he were a child or a simpleton.

"Elim, there's no time to waste. I have always loved you like a son. I wished with all my heart that you *were* my son. But you're not."

Now I felt like the child. "Then . . . I don't understand. Who is?"

Tolan sighed. "Your mother is the one to tell you. I made a promise. . . ." and his voice trailed off.

"I don't understand," I repeated. "Why?"

"Oh, my dear Elim. The soul of a poet, and look at you . . . your closed face . . . all those secrets. . . ." A spasm rippled through him like a sudden wind over still water. "Too many secrets . . . it's like poison." He brought his trembling, clawlike hand up to my face. "Too many secrets poison the soul." The spasm came again, this time accompanied by a racking cough. When his body relaxed he pointed to a table.

"The red box. Open it." I saw what he was pointing at, and rose and went to it. For some reason I was afraid to touch it.

"Open it, Elim." He endured another racking cough.

It was an old lacquered box made from some kind of organic material. I lifted the simple latch. Inside it was the Hebitian recitation mask. I picked it up and felt the coarse material. The neutral face of the mask stared blankly back at me.

"Celebrate Oralius. However you can. The bag also." His voice was barely audible.

A white fiber bag was at the bottom of the box. I picked it up and opened it. Inside were dozens of Edosian orchid tuber cuttings. I looked at Tolan, who was smiling faintly.

"However you can," he repeated with as much energy that remained. "Now take them and go." He closed his eyes and went completely still. I stood there a long time. Thoughts, images, feelings swirled through me, collided, lingered, dissipated—and I did nothing but observe them. I had no choice. To identify with any one of them meant certain chaos. I maintained my detachment as I repacked the red box. A part of me stood off to the side and watched the rest of me pick up the box, go over to Tolan, and press my open palm against his cold, dry forehead.

"Good-bye, Father."

Mila was waiting for me when I came out. Her face was as neutral as the Hebitian mask.

"Why?" I asked.

"It was necessary." She was unapologetic, almost defiant. She looked at the red box I was carrying and sighed.

"Necessary to live this deception for all these years?" She just looked at me. It was a stupid question. In our society, having a child without an enjoined mate marked both mother and child as outcasts. The child needed both parents, otherwise he or she was designated an orphan and taken away to a service institution. The mother was publicly vilified, and the father of the child, if he was ever identified, was severely punished.

"Why didn't you ever enjoin with my real father?" I asked.

"It wasn't possible, Elim."

"And Tolan agreed to this deception?" It was a dangerous arrangement. The Cardassian family is a strictly defined unit, and any corruption of this unit is considered a real threat to our society.

"Tolan is a good man."

"But you had another man's child!" I was angry; I wanted to punish her. She knew this but wasn't going to back down.

"His loyalty was stronger than his disapproval," she answered pointedly. Was this the formality, the distance that had always existed between them? And had there ever been any love between them?

"Who is my father?" For the first time she broke our contact and looked away.

"I'm sorry, Elim." Mother moved to the bottom of the stairs as if she were ushering me out. "Will you come back tomorrow? I don't know how long it will be. . . ."

"Who is he?"

"I can't tell you."

"I have a right to know!" I demanded.

"And I have a right. . . ." She cut herself off and made a wide gesture with her arms that seemed to include everything around her. And then it hit me . . . and simultaneously we both heard his footsteps upstairs. A chill went through me. Of course. I went to the stairs and looked at Mother. Her face was softer, younger. For this one moment the distance between us had dissolved. The footsteps were now directly above us. My entire life had been dominated by his presence. So had Mother's . . . and Tolan's. I nodded and started up the stairs.

"Elim. . . ." I stopped and looked back down at her. I could see how handsome and strong her face must have been when she was young.

"What, Mother?"

"Be careful," she finally warned.

"There's nothing to worry about. I'm just going to say hello to 'Uncle' Enabran." I turned and continued up the stairs.

Tain opened the door. Although I hadn't been here in many years he wasn't surprised to see me.

"Elim. This is like the old days. Come in." And it was

like the old days. He led me through the same dark hallway into the same cluttered study, the focus of his home life. Except there were even more scrolls made from the hide of the *brangwa,* the extinct mountain canid. Early Cardassians from the mountainous region of Rogarin used these hides to record the poetry and stories of their culture. Tain was proud of his collection and was very much involved in a network with other collectors.

"That's an old box, Elim." He pointed to the red box I had forgotten I was clutching. "May I see?" I hesitated. "I don't blame you. It shouldn't be handled by just anybody. Where did you find it?"

"Tolan gave it to me." I never called him Tolan, but if Tain noticed the change he didn't indicate it.

"Ah, yes. How is he? I understand he's quite sick."

"He's dying."

"Oh dear. Such a good man."

"That's what Mother said."

There was a long silence and we just looked at each other. I felt disconnected. What was I doing here?

"Sit down, Elim. Just put that stack on the floor." I cleared the chair he had pointed to and sat holding the red box protectively in my lap. Tain sat in a deep chair that was obviously his favorite.

"I'm glad you've come to me here. We can . . . express ourselves in a way that's not possible elsewhere."

Indeed, the dark room with the piled scrolls and their musky smell, the artifacts and ancient wall hangings with their glyphs and symbols—was any of it Hebitian, I wondered?—was a world far removed from the cold efficiency of the Order. We were sealed away in an ageless cavern.

"Tolan and I shared a love of classic beauty, the old

aesthetics that guided and revealed. He was a visionary, Elim. All those designs at Tarlak, the way the greenswards and plantings contained the monuments, never allowing them to brutalize us with death. Mothers and children are as welcome there as the guls and legates. All were based on classical designs. Oh, yes, he was a dedicated man. You were fortunate to be able to work with him."

I sat in the chair, holding the red box as if afraid it would fly apart. I wanted to cry, to speak from a deep place, to reveal my dreams and desires to this smiling older man who was my father. But I could only sit there and hold the box tighter.

"You're at a crossroads, Elim. You're no longer the young probe we threw into the fray with almost no preparation to see how you would think and react. You're a skilled operative, and ready for the next stage—if you're willing."

I remembered one of the few times Tain had taken me outside the city, when he'd put me on a Cardassian riding hound. He'd held the bridle and walked me around the course. Then he'd given me the bridle and had walked next to me as the hound panted and slobbered. Then he'd said, "It's time." He'd slapped the hound hard, and it had taken off at full speed. But I'd hung on, though frightened by the sudden speed and surging power beneath me. Gradually I'd begun to adjust and learn to roll with the hound's concussive undulations.

"I was never happier in my life," I said out loud. "I turned around to wave to you, and I fell."

Tain studied me for a long moment and nodded. "And you pulled yourself up and continued to ride. I remember."

"But why the secrets?" I asked.

"Without them there's no security. It's as simple as that."

"But that's our work," I protested. "Why the other secrets?"

"It's *all* our work, Elim. To be effective our lives must be the most closely held secrets of all. We're the night people. While the rest of our compatriots sleep that's when we're working the hardest, dealing with the anxieties and fears that would otherwise destroy us. We have to keep the secrets, and store them, and hold them tightly—just like you're holding your red box."

I realized that my hands were cramped from holding the box. I wanted to relax them, but they wouldn't move.

"It requires sacrifice. And each stage of the work requires a renewal of that sacrifice. We have to give up our lives, bit by bit, to these secrets so that people will feel the security to go on with theirs—and do their work. If we tell them everything, if we give them all the information about the threats and dangers that surround us, they'll hate us for disturbing their peace and their ability to function. This requires great strength of character on the part of the operative—to be able to hold these secrets and not let them overwhelm us."

This was the first time I had ever seen Tain possessed by a passion. His eyes were open and alive with his desire to communicate. His facial muscles were unguarded, working naturally as they registered the meanings of his words.

"The truth is, Elim, these secrets must become the source of our strength, the strength that enables our people to withstand their fears, the strength that enables Cardassia to withstand its enemies. Every citizen deserves security, and it's up to the night people to provide it."

I continued to sit for a long time, listening to the sounds of the house. I heard nothing from downstairs, nothing from the outside. I rose and looked at Tain. His face had returned to the controlled half-smile. His jowls seemed to grow larger every time I saw him, and I wondered if I would ever look like that. He remained in his chair as I walked out of the room. I walked out into the night with my red box and all the way to the Tarlak Sector. I went to the children's area and sat across from where Tolan and I had planted the Edosian orchids. At some point I opened the box and took out the mask. I studied the eyeless face and half expected it to talk to me, to explain why my life had become so complicated, so beyond my control. But it was obviously another "night person," guarding its secrets. There were hooks that went over the ears, and I attached the mask to my face. I sat there and waited . . . but nothing was revealed. Finally the tears came.

▌▌

Entry:

"According to my contact on Bajor, Mr. Garak, this woman is not just another pretty face." Quark had that conspiratorial gleam in his eyes, and his voice was ripe with the potential drama. "I should charge you double for this information."

"Really? What have you found?" I tried to minimize my interest, but Quark knew better.

"Why are you so interested in Remara?" He was going to squeeze everything he could out of this situation. I sighed and looked around.

"Will you solemnly promise you will keep this to yourself?"

"Absolutely. You have my word." As children, we were taught that such a bald-faced lie was an occasion for the Mogrund to appear and punish the offender.

"As you know, I lead a solitary existence, and I've been looking for a mate to share my humble existence." Quark's eyes had reached nova intensity; he could barely control his quivering body. "Of course," I continued, "you can't be too careful these days, can you?"

"You certainly can't." Quark slammed his hand against the bar. "You've just given me an idea!" He was positively hopping up and down. "I could broker pairings, Garak. I'd have dabo girls who were looking for mates and match them with clients here on the station who agreed to pay me upon a successful pairing." He looked around to see who could be signed up immediately. "Of course, since you helped me form the idea, this one's on the house."

"That's very generous of you, Quark. Now what about that information?"

"Ah, yes . . . let me see." He punched his padd. "Yes, it seems that she was an art student from Dahkur Province . . . sent to the capital to study . . . married her teacher Tir Karna. . . . They had a child—a son, Berin. . . . Ah, this is where it gets interesting: Tir and the boy were killed when Cardassians destroyed the shuttle they were in as it was taking off. . . ."

"What shuttle was that?" I asked.

Quark punched the padd. "The *Taklan* . . . it was one of their own, bound for Terok Nor. Why would the Cardassians destroy their own shuttle?" Quark asked.

"Go on." I took a sip of my *kanar* and was amazed that my hand remained steady. Is this my hand, I wondered?

"Shortly after this, Remara joined the Resistance. You can't hold that against her." Quark looked up as if he'd just discovered a reason for the deal to unravel.

"Forgive and forget," I said, taking another sip of *kanar.*

"A man after my own heart." Quark refilled my glass.

"Is there anything else?" I asked.

"Not much . . . went back to school after the withdrawal . . . works as a counselor at the Mihan Settlement House in the capital . . . became a part-time dabo girl. I don't know what it is, Garak, but the Klingons love her. And she now works for one of the great entrepreneurial minds in the Alpha Quadrant!" he concluded, with a positively radiant look on his face. I could see that he was itching to embark upon his new business. I drained my glass and declined the offer of another, as Quark's hand snaked toward the bottle.

"No, thank you. I appreciate the help. You've been most helpful."

"Valued customers deserve special service, Mr. Garak." At that moment Morn rumbled through the door, and Quark's eyes locked in. "Speaking of which. . . ."

As I left, I could hear Quark begin his new pitch. "I have the answer for you, Morn my friend. You lead too solitary a life. As I was just saying to Mr. Garak. . . ."

The *Taklan*. And she was a member of the Resistance. The colonel's question returned: what did Remara want from me? I considered paying a visit to Kira but decided against it. I had time to think this through; Remara wouldn't be back on the station for another week. By then I would know what to do.

It was late, and I didn't feel like going back to my quarters. I decided to go up to the observation lounge, where Remara and I had had our first rendezvous. My feelings about her were increasingly conflicted. Up until now I hadn't perceived any danger, but after Quark's information I realized that I was being naïve. As I moved up the narrow circular staircase a huge figure loomed above me. The light from behind him turned him into a giant shadow—but I knew who it was. I turned around, and as I anticipated there were two more Bajorans at the bottom. I berated myself for being so involved with my musings that I had lost my sense of space. That and too much *kanar*.

"Everybody's favorite Cardassian," said Londar Parva, the Bajoran I'd "bumped" into on the Promenade. "What is it about you? Nobody wants to treat you like the animal you are. But if Odo doesn't want to deal with you, I will."

He started down the stairs while the other two held their position at the bottom. I had no choice. I ran down the stairs and threw myself at the two Bajorans, trying to break through them. I nearly succeeded, but Londar was quick and caught me from behind. They dragged me into an isolated alcove.

Londar stood in front of me while the other two had my arms pinned.

"You don't belong here, spoonhead," he growled and hit me across the face with his closed fist. The combination of the insult and the blow set off an inner explosion. I used the two men holding me as leverage and kicked both legs up and caught Londar squarely on his massive jaw. As he staggered back with a loud cry, I freed my right arm and came across and hit the man on my left in the face, then immediately came back with my right elbow and caught the man on my right in the throat. He went down, but the man on my left still held on to my arm. I hit him again, but by this time Londar had recovered and made a wild charge that sent me flying into the wall behind me. This freed my left arm, however, and I was able to square off against the two men with my back against the wall. They hesitated as I took my position. In the pause I could hear the third man still trying to make breath move through his damaged windpipe. I could also hear the three of us panting heavily, and I smelled the sour perspiration of people who exercise little and drink too much.

"That's enough!" Colonel Kira stood behind the two Bajorans with her phaser drawn. Londar and the other man turned. A small crowd had gathered behind the colonel.

"You see?" Londar said to the crowd as if they'd been privy to his logic. "Even Bajorans protect the—"

"What's going on here?" Kira demanded.

No one spoke. We looked at her and continued to pant.

"Garak?"

"Nothing serious, Colonel. We were just having a political discussion and we found little common ground."

"Is that why you're bleeding?" Kira asked. Indeed, I could taste the blood in my mouth.

"Political opinions often have consequences," I replied. The colonel was disgusted.

"Londar?"

"The tailor attacked us," he stated.

"All three of you?" Kira asked, looking at the two other Bajorans. They weakly nodded assent.

"Do you want to bring charges against him?" she asked.

"What good would it do? Odo won't do anything. Nobody will." Londar was back to his old complaint, now doubly frustrated.

"Just make sure that you don't try to take the law into your own hands," Kira warned. "Now if you're not going to bring charges, go on about your business." She motioned them back toward the Promenade, and they sullenly obeyed. Londar shot one last look back at me, and I smiled.

"Pleasant talking to you," I called. Londar was so filled with loathing, I was sure he could spit bile. I knew it wasn't personal, but I also knew that I had to be more vigilant. The crowd dispersed, but Kira stood watching me.

"Are you all right?" she asked. I moved my jaw around and winced.

"I don't think anything's broken. A few loose teeth perhaps."

"Why won't you report this?" Kira asked. "Londar's a dangerous man, he won't forget this."

"It's best this way, I think."

"Suit yourself," she said.

"Well, I should probably return to my quarters and get cleaned up," I said.

"I'm going in that direction. I'll walk with you," the colonel offered.

"A pleasure." We started off, and I knew she wanted to talk about our mutual acquaintance. "So," I said. "I understand you and Remara were old friends."

Kira gave me a sharp look. "What did she tell you?"

"Only that the two of you had once known each other." We walked in silence for a few moments.

"We met at the Singha refugee center," she finally admitted. "She was the only one left in her family, and my father let her share our cramped living space."

"That was very kind of your father."

"He was a kind man. Remara was older and she helped take care of me and my brothers. But we're not friends," she added pointedly.

"She told me that the two of you were close."

Kira nodded. "Until she showed her true colors."

"And what colors were those?" I asked.

"People seem to think you're a clever person, Garak. Perhaps you are. But Remara knows how to use her beauty—especially with clever men." Kira stopped at in intersection of corridors. "I'm going this way."

"Thank you for your company . . . and your assistance," I said in parting.

"The fact that she's a thief and a traitor probably doesn't bother you," she said, looking at me with a pitying half smile. "But trust me, Garak—she's using you for something. Goodnight." Abruptly, Kira turned and moved down the corridor with her martial stride. No doubt going to Odo's quarters.

Of course Remara is using me, I thought. For what, I had no idea. Traitor and thief. The mystery only sharpened my appetite.

12

Entry:

Tzenketh. Each assignment was farther away from Cardassia Prime, and of longer duration. Loval, Celtris III, Lamenda Prime, Kora II, Orias III. If I made a chart of my assignments from the beginning, each vector would penetrate progressively deeper into space. I wondered if this was a sign of advancement in the Order.

I had done what Tain asked, and in the following years no one was as dedicated a night person as I was. I went everywhere they asked me to go and stayed as long as it took to complete the mission, but Tain never said a word that would indicate whether he was pleased or displeased. In fact, I saw very little of him, and even less of Mila. This distance from them, and the fact that I was rarely home, actually made my work easier. My primary contact at the Order was Limor Prang, who became even less expressive, if that were possible, as he grew older. I knew, however, that my dedication, and the absence of any kind of life outside of the Order, concerned him. On those occasions he'd tersely suggest that I visit Morfan Province or some such popular vacation area. I'd tell him

I'd consider it, and accept another assignment . . . or tend to my orchids . . . or walk.

The walking started when I knew I had to find a place to live where I could grow the orchids. Such a place is rare in the city, and when it appears the cost is prohibitive. I explored every sector, inquiring, following up possibilities, sometimes making a nuisance of myself. It was during this process that three things happened: I found a place, I learned to talk to all kinds of people, and I fell in love with the city and its various sectors.

The house was owned by a retired chief archon, Rokan Du'Lam, a man I later discovered was notorious for the sternness of his courts and sentences. He had a back apartment that opened out onto a modest plot of ground. I explained that I had limited means, but that I traveled a great deal and would gladly improve the fallow ground with plantings.

"What kind of plantings?" he hoarsely demanded. I was grateful that I'd never been dragged into his court.

"I am fond of Edosian orchids, sir." He laughed in my face.

"Can't grow those here!" he barked.

"I beg to differ with you, sir. I'm sure that under my care they would thrive." He laughed again.

"I'll tell you what, boy. If you can grow orchids here, I'll let you have the apartment for the cost of the energy and resources. If you can't, then you pay what I tell you." It was clear that this was a man who did not suffer fools or braggarts.

I took a deep breath and agreed. I happily moved out of my basement, and every spare moment was spent preparing the soil for planting. On the day that I put in the sprouted tubers, the archon had invited a friend who lived nearby to witness the event. She was an older woman I had seen with him before, and she tended a small plot in the back of her home with simple, well-integrated plantings. They both carefully watched me plant with pitiless expressions that expected failure. Neither of them said a word to me, but occasionally they would whisper to each other. At one point I heard the woman distinctly say, "I think he knows what he's doing, Rokan." After the last tuber was planted, they just looked at me and went into the house without a word. There was nothing to do now but wait; but I was certain that my new home was now well within my means.

During the waiting period, I often visited the Tarlak Grounds and Tolan's orchids for inspiration. It was still one of my favorite places. I would sit in the same shaded spot where he'd told me about the first Hebitians, contemplating the elegant beauty of the orchids and listening to the children's voices floating to me across the greensward. The magic of these flowers has fascinated me from the moment I first saw them. The mysterious way they reveal themselves, layer by layer. . . . Just when you think they can't get any more beautiful, that you can't learn anything more, another layer of bloom surpasses the previous one and the orchid changes personality. Recently I have developed a new indulgence—clothing—and I know it's because of the influence of the Edosian orchid. Each time I put on another well-designed and well-tailored suit in a fabric with depth and an aesthetic pattern, I feel like another person. One of my favorite duties is to choose what I will wear for each assignment. As I smell the soft pungency emanating from somewhere deep in the soil, and observe the shaded pastels blend and reblend in a continuous flow, I realize that the Edosian orchid defies description and aspires to the condition of high art.

"Kel. Kel! Don't wander off too far. We have to start home."

The voice cut through me like an icy wind. I didn't want to look. The same sweetness, piping and strong. If an Edosian orchid could speak. . . . I looked across the greensward, and there she was, the blue-black hair and the long, dark gray skirt flowing behind her as she chased a little girl who was giggling, trying to escape from her mother but knowing that the beauty of the game was that she wouldn't. Half of me wanted to run after them, the other half wanted to be buried deep in the ground. Why her? Why now? With sudden clarity I saw my entire life as a defense against this very moment. I didn't want to feel what I was feeling; I didn't want this immense burden of desire. I had learned to be satisfied with the occasional brusque sexual contact that quenched desire the way food or water did, and to live without any expectation of that touch that transforms routine into adventure. Watching Palandine and her daughter defy gravity with their dance of love destroyed all my definitions, and my carefully maintained boundaries began to give way, for the first time since Bamarren, to the magic of limitless possibility. I knew at that moment that I'd never be satisfied again. Even my beloved orchids looked like weeds.

I watched like someone unable to avert his eyes from impending horror, as the mother ran down the daughter and gathered her up in her strong arms. They were both giggling, absolutely fulfilled in each other's company, lighting up the grounds with their radiance.

Palandine and Kel. And the other. Not present at this

moment, but of course always there. Oh yes, I had kept track. How could I not? Especially when we have the resources to keep track of any Cardassian. Barkan Lokar was now an important administrator with the Bajoran Occupational Government. As much as my own work remained covertly placed in institutional shadows (and Tain made sure that I was publicly identified as a bureaucrat at the Hall of Records), Lokar's was very much in the full light of the sun. Oh, I knew a great deal about him. Bajor, a planet rich in resources, was being skillfully stripped by his efficient programs. With the help of forced labor, the moribund Terok Nor outpost was being revitalized into a fabulously productive mining enterprise.

Lokar was the favorite of such powerful Cardassians as his father, Draban Lokar, and Procal Dukat, key members of the Civilian Assembly and Central Command respectively. In fact, his prefect on Terok Nor, the ore processing station, was Procal's son, Skrain Dukat. Lokar's ambition and his prospects had no limit. Nor, it seems, did his appetite for using and disposing of people . . . especially women. His tyrannical excesses, visited upon friend and foe alike, were well documented; but as long as his stewardship produced such successful results no one cared. Lokar has quickly become an integral part of the easy corruption I see and smell more and more at the highest levels of our system, and which gives the lie to our stern and moralistic façade. Perhaps, I thought, when I leave for Tzenketh tomorrow I'll erase all memory of the way back.

Palandine's husband and Kel's father.

I watched them leave the Grounds, but I stayed rooted to my spot waiting for a great hole to open up and swallow me. It didn't. Darkness came, and the chill finally drove me to my feet. I started to walk.

Cardassia City is designed as a round wheel with the Tarlak Sector functioning as the administrative hub. This is where the public areas—the Grounds and the monuments, the government buildings—are located. Radiating out from the hub, like unequal slices of pie, are six sectors. I wandered first into the Paldar Sector, the residential area where Tain's house was located, as well as the archon's where I was lodging. It was one of the earliest settlements, and most families had lived there for generations. Government bureaucrats and civil servants who worked in the Tarlak Sector usually lived in Paldar. I walked past Tain's house, stopping momentarily to wonder if other people felt so completely estranged from the home of their youth. There were few pedestrians, since this was the time of the evening when families gathered after a long day of work and school: The good Cardassians. The sector reeked of rectitude and self-importance.

I decided not to return to the archon's, and turned right at the Periphery, which marked the outermost limits of the city; beyond were the dry scrublands that contained shuttle terminals, military training areas, food-producing centers, and isolated factories and settlements. I began to traverse the huge Akleen Sector (named after the putative founder of modern Cardassia, Tret Akleen), where the military was garrisoned. Troops were marching and drilling on parade grounds scattered throughout the sector, and civilian pedestrians were often challenged.

"Where are you going?" the sentry demanded.

"To the Torr Sector," I replied.

"Why don't you take the peripheral shuttle?"

"I want to walk."

"You can't walk here," he stated. "You have to go

around." He pointed the way and I took it. I decided to return to the Periphery, to bypass the rest of Akleen and the adjoining Munda'ar Sector, which consisted of cavernous storehouses. I entered the Torr Sector, the largest and most populated and the place Cardassians come for food, entertainment, artistic displays, and public performances of music, dance, and spectacle. It was originally designed to house the service classes, and over the course of time it became the center of our cultural life. The streets were crowded with young men and women coming to and from the various restaurants and attractions. I thought I could lose myself in the crowds that filled the thoroughfares at all times of the day and night and enjoy the anonymity, but the jostling and the noise only made me more aware of the loathsome self-pity I was feeling. I wanted my life to be arranged without need, to be totally self-sufficient, able to do my work for the Order and find fulfillment wherever I could—to accept my life as enough. But how could I, when my deepest involvement was with orchids?

I moved away from the crowds, and into a quiet neighborhood of modest homes that reflected the Cardassian ideals of cleanliness and frugality. The walkways were narrow and immaculate; even the smallest homes were carefully maintained. Cooking smells filled the air, and I realized that I hadn't eaten since morning. I also realized that I was not yet prepared to leave for Tzenketh in the morning. But what was there to prepare? Decide on my wardrobe, pack it, and close the door when I leave. The archon and his lady friend would be more than happy to tend the orchids. I'll feel better, I decided, when I'm on the shuttle and immersing myself in the assignment. Then I can forget about her and do my work.

A group of people caught my attention. They were entering a larger building on the corner, and trying to maintain a low profile. I had witnessed this before . . . and in this sector, I realized . . . in this neighborhood. It was after the first cell meeting and the encounter with Ramaklan/Maladek. I shivered as I thought of him. Two people were behind me, and I was sure they were also part of this group. On an impulse I "withdrew" my presence, blended into the lower vibrating energy of this group, and entered through the rear of the building. Once inside, we walked down a flight of stairs to a darkly lit but surprisingly spacious basement that had twenty-five chairs facing a slightly raised dais, empty except for a table. I took a seat at the back, and when I had settled I saw the sole decoration on the wall behind the dais: it was the winged creature from the stone carving. The face had the same features as the recitation mask Tolan had given me. I shivered again and wanted to leave immediately. I felt an irrational sense of danger, but the room had quickly filled up and I didn't want to draw attention to myself. I also felt like a fool for following my initial impulse to come here. I looked around. The man next to me smiled. I tried to smile back, but my face was frozen. I couldn't locate the source of my anxiety—there wasn't the hint of a threat in the room—but my stomach was churning and my throat felt tight. I had to use all of my techniques to stem the rising fear.

The door closed from the outside and the lights changed to feature the dais. Two people rose from near the front and stepped up to the table. Without a word they each picked up a mask and held it a long moment, as if studying the mask's neutral expression. They looked at each other, nodded, and fastened the masks to their faces. They took another long moment, now studying each other. Then they turned to us and moved to the edge of the dais, where they stood and made contact with every person in the room. I don't know how long this went on, but a palpable feeling of expectation was growing in the room. Finally, the woman (or, rather, the person who had been the woman, as the masks had transformed them both into variations of the creature behind them) began to chant.

> "The power that moves through me
>   Animates my life
>   Animates the mask of Oralius
> To speak her words with my voice
> To think her thoughts with my mind
> To feel her love with my heart:
> It is the song of morning
>   Opening up to life
>   Bringing the truth of her wisdom
> To those who live in the shadow of the night."

The man responded.

> "It is this selfsame power
>   Turned against creation
>   Turned against my friend
> That can destroy his body with my hand
> Reduce his spirit with my hate
> Separate his presence from my home:
> To live without Oralius
>   Lighting our way to the source
>   Connecting us to the mystery
> Is to live without the tendrils of love."

There was another long moment of silence as the two people, their stature and the power of their presence somehow enhanced to the status of iconic figures, maintained their vibrant contact with each other and with us. Then they moved back to the table and reversed the opening ritual. As they took their seats, I wondered how two such ordinary people were able to expand their presence in such an extraordinary manner. The irony of my withdrawn presence did not escape me.

Someone began to hum a simple melody. After several repetitions, others joined in with haunting contrapuntal harmonies. The intensity of the sound gradually built in strength and insinuated itself throughout every part of my body. Every cell was being massaged by the sound, and without any conscious effort I began to hum harmony that was my own and that somehow fit in with the others. My body began to feel the benign warmth rising along my spine that only occurs with enough *kanar.* My anxiety had evaporated, and I felt connected to this group of strangers. The intensity kept building, and my whole being vibrated with such rhythmic insistence that I found myself swaying in a circular pattern. I was not the only one; the entire room was swaying. Occasionally a voice would shout out the name of someone and the others would forcefully repeat the name. When there were no more names the energy began to subside until we were silent again. I had never felt so in touch with every part of my body.

A woman simply but elegantly dressed in a white doublet, blouse, and culottes stepped up to the dais. Her bright eyes were set wide apart, and her look was somehow stern and at the same time kind. It was difficult to tell how old she was. When she spoke, her voice had an unstudied resonance, slowly and softly projected. She had the engaging talent of making you believe you were the person she was primarily addressing.

"I am your guide tonight," she began. As she continued to speak the room was absolutely still. Her simplicity commanded, without any effort. She told us that the people had been healed, and to make sure that we had more names for the next healing. Looking directly at me, she welcomed the newcomers. I tried to deflect the look, but she was powerfully focused, and easily contained me.

"It takes courage to come here, to look at things the way they once were. And while they can never be that way again, we can extract an essence that will nurture and amplify our own lives. We can strive to be better friends and live with ourselves and others with respect and the recognition that each soul desires to be reconnected with the source. To enslave or prey upon each other is not how we began. We were connected to each other. We did not experience hunger, deprivation, or loneliness. We were connected, and we cared and nurtured and loved. No, friends, it's not how we began. But if we end in isolation and hate, not even a monument in Tarlak will ease the agony of our lost soul."

The meeting went on with more recitations, chanting, and readings from something called the Hebitian Records ("Where everything is written," she claimed). There was a final meditation, and it was over. People rose, but instead of leaving they lingered and spoke to each other. I wanted to leave. The peace I had felt after the "healing" had been replaced by a deep disquietude that began when the "guide" directly addressed her remarks to me.

As I made my way through the crowd, I discouraged all contact others offered to make. I caught snatches of conversation, and by the time I reached the door I decided that it was all sentimental nonsense. Cardassia suffered a great climatic catastrophe—and if we hadn't been strong and determined to adapt, we would have perished with the weak. And the weak *must* perish; otherwise the integrity of the race is compromised and we become the preyed-upon. Poor misguided Tolan. He was a good man but he was a gardener, and the worst thing he had ever had to do was kill weeds.

"Who sent you?" It was the Guide.

"A friend," I replied vaguely.

"Ah," she said with an odd recognition. "You're a careful man. This is good. We're not looked upon with favor by the authorities, you know." She smiled at me, and I experienced an inexplicable surge of hatred. How dare she? How dare she set herself up as superior? This was a superstitious cult that undermined the fundamental tenets of Cardassian life. It deserved to be outlawed.

"I hope you'll join us again." She said this with a detached gravity, nodded and turned back to the others. I quickly went up the stairs and back outside, where I felt I could breathe again. As I began the long walk back to the Paldar Sector, I debated whether I should inform Internal Security about the existence of this meeting.

13

Ah Doctor, Dominion weapons have destroyed us, and as we resurrect ourselves the dead and the discredited are returning. After years of toiling in anonymity and exile, I have become a much sought-after notable. This evening, as I was working on this chronicle, I had a visitor from the past—Gul Madred. I'm sure you know him by reputation; he had a distinguished service record marred only by the unfortunate incident with the Federation Captain Picard. He fell out of favor about the time I was stranded on Terok Nor. I almost worked with him in a proposed joint operation that involved both the Order and the military. It was a daring idea that made too much sense to succeed. The military would behave like a military, and take care of the fighting—and the Order would behave like an intelligence service, and get them the information they needed in order to behave like a military. Madred, however, was a key member of military intelligence and insisted that they did not want any involvement by the Order. He made it clear, however, that he did want certain techniques that we had perfected. We were reluctant, of course, to part with them and after several increasingly acrimonious meetings we decided to part with each other instead. I'm afraid we have never had much regard for their intelligence; the incident with Picard supports our low opinion. If nothing else, an interrogator must have the stamina to outlast his subject.

Still, I was delighted and utterly surprised to see Madred when he appeared at the door. I always regarded him as a cultured and serious man, and despite his troubles of recent years he was still very much involved with the future of Cardassia.

"I'm honored, Gul Madred. I'm also too woefully provisioned to offer anything more than a seat and some clean water."

"You're very kind, Garak." Madred took the offered stool and I poured him a cup of precious water. "How did you find me?" I asked. The harsh lighting in my shed revealed a deeply lined face, with eyes that couldn't hide an intense almost haunted weariness.

"Your necropolis has become the subject of much conversation throughout the sector," he replied. "Or is it a memorial to your former mentor?"

"It's whatever people want it to be. It seems to give comfort to some. For me it meant bringing some order out of this chaos."

"Yes. And that's what brings me here. We've had our differences in the past, Garak, and at times we've come down on the opposite sides." It was rumored that his was one of the powerful families that had supported Dukat's alliance with the Dominion. "But I'm hoping that we can find common ground during this transitional—and crucial—moment in our history. We must rise from this." He gestured toward my "necropolis."

"One billion dead. We have no choice," I observed.

"But we must do it correctly!" He was passionate and emphatic. Something was driving him.

"You have no disagreement from me, Madred."

"I know this. Because, like a true Cardassian, you *are* bringing order out of chaos—which is more than I can say about others in our sector." He looked at me meaningfully, and I waited for him to continue.

"You've heard of the movement afoot to bring in Federation methods for determining our new leadership structure?"

"No, I haven't," I replied without hesitating. I prayed that Parmak wouldn't make one of his unannounced nocturnal visits.

"Each sector will vote for a leader. *Vote*, Garak.

Which means that a hygiene drone will have as much to say about our future as you or I."

"Would this be true for *every* sector?" I asked. I hadn't realized it had gone this far.

"Yes. And then the six sector leaders would form a council that would determine everything from rebuilding the infrastructure to rearming our military—and each of us would be subject to their decisions!"

"Sounds a bit too simple, doesn't it?" I observed.

"Simple? It's unbelievable. Who are these people? Alon Ghemor? A family of traitors. Korbath Mondrig, a rabble-rouser from the service class. I wouldn't have these people clean my shoes, let alone make decisions that determine our future!"

Madred had indeed changed since I last saw him; he was more neurasthenic, given to sudden emotional outbursts. I had to be very careful with him.

"What do you . . . suggest we do?" I asked softly.

"I'm in contact with a group of people—I can't tell you their names yet—and we are in the process of mounting a serious counteroffensive to this . . . Federation model," he nastily spat out.

"And what would you like from me, Madred?"

"Your support, of course. Unfortunately, it's going to get rough, and we'll need skillful operatives." He graciously nodded to me. "We're also going to need information. I understand you're working with a Dr. Parmak who's very much involved with Ghemor."

"I was assigned to his med unit. The situation makes for strange bedfellows," I added.

"Of course." I found it interesting, Doctor, that for some reason it would never occur to Madred that I would actually enjoy my relationship with Parmak. I had the feeling that he was making an assumption about me that was perhaps reinforced by my involvement with the Order and Tain.

"Our work is winding down, however," I shrugged. "We don't see as much of each other."

"Nevertheless, any information would be useful . . . and helpful to your cause," he said with obvious meaning. It was at that moment, Doctor, that I knew I would never help these people. How many times while I was exiled on the station did I hear that expression "helpful to your cause"? I'd comply, time after time, but it never seemed that my cause—returning home—was ever advanced.

"And what do you think my cause is, Madred?" I asked with an ingratiating smile. He hesitated; the question wasn't expected.

"I would think that given the past circumstances you'd want to find favor with . . ." He hesitated again. Who was left? Madred and his group?

"With Enabran Tain?" I suggested. He laughed, but he got my point. How typical of his class (and his military intelligence background) to operate from an outdated model.

"Let me see what I can do." It was time to end the meeting. "It was a pleasure to see you again." Madred rose and barely inclined his head. I was disliking him more and more. I escorted him to the door to get him out as quickly as possible.

"By the way, I bring you greetings from an old schoolmate of yours. Unfortunately I can't tell you his name."

"Ah. Please return my greetings." Madred left, not a moment too soon.

Is it him? Is he still alive?

14

Entry:

While the design of a circle with a hub and six radiating sections is a simple one, Cardassia City is densely laid out with an angular and labyrinthine complexity that only the natives can navigate. As I became expert in my knowledge of every neighborhood and thoroughfare I developed an irresistible desire to secure new lodgings at regular intervals. I would pick an area and look for a place that would satisfy my need for privacy and my passion for Edosian orchids. While my hosts would be deeply disappointed at my departure, they were equally grateful for the gift of healthy orchids I would leave them. With the exception of the archon and his lady friend, however, I had little hope that these people would be able to maintain the orchids.

One of my genuine pleasures was to pick someone in the street to follow. Part of it was to satisfy a desire I've had since Bamarren to move through places and among people undetected, a desire that increased significantly after seeing Palandine and her daughter. In the intervening years, I'd pick someone who looked like a walker and follow him or her as long as they walked. I'd make sure my presence was minimized and I'd take on the person's physical carriage and behavior. After a while, once the physical mimicry felt complete, I'd also take on the thoughts and feelings of that person. In this way I not only felt connected to another, but I was divested of my own thoughts and emotions—especially the painful ones.

Because I could never stop thinking about her. It was

a terrible possession, and the more I told myself to stop or tried to employ gimmicks to distract me, the worse it got. I often returned to the Tarlak Grounds in hopes of seeing her; most of the time I sat among Tolan's orchids in vain. And the few times she did appear . . . ah, how can I describe the feeling? A poet once described, "an exquisite pain/ Churning the heart, the stomach, and the genitals." Crude, yes, but anatomically correct. It is so curious how we can learn to live with just about any condition or situation if we believe we have no choice.

Palandine and Kel appeared on this day, and I realized that Kel was getting too old for the children's area. I could see that it was Palandine more than Kel who wanted to come to the Grounds. Palandine would stretch into the sunshine and try to encourage her daughter to run and wrestle with her. Kel, however, had developed a taste for novels and rebuffed all her mother's efforts to play. The spaces between their visits to the Grounds were widening, and sooner than later they would stop coming altogether. By my calculations it wouldn't be much longer before Kel was sent to an Institute. As I watched them, I became consumed with these inevitable changes and wasn't sure what I would do.

As they left the Grounds, my body had no problem deciding on a course of action: it followed them. I knew this was dangerous, and my anxiety made me unsure how to proceed. I knew where they lived in the Coranum Sector, the oldest and most prestigious neighborhood in the City. But what was I going to do? Stand outside their home and live off the occasional glimpse? This was folly. But there was no turning back . . . my body kept following. We passed through the crowded great public area, where Palandine ran into two women she knew. They were standing in the shadow of the Assembly building, and I had to be watchful for colleagues. Finally they moved on, and for a split second I considered retiring to my cubicle in the Hall of Records and distracting myself with a huge amount of deferred work, but my body followed. I couldn't let them go.

We entered the Coranum Sector, and the contrast was dramatic. Stately old buildings dating back to the early Union faced wide thoroughfares; they weren't cramped and pushed together as in the Torr. The care and craftsmanship lavished on the facades made even the fine homes of the Paldar Sector look boring and drab. These were the homes of the families who had ruled Cardassia for generations, and they were built to reflect the solidity and continued longevity of that rule. Of course the Lokars would live here.

Foot traffic was minimal, and I realized that I was too close when Kel looked back and almost made eye contact with me. I stopped, pretending I had lost my way while they went on further. Finally they came to their building, a three-storied newer version of the early Union style, but with the same classic angles and high windows. They entered, and suddenly I was alone on the street, a conspicuous loiterer. Determined that I would never do this again, I continued in the same direction. As I passed the building I glanced at the heavy door, which gave no promise or sign of opening for me. My plan was to take my next left and cut through the Barvonok Sector, the center of business and commerce, on my way to the Torr and yet another new home. It was a trained habit never to retrace my steps.

"Elim. Elim Garak!" Her voice came from behind,

and I quickened my step. I didn't want to stop. I didn't want to look at her. My mind was desperately looking for a way to slip off, to lose her. But the whole enterprise was a fiasco. Of course, she had spotted me. It was almost as if I had begged her to.

"Elim!" Her voice was winded, exasperated, and amused. She was a magnificent athlete, and her long legs had very quickly caught up with me. I turned.

"Palandine?" I winced at the utter woodenness of my feigned surprise.

"First you follow me, and now you're trying to run away." Her frankness was as disarming as ever. "Still the same bundle of contradictions, aren't you?" I could see that she was trying to measure the Elim she knew from Bamarren against the one who stood before her.

"I assure you, I just happened to be walking in this sector," I struggled to reply.

"And the screech crake has a pleasant voice." She was still catching her breath. "But I suppose the fact that you were also at the Grounds and the Assembly building could be an extraordinary coincidence," she said with a look that challenged me to come up with an answer. I couldn't. I felt exposed and ashamed.

"I'm . . . sorry. I tried to be discreet." There was no point in pursuing the deception.

"Elim, you forget—I studied with the same teachers. Old habits die hard," she added with a self-deprecating laugh.

"I was not going to do it again," I assured her.

"Let's walk," she suggested, noticing a couple coming out of a building. We continued in the direction away from her house.

"You've changed," she said.

"It's been a long time. Would you expect me to stay the same?" I asked.

"No," she replied softly. She had changed, too. Close up, her face was thinner and faint lines were drawn around her eyes and mouth. It was more than just middle age. As genuine as her pleasure was in seeing me again (a pleasure that relieved me enormously), the old delight that would always animate her face instantly was a thing of the past. There was a sadness about her, as she led me through an area of Coranum I'd never walked before. The streets narrowed and the houses were older.

"I love this area. This is the earliest settlement in the city. Turn here," she instructed. A narrow passageway, almost hidden by an outer wall, led between two houses and opened up into an unexpected public grounds that was remarkable for the mature size of the shrubbery and plantings. It was a small grounds, but the profusion of growth gave it an insularity that reminded me of another place.

"This is extraordinary," I said.

"Yes. Kel and I spend a lot of time here. Or we used to," she added with that same softness as if she were talking to herself. "I feel safe here."

"It reminds me of the enclosure at Bamarren," I said. She laughed, and the old delight momentarily flashed.

"Yes! That's why I love it here." But her expression changed and she gave me a look that creased the lines in her face. "We treated you so terribly."

"Please. . . ." I started to say.

"We did, Elim. You know that. We believed . . . or at least *I* believed. . . ." she stopped herself with a bitter laugh. I didn't ask her what it was she had believed.

"That's finished now," I said.

"Is it?" she asked with a wry smile. "Well, that's good news."

"We were children, Palandine."

"Yes, we were. Aspiring to be grownups." She gave me that creased look again. "You were the grownup, Elim. We were only pretending."

"Please. . . ." I tried to stop her again.

"No! I lost you as a friend. I think you understand this . . . unless I'm very much mistaken." Her look made me uneasy. "Why were you following me? Why've you been watching me and Kel all this time?"

"You knew?" I was incredulous. I had come to believe that I was virtually undetectable in these situations.

"Of course I did. I may not have a career, but I learned my lessons well." She said this with a bitterness that took me out of my own feelings of failure. "At first I didn't know what to do. There you were, sitting like your *regnar* among those magnificent orchids. It unnerved me at the beginning, but after a while I looked forward to your being there . . . watching us." As we held each other's look I didn't try to hide my conflicted feelings.

"Why did you decide to follow me today?" she asked. I struggled to find an answer. She nodded as if confirming something to herself. "Tell me, would you have ever . . . declared yourself to me if I hadn't?"

"No," I replied. She nodded again, this time with a sad acceptance. "You keep your own counsel now, don't you? This must be very dangerous for you."

"For us both. I'm sure I don't have to remind you," I added.

"No," she smiled. "Where do you work?"

"At the Hall of Records."

"Doing what?" she asked.

"I'm a research analyst," I answered.

"What kind of research do you analyze?" She was not going to be put off with vague answers.

"I'm a bureaucrat, Palandine. I no longer try to make my work sound interesting. The best part is that I travel a great deal to gather data on population shifts—births, deaths. Most of my work is statistical analysis—making sure the facts match the reports we receive." I delivered this with appropriate flatness.

"Do you like it?" she asked.

"I like the travel," I answered. Her face was now a grimace.

"Was Barkan the reason you left Bamarren?"

"I was asked to leave."

"Why?" she demanded.

"I was never given a reason. When I got home I was placed in the Civil Service Institute."

"Well, you certainly don't look like a bureaucrat who sits in a chair all day."

"I walk as much as possible. I know the City as well as I knew the Mekar." Palandine forced a smile and walked to a low bench set amid the shrubbery. I could see that she was upset by what she perceived as my fall from grace. Promising young man forced by circumstances to live the life of a lonely functionary.

"What about you?" I asked as I sat on the ground across from her.

"Barkan and I were enjoined. For a while I worked in security at the Ministry of Science. I enjoyed it. Lots of intrigue and bad liars. But women dominate the Ministry, and I did very well. My prospects were encouraging."

"What happened?"

"It's complicated, Elim," she shrugged. "Do you have a family?"

"No."

"You really do keep your own counsel, don't you? Part of me envies you." She made an abrupt gesture with her head as if shaking off a pest. "Barkan progressed more rapidly than we'd expected. He established himself on Bajor, and we began spending a lot of time apart. He thought that we should work together, but before I could work out a transfer Kel was born." She shrugged again. Such uncharacteristic diffidence.

"Why aren't you living on Bajor now?" I asked.

"Too dangerous. By the time I felt Kel was old enough to make the move, the Resistance was targeting Cardassian families, and Barkan insisted that we stay here until they could control the situation."

I immediately questioned his motives and tried to hide my thoughts, but the effort was as futile as trying to hide my presence from her.

"Do you still hate him?" she asked.

"Hate's a strong word."

"But we're all capable of feeling it, Elim. How do you feel about me?" she asked with a direct simplicity that went through my body like electric shock. The churning I experienced earlier at the Tarlak Grounds returned. I was afraid to answer. She nodded again with resignation. This time she had completely misread my thoughts. I realized that she not only expected my hate, but accepted it. She stood up and seemed smaller.

"This wasn't such a good idea after all, was it?" And when had she ended so many of her sentences with a question?

"What happened to you?" I asked sincerely. "You were the most confident person I'd ever known. Even when you made the decision at Bamarren there was no doubt—no apology." Her eyes suddenly fractured and tears filled the cracks. "Do you think I followed you because I hate you?"

She couldn't answer. She just stood there shivering. I moved to her to hold her, and she didn't resist. She didn't move. She let me put my arms around her and draw her vibrating body to mine. The touch, the feel of her against my body was something I had never expected to experience outside my imagination. For the first time since Bamarren, I wanted to expand my presence, to feel everything that was coming through this moment and joining us. Inexplicably, I had a sudden vision of the Guide, the woman from the meeting.

"This is our secret, Elim," Palandine whispered.

"Yes," I answered. "Our secret." Another one. But it didn't feel like it would poison me.

15

Entry:

The encryptions were getting harder to decode, but the information being pieced together indicated that a significant resistance was beginning to form on Cardassia itself. I had anticipated this happening, and wondered why it had taken so long to coalesce. Unless the entire planet had somehow gone mad, there were too many good and intelligent people who would be able to see the Dominion promises for what they were and take an action to forestall the inevitable betrayal. Odo confirmed my belief.

"After Tain's attempt to destroy the Founders' homeworld, there's no chance the Dominion will allow an autonomous Cardassian state to exist." It was the middle of the night, and we were finishing up the last transmissions in Odo's office. I was exhausted. Sometimes we'd work through to the morning, but thankfully tonight I'd be able to return to my quarters and get a few hours sleep.

"But surely, Odo, the Founders must know that this was the action of a few desperate people," I reasoned.

"I hope you haven't forgotten that you were one of those desperate people," he reminded me. I was too tired to argue. "Besides, Garak, this action only confirms their belief in the treachery of the solids. They've seen what Cardassians have done to other races; it's not as if their fears are without foundation." Odo looked as if he could use a spell in his bucket; I had rarely seen him looking so run-down.

"No," I sighed. "We have not inspired the confidence of our neighbors." I began to push myself away from the computer when a rescramble suddenly formed into a coherent communiqué.

"Look at this, Odo," I said. The renewed energy in my voice brought him over. "It's from the Vorta—Weyoun." We studied the message in silence.

"He doesn't know where Damar is?" Odo was as perplexed as I was.

"Yes. And judging from this, he's quite eager to find him." I wondered, could it be possible? Odo was thinking the same thing.

"Do you suppose—?" he began.

"Yes. Damar's broken with the Dominion. Either he's on the run . . ."

". . . or he's gone over to the Resistance," Odo finished.

"This would be significant. Damar's a dedicated soldier who commands the loyalty of much of the army. He's not a politician who changes sides like coats." I hated the man, but I knew that he lived by a strict military code of honor: The Cardassian Union, right or wrong. How else could he have followed that psychopath Dukat for so long? And how else could he have justified his murder of an innocent like Ziyal?

"Unless it's a trick to expose the rebels," I added.

"I'd better get this information to Captain Sisko," Odo decided.

"Would you rather I tell him?" I offered. Odo looked positively drained; he needed to return to his liquid state.

"No," he declined after a moment. "There are certain protocols. . . ."

"I understand." And I did. They had codes that I was not privy to, and they wanted to keep it that way. "In that case, Odo, I'm going to get some sleep. You know where to find me."

"Thank you for your help, Garak," Odo said, with his sincere formality.

The Promenade was empty at this hour. I made my way up to the second level, to spend a few moments in the observation lounge before retiring to my quarters. It was the one place on the station where I felt a sense of expanded space. The ironies of the situation both amused and irritated me. Here I was, the invaluable decoder of Cardassian encryptions containing life-and-death information for the Federation—and they won't trust me with the code to wake up Captain Sisko. Ah well, it was never easy being a Cardassian on this suspended chunk of desolation. And then I laughed out loud. But what about Odo? The last time I looked he was a changeling, a member of the race of Founders that was determined to destroy the Alpha Quadrant. Not only did he have the captain's wake-up code, he also slept with the station's second-in-command.

I found myself staring at the escape pods that had recently carried the *Defiant*'s crew to safety before that noble vessel was destroyed. They were temporarily tied to a docking arm and looked like small, vulnerable orphans waiting for another home. A noise at the other end of the level reminded me to pay attention, in case Londar Parva and his friends were looking for another opportunity to put the "spoonhead" in his place. The turbolift was nearby, and I made sure it was empty before I entered.

But if Damar had thrown his support to the rebels . . . if it wasn't a ploy . . . I wanted my revenge on him, yes, but not at the expense of liberating Cardassia. And it wasn't just liberating the planet from the control of a foreign power. It was closer . . . more personal. I wanted something that was even more difficult to attain—redemption.

The doors opened, and once again I was alert as I stepped into the deserted corridor and moved past the sleeping quarters to my own. It was time, I kept repeating in my head. It was time to take our place among the planets and peoples of the Alpha Quadrant as a civilized and open society. It was time to repair the damage. "A stitch in time saves. . . ." What? What was that expression?

As soon as the doors to my quarters closed, I felt her presence. Smelled her. She was standing against the window behind the desk. This was not the first time she had come here and waited while I worked late into the night. But something was different tonight. The distance between us had opened up again. I gestured to raise the light level.

"Don't," she said.

"I didn't expect you until tomorrow." As my eyes adjusted, I saw the phaser in her hand. "Who were you expecting, Remara?"

"You, Elim."

"Am I in some kind of danger?" I looked around to make sure we were alone.

"Sit down," she said quietly. I tried to maneuver around so that my back would face the window.

"Over there, Elim." She indicated the chair in the corner near the door. "And don't be foolish."

"I'm afraid your warning comes too late." She came around the desk and perched on the edge facing me.

"Is this an interrogation?" I asked.

"I was instructed to kill you without questions," she replied flatly.

"Obviously people who don't value the art of conversation." She just looked at me. The distance had never been greater.

"And you lied to me about Bajor. You know my homeworld very well."

"I wouldn't say that. I was there only for a short period."

"Long enough to kill my husband and son." Every-

thing about her—her hair, face, the clothes she wore—
was stripped down, severe. No one who knew her as
a dabo girl would recognize her at this moment. I'd always known that spinning the wheel at Quark's was a
cover . . . and I'd chosen to ignore it. And I knew
enough about myself and my craft to know that my
lapses could no longer be considered accidents.

"You know what I'm talking about, don't you, Elim?"
Her eyes burned with an anger that would never subside in this lifetime. She wasn't a collaborator; Kira
had gotten that all wrong. She was a terrorist.

"You're Khon-Ma, aren't you?" She didn't respond.
"Being the only Cardassian on this station, I expected
you a long time ago. What kept you?"

"They were on the *Taklan* when you ordered it to be
destroyed. With seventeen others who were just trying
to free themselves from being sent to work as forced laborers here."

"In a time of war, when you commandeer an enemy
ship and attempt to escape. . . ."

"That wasn't a war!" she snapped. "It was rape.
Murder. Genocide. One day we had our lives and the
next Cardassians were taking them away!" Remara's
anger dared me to deny this. I wondered what it had
cost her to constantly bridle her true feelings as she
was passing herself off as the remote and desired sex
object. Perhaps the Klingons were unconsciously attracted by what was underneath the makeup and
skimpy costume. Usually the experiences that drive a
person into any kind of resistance movement are also
ones that can anesthetize all feeling. But Remara's passion appeared undiminished. Of course, this passion
was my opening, my chance for escape from her re-

venge disguised as Khon-Ma justice. But I was weary beyond caring. Moments before, I had been fantasizing about redemption, and now I was about to be executed for the Cardassian Occupation of Bajor. And all along I had been clearly setting myself up, ignoring every sign like an inexperienced probe. Perhaps this was the redemption I was looking for.

"I was on Bajor a short time to interrogate possible Resistance members. The occupation was a strictly military affair and they brought in . . . my group. . . ."

"What group?" she interrupted.

"It's not important—it no longer exists. We were given children to interrogate. They were starving, dressed in rags. It was a disgrace, beyond the usual incompetence of the military. The guls were out of control, grabbing anyone they thought was Resistance. I took one look at them and saw that they were just angry rock throwers. I gave them latinum and threw them back onto the streets. We told the military that either we do things our way. . . ."

"Which way is that, Elim?" she sneered. It was one of the few times that I found her unattractive.

"The right way, Remara. Find the right people, get the right information that can be used effectively against the Resistance. But that meant the military had to give up control, and of course that was out of the question. So we were sent home."

"You were seen at the shuttle!" she insisted.

"We were at the terminal when the Bajoran prisoners overwhelmed their captors and took over the shuttle. They had hostages and wanted to negotiate. I could see that Gul Toran was over his head—making ridiculous threats to people who had nothing to lose."

"They had everything to lose," she said, shaking her head at my assessment.

"In that situation, my dear, they had everything to gain and nothing to lose," I wearily explained. "The trick is to give up as little as possible and make them believe that they've won a great victory, but that was beyond Toran's ability. I volunteered to negotiate. The people inside seemed reasonable. The fact that they hadn't tried to escape immediately or begun executing prisoners told me they were looking for a way out. An exchange. . . ." I stopped. What's the point, I thought. All the stories were beginning to run together and they all had the same ending.

"What happened?" she asked softly. The sneer was gone; she, too, was probably weary of the burden of these stories.

"You know what happened, Remara. Gul Toran wasn't going to let me negotiate. And he certainly wasn't going to do it himself. 'Never with terrorists,' he announced; but the truth was that he didn't know how. They had no choice but to try to escape."

"And they were all killed," she said even more softly.

"End of story, Remara." I considered telling her how I had exacted my own revenge upon Toran, and that my only regret was that his death hadn't come sooner . . . but what was the point? Another treacherous opportunist dies after tearing another hole in the fabric. What's gained except the potential for more damage? I rose. The station's gravity felt like it had increased threefold.

"If you're going to kill me, get it over with. One way or the other I'd like to go to sleep."

"Who gave the order?" she asked.

"What difference does it make? I did, if you like."

Remara just looked at me. She lowered the phaser. Part of me was deeply disappointed. "I was at the terminal," she said in that soft voice. "I was in line to get on the *Taklan*, but I was delayed and got separated from Karna and Berin. We had been assigned as a family to Terok Nor. I was just a few people from the door when the guards were overwhelmed and dragged inside. The door closed, and I was left behind. I panicked. I screamed and banged on the door along with the others. Cardassian soldiers started beating us away, and I was thrown to the side, where I hid behind a barricade, hoping that the door would open and I could rush inside. It was from there that I watched you and Toran argue. I couldn't hear you, but it was clear what was happening. You knew each other from before, didn't you?"

"Yes," I replied.

"I could tell you hated each other. When you walked away I knew that they were all going to die." Remara walked to the window and looked out. How much of my life, I thought, had been spent at that window, longing for release from this sad and deadening place.

"Tahna Los told us you were here. He's still in a Bajoran prison, and believes that you were somehow involved in his capture. It certainly wasn't a secret, but nobody knew who you were or why you stayed after the Cardassian Withdrawal. You were very low on the list for termination." She turned and smiled apologetically. "It wasn't until I came here and saw you . . . and recognized you. When I went back and told the others, they put you at the top of the list, and I was assigned." She shook her head sadly and slipped the phaser inside her tunic. She moved away from the window to where I still stood.

"You're going to have to leave this station. They'll keep coming after you until someone succeeds. Goodbye, Elim." She put her hand against the side of my face, and I felt the heat coming through. Perhaps her passion was a curse as a terrorist, but she was a whole person . . . and she had found redemption.

"Why does Kira think you were a traitor and a thief?" I asked as she moved to the door.

"Because I was."

"Did you collaborate at the refugee center?"

"Nerys told you about Singha." Remara sighed and looked past me as if seeing something that only deepened her sadness. "Her father, Taban, let me live with them in their part of the cave. In return I betrayed him." She looked at me with that distant smile I found so attractive when we first met. "No, I didn't collaborate, Elim. I thought Taban was the collaborator. I discovered that the reason he was able to take me in was because he received extra food and medicine from the Cardassian authorities. At the time I had a friend in the Resistance. When I told him about the supplies, I was instructed to keep an eye on Taban's activities . . . and to steal whatever I could to pass on to people who were in need. One day, Taban caught me in the act. I think if I'd just admitted what I was doing and why, he would have forgiven me. He was that kind of man. Instead, I accused him of betraying our people and ran away." Her voice trailed off, and we stood in the vibrating silence of the station.

"You were very young," I observed.

"It was later when I found out why Taban received

extra supplies. His wife, Nerys's mother, was a comfort woman for the Cardassians. Did Nerys tell you that?"

"No."

"In fact, she was the mistress of your old friend, Dukat, before she died."

"Dukat," I repeated softly.

"So they gave up their extra rations. Either that, or be hounded as collaborators. I don't blame Nerys, Elim. In her position, I'd be just as unforgiving."

She turned and went through the opening door. A part of me wanted her to stay, but in my weariness I could only watch her leave.

16

Entry:

Gray, humid, and lush. Sometimes I'd stand up from my gardening work and feel my head bump against the low Romulan sky. Tain told me this was an ideal assignment for me, and when I disembarked on Romulus I partly understood why. Vegetation thrives in this climate. Everywhere you look, shrubs, trees, flowers all grow in a profusion I'd never seen before. And it's that very sight that produces the most amazing reversal of expectation. At first I was convinced there was something wrong with my eyesight: instead of being predominantly green, Romulus is gray.

My cover at the Cardassian Embassy was master groundskeeper. The regular groundskeeper was sent back to Cardassia for an extended leave, during which time I would introduce Cardassian plantings. Tolan had prepared me very well for this cover. My name was Elim Vronok, and my deep mission was very clearly stated: eliminate Proconsul Merrok, Tain's nemesis in the Romulan Empire. No one knew—or would say exactly—why this antipathy between Merrok and Tain existed, but it was fierce and abiding. I knew that part of the reason was that Merrok had previously urged a Romulan alliance with the Klingon Empire to contain the Cardassians, and he had even gone so far as to share cloaking technology with the Klingons. It was this technology— arguably Romulus's most important scientific achievement—that we still coveted; specifically, the improved interphase generator that rendered the interphase scanner (the device developed by Federation scientists to detect cloaked phenomena) virtually impotent. Romulans and Cardassians were tentatively exploring an exchange— cloaking technology for advanced Cardassian weaponry— but any progress in those negotiations was constantly thwarted by Merrok, the prime defense minister.

But there was something else: the rivalry between the Obsidian Order and its Romulan counterpart, the Tal Shiar, an intelligence organization led by the implacable Koval and sponsored by Merrok. The rivalry had become so intense that a virtual state of war existed between the two organizations.

"Vronok!" And my biggest surprise on Romulus was the identity of the embassy's first secretary: Nine Lubak, the instrument of my Bamarren betrayal in the hands of his cousin Barkan Lokar. Krim Lokar had obviously been left in the dust of Barkan's rapid rise, and had found another liaison position, this time dispensing appropriate and carefully prepared "information" to the

Romulan Bureau of Alien Affairs. He was a puppet: his mouth moved whichever way it was pulled. When I first saw him, I thought the mission was compromised. Only the ambassador and my contact knew who I was. But thanks to Lokar's arrogance and self-involvement (which had deepened over the years) he didn't recognize me.

"The ambassador wants to see you," he announced from his lofty position.

"I'll be right in," I assured him with all due deference.

"Make sure you clean yourself before you do," he instructed me, as if I were a child.

"Certainly." I bowed my head.

"First Secretary!" he corrected.

"Excuse me?" I knew what he wanted.

"You will address me as First Secretary," he explained. He was convinced that because I was a gardener I was also a dolt.

"Of course . . . First Secretary." I smiled.

"Do people know what you're doing here?" he asked with distaste.

"I beg you pardon, First Secretary?" I felt a slight twinge. He's not supposed to know anything.

"Out here. The grounds," he gestured impatiently to the plot I was preparing. "Do you have permission to do this work? It seems rather excessive. The grounds were perfectly acceptable with Kronim," he said, referring to the former groundskeeper.

"I assure you, I have the authority . . . First Secretary."

"Well, hurry up!" He actually clapped his hands. "We haven't all day." He turned and entered the building. I marveled how the years had turned him into a fussy middle-aged androgyne. I wondered if anyone would really mind if I put him on the list after Proconsul Merrok.

When I entered the ambassador's office, he was sitting at his desk with an older Romulan woman. Neither of them rose.

"Elim Vronok, this is Senator Pelek." I bowed and waited respectfully to be addressed. The senator completely ignored me, and the Ambassador continued. "The senator has created a renowned arboretum, and she's curious about the native Cardassian plantings you are introducing to the Romulan climate. Especially the Edosian orchid."

I nodded. My expression betrayed nothing, but here was my "contact": a Romulan senator. That Tain managed to turn such a high-ranking official was a feat, considering the hermetic nature of Romulan society. These people regarded aliens as lower forms of life, and the condescending attitude all Romulans reserved for the outsider was never covert. Indeed, as I stood there in a work uniform identifying me as an Embassy service drone, the senator looked right through me. I wasn't even worthy of her disdain.

"Send him to my residence," she commanded the ambassador as she rose. "My groundskeeper will meet with him and get the necessary information." The ambassador started to bow, but Senator Pelek was already on her way out the door. I began to wonder if she was indeed the contact. Could her interest in my orchids be a coincidence? This felt more like indentured labor than an undercover assignment.

"I've been posted here for two cycles and I still can't get used to their arrogance." Ambassador Bornar was a massively overweight man who appeared to be constantly falling asleep. This time, however, when I looked at him he was awake and very present. I wondered how much he knew about my mission. When he saw me studying him he quickly went back to sleep.

"Thank you, Vronok," he rumbled. "Why don't you clean up and I'll have you transported to the senator's residence."

"Yes, Ambassador." As I left I heard him call for Lokar, who was waiting outside the door. He sniffed at me as we passed. First Lackey would be a more appropriate title, I thought. But he didn't concern me. After weeks of nothing but the daily manual labor of reorganizing and maintaining the embassy grounds, finally contact had been made. But the time hadn't been wasted. I had worked hard, lived simply, and gotten myself in excellent physical condition. I'd studied the sketchy information on Merrok provided to me by Prang, but I'd been able to pick up little more on my own. It was going to be a challenge to get to him; he was a careful man, and devoted to his family, and if he had any vices they were effectively masked. A man who kept his habits to himself no doubt organized his life with the practiced attention of an experienced security operative. It was a closed system. But that's why we had contacts: they were supposed to know the way in.

I also spent the time with my poetry, an interest that had revived along with my relationship with Palandine. It not only enabled me to express my passion, it was also the most effective way to alleviate the pain of our separation. Before Palandine came back into my life I had embraced these long assignments. Now all I wanted was to complete my work and return to her company.

"You will wait here," the elderly Romulan groundskeeper instructed me. I barely noticed him leave: the massive outbuilding where I was told to wait was a controlled environment containing the most impressive collection of flora I have ever seen. The technology that allowed for such diversity to exist in one space was ingenious and visionary. I understood why the senator's arboretum was renowned. The grayness that permeated the rest of Romulus was held in abeyance, and various shades of red, purple, green, yellow and blue flashed and vibrated with an energy—an awareness—that quickened every time I moved or changed focus. As I scanned the vast enclosure and the dense growth of shrubs, trees, flowers, and vines I shivered with the recognition that I was also being watched. Besides the visual beauty, there was an overwhelming sense of intelligence . . . and danger.

"Step back!" the voice sharply ordered. I turned and saw the senator standing at the entrance.

"Excuse me?" I didn't understand.

"Unless you desire a stinging experience you won't forget for days, I'd advise you to step back from the Romiian striker." I followed her look, and saw a quivering vine snaking along the ground toward me and displaying sharp spikes along its spine. I stepped back, and it immediately retracted to the concealing bush where it obviously lived.

"It can attach itself to small creatures attracted by its scent and quickly drain them of fluids," she said, as she examined me with a scientific detachment that made me feel like one of her new exhibits. Her sharp features accentuated the clinical attitude.

"We have a similar plant that. . . ."

"The Mekarian sawtooth, yes," she interrupted. "There's one just behind the Terran gum tree. But it actually breaks down the flesh of its prey. The striker leaves a desiccated husk." Her speech was as precise and lean as her trim, ascetic body. "Other than the initial puncture, the dead creature looks untouched. Your Mekarian sawtooth leaves a very messy corpse," she said with disdain.

I made no response, but all my awareness was in play. This was a dangerous woman, and it occurred to me that this dense collection of botanical life from every part of the quadrant was an instructive outpicturing of her own mind. My voice warned me to use my wits every step of the way. I wanted to turn around, to see what else was creeping toward me.

"I was assured that you know what you're doing," she said, breaking the humid silence.

"I'm honored by the generosity of that assurance. . . ."

"How quickly can you bring Edosian orchids to maturity?" Conversation was not at the top of her agenda. I looked around.

"I'll have to bring in some specially prepared soil . . . early morning light is essential. . . ."

"How quickly?" she repeated with a sharper edge.

"To full bloom . . ." I made some rapid calculations . . . "it would take . . . six months at least. Unless . . ."

"Unless what?"

"We were able to trick them." The Romulan gravity is heavier than ours and her constant pressure made it even more oppressive.

"By accelerating the cycles of light and dark," she stated. She was no novice.

"Yes, if we could compress two cycles into one . . ."

"Three months." She nodded, confirming something

to herself and looking through me in that maddening way. I felt more and more like a holographic display. She suddenly walked past me.

"Come with me," she ordered. I followed her down a central aisle, careful to step exactly where she did. I recognized some plants and shrubs either as Cardassian natives or ones I had encountered on other assignments. At one point I stopped when I saw a ground creeper—the indigo sunsearcher—also from the Mekar. It was like seeing an old friend, and brought back a flood of memories. *Regnars* establish their colonies next to the sunsearcher's roots, but I decided not to share this with the senator. Finally we came to a cleared space, where a common-looking plant with small white flowers and oval oily leaves tinged with an iridescent green was isolated from its neighbors. I looked to the senator for an explanation.

"I understand that under the correct conditions your Edosian orchid can be extremely toxic," she said. I was puzzled by the comment. Tolan had once mentioned that the orchid had been used in the past for nefarious purposes, but when I'd pursued him for details he'd maintained that this was information I didn't need. For him, it was a cruel irony that a flower that offered such beauty and aesthetic pleasure could be used for evil. As I studied the plant, the ridges of my neck and shoulders began to buzz with an anxious excitement.

"This is something I know nothing about," I confessed. She looked at me to determine the truth of my reply.

"No one has been able to grow the orchid here," she said, still probing me with her dark eyes. "I told your superior that it was absolutely essential that we be successful. It's bad enough having an alien come in here to do this work, but it would be intolerable to fail. Do you understand?"

"I do," I assured her.

"Do you?" she maintained the pressure.

"Just tell me what you want, senator. My time is also precious, and I have come to your charming planet to do the best work it's in my power to do." I had had enough of her veiled threats and supercilious treatment for one day. I had no idea how she would react to my thinly disguised ultimatum, but she was not the woman I wanted to be spending my time with.

"All right, Elim Vronok," she nodded, almost approvingly. "I want you to start growing your orchids immediately. Tell my groundskeeper, Crenal, what you need and use your 'precious time' to ensure that these orchids are in full bloom in no more than three months." She started to walk away, but something stopped her.

"Where do you want to establish your beds?" she asked. I looked around and realized that where I was standing was ideal.

"Right here would be fine." I replied.

"That's the whole point. Anywhere but here." Her laugh was dry and mirthless. She turned and made her way through the flora, which seemed to recede from her careful, mincing tread, making a path. I looked again at the star-shaped white flower and the oily—almost garish—green of the leaves. I wondered how Tolan would feel if he knew how I was using his gift.

As long as I was able to immerse myself in the work, the time passed quickly. Crenal was a naturally reticent man, and I'm sure taking orders from a "barbarian" only made him more so; but he was knowledgeable and forth-coming with the necessary assistance and information. With his help I devised a simple cover that we used to block out the light in the middle of the day for a period equal to the short nights of this time of year. As expected, it doubled the speed of growth. At first I was concerned that the orchid stems were appearing too reedlike because of the accelerated push, but Crenal created a nutrient supplement that accommodated the speed. He generously gave me the formula, and I used it to supplement the orchids I was growing under normal conditions at the embassy. While the added nutrients made the plants stronger and more resistant to disease and predators, the problem was that they added too much body to the stem and branches, thereby compromising the orchid's lissome elegance.

Crenal was also generous with information about the many plants that were unknown to me. His patience with my unending questions was testament to his devotion and pride. But when I asked him about the isolated white flower, his generosity turned off like Quark's smile when you announce that you can't pay your bill.

"You'll have to ask the senator," was all he said.

And one day I did ask. It was toward the end of the prescribed time period and Senator Pelek, during one of her periodic inspections, had expressed satisfaction with our progress. She was about to make one of her abrupt departures.

"What is the orchid's relationship to the white star flower?" I asked. She stopped and gave me that searching and skeptical look she often used with me.

"Who was your mentor?" she asked. I didn't quite understand the question.

267

"My father," I replied. I knew I couldn't go wrong with that answer.

"He was a gardener."

"Yes."

"What else did he do?" she asked.

"That's all he was," I replied.

"And he taught you how to grow the orchid and didn't tell you of its use?" She was still skeptical.

"He . . . was a simple man. He didn't altogether approve of my choice of career." She nodded, still probing in her expert but rudely exasperating manner. I decided to give her access and momentarily removed my mask. The light in her eyes changed.

"Follow," she instructed. She led me to the white flower. "Look very carefully at the stamen. Are your eyes good?" Without answering, I inspected the stamen, where I saw a tight ball of adhering seeds nestled in against the filament and anther.

"It's called the White Star of Night. Originally, on Vulcan, it was called the Death Star." I involuntarily moved back. "It won't harm you. Or it could, but only indirectly. It produces a limited supply of seeds, which it sends out searching for the proper receptacle. When a seed does find a . . . 'mate', shall we say, it does what pollen is designed to do—it enters the pollen tube of the receptor plant and moves into the ovule, where the egg is fertilized. With certain flowers, however, the process has a significant variation. The resulting blossom of the mated flower is so deadly that just to be in its immediate vicinity is a fatal experience."

"And the Edosian orchid is one of those flowers." The Senator just looked at me. "Why have you separated the White Star from its neighbors?" I asked.

"Because if the flower sends out its seeds and they fertilize others, after a time it will stop producing seeds. I said the supply was limited. We're saving them. Or have you forgotten why you're here?" she asked, as if I were not only stupid but a coward as well.

"No, senator. I know why I'm here," I said with a sweet smile that made her lips curl. She turned and walked away. "Thank you for the lesson," I said to her retreating back.

The Death Star. At that moment, I remembered a time after I had left Bamarren, when I was working with Tolan in Tarlak. I had asked him if he wasn't bothered by his status.

"What status is that, Elim?" Tolan was amused, but his response had made it clear that my question was an unpardonable rudeness. I attempted to apologize; but Tolan wanted to pursue the question. "That I work in a service profession?"

"Please don't be offended," I tried to explain. "I just think that you're . . ."

"Better than this?" he gestured to the bed he was working in. I didn't respond.

"If somebody asks you to do something, and you know that to comply would go against what you believe, even subject you to pain, how would you react?" he asked.

"I would . . . refuse . . . if I could." For a young Cardassian with a deeply ingrained sense of duty, this was a difficult question.

"In all the years I've spent maintaining these grounds I have never felt that pain. That is my status, Elim."

Either Tolan had refused Tain's request, or Tain didn't know about the White Star of Night. Why else would I be here getting this lesson from a Romulan crone?

We were coming close to the moment of maturity Senator Pelek was waiting for. I wasn't sure how it was going to actually happen, but I had learned through discreet inquiries that she had decided Proconsul Merrok was dangerously out of touch with Romulus and its future needs. It was a complicated political opposition, but it came down to the scientist, Pelek, who wanted a more open exchange of information with a technologically advanced civilization, Cardassia; and the warrior-politician, Merrok, who distrusted Cardassians and believed he could manipulate a Klingon alliance through the Tal Shiar. Usually, Romulan rivalries were out in the open, and decided by what they called a "confrontation of honor," but the senator believed that too many of the old guard supported Merrok and so such a confrontation would result in a destructive blood bath. No one would expect this kind of covert conspiracy, and certainly no one expected it from the senator, who was regarded as a brilliant if eccentric scientist who loved to collect plants. The irony, of course, was Pelek's personal alliance with Tain and the Order, and while I wasn't privy to their arrangement I was certain that the senator was acting out of strongly felt principles, and that her political ideals were more important than the latinum to be gained from a potentially lucrative trade agreement.

As I came closer to the end of my mission, my thoughts increasingly dwelled on my much-anticipated reunion with Palandine. Even my poetry, as its passion spilled over the restraints of all structure and form, couldn't focus my desire and calm my impatience. Sometimes I'd be digging in the soil, and I'd notice that my hands were shaking like the leaves of a jacara tree. At such times I'd stop, wherever I was, and attempt to center my concentration with a breathing meditation I'd learned from Calyx. Four quick inhales through the nose . . . hold . . . four exhales through the mouth. Now slower . . . longer . . . run them together. . . .

"Ten Lubak." The gruffness was disguised by a veneer of refinement, but I could still hear it. This was either the extent to which I had lost control of my concentration— or my worst fear had just come true.

"Sleeping on the job, are we?" The voice was playful, confident, superior. Be careful of what you fear most, Calyx had once warned. I opened my eyes.

"One Charaban." He was fuller, and even with the refinement, crueler. A predator at the peak of his maturity. With him was a military gul with a sneering look and the longest neck I have ever seen on a Cardassian. I was suddenly calm. Whether it was the meditation or the realization when I made contact with Lokar's eyes that he knew nothing about my relationship with Palandine, I was able to calmly stand and face him.

"This is a surprise, Elim." And he knew nothing about me. As far as I could read in his eyes, I was nothing more than a gardener working at the embassy . . . a story he could tell at some dinner about running into an old schoolmate who had such promise, and ended up growing flowers.

"What brings you to gray Romulus?" I asked, genuinely curious.

"Skrain Dukat. . . ." Lokar presented his long-necked companion, who barely nodded. ". . . Elim . . ."

"Vronok," I added quickly. Lokar looked at me with surprise. "What can I say, Barkan? Part of my problem when we knew each other was the question of my . . . origins, shall we say." I made a resigned gesture. "It was, as you can imagine, a bit of a scandal, and accounted for my abrupt departure from Bamarren. But at least I met my real father before he died. It was only appropriate that I take his name."

"I see," Lokar almost whispered. The story was getting even better. Dukat's sneer had expanded to a grotesque grimace that was probably his version of a smile.

"If you'll excuse me," Dukat said to Lokar. "I'll go in and clean up before we present our credentials." He gave me one last sneer before he entered. I may have gone to school with Lokar, but as far as Dukat was concerned I was still an illegitimate service drone.

"I'm on Bajor now. Vice Prefect of the Occupation Force. Very rich planet, Elim. And it's my job to make sure the riches are wisely exploited. Dukat runs the mining operations on Bajor, and we're here to complete a trade agreement." All this was told with a conversational ease, as almost a confidence between old friends. He was so much more accomplished in the subtle way he established his superiority.

"Your cousin Krim must be a very useful liaison in this process," I said, observing his reaction to the use of "liaison."

"Yes," he replied with unruffled poise. "The two of you must have had some interesting reminiscences."

"I'm afraid he didn't recall me."

"He didn't?" Lokar laughed. "That's not surprising. I'm afraid Krim's mind can retain only so much. And you didn't remind him?"

"I chose not to." I smiled.

"I understand." He returned my smile with a look of such false sympathy, it almost made me laugh. I was no longer a worthy opponent, and he was exhibiting the complacency of a well-fed predator. This suited my purpose; as long as I posed no threat to his superior position he would soon forget me. Still, I reminded myself, I must rearrange my records to corroborate the Vronok story of illegitimate disgrace.

"Are you here for an extended visit?" I asked.

"No, I'm afraid not. The agreement is fairly well secured, and we're just here to sign and drink their foul ale." I nodded with a knowing laugh. Ah, yes, how difficult the obligations of the powerful can be. But I was relieved that his stay would be brief.

"And how does your family enjoy living on Bajor?" I asked.

"That's right, you know Palandine," he said brightly, as if he'd just remembered. I was tempted to tell him just how well. "It's difficult, you know. The Occupation has become quite dangerous for our families. Especially with the vicious and cowardly tactics of the Bajoran Resistance." I nodded again with a good servant's understanding: for the privileged, power is indeed coupled with awful responsibility and sacrifice. This "sympathetic" moment was broken by the hurried approach of a young Cardassian woman.

"I'm sorry I'm late, Barkan. The transport...." Lokar's sharp look stopped her. She looked from him to me, not quite sure what was going on.

"Gul Dukat is already inside. Organize our presentation and I'll be right in," he ordered coldly.

"Certainly, Vice Prefect." She bowed and entered the embassy.

"My administrative assistant. She's young, but very good." I smiled. I'm sure she was. This one awkward moment confirmed all the reports about his philandering, and allowed me to fully rationalize my own intimate involvement with a married woman.

"It was a pleasant surprise to run into you again, Elim." The conversation was over, but not before he looked around. "Very good work. The grounds are quite presentable."

"That's very kind of you, Barkan. Thank you." I inclined my head to this pure expression of the aristocratic obligation to recognize when Cardassian standards are maintained. I then decided to ask one final question.

"How did your Competition turn out?" I asked with innocent curiosity. He paused at the door. Other than the light disappearing from his eyes, his affable expression never wavered.

"Extremely well, Elim. It got me here." A brilliant answer. I bowed again in genuine appreciation, and he entered the building. In fact, the Competition resulted in a draw. My sources informed me that Pythas Lok, the challenging One Lubak, had been betrayed during the battle by one of his team leaders, Four Lubak. Four had been chosen as a leader because he'd been part of our successful and undetected penetration during the previous Competition. This time, however, he'd been detected at a crucial moment. Betrayal had been suspected, but it wasn't confirmed until Four showed up on Bajor as one of Lokar's chief assistants and promoted to gul. Gul Toran is someone Tain has warned me to monitor periodically.

As I returned to my work, I noticed that my hands were completely steady. Lokar's weakness—underestimating his enemies—had allowed me to pass through his vigilance undetected. Even so, I debated whether or not to have flowers delivered to his quarters.

Crenal and the senator were waiting for me when I arrived at the arboretum.

"How long will it take to prepare the orchids for transport?" she demanded. I could see from her tense body language that we were now at the endgame.

"We've arranged to have everything ready for delivery before afternoon. That gives Crenal and his assistant plenty of time to transport and plant before dark." Crenal nodded in agreement.

"There's one change," the senator stated. "I want you to accompany Crenal."

"Me?" I was shocked. This was not what we had planned.

"I've made no secret of the fact that the groundskeeper from the Cardassian Embassy is teaching us how to grow Edosian orchids," she explained, fully aware of the distasteful irony. "In fact, I've used it as an example of how our two cultures can learn from each other. It's also no secret that the proconsul would like to downplay his anti-Cardassian feelings, and when I suggested that he incorporate these orchids into his own collection, he readily agreed. He also expressed a strong desire to meet you."

"What do my superiors think about this change?" I asked.

"They are not my superiors, and I don't care what they think. The only superior you should worry about right now is me!" Her tension made her features even sharper and her eyes bigger. She was pure will, and would suffer no opposition.

"And do I have to remind you that nothing can be traced in a causal manner?" she asked rhetorically. I simply smiled in the face of her contempt for my inability to think clearly. That absolute belief in her own logic reminded me that the Romulan connection to the Vulcan antecedent was still very active.

"Get to work!" she commanded, and Crenal and I obeyed. I realized as I put gloves on my hands that I was actually grateful to the senator. She indeed was one of the most efficient contacts I had ever worked with. I was also grateful to be participating. This way, I knew the job would be done correctly—and I could return to Cardassia.

Merrok was standing at the entrance of his grounds when we arrived. He was not what I had expected. In fact, the similarity to Tain was at first unnerving. Merrok, too, was overweight and somewhat rumpled, unusual for a Romulan. He had that same avuncular manner when listening, and his unaffected courtesy made me forget that I was a Cardassian. His simple and worn work outfit told me he was a serious gardener.

As Crenal and I worked unloading the different plants the Senator had sent and preparing the soil, he peppered us with intelligent questions and listened carefully to our answers. Two children came out of the house and my heart sank. I had been told that he lived here with his wife, who was bedridden with some mysterious malady. But when he introduced us to his grandchildren and told us that they were returning to their home today, I was enormously relieved. Because by tonight the cross-fertilization would have taken place, and shortly thereafter the orchids would be lethal for one cycle of light. By tomorrow night they would revert to the innocent beauty that makes them a coveted possession of the dedicated groundskeeper.

Merrok watched me carefully as I transplanted the orchids. He intuitively knew to suspend his questions while I performed the delicate operation. I could see that he was enchanted by them.

"Tomorrow you might give them a supplement I'm going to leave with you. Four parts water, one part supplement. That will aid the transplant." Obviously it was vital to our plan that he be near the orchids on the first day, but I recognized from his fascination that he didn't need any encouragement.

"Not today?" he wondered.

"No, I don't think so. They have enough to adjust to already. By tomorrow they'll be receptive," I explained as I put on the finishing touches. He nodded approval at my logic. I rose to make sure that Crenal was placing the White Star far enough away from the orchid. The seeds had already been sent and accepted; there was no point in establishing this lethal fertilization as a periodic event.

"What is he planting?" Merrok inquired.

"I believe the senator said it was called Starlight Sweetness," I replied.

"Women," he chuckled. "Where's it from?"

"Somewhere in the Klingon Empire, I believe," I answered.

"At least my grounds will live in political harmony," he laughed, enjoying the irony. If only he knew how deadly the irony was. But his pleasant company made me curious as to why Tain harbored such antipathy for the man.

When he finished, the proconsul invited us in for a refreshment. I politely declined, but he insisted.

"I've never had a Cardassian in my home before, Vronok, and I'd like you to be the first." There was no way I could wiggle out of this. Crenak and I obediently followed him, brushing our hands against our clothes.

"Don't worry about that. It's honest work and honest soil," he said as he led us inside. A young man dressed in the black uniform of a high-ranking Tal Shiar officer watched me coldly as I entered. I could feel Crenal shrink away from the young man's presence. The proconsul proudly introduced him as his son, Colonel Merrok. The colonel looked at me and shook his head with hostile disbelief. Obviously the rank of proconsul would be far beyond his diplomatic prowess. I was sorry he wouldn't be around to help his father tend to the orchids the next day.

"Tameenar!" Merrok called, and a liveried servant immediately appeared. "Bring some ale." The servant soundlessly disappeared. The room was cavernous—Romulans, it seemed, valued large spaces—and simply but elegantly furnished. As he continued to stare at me, I knew it was only a matter of time before the colonel expressed his disapproval of my presence. Romulans wore their rudeness like a badge of honor.

"Was this necessary, Father?" He referred to me as if I were a mute display. "This passion for your plants seems to attract other lower life-forms as well." The gesture was so outrageous that I began to laugh. Crenak was shocked at my reaction, but Merrok laughed even harder. The old proconsul was not making me feel too terribly pleased about my mission. I was genuinely liking this man.

"Our friend Vronok is not only an accomplished floriculturalist, Toral, but he is the bringer of an exquisite creation whose cultivation few people in the quadrant have mastered." The Colonel snorted. "Besides, he's part of the good senator's reconciliation gesture," he added with heavy irony. At that both men laughed. Ah yes, I thought, another case of fatal underestimation.

The servant returned with the Romulan ale, and we each accepted a glass. The proconsul proposed a toast.

"Here's to the success of the plantings. . . ." He paused, and just as I was about to drink he continued with a twinkle in his eye. ". . . And to the spoonheads staying within their own borders." I smiled, and without hesitation drank from the glass. Lokar was right, Romulan ale was a foul drink. But I must confess that the toast proposed by proconsul Merrok left me feeling much better about the whole affair.

"So you spent some time with him, Elim. I hope it was edifying," Tain said at the end of my report.

"At first I couldn't think why you hated him," I confessed.

"I don't hate anyone, Elim," he carefully explained. "I have a job to do—and sometimes it's necessary to eliminate those enemies who can't otherwise be dissuaded. And he was determined to block our interests at every juncture."

"Was?" I queried.

"Oh yes, you did your job. With the help of a far-sighted Romulan patriot like Senator Pelek, we were able to significantly slow down their anti-Cardassian faction. Merrok was found two days after you left in a tool shed. By then there was no way to trace the cause and it was determined that he died of complications due to age." I had never seen Tain so animated. He radiated glee.

"It was reported that a few other people decided to smell the flowers that day," Tain chuckled. I hoped it hadn't been the children. "Oh yes, my boy—yes, you did excellent work. A job well done." He had never complimented me with such unconditional enthusiasm. It was almost a demonstration of paternal pride.

"You see, I had this planned for a long time, Elim. But Tolan wouldn't agree. He wouldn't take on the assignment, and he wouldn't pass on the information. But thankfully he trusted you, Elim." Tain patted me on the shoulder, which meant I was dismissed.

As I walked to my rendezvous with Palandine in the Coranum grounds I felt empty. What remained of the pride that filled me was nausea and a bilious taste in my mouth. I was the one poisoned. Perhaps by the pain that Tolan refused to suffer.

17

Fear and isolation, Doctor. You can't have one without the other. Fear isolates and isolation is fear's natural home. Just as my orchids need carefully prepared soil to protect them against disease and pests, fear needs the isolated circumstances to deepen and grow without connective or relational interference. When fear is allowed to flourish in its dark and lonely medium, then any evil that can be conceived by the fearful imagination will emerge.

The death toll rises every day. We are now over the one billion mark. This is a numbing, dry statistic. I'm certain that when you read this, Doctor, you will have a disturbed reaction. Others will rationalize that the figure is commensurate with Cardassian complicity. And a third group will simply shrug: it's not their problem. My reaction would probably have been a combination of the latter two. Like most people, I want to get on with the business of my life and what's done is done and doesn't warrant any further loss of sleep or appetite.

Our med unit has been converted into a burial unit. It's a logical progression; the survivors have all been accounted for and only the dead remain unclaimed. More immediate, of course, is the potential for decaying corpses to spread disease. So every day now I am engaged in the hardest work of my life; I find that nothing has prepared me for this. My feelings are spent, my moral rationalizations are empty, and I can't say it's not my problem when I'm pulling and lifting and throwing bodies of people who once only wanted to go about the business of their lives.

A Federation official suggested that we simply vaporize all corpses. Underneath the suggestion was the judgment that our burial customs are archaic and morbid. At first I became angry and wanted to berate him for his lack of sensitivity as well as for his own culture's morbidity in representing death as sanitary and disassociated from life. But I realized that we were no better. We created technologies that dispensed death efficiently and from a distance; we never took responsibility for our personal actions because we were in the service of a greater good—the Cardassian state. Colonel Kira once told me how many Bajorans died during the Cardassian Occupation, and my mind rejected the figure like a piece of garbage. We'd been in the service of the state, I had told myself, and the state had determined what was necessary. But now I understand why she hated me. More important, I now understand that constant burning, almost insane look in her eyes.

Most of us who are left, Doctor, are insane. We have to be in order to survive and emerge from our isolation. It's the only way we can live with the pain of what we did. Or didn't. Each of us accepts the amount of responsibility we are capable of bearing. Some accept nothing, and these people are quickly swallowed by their isolation, their insanity transformed into a rationalized evil. A smaller group accepts total responsibility, and their insanity is an unbearable burden that cripples and eventually grinds them down. The rest of us carry what we can and leave the rest. For myself, Doctor, when a corpse is too heavy to bury I try to remember to ask someone to help me.

18

Entry:

"Was he a member?" Palandine asked.

"I don't know. I've often wondered myself. I suspect he probably was. He was a simple man." The sun was going down and we were completely immersed in the shadows cast by the foliage.

"You make his simplicity sound like a defect," she observed.

"Tolan was ... somewhat gullible ... superstitious. ..." My feelings about the man had become conflicted, and Palandine picked up on this.

"Was he your real father?" she asked.

"Why do you ask?" Ever since Lokar had reported our encounter on Romulus to Palandine there'd been any number of questions she'd tried not to ask.

"I don't know. I suppose I'm just trying to reconcile statistical analysis with Romulan gardens." We lapsed into a long, stony silence. Usually she knew better than to expect a real answer when she did ask about my working life. We both tried not to venture into certain personal spaces; often the attempt functioned as a barrier. I'm sure she knew that I was more than a data analyst at the Hall of Records. She also understood that the less she knew about what I did the more chance our relationship had to survive. For the same reason I never asked about Lokar. The less information, the less damage if either one of us was betrayed.

"What do you hear from Kel?" I asked, trying to find a way around the barrier. She was completing her first Level at the Institute for State Policy.

"She may transfer," Palandine said.

"Really?" I was surprised. Everything I had heard indicated that she was doing well. "To another discipline?"

"She doesn't know. She's not happy with the course orientation. She feels that the political education she's receiving has been reduced to learning how to serve the military. She feels that it should be the other way around." I could see that Palandine was concerned.

"A radical idea, but many people feel the same. How does her father feel?" I asked.

"I'm afraid she won't get much support from that side of the family," she replied carefully. I wasn't surprised. Besides knowing the close alliance between the Lokar family and the military, I was also aware of a group called the Brotherhood, which was made up of elite Cardassian families traditionally associated with the aristocracy and the military. The Lokars were a mainstay of the Brotherhood; Barkan's father, Draban Lokar—a venerable member of the Detapa Council—made little effort to hide his contempt for the civilian-led government and fully supported the autonomy of the military's Central Command. The Brotherhood claimed to be a friendly organization engaged in sporting and social events. As it turned out, I was alerted that at any moment I'd be assigned to investigate the Brotherhood and rumors of a conspiracy to disrupt the current tenuous balance between the Civilian Assembly and the Central Command.

"What about your family? Do they have any advice on the matter?" I asked. Palandine laughed.

"My parents are older people, Elim. When I enjoined with Barkan and gave up my career they felt that their work was done. They hold the Lokars in such high esteem that whatever old Draban decides is just fine with them." The darkness and rising chill weren't helping the mood. I stood up.

"Kel's a very resourceful young lady. I'm sure. . . ."

"Have you been to one of their meetings?" Palandine suddenly asked.

"What?" I thought she was referring to the Brotherhood.

"The Oralian Way. Have you been?" Her heaviness was replaced by active curiousity.

"Yes . . . once," I replied.

"Well? What did you think?" she pursued.

"I . . . it was a mistake. I shouldn't have been there," I struggled.

"Why not? Because they're outlawed?"

"No . . . although . . ."

"What, Elim? Just tell me." She was growing impatient with me.

"I'm of two minds. I know, that's just another way of saying that I'm confused. One mind says these people are as deluded as Tolan Garak in thinking the Hebitians were a spiritually advanced civilization. They couldn't adapt and they died—that's the lesson, and I think we've learned it very well!" Very rarely did my emotions race so beyond my control. I was almost breathless. It was more than just anger at what I believed to be the weakness and delusion of these people. I suddenly wanted to throw a tantrum.

"And the other mind?" she asked quietly. I shook my head.

"I'm sorry," I managed. I couldn't even begin to put the other thoughts into words. Palandine smiled.

"Yes. What if they're right? What if they *could* help us reclaim something noble in ourselves? Where does that leave us?" We stood looking at each other. The night wind gusted through the foliage and I wondered where I'd be if I didn't have this woman's friendship.

"Do you remember where they are?" she asked.

"What? Now?" I began to panic.

"It's either that or a meeting of the Bajoran Occupation Support Group," she laughed with a delight I hadn't heard in a long time.

"It was a while ago, Palandine. I don't know if they're in the same place . . . or if they even meet tonight." Her enthusiasm rendered me as helpless as it did when I first met her.

"We'll find out, won't we?" She started to leave. I had no choice but to follow.

"What is this . . . support group?" I asked.

"Abandoned women whose children are either grown or away at school. We're supposed to support our heroes, but we end up supporting each other."

"To do what?" I asked naively.

"You don't want to know, Elim," she replied. As we left the grounds, I thought I heard a snapping sound. When I looked back all I could see was the shadowy outline of the foliage dancing with the gusting wind against the dying light.

It was no trouble finding the house again, but as we stood on the walkway everything was quiet and dark.

"Is this the entrance?" Palandine asked.

"No, it's along the side," I pointed. She moved quickly along the building and stopped in front of the door. As I caught up with her, the door opened and the Guide was standing there as if she'd been expecting us. I couldn't tell if she remembered me, but she reacted warmly to Palandine's delighted look.

"Come in, please," she offered, and without hesitation led the way down the narrow stairs. This time instead of turning left into the main room we passed through a curtained entrance to the right. We then followed her into a dark hallway that opened up into a small room with a few low cushioned chairs and soft indirect lighting. The Guide invited us to sit. Palandine immediately complied, and for a moment my discomfort was so acute I wanted to bolt. Although we were the only people in the room, I was aware of movement all around me. As my eyes adjusted, and I reluctantly and awkwardly settled into the low seat, I saw that the walls were covered with a frieze, and that this was the source of the movement. It began at the bottom of one corner and ran continuously around the room, moving gradually higher until it finished at the top of the same corner. It depicted what looked like the daily activities of another time and culture, performed by half-naked people who were Cardassian, but leaner and somehow more refined. My discomfort with this unaccustomed low style of sitting and with the Guide's smiling silence was replaced by fascination with the frieze. As I studied the figures I realized how heavy and restricting my clothes were. How protected we were, I thought. And from what? I tugged at my pants to cross my legs. There was nothing salacious about these people, but they were all attractive. The limbs and torsos of both young and old were exposed as they went about their duties of growing, hunting, gathering, building, communing, raising their families in postures and attitudes that were similar to our own but different enough to be considered archaic. The sequence of these rites and activities began with the miracle of birth and ended with the mystery of death. Palandine and I were spellbound as we followed their sensuous movement along the frieze. It was clear that these people had embraced their lives with vitality and joy.

"Hebitians," Palandine murmured.

"Celebrating the cycles," the Guide added.

"I want to get up there and join them," Palandine said. "But we're a little late, aren't we?" Sadness passed like a cloud over her radiant face.

"For them, yes," the Guide laughed. "But not for us. Look at the way the frieze spirals up as it moves around the room. Because it ends at the top only means that their cycle has ended. What you can't see is that another cycle begins at a higher spiral appropriate for the next age. Our age." Palandine and I looked at the place where the visible spiral ended, and we tried to imagine the next.

"You seem less careful this time," she suddenly said to me. She did remember. Somehow I wasn't surprised. The threat I had felt years before in this woman's presence—the fear—had evaporated.

"What's your name?" Palandine asked.

"Astraea," she replied.

"Elim says that you're a guide."

"Sometimes."

"My name is Palandine. Can you help me?"

"It would be my pleasure, Palandine."

"What do I do?" Palandine was unashamedly childlike in her openness.

"Come back. Both of you," she simply replied. Palandine nodded agreement, and something was sealed between them. Just like that. Now the sadness passed to me. I wanted to cry, and my throat began to constrict.

"It's all right, Elim. When you can. Everyone moves along the cycle according to his or her fateline." Astraea looked at each of us. "Both of you have work to finish." There was a long moment that felt like a lifetime, as we sat in the room, thinking about our work. The frieze now began to move in the upward direction. I was too amazed to ask if this was truly happening. People would disappear at the top while more would enter from below. Certain faces were recognizable, but I didn't know why. Something was also rising within me, an energy moving up my spine to my head, and I began to feel dizzy. Two of the figures could have been Palandine and me, but I couldn't be sure. I was almost nauseous with the energy surging within me. The figures completed the cycle and disappeared at the top. The frieze stopped moving.

"Thank you for coming." The dizziness and nausea passed. My head was lighter, and I felt cleansed. I looked at Palandine, and she now radiated with such light that I turned away, inexplicably embarrassed as if I had seen something I shouldn't. Astraea led the way back up the stairs and ushered us out.

"Come back," she said with the same warmth. "You're always welcome."

As we took the long walk back to the Coranum Sector, neither of us spoke. When we had left Astraea at the door, Palandine was as serene as I had ever seen her; but when she stopped not far from the Tarlak Grounds and looked at me, her face was troubled. The evening had been like a dream that contained an important message I struggled to remember.

"I care for you, Elim—deeply. But even with her help . . . how can we undo the choices?" Such a simple question, and everything inside me began to shrink. She held her hand up and I attached my palm to hers. We held for a long moment. She nodded and walked off into the night, leaving me undefended against questions I couldn't answer and feelings I couldn't control.

"Tonight?!"

Prang looked at me. He immediately knew I was not in full possession of myself. This was not the way an operative embarked upon a vital mission. His face reflected a concern I had never seen before. I summoned every resource within me to gather my scattered emotions. After Palandine had left, I had spent the rest of the night sitting in the Grounds near the children's area. When Prang informed me that I was leaving for the Morfan Province on Cardassia II on an assignment whose termination was "yet to be determined," I couldn't control my reaction.

"You knew this was imminent," Prang said.

"Yes, of course," I replied. I took a deep breath, and my disparate parts began to snap back. "I was up most of the night. Perhaps something I ate," I shrugged.

"You look like you're not eating anything," Prang observed. If Tain was the father of the Obsidian Order, Prang was its mother.

"I'm fine, Limor. Please excuse me." I was now in full possession, and relieved that the demands of work would now push everything else to the side. Prang watched me for another moment to make sure.

"You're going to the Ba'aten Peninsula in Morfan, where you'll meet your contact. All the information is on your chip." The Ba'aten was the last remaining rain forest in the Union, which made it a much-desired vacation area for Cardassians. How the Peninsula had resisted the great climatic change was still a scientific mystery.

"There is one procedure we need to complete today. Come with me." Prang led me out of his bare office and took me to the research department, where all the new technologies are developed and tested. Mindur Timot, the cheerful and ancient head of research, was waiting for us. He thumped a raised pallet with one hand while working a computer panel with the other.

"Ah, Elim. We have something special for you today. Lie down here, if you will. Head close to me." I complied, as Timot now thumped me on the shoulder.

"I've just about calibrated the connective adjustment. . . ." Timot mumbled, as he continued to work the panel. His other hand was now probing my skull behind the right ear. The man's ambidexterity was impressive.

"Yes. That's your molecular structure. Otherwise the brain would never accept the little coil." Timot held up a small wire device with four or five coils that began with a tight one and widened out. "And that wouldn't be very good, would it, Elim?"

"What is it," I asked.

"Well, I don't have a name for it yet," he realized with a laugh. "For the time being we'll just call it the wire. Simply, I'm going to attach the small coil to the cranial nerve cluster that transmits feelings of pleasure and pain." He held the wire in front of me and demonstrated. "The wider end will be placed just beneath the cranial subcortex, where the Cardassian brain—in its infinite wisdom—" he laughed again as he pressed the actual point, "decides what to do with this pleasure or pain. With the wire, Elim, your pain, at a certain point, mind you, my boy, we can't take away *all* your pain—that would be monstrous—at a certain point, before that critical moment when the pain would induce you to do or say anything to relieve it, at that point, Elim, the wire is calibrated vibratorily to stimulate enough of an endorphin flow to actually *convert* the pain into a pleasurable feeling, which would enable you to endure the most vigorous interrogation and, dare I say, torture." The old man's enthusiasm raced like a hound to his triumphant conclusion. I was less enthusiastic, however. I looked at Prang. I knew why I was being fitted with this "wire."

"It's because of my threshold rating on the enhancer, isn't it?" I stated more than asked.

"Eventually every field operative will be fitted with the device," he replied.

"You mustn't take this personally, Elim," Timot cautioned kindly. "Your pain threshold, contrary to certain received wisdom, is something that can neither be considered a sign of character strength or weakness nor 'improved' by practice. It's given to you along with your height, weight, and fateline, my boy. When I tell you that this wire will give you no trouble, as long as you don't meddle with it, you can believe me. You know that, don't you, Elim?"

"Yes, I do, Mindur." The man had never given me anything but superb technology and sound advice. "Please continue," I submitted.

"Good boy." Timor thumped my shoulder again.

As I stood on the Promontory, which overlooks the southern end of the Peninsula and the Morfan Sea, I understood that nothing could have prepared me for this sight. Surrounded on three sides by the aquamarine waters, the lushness and green vibrancy of the vegetation formed a dense canopy containing a teeming variety of life underneath. It was fed and nurtured by an abundance of rain that fell nowhere else. Above the canopy, complex patterns traced by innumerable species of avian flight made me dizzy. At one time these forests and the life they sustained had covered much of the surface of our planets. I remembered the Hebitian frieze and its lush background. Of course we were different people: it was a different world. The more the forests receded, it seems, the more we covered ourselves. Their world didn't need an agent of the Obsidian Order to investigate a group of prominent Cardassians who "happened" to be spending their vacation together. It didn't have Enabran Tain targeting one of his bitterest enemies, Procal Dukat, a powerful member of the Central Command. And I'm certain it didn't have fathers who refused to acknowledge their sons. If we lived on the next spiral of the cycle of life, how did we know it wasn't going downward?

"It's a beautiful sight, isn't it?" the familiar voice asked from behind. The stealth as well as the familiarity startled me. I was waiting for my contact, and not to hear him approach was embarrassing. I turned . . . and there he was.

"Pythas Lok." His slight frame and the shadow of a mocking smile stood surprisingly near.

"But you can't afford to get too lost in the scenery," he said. "Otherwise people can creep up on you."

"Or ghosts from the past."

"Did you think I was dead, Elim?" he asked.

"I didn't know what to think. I kept track of you until Orias and then every trace of your existence was erased. It was like you never existed."

"True, but I was never a ghost."

"Whenever I made an inquiry it was blocked. And then I heard a rumor that the Order had organized an 'invisible' cadre. I couldn't confirm it, but I always had my suspicions." Pythas didn't answer—and I didn't expect him to. "It's good to see you, Pythas."

"It was just a matter of time, Elim. Come inside. I think I have some information that can get us started." His grace was even more refined as he moved to the small house that was our assigned base of operations. If anything could have taken my mind off downward spirals it was the appearance of Pythas. As I followed his light and soundless tread, I felt invigorated for the task at hand.

* * *

"Draban Lokar?" I repeated.

Pythas nodded. "He and Dukat are the primary motivators of the Brotherhood."

"Are the sons, Barkan Lokar and Skrain Dukat, also involved with this business?"

Pythas nodded, again. "I've had the opportunity to watch them both in action," he said.

"On Bajor?"

"And on Empok Nor. They're definitely members of the Brotherhood, but they're not part of this gathering at the compound," Pythas assured me. The "compound" was a vacation resort privately owned by the Brotherhood for the benefit of its members.

"Did you also observe Gul Toran on Bajor?" I asked.

Pythas looked at me with a thin smile. "I would have been surprised if you hadn't heard."

"And shortly after the Competition Tain recruited you," I said.

"What was good for you, Elim, was usually agreeable to me as well," he wryly observed.

"Do you suppose Tain recruited other people who were betrayed by Lokar?" I asked.

Pythas shrugged. "What better way to motivate your agents than to give them the opportunity to settle old scores?"

"All right, my friend, let's see if we can't settle some of our own," I said as I rubbed my hands together.

Pythas had spent enough time in the Peninsula to become habituated to the mysteries of the rain forest. It was an assignment ideally suited to his temperament. Over the years, his modest demeanor and quiet ways had turned him into more of a solitary person than I ever was. I had learned to withdraw my presence as a tool, but I was always aware of my need for contact, and that my value as an operative lay in my ability to engage others in a nonthreatening manner that drew them out. Pythas had learned to withdraw his presence as a way of life—and he moved through the world like a shadow. I was not surprised that Tain had recruited him for the "invisibles." It took a special person to be able to operate in such unrelentingly anonymous circumstances—no family, no fixed base or identity—and there was no doubt in my mind that he was one of the most brilliant agents in the Order.

Our relationship picked right up where it had left off at Bamarren. Other than Prang, I have never met anyone where so much was communicated with so few words. His eyes had a depth and eloquence that told me everything I wanted to know. How ironic that my lust for conversation was satisfied by someone who rarely spoke. When he was betrayed in his final Competition at Bamarren, he had considered taking his revenge on Four Lubak, but soon came to realize instead that Lubak and Barkan Lokar had done him a favor. Pythas not only admired Lokar's ability to seduce others to his will, he recognized it as an indispensable trait of leadership that he didn't possess. He'd been about to resign his One status when Tain entered his life. It was almost uncanny how Tain stayed so thoroughly informed of our Bamarren progress; I've often wondered if Calyx had been involved. With the invisibles, Pythas found his life work and seemed genuinely fulfilled. If he missed the intimate connection to a family, he never said.

Our assignment was a simple one: we were to gather indisputable information that we could present to the Detapa Council and the Civilian Assembly to discredit both the Brotherhood and Tain's enemy, Procal Dukat. To this end, Pythas used the cover of Tonarkin Bine, an experienced forest guide who'd been recommended to the Brotherhood as someone who would be invaluable in planning their recreational activities. Dukat was an avid outdoorsman, and he met with "Tonarkin" several times to arrange ambitious forest treks. Pythas won him over with his unassuming confidence and familiarity with the forest. This was no mean feat, for hidden within the beauty and endless variety of the flora and fauna that attracted people to the rain forest were innumerable dangers that posed serious threats to the uninitiated. It was planned that before the main trek, which would involve several members of the various Brotherhood families vacationing at the compound, Pythas and Dukat would take a shorter trek to explore some possible routes. This suited Dukat, who wanted to have a more authentic wilderness experience before the "women and the complainers" got involved.

After they had settled in at the campsite, located near our base, Pythas would find a way to expose Dukat to a numbing drug that would enable us to abduct him and bring him back to the house. With the help of the enhancer I would have until the middle of the next morning to complete my interrogation and extract sufficient damning intelligence before I returned him to a specified area. During the interrogation, Pythas would return to the compound and organize a search team. It would be determined that the old man had gone to relieve himself away from the campsite after dark and been attacked by a poisonous *plaktar.* Delirious, he had wandered even farther away, until he'd passed out in the designated spot. When he would return to consciousness he would never remember what had happened to him.

"As you can see, the *plaktar* has a flatter body and longer legs than the tortubial." Pythas pointed out the differences on his own carefully detailed drawings. "It's very easy to confuse the two . . . and potentially deadly if you do. One lick of the *plaktar*'s tongue, depending on the amount of toxin released. . . ." It was another late night, and the information was beginning to bounce off of my skull.

"Please, Pythas, tell me it's not necessary to know as much as you do," I begged.

"It is. This is not the Mekar, Elim. And it's not Cardassia City. You have no idea what's in that forest. Whether you trek for a week or carry an old man a short distance. . . ." Pythas was merciless. He was determined to teach me in days what it had taken months for him to assimilate about the forest and its denizens.

On the eve of the celebration of Gul Minok's victory over the Samurian invaders, which traditionally ushers in the beginning of the longest Cardassian holiday period, Pythas organized the equipment in preparation for the overnight trek with Dukat. He handed me a small vial filled with greenish liquid.

"I think it best if you kept this." I nodded and took the vial.

"If they do an analysis . . . ?" I started to ask.

"It's a synthetic that'll match the *plaktar*'s toxin," he answered as he tied off the last pack. "Anything else?" he asked.

"No," I assured him. I could see that he wasn't altogether convinced.

"It's important that you cover all tracks between the base and where Dukat will be discovered. And make sure you arrive at the campsite before dark. . . ."

"Pythas, we've been over this how many times? I'm no longer a probe." Perhaps it was because he was accustomed to working by himself, but his incessant repetition of details led me to believe that he could never completely trust others. Either that or he was the most compulsive person I had ever known.

"Good luck," he said as he lifted the packs. His wiry strength was always a surprise.

"And to you, Pythas," I replied.

"Who are you?" The old man's eyes snapped open and immediately focused on me. Either the antidote produced this kind of sudden reaction or Dukat possessed a great ability to recover his self-control. I suspected the latter. Everything had gone according to plan. I arrived at the campsite shortly after Pythas and Dukat—just before nightfall. Dukat was eager to explore the immediate vicinity; he was energized by the day's exertion and by being in a place he clearly loved. Pythas had a difficult time convincing him there wasn't enough light and that the forest was too dangerous after dark.

"The time could be better spent going over possible routes, and getting some rest for an early start," he reasoned.

Dukat reluctantly agreed, and after they spent an interminable amount of time going over topographical diagrams, and Pythas had patiently answered Dukat's unending questions (the old man's reputation as a brilliant military strategist indeed had merit), they finally settled into their camp shells. There was another interminable wait for some sign that Dukat had fallen asleep. Finally, a muttering snore set Pythas and me into action. He moved like a shadow to Dukat's shell, raised the side panel and applied the *"plaktar* toxin" to the back of his right hand. All of this happened without a sound. As Pythas moved back to his shell to dress, Dukat grunted.

"What's this on my hand?" he demanded.

Pythas and I froze in our tracks. Could he somehow be resistant to the drug? We waited in tense silence until we heard the long sigh of a body surrendering to a point just before death. Immediately we were mobilized. According to our plan, I attached Dukat to an infantry sling and shifted his weight to the top of my back across my shoulders. Thankfully, he was a thin, wiry man. I carried him in the direction that a later investigation would determine was the route he took when he awoke in the middle of the night to relieve himself and lost his way trying to get back to camp. Pythas laid the tracks of his own search route and we rejoined at the place Dukat would later be "discovered." From there it was a relatively short distance to our base.

After I left the campsite with Dukat, I panicked when I found myself alone in the forest at night. The blackness was so thick I felt like I had been swallowed by a huge beast. Dukat's inert body and the enveloping foliage and humidity made it difficult to breathe. I had to stop and allow my body and eyes to adjust. Slowly the illuminating marks we had previously established to determine my route began to appear, and I made my tentative way, alerting my senses to be aware of those nocturnal creatures looking for prey. Pythas had taken me into the forest many times during daytime, but it was a different world at night. Every sound, every unexpected touch of a branch or ground creeper stopped my heart. The soft, canopied light that made this world so benign and life-enhancing during the day was transformed into a killing ground of competing predators, and those of us who relied on a highly developed sense of sight were the prey.

"Are you all right?" It was Pythas, but I couldn't see him.

"Yes," I lied. I wanted to weep for happiness that I had found him.

"This way." I moved in the direction of his voice, and just as I wondered how I would follow him, I noticed that he had placed an illuminating mark on his back. At that moment I truly appreciated his obsession with detail. After a tense but steady march, we came to a trail that took us up along a steep ridge. It was a hard climb, but at one point the forest discernibly thinned out and I felt I could breathe again. Even though my body ached with the strain of carrying Dukat to the top, I was relieved that I was no longer being slapped in the face by malevolent vegetation. Once we reached the top of the promontory, it was a short distance to the house.

"Who I am is not important," I said as I raised the level of the enhancer. "It's all a dream and as soon as you answer my questions you'll wake up and return to your beloved forest."

It was an advantage, I realized, to have connected him before he regained consciousness. Along with the drug and the light containment field, the suggestion of a dream reality was more threatening to a soldier like Dukat than the familiar context of a hostile interrogation. He sat on a chair with a low back in the middle of an intense cone of light while I remained in the outer dark. His squinting eyes told me that it was difficult for him to see me with any clarity. But his eyes also revealed that he would match the power of his mind with anyone who dared. My best chance with such an experienced and proud adversary was to press my advantage.

"PROCAL DUKAT!" I screamed harshly. He winced and tried to follow me as I receded deeper into the darkness of the room and moved around behind him. His head stopped and snapped to the other side where the containment field also prevented him from turning around to follow me.

"Why did you come here?" I whispered. He tried to shift the weight of his body to stand up and when he realized that he couldn't, that even the range of his arm movement was limited, he rested his hands in his lap and tried to move into a deep relaxation. In a way it was touching: the old man reverting to the mind control exercises he had learned as a child. I remained still and let the silence extend as I very gradually raised the level of his subliminal anxiety.

"Why was it necessary?" I asked softly.

The silence continued to the point where I had to fight my own impatience. Usually the effectiveness of an interrogation is assured by its sense of timelessness; the maddening possibility that it could go on forever. In this case I was acutely aware that we had to finish by first light when Pythas would have to contact the compound and inform the others of Dukat's "disappearance." And yet I had to wait for his response, for some kind of reaction, before I could continue. To force the procedure would only betray my limitations. His breathing had a maddening regularity, and I wasn't even sure if he was still conscious. I had modulated the enhancer to the upper end of level three, far past the point of no reaction. I wondered if I had attached the filament at the base of his skull correctly.

Suddenly he caught his breath in a ragged gasp that sounded like fear. His body shivered violently, and he held his breath longer than I thought possible. Whatever he was experiencing was terrifying and only his bedrock discipline enabled him to contain it. To admit that fear would have any effect on him was the equivalent of an act of cowardice to a man like him, and I began to suspect that he would literally go mad or die before he'd give me the cue I needed.

"Get inside! Get inside their appendages!" he yelled. "It's your only chance! You're going to die—at least die with honor not running away with your backs exposed to their death and ridicule—get inside! Use your hands, your teeth whatever is left is nothing but the last knowing that you died not running like gutted cowards but get inside!" he babbled on one long breath, his face turning red with the effort to control a horror that was uncontrollable. He began to cough and flecks of blood appeared on his lips. "Get inside! Embrace them your lives are not important nobody cares if you live but how you die in the face. . . ." His coughing turned to gagging and choking. He was apoplectic, and tears began to appear. His rage was impotent, and he knew it. He was crying like a little boy whose tantrum was having no effect whatsoever on the outside world. "You cowardly bastards!" he sobbed in a hoarse whisper. His voice was going. "Why won't you die like men?"

I made the decision to modulate down to the lowest level. I knew the risk I was taking—this might give him the respite he needed to outlast the night—but his threshold was high, and he was perilously close to snapping into insanity or worse. I had to reinsert myself in his process somehow. He would try to match his will with anything I imposed from the outside and fight to the death; I had to become involved, even at the risk of imprinting my identity on his memory. I moved back around into his purview. His eyes were closed, his body clenched as if trapped by the horror of his last image. I came to the edge of the cone of light.

"Why are you frightening me like this? What have I ever done to you?" I asked simply.

He opened his eyes and squinted at me. "You." Was there recognition?

"Yes, it's me." I squatted so that I was at eye level. I tried to soften myself, round off all the sharp edges. "Why are we here? Why have you brought me? I was asleep and safe."

"There is no safety. You saw them!" he whispered fiercely, his eyes burning with his vision. "We can never sleep. How many times have I warned you? They even invade our dreams and we have to fight them there." He was feverish, but there was definitely a look of recognition. I had a sudden intuition.

"But what can we do?" I asked like a child. "We're asleep. How can we defend our dreams?" The clenched muscles of his face began to slowly give way to a smile. I was right.

"Tell me, Father. Please." A hint of the real son's overenunciated and ponderous diction began to creep into my voice. I even tried to lengthen my neck. I was summoning up the image of Dukat's son as much as I could from just that one meeting on Romulus.

"You have to be strong on every level. Cowardice is like a disease and these people will infect you any way they can. Look what happened at Kobixine. They said negotiate with the arachnids. I said no." The voice was harsh, whispered, but he was going to communicate at any cost. "We have the advantage. Exterminate them. That's what they want to do to us. We're outnumbered, but we have the element of surprise on our side. We have to use it!" The old man began to cough again and flecks of blood and spittle flew into my face. "Gul Karn caved in. He became infected. We lost our advantage and the arachnids slaughtered us." The memory was fresh and bitter. "That's why Karn had to die, son. That's why we need the Brotherhood. They must not be allowed to infect us!"

I began to breather easier. Now we were getting to the crux. "Who are they, Father? Tell me so I can recognize them," I pleaded.

"You know them!" I could feel the heat of the old man's anger. "How many times have I warned you? Only fools don't listen!"

"I'm sorry, Father," I whispered.

"They're the same people who now want to kiss the Federation's ass and sign treaties that turn us all into women. Again, we have the advantage and the civilians and the traitors are pissing it away." His disgust was corrosive. "We have two implacable enemies, son. How are we going to fight them if we turn our warriors into women? That's what the Assembly wants to do!"

"The Federation . . . yes," I said. "They only understand power . . ."

"And the Klingons, boy! Don't forget them!" he commanded as if they were surrounding us. "They understand power, too, and if they think we'd rather talk than die. . . ." Dukat trailed off.

"I won't forget them, Father." I started to modulate the enhancer up. I didn't want to lose him. His eyes widened with a new thought.

"Did you go to Romulus?" he asked.

"Yes, I did. With Barkan," I added.

"He's good. He's good, son," the old man nodded. "But watch him. He's like his father. If a better deal can be made. . . ." I modulated higher. He was seized by a spasm and his face contorted into a rictus. "That's what they look like!" he screamed. "That's what they really look like when you strip away. . . ." His breath ran out and he began to choke in an attempt to refill his lungs. I chose not to modulate down. "We have to . . . kill them. Carriers . . . they carry the disease. Every one of them. Surround the Assembly . . . let everyone watch so they never forget. Ghemor . . . Lang . . . the guls who stand with them . . . especially the traitors!" Dukat was energized and tried to rise as if he were exhorting his troops. The frustration of not being able to poured into his words.

"The Brotherhood has to move now! The families must take their rightful place. Support the Directorate or die. And no exile! Exile is just deferred treachery. Those who were meant to rule must rule. End these negotiations with the Federation. Use the Romulans to drive the wedge! What did they say?" he suddenly asked me. "Will they move with us against the Klingons?"

"They said . . . yes. Yes, they will." I didn't know if this was the right answer, but I had to keep moving. Dawn was breaking.

"Good. Cripple the Klingons and then we can move against the disease itself."

"The Federation," I said.

"Yes, boy. The Federation. But first we have to root it out here . . . we have to purify Cardassia before. . . ." His breathing was becoming increasingly tortured, and his voice was reduced to a painful rasp. I was afraid that the sustained exertion would seriously injure him to a point that aroused suspicions. I shut the enhancer down. His eyes closed and his ashen face relaxed. I left the containment field in place and stepped outside to clear my head. No matter how objective I tried to remain, I could never remain totally unaffected by another man's horror. Fear was a contagious disease. It was nearly full light now, and I knew that I had little time to bring him back before the others arrived.

When I stepped back inside he appeared to be sleeping. I turned off the containment field and hid the enhancer and the recording devices which would document Dukat's "confession." I prepared a lighter dose of the *plaktar* toxin and reattached the sling to my body. When I turned back I was shocked to see him standing and looking at me with a clear and level expression.

Suddenly he attacked me, and as I stumbled back to avoid his furious rush I nearly spilled the toxin on myself. I slammed him into the wall and he sagged. He had no reserves with which to maintain his advantage. I twisted his right arm around to his back and administered the toxin. As I was attaching him to the sling he turned his head and faced me.

"Who are you?" he asked for the second time, fighting against the toxin's effect. This was one tough old warrior.

"Your worst nightmare," I replied.

"Ah," he croaked. "Then Tain sent you." He gave me one last murderous look before he lost consciousness. In a flash I realized that I hadn't got him to name any members of the Brotherhood. But I was more concerned about his associating me with Enabran Tain.

Entry:

Hands yanked and ripped the clothes off my body. I was unable to make any effort to stop them and couldn't make out their faces.

"Strip him completely. He's dead." It was Doctor Bashir's voice. But I'm not dead, I wanted to say. I couldn't form the words to voice them. I was absolutely helpless as they lifted my naked body and threw me into the deep pit on top of the other bodies.

"Ah, Elim," the body next to mine said. "You, too." It was Tain.

"Sooner or later we all end up here," the body beneath me observed. It was Tolan. All the bodies in the pit were murmuring.

"But we're alive," I protested above the babbling drone. "What are we doing in here?"

"This is the final strategem, Ten Lubak." It was Calyx. "If you can master this one, you've found your place."

"But this is horrible. This can't be my place. How can I master this?" I pleaded.

"This *is* your place," Lokar's voice informed me. "And you must never forget it."

"Just tread lightly, Elim. Use the silences," Pythas's voice advised me. I tried to move so I could see him, but I couldn't.

"Accept, Elim," Mila told me. "Stop fighting who you are and then you can move ahead."

"But why? Why are we here? And where's Palandine?" Before anyone could answer I felt a load of soil and rocks fall on my body.

"That's the last one," Doctor Bashir called above me. "Cover them up and seal off the pit. For the good of the quadrant they must never be allowed to return."

"But why?" I cried. "Calyx, how do I master this?" My questions were answered by the falling soil and the murmuring babble. "How? Tell me! How?"

I pushed myself away from the desk, bathed in sweat and gasping for breath. I stood up and looked around the room. Slowly, I came back to the station and the night silence. I had fallen asleep working at the desk. I rubbed my head where it had rested fitfully against the hard surface. This was probably my last night on the station. Perhaps forever. I had so much work I wanted to complete. It was late, but I punched a code on the station comm.

The voice cleared a passage in the throat to be able to speak. It was exactly what I couldn't do in the dream. "Yes?" the Doctor asked.

"Doctor, forgive me, but I need to see you," I said as calmly as I could.

"Garak?"

"I do apologize, but it's important."

"What's wrong?" the Doctor asked, trying to gauge the level of importance.

"It's not a medical emergency. Please, I realize this is an imposition." There was a silence and I heard another voice in the background. Ezri Dax. A muffled conversation. The Doctor cleared his throat again.

"I'll be right over," he said.

"Thank you, Doctor." I turned to the window, and the eternal night of space. My beloved stars. Only a nightmare as terrible as this could make me so grateful to be alive on this station. How ironic that I would be leaving it in a few hours.

"It's the anxiety of going back to Cardassia," the Doctor assured me. "And it's a very dangerous mission. Does one ever become inured to the possibility of death?" the Doctor asked.

"Not really," I answered as I served the Tarkalian tea. "If we lose our fear of death, we lose an important ally."

"I don't know, Garak." The Doctor sipped his tea. "Perhaps you should talk to Ezri about this. I don't know how much help I can be."

"Ezri, with all due respect, wasn't in the dream."

"Neither was I," the Doctor replied.

"On the contrary, my friend, you were." He gave me his puzzled look, which wrinkled his brow. I was always amazed at how deep the furrows were for one so young.

"I trust you don't mean that literally."

"You were in my dream," I maintained.

"Garak, you can't believe. . . . Look here." The Doctor took a deep breath. "My . . . persona . . . my symbolic representation was in your dream to . . . serve a purpose devised by your subconscious mind to satisfy some . . . need. It had nothing to do with me other than how your psyche used me . . . the way a . . . playwright uses a character." The Doctor paused and shook his head. The idea of his participation in my dream had ruffled his science. "This area has always been a great mystery. If I had a dream about . . . Hippocrates, you can't believe that this ancient Greek healer actually showed up," he challenged.

"We exist on many levels at the same time, Doctor. This level. . . ." I gestured to the room and its objects. ". . . the space/time continuum, I believe you call it, is perhaps the narrowest and least dimensional of all. But it's the one in which we choose to relate to each other as corporeal beings in a defined material space measured by units of time. It serves a purpose, yes, but it's a purpose that's been determined by our interaction on *other* levels, deeper and more complex than this one."

"What's the purpose of this one then?" he asked impatiently.

"To consummate the agenda created by our more dimensional selves!" A passion had crept into my voice, and the Doctor just looked at me.

" 'There are more things in heaven and earth, Horatio, Than are dreamt of in your philosophy.' " he quoted.

"Who's that?" I asked.

"Shakespeare," the Doctor replied.

"Hmmh." I nodded in agreement, surprised that for once the author of the politically misguided *Julius Caesar* made sense.

"I've never heard you talk like this before," he said. "I had no idea Cardassians held such ideas."

"Most don't. But we once did."

"So you're saying . . . what? That this level is the concrete manifestation of . . ." he stopped.

"Of who we are, Doctor. Our being. Human being. Cardassian being. But we have become these beings—*are* becoming, always in the *process* of becoming—on these other dimensional levels that are not limited by the measures of time and space. And the great determining factor of our becoming is relationship. Unrelated, I become unrelated. Alienated. Opposed, I become an antagonist. Unified, I become integrated. A functioning member of the whole." The Doctor was thoughtful; his previous agitation had dissolved.

"You're a scientist, Doctor. You have a deep understanding of *this* level. I don't mean just the mechanics. You understand about relationship, the laws that attract and repel, the combinations that nurture and poison. Health and disease. Integrity and breakdown."

"In your dream," he said, "I presided over the burial of yourself and the people you were most intimately related to. Why?"

"You said, 'for the good of the quadrant . . . they must never be allowed to return.' Why would you say that?" I asked.

"I can only think that. . . ." He stopped and shook his head. "I'm sorry, Garak. This is not easy for me. I still can't help thinking this was *your* dream. Even if I was invited . . . you were the playwright."

"Yes, but put yourself in that part. Why would you bury these people and cover up the pit?" The Doctor looked at me in frustration. "Please. Indulge me. It's vital that I have your answer."

"If you and the others were carriers of some disease," he shrugged. "In our fourteenth century on Earth there was a terrible plague, the Black Plague, which wiped out half of Europe's population. People believed that the dead bodies had to be destroyed, burned . . . buried . . . because it was the only way to prevent the spread of the disease. . . ."

My comm sounded. "Garak." It was Kira.

"Yes, Commander."

311

"Can you be ready to leave at oh-seven-hundred hours?"

I sighed. It was less than an hour, but I had no choice. "Certainly."

"See you in Airlock 11. Pack lightly."

"Just my hygiene kit and a change of undergarments," I said lightly. We clicked off. The Doctor was studying me with an interest in his face I hadn't seen in years.

"Well? Is it the Black Plague, Doctor? Or just the ramblings of an old spy on the eve of battle?"

"You're an amazing man, Garak."

"And my gratitude to you can never be adequately expressed. But I shall try," I promised.

"Please. What have I done?" he asked genuinely.

"That time you extended yourself so generously and found a way to remove the wire from my brain without killing me . . ."

"I would have done that for anyone," the Doctor interrupted.

"I'm sure that's true, but that's not what I mean. All during the time the device was deteriorating, I was convinced I was going to die."

"You were even resigned to it," he reminded me.

"I was also convinced that it was all a dream, and I kept asking myself what you were doing there."

The Doctor was puzzled. "But what you just told me, that our dreams are just another way we relate . . . ?"

"I had forgotten. That point of my life was perhaps the lowest. I had forgotten many things. When I 'woke up' and realized that because of you I was going to live—at that moment, I began to recollect some valuable information."

"About dreams?" he asked.

"Yes. But specifically about relationships, and how they set the course of our lives. You not only 'saved' my life, you also made it possible for me to live it." The Doctor's face darkened.

"What is it, Doctor?"

"The time I wounded you in that holosuite program. . . ."

"Yes," I prompted expectantly.

"I never apologized for my action."

"And you must *never* apologize!" I urged.

"Please, Garak. This is not the time to give me a lesson on how to behave like a hardened spy. . . ."

"No, no, no. On the contrary, when you shot me, my dear friend, that was the next step in my process of remembering. I was going to sacrifice the others, the people you considered your friends, because that was the only way I could be sure to save myself. You opposed me. Indeed, you would have killed me if necessary."

"I'm sure it would never have gotten to that point," the Doctor muttered.

"You would have killed me," I repeated. "For the greater good." The cliché suddenly had another meaning for both of us. "This is my last trip to Cardassia. I'm not returning. You were in the dream for a very specific reason. Once again, you helped me remember. Thank you, Julian." I put my hand on his shoulder.

"You're welcome," he smiled warmly. "And by the way. It wasn't the dead bodies that carried the disease. It was later determined that it was the rats feeding on the bodies who were the transmitters."

"Then I guess we'll go to Cardassia and look for the rats," I said.

"Be careful, Garak. And look after my hot-headed friend, will you?"

"Don't worry. We'll look after each other," I answered him. He moved to the door. "Did you really have a dream about Hippocrates?" I asked.

"Yes. Actually I did."

"Why am I not surprised?" I replied.

Kira was waiting in front of the airlock when I turned the corner.

"Odo's on his way. How are you feeling?" she asked.

"I've never been better, Commander," I replied with fervor. Kira gave me a long look.

"I don't think I've ever seen you so enthusiastic, Garak."

"I've finally remembered why I'm here."

20

Entry:

"Let's walk, Elim. It's a lovely day." Tain was waiting for me in front of the Assembly building.

"As you wish," I agreed with pleasure and mild surprise. Over the years we rarely met outside his office; only an emergency or drastic change of plan would alter the routine. Now as we walked through the late morning sun and pedestrians at a leisurely pace I experienced a connection to the surrounding bustle and energy in a way that felt almost normal. A father and his son taking a stroll. Tain was heavier, and I could hear his breathing labor with the effort. He's an old man, I thought. He's mortal. I'd never thought about Tain in this way, and I became protective as we approached an aggressive knot of pedestrians at the edge of the Coranum Sector. One man was about to run Tain down when I intercepted his path and bumped him to the side. I ignored his challenge as we continued.

"Yes, Elim. I'm getting old." It wasn't the first time he picked up my thoughts; this was how our conversations usually went. "It'll happen to you, too. You'll wake up one day and realize that you have just enough energy."

"For what?" I asked. I was alerted.

"To leave your affairs in order," he replied. "But you have to start thinking about these things long before that day arrives." Behind the hooded half-smile was the steely focus that always challenged me to rise to the occasion.

"You're leaving the Order," I said.

"I am."

"Where are you going?" I tried to control the sudden sense of dislocation that had usurped my newly found connection to the community.

"To the Arawak Colony." Of course. His beloved mountains in Rogarin Province.

"Is Mila going with you?" I asked.

"She is." I struggled to put all the forming questions into some kind of order. I wasn't paying attention to our surroundings, and it was only when Tain stopped that I looked around and realized where we were.

"There is the matter of succession, Elim. The Order has managed to steer a course that's been consonant with Cardassian security. The new leadership must maintain that course." I didn't know if it was the uncertainty about my own future or the fact that we were standing in the grounds where Palandine and I had spent so much of our time together, but I felt the inevitability of some kind of final reckoning. This was so typical of his manipulation. Just moments ago I was feeling protective of this benign old man, my father. And now . . . the irony filled my mouth with a bitter taste.

"Yes, you see. It's a problem," he nodded. "Two problems, actually. The less serious is that you've been connected to the incident with Procal Dukat. But we expected that he might retain enough memory of the interrogation. What was not expected was Barkan Lokar's recognition. While there's nothing they can prove, still, you've made some powerful enemies. Lokar has determined who you work for and he and the young Dukat now have you in their sights. Of course our stature is measured by the enemies we make, and that would be reason enough to allow you to succeed me," he said in a gentle, almost paternal tone that was keeping me off balance. He moved to the covered seating area, where the sun filtered through the old vegetation. I had never been here with anyone but Palandine. With a long sigh he settled into a patch of sunlight on the low bench.

"This is a beautiful place. I can understand why it's an ideal rendezvous," he observed.

"I always expected that you'd find out," I said.

"But what were you thinking? Not of the long term, certainly. And it's not just *any* woman. She's Lokar's wife. Sooner or later he's going to find out. You know that, don't you?" he asked with a sharp edge.

"Yes," I answered. The benign mask was slipping, and I began to see the depth of his anger.

"And when he does, your powerful enemy now becomes an implacable one. He won't rest until he has destroyed every trace of you." He was spitting his words at me. "What are you going to do?" he demanded.

"I don't know," I admitted with tightly wound control.

"You don't know!" he repeated with a disgust I hadn't heard since I was a boy and failed to record all the details of one of our walks. "And I'm supposed to pass my life's work on to someone who can't think beyond his lust?"

"It's not lust," I argued.

"Sentimentality," he hissed. "Even worse. You jeopardize our mission, the security of our people because of pathetic sentiments. And all this while, instead of giving up your life to the work, hardening yourself into a leader who could inspire others and expand the vision, you're playing out Hebitian fantasies with another man's wife!"

"Yes. Just like Tolan!" I exploded. "Perhaps he *was* my real father after all."

Tain rose like a man many years younger and grabbed my shoulder in a powerful grip. His anger was now a murderous fury and it was all I could do to hold my stance against the pain of his grip. His cold eyes told me I had betrayed him. Worse, I had failed him. He let go of my shoulder and turned away from me. My entire body trembled. When he turned back he had regained his composure.

"You've been returned to probe status. You will be given a period of time to prove whether you have anything of value to contribute to the organization. This, of course, is contingent on your never seeing the woman again and immediately setting into motion a plan to eliminate Barkan Lokar. A plan that will not implicate the Order. From now on you will report to Corbin Entek." He could have been speaking into a comm chip.

"And who will be succeeding you?" I asked.

"He already has. I leave for Arawak tonight."

"Who is he?" I persisted.

"Pythas Lok." He watched me for a moment. His mask was back in place. "Goodbye, Elim." He turned and walked away.

As I watched him leave, I felt completely empty and wondered how I could feel such emptiness. This sudden, wrenching reversal of fortune . . . everything changed beyond recognition. . . . And yet . . . there was no anger, no self-pity . . . no fear. Only release. Release from the secrets. Release from the limbo where, ever since I was a boy, I had been trapped between imposed obligations and feelings of mysterious longing mixed with shame. I felt empty . . . and free.

I had to see her again.

"I was expecting you," Mila said when the door opened. I followed her inside, and instead of the customary trip down to the basement she took me to the large central room, which was filled with stacks of packing bins.

"I'm afraid we're not leaving you much," she said. "The furnishings have already been taken away."

"I wasn't expecting anything." I tried to keep all irony out of my tone.

"It's your choice, Elim." Her voice was just as neutral. "The house is yours to live in."

"I assumed Pythas would be moving in."

"The house belongs to Enabran, not to the Order," she explained. "Under the circumstances you have the choice to live here."

"Do you know the circumstances . . . Mila?"

She looked at me. It was the first real contact we'd had in many years. She nodded slowly.

"Before I make my 'choice,' I need your help," I said, surprised that the request emerged so simply. I wasn't as angry with her as I wanted to be. Mila saw this and softened perceptibly.

"How can I help you, Elim?" It was an objective question; she was careful to maintain distance between us. "Housekeeping" for Tain, after all, came with certain obligations.

"You know about . . . this woman." I felt ungainly discussing this with her; like a little boy defending his wayward behavior.

"Lokar's wife." She revealed nothing, but at least I was discovering that she and Tain spoke to each other. Perhaps Mila was more than just an efficient housekeeper who dusted his brangwaskin books and scrolls.

"I need your help," I repeated.

"You saw him today," she stated as she arranged two cups in the drink replicator. I nodded. "He was angry when he left this morning."

"I love her, Mila."

"You're a grown man, Elim." I couldn't decide whether she thought I didn't know this or was seeing it for the first time herself.

"And Palandine's a grown woman," I replied.

"I don't care about her. It's you! You have to learn . . ." She broke off and passed me a cup which exuded the herbal aroma I've always associated with her and Tolan. Bitterbark and sweet groundroot. Moist rich soil.

"To control myself?" Mila blew on her tea. I shrugged at the obvious irony; I didn't want to get into a fight. "I know. I really do know this, and if there were a way I could . . . just . . . let go . . . convince myself it's a bad idea and walk away . . . I would." Mila made an impatient movement with her head. She was struggling for control herself.

"I mean it, Mila. I would. But I think about her, feel her, all the time. Especially when I'm alone." Mila sat on a bin and sipped her tea. She avoided my look. As I positioned another bin across from her, I experienced a deep pain in my shoulder. It was still throbbing.

"Tain's angry . . . with me. He wants me never to see her again and . . . to kill Barkan." Still she avoided looking at me. "But you know this, don't you? And you know what's possible. Because you have your own . . . thoughts about this. Don't you Mila?" I persisted.

Again she jerked away from me. Tea from her cup slopped onto the floor. "There's no time, Elim." She put the cup down, wiped her hands on the protective smock she wore, and looked for something to clean the floor with. "There's no time for this."

"But here we are," I shrugged. "I've been reduced to probe status, my work dismissed as counting for nothing. . . ."

"It will count when you *choose* to make it count," she said, as she picked up a piece of fabric and rejected it.

"But what about the sacrifices I made? Don't they count?" I demanded.

"Sacrifices?" In frustration Mila took off her smock to wipe the tea from the floor. "Elim, you amaze me." Shaking her head, she got down on her knees and began scrubbing vigorously, as if the spilled drops of tea were hostile agents capable of spreading disease and destruction.

"Really? Well, I'm pleased I still have the ability—"

"Sacrifices," she hissed, her control escaping like steam from a narrow rift. "What was the name of that book you once gave me? When you first came back from Bamarren. The one you proclaimed as the greatest Cardassian novel ever written and insisted that we read it." Mila was still on her knees, but now I was the offending spot she vigorously rubbed with her words and eyes. "Generations of one family, each faced with the same choice at a crucial moment. Do they serve their personal needs or do they serve future generations? Do they choose the comfort of their own lives over the life of the state and its mission? I read it, Elim. You told me to and I did."

The Never-Ending Sacrifice," I answered.

"Yes. That's the one." She made a sighing sound as she stood up. Mila was heavier now, and moved with greater deliberation. She, too, had grown old. "I suggest you reread it."

"Tain always came first, didn't he? I suppose that was *your* never-ending sacrifice." I no longer reined in the irony.

"Yes, he did. And if you know anything about sacrifice you'd understand why. The man gave selflessly, constantly. He never asked his people to do anything he wasn't willing to do himself. He never asked for anything but the devotion and loyalty that he gave to his work."

"How fortunate he had Tolan."

"Tolan understood and accepted his obligations," Mila said coldly. "But he was sentimental. Like you. That was the one thing Enabran worried about."

I smiled in sad recognition. Sentimental. Yes, Tain and

Mila had definitely shared their confidences and judgments with each other.

"But I don't blame Tolan. He was a good man." Mila watched me as I rose.

"Yes. So you keep saying." I wanted to leave.

"She's nothing but trouble for you, Elim. End it now. Do what Enabran says and reclaim your rightful place."

"My place," I repeated.

"*Now*, Elim. Otherwise you're in real danger," she warned with a certainty that reminded me of the time she'd brought me to Tain after I'd left Bamarren. Mila always knew what was at the heart of the never-ending sacrifice.

"Thank you for your help," I said, too weary for irony.

"What did you expect from me?"

"To be honest, I can't remember," I answered. "Have a pleasant trip." I smiled and bowed.

"Let Limor know if you'll be living here." I nodded. Yes, I thought, that would be my answer. My choice. She shook out her smock to determine whether or not to put it back on.

"Mila." She looked at me and took a deep breath, as if preparing herself for my question.

"Who was Tolan?"

"My brother." She decided to wear the smock, and I left.

It was a clear night; I sat among "Uncle" Tolan's orchids and watched the Taluvian Constellations pulse with undiminished strength. More than ever, I believed not only that they were sending us subliminal messages containing vital information, but that our ability to decode these messages would determine our fate. At Bamarren, Docent Rilon had passionately maintained that if we were only willing to let go of the busy preoccupations of our conditioned minds and concentrate instead on receiving the energy pulse of any given star configuration, the newest and ever-developing part of our brain would be guided by the creative wisdom of the Primal Plan.

Without any effort, my choice was made; the plan lay before me like a diagram. Whether it was my decision or one inspired by the Taluvian pulse was a question I didn't ask. At this point I had to accept the givens and take action. The difficult part would be staying away from Palandine; if I could do that, the plan would succeed.

In the weeks that followed, I submitted to my punishment. I informed Limor Prang that I would be living in Tain's house, and he accepted my decision with the usual absence of reaction. I then reported to Corbin Entek, who had been in the Level above me at Bamarren and one of Lokar's trusted adjutants, One Drabar. We had worked together very closely during the Competition, and I had enormous respect for him. I once asked him why he hadn't stayed with Lokar and become a part of the Bajoran Occupation.

"Everyone has their work," was all he would say. Considering the plan I had set into motion, I had to be extremely careful in my dealings with him.

"You've been assigned to a new cell, which meets tonight," Entek informed me. I had expected the reassignment: a probe begins at the bottom, and up until this moment I'd been the leader of my cell. "I've also recalibrated your comm chip. May I have your old one, please?" he asked.

"Certainly," I replied and gave it to him. It could have

been worse. Entek was tough and ambitious, but he was not one of the agents who feared and resented my former status as a "son of Tain."

"I appreciate your attitude, Elim. This could have been awkward," he said with honest relief.

"We're professionals, Corbin. We make our adjustments when necessary." No one knew the real reason for my humiliation; everyone assumed that Tain had not been pleased with my results, and that I was being used as an example of how failure is punished.

"If you need anything, don't hesitate to ask," he said.

"That's very kind of you. Some information, if you're allowed." My request was disguised as an afterthought. "I assume tonight's meeting will involve a mission. I don't want to know what it is, but I'd like to know how much time I have for my personal transition before I'm assigned." I was as reasonable and unattached to the request as possible, but his answer was vital to my plan. Entek hesitated. It was awkward for him after all, I thought. This was not only a question I would never have asked Limor, but it was complicated by the fact that until this moment I had been Entek's superior.

"You leave in two days," he finally replied. My heart sank. Lokar would not be back on Cardassia Prime until the following week for the beginning of the negotiations regarding the Bajoran Occupation.

"Thank you, Corbin."

"Will that give you enough time?" he asked. His consideration was highly unusual, but I assumed he was going out of his way to make sure I was not unnecessarily humiliated by my demotion to probe status.

"Some adjustments will have to wait." I inclined my head and started to leave.

"Would it help to know that the assignment is on Bajor?" Corbin asked. At that moment it hit me. Ah yes. I had misread Entek's awkwardness and consideration. I still felt Tain's hand on my shoulder.

"Yes, it does, Corbin." I bowed again and left. On an impulse, instead of leaving immediately, I went down the corridor to Tain's old office. The door was open, and I stopped at the threshold just as Pythas looked up from a now much cleaner desk. He smiled shyly and stood up.

"Please come in, Elim," he offered. What surprised me was how pleased I was to see him. Just as I had felt he was the only other person who deserved to be One Lubak, I now believed he was the only other person who deserved to occupy this office.

"Welcome to the visible world, Pythas," I greeted.

"I didn't campaign for this," he said without apology.

"If you had, Tain would never have picked you. He deeply mistrusts politicians. Of course," I added, "he was a superb politician himself." Pythas appreciated the paradox.

"I was hoping you'd choose to stay," he said.

"I had no choice. At my age what was I going to do? Lead wilderness treks in Morfan?" As we stood in the tiny, nondescript office, the planning center of so much activity affecting the lives of all Cardassians, I wondered how much, really, the generation of Tain and Prang had yielded to ours. I looked at Pythas' *kotra* board, which was set up to be played on a separate table. As far as I was personally concerned, Tain was still attempting to control the pieces.

"And what makes me happy, Pythas, is that I can continue to dominate you on the *kotra* board."

"Ah, we'll see, Elim. We'll see."

"Well. I better be off."

"Yes," Pythas nodded. "Be careful, Elim."

"Thank you. I'll do my best." As I walked back down the corridor, the message Tain had sent me when he made Pythas his successor became quite clear.

I waited in the darkness, this time across from Tolan's orchids, on the other side of the children's area. Mila and Tain were right about my sentimentality. I hadn't dared go back to the Coranum grounds after my last meeting with Tain; now I was hiding in these bushes like a naughty boy hoping anxiously to see the object of his forbidden desire. Tain had arranged the mission to Bajor. Once I told Prang I would live in the house, Tain was going to facilitate my move against Lokar. And how elegant it was. My contact was a Bajoran double agent who would help me arrange Lokar's assassination and make it look like the work of the Bajoran Resistance.

But I couldn't stay away from Palandine. Yes, I was sentimental. But after Lokar's death we'd be able to call it something else.

And there she was. The shadowy outline of my desire. My love. She had gotten my message. Palandine was facing toward the Edosian orchids, and I could see she was in a tense state from the way she moved and held herself. As I was about to signal my presence, I sensed faint movement in the shrubbery behind the orchids. It could have been voles, but I don't think I would have been aware of their movement from this distance. Of course I was under surveillance—that was no surprise. What was surprising was my foolishness. Reluctantly I decided not to signal. It was time to stop behaving like a reckless child. It would have to be enough to watch her shadowy outline and remind myself what was at the other end of my Bajoran mission. Giving up Palandine would not be part of my never-ending sacrifice.

After an unbearably long period of time, during which Palandine grew increasingly agitated, she suddenly stopped her pacing not far from where I was well hidden, and looked sharply in my direction. I was convinced that she could see me, even though it was rationally impossible. But she began to walk toward me, and whether or not she could see me, she somehow knew I was there. She stopped just short of my covering shrub, and the sight of her face shocked me. It was swollen and bruised. One eye was completely closed, and the other contained enough pain for ten. It took every bit of my willpower not to reach out and hold her. Her one eye held mine, I knew she wanted to tell me something so important that she was willing to wait all night if necessary. But I was certain that someone had followed me here, and that any contact would fatally expose us. Not now, my darling. Soon, I signaled. She barely nodded, sadly, and walked away. As I watched her recede into the darkness, every cell of my body was so quickened with hatred and the a desire for revenge that I barely heard the noise behind me.

I could see the light above me. I pushed my way toward the luminous white center surrounded by a rosy corona. The medium was heavier than water, perhaps a liquid gas, warm and buoyant, but miraculously it wasn't suffocating me. As long as I pushed and stroked and kicked my way up to the center of the light I knew with certainty that I would arrive at my destination. I didn't dare take my eyes off of my lighted goal for fear of losing it, but I knew there were bodies all around me. They drifted in and out of the edges of my periphery, and I wondered if they were going to the same place. While their presence was strongly felt, it was too dark to see who they were. They never made any physical contact, but we were deeply and pleasurably connected to each other.

The light was growing more and more intense the closer I came to it. Blinding white and painful. I couldn't keep my eyes open and I was afraid to close them. Finally the light shattered as I broke the surface and heard someone scream. The shards of light gathered at several magnetizing points, where they formed shapes.

"If he screams like that again, we'll all be deaf." A voice emanated from the shape of a person standing in front of me. A hand flashed out from the body shape and slapped me across the face. A warm feeling of pleasure flowed through me; the liquid medium I had moved through to arrive at this place was now inside me, filling me with its tender nurture.

"He's conscious now." Another voice spoke from a body, which moved out of the surrounding darkness into the penumbra at the edge of the pool of light. The hand flashed again and slapped my face. Another release of warm pleasure. The wire, I thought. This is an interrogation. Military interrogators. They have no idea. I wanted to laugh, and it took a concerted effort to gather my disparate parts in order to integrate my will. Was I on Bajor?

"At least the smile's gone," the first voice said. I was fully awake now. I let my jaw go slack and my eyes glaze over, but I could make out a good two hundred degrees of the room. Besides the two Cardassian soldiers, I was able to discern a third man standing in the darkness to my left. I sensed he was the focal point of the others. I couldn't sense anyone behind me. The hands of the closest soldier grabbed me by the shoulders and pulled me into a more erect sitting position.

"Pay attention now!" he shouted in my face. I cleared my eyes to indicate more awareness.

"He's ready now, sir," the soldier confidently reported to his superior. To think that they give these brutes the delicate task of an interrogation.

"Why are you shaking your head, Elim? Regret for the foolishness that brought you here?" I was not surprised to hear his voice. Only surprised that it had taken so long. I had been very careless. Sentimental.

"Leave us," Lokar ordered the soldiers. They looked at each other.

"He's not secured, sir," the one closest to Lokar warned.

"Elim and I are old friends. We're just going to have a chat," Lokar said with a pleasant smile. "You may go." The soldiers left and Lokar studied me in silence. "Quite impressive," he said. "The amount of punishment you absorbed. I'm afraid, however, that that smile of yours only infuriated the glinn. Do you remember the first time we met? The same smile." I made no response. Was it coincidence that Lokar had made his move as I was about to make mine? Or was I betrayed? Someone must have known that he had come back from Bajor. That's what Palandine had wanted to tell me with her battered face. They must have followed her. Where was she now? The wire wasn't designed to alleviate the anxiety I felt for her safety . . . and my hatred. If I could somehow get to him here. I began to calculate the risk. At that moment, Lokar circled around so that he stood directly behind me, but at a distance to easily deal with any move I would be foolish enough to make. I continued to look straight in front of me. I had to channel this hatred along a finely tuned band of intention.

"How is your gardening these days? Or do you get much of a chance in your new profession? You did that very well. I left Romulus feeling sorry for you."

"Your arrogance made it easy, Barkan."

"Indeed. I underestimated you. It wasn't until many years later that I discovered you'd been recruited by the Obsidian Order. I'd always assumed you'd . . ."

"You assumed that it was because you gave me a low rating in your Competition evaluation that the Prefect asked me to leave. And then you assumed that I had disappeared into the service class." I allowed the ancient resentment to color my tone; it was a tacit acknowledgment of his superiority I knew he wouldn't miss.

"Ah, yes. Still bitter, are we?" And he didn't. I could feel his initial defense relax. In his mind I was still Elim, the naïve murk. "It's clear you never learned to build on these lessons. It's a pity. You're a clever person, but a petty one; harboring your slights and jealousies, plotting your revenge. And it made you sloppy and self-indulgent. Yes, I underestimated you. I'd lost track of you, I had no idea what you were up to, professionally . . . or personally. Imagine my surprise." Resentment crept into Barkan's tone. Here was the opening I wanted.

"How did you find out?" I asked.

"Please, Elim. That's when you underestimated *me*. Flaunting your 'relationship' in public like infatuated schoolchildren."

"Yes, I suppose it would have been wiser to behave like experienced adulterers," I replied with a sigh.

"You're the lowest form of scavenger, Elim. You have no attachments of your own, and so you feed on the emotional vulnerabilities of others." The resentment gave way to the implacable hatred Tain had anticipated. It wouldn't be long now.

"What are you going to do with Palandine?" I asked.

"That's not your concern. I'm sure you're accustomed to being the one to ask the questions, but I'm afraid that's no longer your privilege. You are now obligated to answer mine." His voice hardened and he moved closer to me, a sign that his desire for revenge was outstripping his objective.

"I'll answer what I can, Barkan." I tried to sound defeated.

"Who else was involved with the abduction and torture of Procal Dukat?" he demanded.

"Are you implying I was involved?" I asked incredulously.

"Don't play me for a fool here. I warn you. Perhaps you possess this impressively high threshold for pain, but there are other ways I can hurt you," he warned.

"Barkan, I would have been proud to have exposed a traitor like Dukat. He deserved his fate."

"Is that why Pythas Lok was chosen over you to replace Tain?" Lokar had a source within the Order. "It seems everyone is chosen over you. Don't you grow weary of being bypassed?"

"Only betrayal makes me weary," I replied.

"But you're a failure, Elim. You even failed in your attempt to assassinate me."

"I didn't fail with Palandine," I said quietly.

There was a silence. I hadn't meant to make my move this quickly, but I prepared myself. His footfalls approached me and a tremendous blow to the back of my head sent me sprawling on the floor.

"You did, Elim. You can't even begin to measure your failure," he said with murderous chill. He kicked me in the small of the back. Pleasure instead of pain; a strange sensation. I groaned and remained motionless.

"Get up!" I didn't move. Barkan aimed a kick at my genitals but he was too angry to be accurate and my upper leg absorbed the blow. A harder, better placed kick between my right hip and ribs knocked the air out of me and let loose another flow of endorphins. I groaned louder, and rolled to a position where I could keep Lokar's legs in my lidded sight. He was breathing hard, not so much from the exertion as from the rage it was releasing. His weight shifted to his left leg, preparing for his right to kick again. My opportunity—a word Lokar had taught me to respect. As his foot came straight along my line of vision toward my face, I shifted slightly away, grabbed his approaching ankle with both hands, twisted with all my strength and brought him down on his face. He struggled for his phaser, but I had him by the throat from behind and cut off his windpipe. He grabbed my forearm, and the strength of his effort to free his breathing rolled us over and over until he began to weaken from the lack of air. Everything turned red as I poured my last ounce of energy into Lokar's death. And then black.

The corona of light was now receding from me. I was returning. This time there was no effort involved; I floated in a gentle current of the soothing balm and didn't care where it was taking me. The others were there—my fellow travelers, their voices murmuring tonelessly, producing a steady sound that permeated the medium and intensified our connection. Their voices speaking to me. Their faces, serene and loving, illuminating the darkness as they floated by. Everyone I have ever known. Family. Faces from childhood. Bamarren. People I had known briefly. People I have known forever. Loved. Hated. We were all just together now, sharing the same nurturing medium as we traveled along our currents until we gradually separated.

I was alone now. The blackness was complete, with the exception of a pinpoint of light above and behind me. I wasn't afraid. I wasn't lonely. The caressing motion of the medium continued to soothe me. The blackness began to pulse with a soft rhythm. And the voices were still with me. I was being prepared. Thump thump thump. No matter what happened, they said. Thump thump thump. No matter the damage. Thump thump thump. Everything can be repaired. Thump thump thump. Don't surrender to the appearance. Thump thump thump. Trust the mystery. Thump thump thump! Don't surrender, they said as they began to fade. Thump! Thump! Thump! Everything can be. . . .

I opened my eyes. I was on the floor. Someone was banging from far away. A bare room. Dark. My vision blurred. . . . I turned my body with great effort. It was so heavy and exhausted, if it hadn't been for the pain I would have believed that it didn't belong to me. My eyes began to focus. This was a different room. I made out the outline of someone sprawled on the floor near me. Shouts and further banging coming closer. Where were we? I crawled with difficulty to the other body. Is he still alive? I felt leaden and drugged. The body was face down. I reached out and pulled it over, and the head flopped toward me.

Faces formed and reformed. Each one superimposed on the next in a long line emerging from blackness. Maladek. Merrok. . . . The molecular structure of one giving way to the next. . . . Procal Dukat. Tolan. Floating into focus, receding back into the darkness. I shook my head, trying to stop the flow. The Hebitian mask. *My face.* I grabbed my "face" and screamed into it. The flow stopped. The molecules rushed together and instantly formed Barkan Lokar's death mask.

The door burst open and several hands grabbed me.

PART III

*"Mister Garak . . . why is it that no one
has killed you, yet?"*
"My innate charm?"

I

Entry:

When I was first "assigned" to Terok Nor, I thought that the Order and Tain would design my punishment in such a way that I would not be wasted. Why let me live if I couldn't be used? After all, I reasoned, they needed a representative on this forsaken outpost. Lokar's ore-processing operation had created a lucrative commercial enterprise on the edge of the quadrant that attracted all types for all reasons. What better place to employ the services of a disgraced but still useful operative?

The military, under the command of Gul Skrain Dukat, had treated the station as its own private fiefdom, but no one complained as long as the mining operation continued to process twenty thousand tonnes of uridium ore each day. And with these high numbers no one was going to object to "excesses" in the treatment of the Bajoran laborers. It was clear that the station's enormous profits were created by the free labor of a people who had been reduced to mere slaves. It was also clear—as I followed my escort like a sleepwalker, devoid of all feeling, stripped of my past and any hopes for the future—that this was a soul-deadening environment. An ideal match for my benumbed state. As we entered Dukat's office, I was greeted by his undisguised contempt.

"Elim Garak. How the mighty have fallen. Welcome to Terok Nor."

"Oh, I try to visit even our humblest outposts, Dukat."

"This is going to be more than a visit, trust me. You'll soon wish that the execution had not been commuted," he said, regarding me like a lower life-form he was considering as a source of food. With his long neck and oversharpened features (his ridges, I'm certain, could cut to the bone) he had the look of a predator waiting for the right moment to make the kill. Engaging this look dispelled my previous lethargy; I knew that he held me responsible for his father's execution. As the moment extended I could almost taste the noxious combination of his hatred and frustration. Obviously it had been ordered that I was not to be touched, and the prohibition only sharpened his predatory hunger. Dukat broke the look and turned to an underling.

"Take him to his new life." He dismissed us.

As the underling led me along the filthy Promenade, where Bajoran laborers and their Cardassian overseers played out the daily dramas of slave and master, I wondered how my "new life" would fit into all this. Laborers and overseers were equally baffled by the sight of a disgraced Cardassian, as we passed through the cluttered, makeshift living conditions. I could hardly believe that this was a station run by Cardassians. We stepped over the trash that even now Cardassian guards on the upper Promenade level were raining down on the Bajorans who ate and squatted below. Our racial policies were harsh, but Dukat evidently took them to an extreme that reduced the workers to beasts of slavery. This was truly the dark side of the Occupation, and I moved through it all completely in tune with the misery and the pain and the despair. This world was the perfect extension of my inner self.

At the end of the Promenade I was led down some steps into a dreary workshop littered with articles of clothing, uniforms, and bolts of rotting fabric. Everything was covered with the same patina of oily muck that encrusted the entire Bajoran section.

"What is this?" I asked.

"This is where you will carry out your assignment." It's bad enough when a toady assumes the behavior of his superior, but when the superior has the rhetorical grace of a Tarlak monument . . .

"And what is my assignment?"

"This is a tailor's shop," he announced.

"That's keenly observed," I said. He accepted my remark as a compliment. The type of toady who gives all Cardassians the reputation for having no sense of irony. "But do you want me to clean it, to burn it, to turn it into the Terok Nor information center . . . ?"

"This is where members of the occupation force brought their garments to be mended." It was a challenge for the boy to get to the point, but I remained silent so as not to confuse him any more than he was. "The station has been without a tailor since the last one—a Bajoran—decided one day that he would no longer mend our garments."

"I'm sure you gave him a more ennobling position," I said.

"He was executed," the toady replied.

"A promotion of sorts," I muttered. "Certainly in this place." I could see that he was growing more uncomfortable in my presence. As much as he wanted, he was unable to assume Dukat's sneering superiority. A

natural-born toady. "And I have now been given the privilege to mend the holes in your uniforms."

He nodded in agreement. "You will be providing a
vital service to the Cardassian effort on Terok Nor."

"A stitch in time, eh?" I smiled at him. I'm sure I must
have looked positively demented. He shuffled nervously,
mumbling something about quotas and standards and
filthy Bajorans. I continued to smile and to calculate the
dozen or so ways I could end his miserable life in an instant. Finally he made an awkward exit, leaving me
alone in the middle of this pile of rags and filth.

Yes, I thought, this is more than punishment; this is
humiliation. I am the first Cardassian slave on Terok
Nor. My new life. My place.

Entry:

Cardassians design everything carefully. Nothing is
left to improvisation or chance. Everything has a function, and every function serves a purpose that fits into
what the Bamarren prefect called the mosaic of the state.
Just study the architecture of Terok Nor, for example.
The diagonal angularity impels the inhabitants, workers
and overseers alike, to move on to their next duty. There
are no ninety degree angles, certainly no enclosed
squares to capture one's thoughts and energy in any kind
of meditation. Everything is designed to guide and direct
subliminally so that conscious choice is kept at a minimum in our daily lives.

But exile changes all that. You can only be subliminally controlled when there is a rationale, a meaning to
your existence. A tailor. On Dukat's Terok Nor. Is this
Enabran Tain's sense of humor? The punishment that fits
the crime? He must be very angry with me indeed, not

only to deny me the dignity of a summary execution but to bury me on this death station and render me as useless as one of these filthy rags.

Don't surrender to the appearances.

I shook my head as I began to sense the stirring of feelings I didn't want to emerge and slipped the device from a hidden pocket that eluded the fools who'd searched me. I had ignored Mindur Timot's warning never to tamper with my wire, and had devised a control that allowed me to activate the mechanism myself. I had become quite devoted to the wire's anesthetic power, and as I stood in my new home I could feel the endorphins rush through my nerve nexus and into and throughout my perceptual body. Suddenly I was standing outside of my body, watching my reactions—and marveling at how much I had aged.

Entry:

The doors opened, and a soldier walked into the shop holding a bundle. I had my head buried in the innards of the computer, where I was rerouting the circuitry in order to connect it to the station terminal, and I only saw his outline. I was at a delicate point and I didn't want to lose my focus.

"Just put it in the corner with the other uniforms," I said without looking up. Before I could react, the bundle hit me with force on the side of my head. It was Dukat.

"What is this?" he demanded as he looked around the shop and saw the pile. "Are you mending these garments or collecting them?"

"I will begin the repair process once my workshop is in order," I replied as I stood up.

"And how much longer will that be?" he asked.

"When I have the tools I need," I answered. Dukat looked at me with his mean and deadly smile. He knew that I'd been taking my time "cleaning" the shop. The pile of garments waiting for my ministrations was growing bigger every day, and there had been numerous complaints. One soldier walked in and threatened me with bodily harm when I told him that I didn't know when his uniform would be ready. The truth was that I had neither the expertise nor the will to launch my new career, and when I wasn't sleeping I was rebuilding the neglected computer that appeared to have been damaged by the Bajoran's pathetic attempt at sabotage.

"If I wanted a computer engineer, Garak, I would have given you the assignment. I want a tailor. Do you know the difference?" he asked with overdone sarcasm. "Get this operation going in two days or you will become the first Cardassian to work in the ore-processing center," he warned. "I'm sure the Bajoran workers would enjoy your company."

"Yes, you've certainly won their hearts and minds with your benign administration," I observed pleasantly.

"Two days, Garak, or you can find out about their hearts and minds yourself. I'm afraid there's not much call for a gardener on Terok Nor," he said with disgust. Instead of leaving, Dukat moved to the panel where I was working and picked up one of the disconnected circuits.

"Who gave you permission to do this work?" he asked, inspecting the circuit as if he understood what he was looking at.

"You did."

"When?" He arched his brows in a manner that told me he'd worked long and hard in front of a mirror.

"When you assigned me to rehabilitate this sad shop. Beside tools, I need instruction and information. Where do you expect me to go? My Bajoran predecessor, I believe, is now with his Prophets." Dukat snorted, and dropped the circuit on the floor at my feet. His eyes were cold, almost dead.

"Your life means nothing to me. Just as my father's meant nothing to you."

"I beg your pardon? Do I know your father?" Dukat made a move to grab me and immediately stopped himself. I was impressed by his self-control; I knew how much energy fueled his hatred.

"No offense," I went on, further testing his control. "Of course, Procal Dukat was a famous military figure. We all mourned his passing. But I never had the pleasure personally. . . ."

"Two days," he repeated with deadly emphasis. "Get what you need—clear all purchases through my aide, Hadar—and begin work in two days. There's a point beyond which you won't be protected." He nodded. "You'll get to that point . . . and I'll be there, waiting for you." He turned and strode out of the shop.

Entry:

I have been taught ever since I was a child to believe that every event, every circumstance, every action and reaction in my life is an intertwining thread in my fateline, and that each person's fateline is just another piece of that carefully designed Cardassian mosaic. In my current circumstances, the more I try to deny the past and the history that has informed me the more it overwhelms me. Even the wire can't let me forget that this exile has a meaning: otherwise life on this station is even worse than death.

"Silence, exile, and cunning." An expression which comes from a human someone urged me to read. His writing was too childish for my taste, but the expression always had meaning for me. Silence. Exile. Cunning. After all, we do have to get on with our work, however we can and in whatever circumstances. If mending the garments of our military occupation was the work designed for my survival in this time and place, then it would not be terribly cunning of me to refuse it. No, I decided that I was not going to sacrifice myself to Dukat's desire for revenge. I would do this work; I would do it so well as to become indispensible to the station . . . and I would survive. I refused to be buried alive in this humiliation.

For the first time since I had arrived on Terok Nor, I felt an energy, an appetite for meeting this challenge, and I began to construct a course of action. Once the computer was up and functioning, I could get all the necessary information and guidance, but I still lacked state-of-the art tools. I quickly discovered that there was only one person on the station who could help me procure what I needed: the Ferengi publican, a Mr. Quark.

I found Quark's establishment noisy and tiresome, filled with people looking for quick fixes and easy answers. And yet, here I was, looking for a shortcut of my own. I certainly didn't come for rewarding conversation.

"I'm looking for a Mr. Quark," I asked a Ferengi barkeep.

"And who's looking for him?" he replied with unpleasant suspicion.

It turned out to be Quark himself. As I made my proposal, I was somewhat unsettled by the unblinking avarice in his eyes and the metallic assault of his voice. But as we got further into the negotiating details, I found him to be a reasonable man. Quark makes no pretense about his priorities, and woe to the person who enters into negotiations with him who doesn't have his wits about him. And who doesn't have a capacity for the drink Quark liberally pours during the haggling. But he delivered, Hadar paid, and I was soon set up with the tools of my new career.

Entry:

I pride myself on being a quick study, but even I am pleased with the progress I'm making in learning the tailoring craft. Indeed, I'm able to use many of the qualities I developed in the Obsidian Order: patience, precision, the ability to calculate how each part fits into the whole pattern. I suppose I should be grateful Enabran didn't have me assigned to the ore-processing center.

But the best part—which nearly drove me mad at the beginning—is the solitude, the silence in which I work. Although I did my best to use this work to blot out every thing and person from my past, I couldn't help but recall that initial joy I found in the Mekar Wilderness. For it's in this silence, as I cut and sew and measure, that I'm relearning how to listen. Not to the prattling of others, certainly not to the fantasies that my memory provokes when I try to rewrite history. But to the deeper voices in myself. What is pain, for example, but another voice to be listened to? Don't identify. Keep your distance. But listen! There's information that can help me find the missing piece to any puzzle; that can save me from this waking nightmare. Because it's in this silence—as I listen to these voices—that I'm learning how to reinvent myself.

As my tailoring skills increase, so do the interruptions of my solitude by people who throw their garments at me as if their imperfections were my fault. Dukat has spread the word that I am a disgraced traitor, and I have become the receptacle for any ill will that walks into my shop. But I say nothing. These are only more voices that command my attention. I pick up their garments and mend them flawlessly. When they complain that the price is steep (because I'm treated like a slave doesn't mean I'm going to start undervaluing my work), I just give them the smile—the smile *she* taught me. It somehow tranquilizes them while I pick through their psyches. Oh, they pay, one way or another. When Quark found out how much I was commanding for a simple alteration he asked me how I was getting away with it. I assured him that I didn't know what he was talking about . . . and smiled while he poured another glass of *kanar.*

But the silence in which I reinvent myself (out of whole cloth, as it were) is not easy. For someone who values the art of conversation as much as I do, establishing a new life based on the power of silence requires a cunning of which I never dreamed. But it's my only chance to reassemble the mosaic. So I sit here, day after day, and work and watch and listen . . . trusting that sooner or later all the information I need to return home will come to me.

2

We live in an eternal twilight, Doctor. Because of the wind currents, the dust clouds produced by the innumerable detonations all over the planet have joined and created an unbroken atmospheric cover. For a while it seemed that the clouds covering the city were lifting and dissipating, but it was only a temporary clearing as they were soon replaced by others that had grown thicker and larger from their travels. We are now as gray as Romulus, but without the mitigating lushness.

Now that the thoroughfares have been cleared, I have resumed my long walks. Just in time, I might add. My dreams have become increasingly disturbed of late, and I wonder how much my involvement with what Gul Madred calls my necropolis has to do with it. And then there's the invitation Madred has extended to me to join him at the next meeting in order to meet his colleagues . . . and my old schoolmate. Could it be him? After my exile, both Pythas and Palandine dropped out of sight. No matter how hard I tried to track them during my time on Deep Space 9, I could get no information. Either my attempts were stonewalled or I was told that they'd been victims of internecine warfare during the Dominion Occupation. At this moment I am almost afraid to discover that they'd survived. A part of me has wanted to bury that part of my life. The defenses I set up to survive my exile are obviously still intact.

I am often joined on my walks by Dr. Parmak. He's a charming conversationalist, with a first-rate mind. His perspectives are always provocative. He does, however, have a tendency to proselytize for Alon Ghemor and the "Reunion Project" (the name they've given their group to remind people of the principles that formed the original Union). Whenever we encounter other pedestrians along our route, Parmak engages them and attempts to win them over to the Reunion side. This often makes for spirited exchanges, and although I am subjected to the opinions of people who should be given a new brain, I rather enjoy this peripatetic politicking. It's something I would never have done on my own. In some respects he is so much like you, Doctor. If I've found someone's opinion insufferably boring, he'll kindly but sternly lecture me on the value of tolerance.

" 'Reunion' is about bringing together *all* points of view, Elim."

"So we can spew forth whatever nonsense comes to mind?"

"In a context, my friend. There must be a political context, so that one opinion doesn't dominate to the point of shutting out all others," he patiently explained.

"The 'anarchy project' would be a more apt name for your group, Doctor," I replied.

"Oh, my dear Elim," is his favorite expression, usually delivered with a sigh and a sad shake of his head. But I listen to him because it's bracing to have a genuine voice of optimism in the midst of this dust and devastation.

One day I asked him how he had been brought to Enabran Tain's attention. He never struck me as being a dangerous radical. It turns out that he was Tain's personal physician, and that the great man had him interrogated because, the Doctor assumed, "he was concerned that I was in an ideal position to assassinate him."

"I think he was more threatened by the fact that you were intimate with his weaknesses," I pointed out.

"Well, certainly his physical infirmities," he admitted.

"Which are also a man's weaknesses," I reminded him.

"The paranoia, the secrets, the power he held. . . ." The doctor shook his head. "He must have been a difficult man to work for." I smiled at his understated tact.

"He once tried to have me killed," I said.

"Really? What did you do, Elim?"

"I survived." The Doctor gave me a confused look.

"Survived . . . what?" he asked.

"Working for my father," I replied. The Doctor stopped and just looked at me. His former fear of my eyes was long gone.

"A father who would murder his own son?" The idea horrified him. We were in the Barvonok Sector, where the tall structures of business and finance once dominated. "Oh, my dear Elim," he said, this time with an empathy that stripped me of any illusions I had about Enabran Tain as a father. Surrounded by the piles of debris, oppressed by the low leaden sky, I finally began to surrender to the loneliness and loss that has preyed upon my dreams ever since I can remember. Even nothing is better than the ideas that have brought us here.

"Perhaps there's a way I can help your project, Doctor." As much as I tried to deny it, there was another "assignment" for me. Tain would have been amused by the irony.

3

Entry:

My life has taken on a rhythm and a routine I would never have anticipated when I was exiled to Terok Nor. Once I made the decision to pursue my new profession vigorously, and had set myself up with the proper tools, I was working all day and well into the night. Being the only tailor on the station meant there was never a shortage of garments to be mended and altered. As I became more proficient I found that unless I challenged myself, I would soon suffocate in the monotony of repeating the same basic actions. Again I went to Quark with a proposal: I would gladly make a new outfit for him, if he'd be willing to spread the word that I was also a designer of clothing. He countered my offer with the suggestion that if I would also design and build outfits for his waiters, he would make sure that any visitors to the station in need of clothing would be directed my way. I explained that such a project would leave me with little or no time to deal with the backlog of repair work I had. We compromised, and I agreed to create outfits for him and his brother Rom. (I later discovered from Rom that Quark had charged him for the outfit. When I expressed outrage, Rom assured me the price he had paid was reasonable.) Quark also got me to agree that for every client who came to my shop on his recommendation I would pay him a percentage of the agreed price. He was true to his word, and with his help I began to build a clientele for my designs.

Entry:

One day a human woman came into the shop. She was in a state. It turned out that she was a member of the Federation's negotiation team that was working out the details of the Terok Nor transfer of power from the Cardassians to joint Bajoran/Federation administration. The garment carrier containing her uniforms had been lost or stolen in transit, and the first negotiating session was to begin the next day. Here was an opportunity. Not only was I deeply curious about these negotiations for my own personal reasons, but this might be useful information I could pass on to interested parties at home.

I calmed her down with some tea and the assurance that she had nothing to worry about. We specified the type of uniform, discussed various details, and when she was ready I took her measurements. She, of course—in that endearingly literal-minded way humans have of assessing others—assumed that a tailor was always a tailor and would never be anything else. Consequently, she revealed more to me than just her bodily measurements. In fact, she was more protective and shy about her body than she was about vital state information. Why the Federation doesn't train their people better I'll never know. I suppose it's the arrogance of believing that no one is smart enough to outsmart you. In any case, this was an opportunity. Silence, exile, and cunning.

Entry:

"I'll deliver the information," the nameless contact said after I had made my report.

"I trust you'll find it useful. . . ." He cut me off before I could finish. I rescrambled the signal, to make doubly sure the transmission wasn't picked up. I expected that Entek would use a subordinate to receive my offering. And I expected no promises or "news from home" in return. They must have somebody from the Order on the station monitoring the meetings, but obviously my information was more interesting than what they were gleaning. I wondered if they would try to make contact with me. In the meantime, however, I was determined to press my unique advantage and keep them interested.

I was also determined not to overvalue the information and congratulate myself prematurely. I had to make sure that *I* wasn't the one being used. The woman is a charming and clever conversationalist, and she's providing something I have deeply missed since being exiled to this floating arachnid. She told me that she has never met anyone who listens as attentively as I do. I would dismiss this as gross flattery, except that she responds to my silences as if they were words; I sometimes feel that she's able to read my mind. All the more reason to be careful. She's either a skilled operative who has enough information about me to manipulate an ingenious strategem . . . or a lonely woman who needs to talk to someone who will listen. And if it's the latter, why would such an attractive person, even for a human, not already have a mate or a confidante?

Careful, Elim. You know perfectly well that the surest way to your heart is through conversation.

Entry:

Over the last several days we've been meeting every day, ostensibly to furnish her with a new wardrobe. Quark's going to be very pleased with his commission. We pretend that the time spent together is necessary. I know why *I'm* pretending, but as for her. . . . At one point yesterday I nearly made a childish mistake. Her personality sketches of the Cardassian negotiators (most of whom I know) are wonderful, but when she mentioned that one in particular was most definitely making sexual advances I blurted out, "It's probably Gul Dukat." She was surprised by my immediate response. How did I know? I told her that his behavior in these matters was notorious. And indeed it was. The imperious manner in which he exercised sexual sway over the Bajoran women laborers was disgusting. When she asked why I seemed so disapproving, I controlled my response and explained that on Cardassia we value the integrity of the family, and that married men were held to certain standards. Of course I was aware of the irony of my current circumstances as I explained Cardassian sexual morality. She accepted my explanation and became thoughtful, almost sad. At that point I had to bring our session to an end.

After she had left, I realized that it was becoming increasingly difficult to maintain my professional silence. I, too, was filled with a sadness . . . and an inexplicable desire to share feelings that had lain dormant since my banishment. Her openness invited my exploitation, but it also tempted me to reveal the pain and the bitterness of my current circumstances.

Entry:

"All I can tell you is that the authorities are satisfied with your intelligence," the officious young contact informed me. I had to admire how his mask revealed nothing about my present status, or whether or not I would be allowed to participate in the almost certain Cardassian withdrawal from Terok Nor.

"I appreciate your help, but if you could pass on a message to Pythas. . . ." Once again I was rudely disconnected. I slammed my hand against the console in frustration. How dare he treat me like a common drone! This child. I poured myself a glass of *kanar*. I could not allow the tenuous truce I had arranged with the circumstances to be compromised. It was too easy for me to slip back into despair. I then made a decision. I had to have an answer to my question, and it meant using a resource I'd been saving. I punched a long code into the computer. I waited. When I read the response, it was just as I had suspected: the personal codes I had created and rarely used when I was active were still in place. I rescrambled and punched in another code. I waited again, and the response told me there was no danger of being intercepted. Then I punched in the final code. I waited, praying that Pythas would be accessible. A face appeared; but it was Corbin Entek.

"Garak!" Why was Entek in Pythas' office? At his desk?

"Where's Pythas?" I asked, my heart sinking.

"How did you . . . ?" We were cut off in the middle of his question. His stunned reaction revealed that contact with me was the last thing he expected. I immediately scrambled the transmission to mask my code, but they had other ways of resealing their integrity. Where's Pythas? I repeated to myself. Had Entek replaced him as head of the Order? Had my last possible link been broken? I had to focus my breathing and reestablish my tenuous truce with the circumstances . . . and with the despair that hovered like the Corillion Nebula.

Entry:

In the middle of today's fitting my client broke down. It was an extraordinary moment. She confessed that she had just received word that her father had died. As her grief spilled out she also revealed that she had separated from her husband just before the negotiations began. It seems that he was a philanderer who had betrayed her trust from the beginning, and that she had tried for years to deny the truth of their relationship. I was nonplussed. This outpouring of emotion . . . I offered her a glass of *kanar,* and to my surprise she accepted it . . . and several others. Out of courtesy, of course, I joined her.

I don't do well with the kind of emotional exchanges humans seem to engage in regularly, and I have little sympathy for those who confuse the responsibilities of family with their duty to the state; but I confess that I am deeply moved by this woman's plight. Here is a high-ranking officer in the Federation hierarchy—a politically astute woman able to converse with depth and intelligence on any subject—revealing intimate details of her life to me, her "tailor." At one point she looked at me and asked me to hold her. I did. As I tentatively put my arms around her, I was so afraid of her need that I tried to keep her body at a distance. She would have none of it. She collapsed against me, and the sobs that convulsed and rolled through her body found correspondence in mine. I bit my tongue until I could taste blood in the effort not to surrender. Gratefully, the door to the Promenade was closed.

Eventually she regained her composure. She was embarrassed by her behavior and apologized. I assured her that apologies weren't necessary. I suggested that we finish our business for the day and pick up again tomorrow. She agreed and left. I didn't report this meeting to my contact. I just stood in the shop as mute and frozen as one of my display dummies. The one dominating thought was that I looked forward to our next appointment. The near empty bottle of *kanar* was sitting on the desk and I decided to finish it. Oh yes, I sighed, getting involved with a subject of investigation. Violation of a cardinal rule. I laughed. Enabran would be very disappointed with me. If he thought I was sentimental before. . . . I emptied the bottle, but I still couldn't get this woman out of my thoughts.

Entry:

She didn't keep our appointment today. Instead, two Federation investigators, one human and one Vulcan, came to the shop and asked me questions about her. The short human, with a face like a hungry vole, was openly suspicious and at times insulting, while the Vulcan conducted himself with a formality I'm sure must have been encoded in the rules regulating Federation investigative procedures. I quickly realized from their clumsy methods that they knew nothing. Their unskilled questions told me that they were investigating a newly discovered and serious breach of security surrounding the negotiations. Because of my contact with her, I was a suspected source of this breach. When they asked why we met so often and what we discussed, I assured them that as a plain and simple tailor our conversation dealt with the business at hand and nothing else. When I suggested that their uniforms looked a little worse for wear, they sniffed at the suggestion, dismissed me as someone obviously lacking taste, and left the shop. They don't have a clue. Where do these people learn their craft? A holosuite program?

However, I was concerned about her. The investigators were probably checking on all members of the Federation's negotiating team—but I wondered if the stress she'd been experiencing had betrayed her. I waited until afternoon, and when she still didn't appear I closed the shop and went to Quark's to see what I could discover for myself.

Unless I have business I rarely go to Quark's; I have little tolerance for noise and stupidity. So when he saw me he assumed that I had another proposition, and I observed him shift into his engage mode. After all, he was making a tidy sum from the shop. I rejected his offer of *kanar* and asked for red-leaf tea instead. This put him on the alert; he didn't know what I wanted, and his Ferengi suspicions were aroused. As I weighed how best to enter his information bank, the same two Federation investigators entered the bar and asked to speak with Quark. I pretended I had never seen them before, and I'm sure that they thought I was just another Cardassian. To humans we all look the same.

They moved out of earshot with Quark, but I could see that he was initially defensive with them. The suspicions I had aroused in him were now directed at the investigators. I'm sure he assumed that one of his "enterprises" had violated Federation law. But he calmed down, and after a short while the investigators left and Quark returned to where I was sitting at the bar. I didn't have to say a word; he was eager to share the experience.

"One of the Federation negotiators is a spy!" His eyes were bulging with drama.

"Really?"

"Yes. I'd heard something about this two days ago from a . . . a source," he whispered as he looked around. "It seems that the Federation negotiating position is being leaked to the Cardassians, and everything is in an uproar." Quark's eyes had a glitter that reflected the concern shared by all the inhabitants of the station. These negotiations would determine their future. My future.

"I'm shocked. Any idea who it is?" I asked. Quark leaned over the counter in that melodramatic and confiding manner of his.

"My . . . source says they have a suspect, but before they make a move they want to uncover the suspect's contact as well."

"Contact . . . you mean . . . ?" I gave him my best puzzled expression.

"Whoever's taking the information and passing it on," he explained as if I were a child.

"And quite right they are," I replied. Quark leered at me. I thought he was going to tout me on one of his more salacious holosuite programs.

"What have *you* heard?" He brought his face even closer to mine. Any interaction with Quark was always a *quid pro quo* exchange.

"In my shop?" I finished my tea. "My dear Quark, all I hear is the sound of footfalls that drift in from the Promenade." I smiled and nodded, and made my way to the door.

"Very poetic!" he yelled after me. I'm afraid Quark was as disappointed with my response as I was disturbed by his information.

Entry:

For the second night in a row I didn't sleep. On my way to the shop that morning I felt a tension in the atmosphere. Was it just me, or was the Promenade in a remarkably unsettled—even agitated—state? It was certainly swarming with people and creatures of all sorts. At the Replimat I debated whether or not to stop for what passed there as food. However, my favorite table—ideally placed directly opposite the airlock doors that lead to the docking ring—was empty, and I decided to indulge myself and order an Idanian spice pudding. I enjoyed sitting there, watching the comings and goings of every traveler to and from the station. It's very relaxing . . . and sometimes very rewarding, when people appear whose whereabouts are valuable information.

I had no sooner settled into my seat with my pudding when I heard the sounds of a commotion coming from the middle of the Promenade. It was still crowded, and I couldn't tell what was creating the disturbance. I took a bite of pudding and turned back to the source of the noise—and there she was. The pudding turned to chalk. The crowd had momentarily separated her from her escort, the two investigators and Constable Odo, and she stood there, looking at me with an expression that froze my blood. Not angry, not reproachful. . . . not even disappointed. An even expression, relaxed, clouded by that tinge of sadness I had first noticed when we discussed Gul Dukat and the expected morality of Cardassian men. My first thought was that she must be a formidable negotiator. My second was that she was about to expose her "contact." But she just continued to look at me with her intelligent, gray eyes as if my skin were transparent and she could see all the way down to the bottom of my soul.

The investigators caught up with her, and she turned away from me as Odo led them through the airlock. I realized that I had stopped breathing.

I left my pudding, stopped at Quark's to buy a bottle of *kanar,* and retired to my quarters. It took half of the bottle before I began to breathe again; and only when it was empty did I finally ask myself the question: Why hadn't she betrayed me as I had betrayed her?

4

A deep sadness I had not felt in a long time reemerged as I walked through the Coranum Sector to my meeting with Madred and the group he referred to as the Directorate. Not one of the old, stately buildings had been spared by Dominion revenge. Perhaps there was a cruel justice at work here, Doctor, since these were the families that had initially agreed to the alliance with the Dominion. But if anything marked the end of Cardassia as we remember it and symbolized the stripped and naked state of our civilization, it was the devastation of this first settlement, the "birthplace" of the Union.

The sadness was most keenly felt when I passed the Coranum Grounds. Every bit of vegetation had been engulfed by the firestorm, and any evidence of that soft and protected place of assignation had been reduced to ashes. I quickened my pace.

As I stood in front of the building debris I tried to locate the entrance to the basement Madred had described. Judging from the enormous amount of rubble that had already been cleared, this had been an impressive home. Finally, I made out a path that led to the rear of what would have been the ground floor, and followed it to a temporary structure that functioned as both an entrance and a cover for the staircase. The darkness swallowed me as I carefully made my way down the stairs and into a makeshift anteroom. At that moment a door opened and Madred appeared.

"Ah, good. I was concerned that you weren't coming," he said with some irritation. I realized that I had gotten lost in my thoughts as I'd walked through the sector. In a sense, Doctor, my new world has become timeless, especially in the absence of all my old routines and landmarks.

"I wanted to make sure no one was following me," I lied. At our previous meeting, when I'd suggested that I might be able to provide some helpful intelligence about the Reunion Project, Madred warned me to maintain absolute secrecy about the meeting and its whereabouts.

"Did you notice anyone?" he asked with concern.

"No," I replied. Actually I could have been followed by an army and I wouldn't have noticed. I'm afraid I've become careless as well as timeless, Doctor. Madred led me down a short corridor that had formerly been much longer but truncated now to adjust to the new living circumstances.

"Is this your home?" I asked as I followed him.

"What's left of it," he replied. A door opened, and we entered a large room badly lit by several emergency lamps. The city had to live with intermittent blackouts as the power grid was being realigned. As my eyes adjusted, I was able to discern the shapes of seven people arranged around a table in the center of the room. Most of them looked familiar, and I wasn't surprised to see them here. One person, however, did surprise me. Two people I didn't know. My "schoolmate" wasn't here.

"This is Elim Garak. Some of you may know him," Madred said as introduction. He offered me a seat and took his place to my right.

"Elim Garak," the person to my left repeated with amused wonder. "How are your tailoring skills these days?" he asked. It was Gul Hadar, who had been one of Dukat's aides on Terok Nor; a man of weak character who easily participated in the worst excesses of the occupation.

"Under the present circumstances, Hadar, they come in quite handy," I replied. He nodded, studying me in his diffident manner. He also came from one of the old families.

"I wonder if that's why Madred invited you here." He turned to the others. "Because Skrain Dukat claimed Garak was a dangerous traitor who was responsible for the deaths of his father and Barkan Lokar. Are we in need of a tailor?"

"Skrain Dukat was the traitor," said the voice across from me. It was Gul Evek, a blunt, unsmiling soldier who I'd thought had been killed pursuing the Maquis in the Badlands. "I think we can safely say that anyone who was his enemy has a right to be here. Especially anyone who fought with Damar." He looked at me with his stern face, and I acknowledged his support. I heard Hadar sigh, and understood that the "Directorate" was far from unified.

"The issue is not Dukat. It's the future of the Union!" the man next to Evek maintained. This was Legate Parn. He challenged the group with a look that made me believe that he was the leader in this room. Parn had administered the Cardassian colonies in the demilitarized zone after the treaty with the Federation, a treaty he and Evek had believed was the beginning of the end when Cardassia signed it. They were outspoken in their view that accommodation with the Federation had fatally compromised our resolve.

"The dead are dead. Those of us left—who believe in the ideals that have guided our race for millennia—are faced with the threat of utter annihilation by the very disease that has brought us to this sad place. Federation ideas will finish the work the Dominion began." Again he challenged each of us. I followed his look. On the other side of Madred was Nal Dejar, a sharp-faced, saturnine woman who had been a member of my last cell at the Order. She once came to Deep Space 9 on an assignment with two scientists, and refused to make any contact with me. Judging from her averted look, she was still refusing. Next to her was a man with a severely disfigured face that was still recovering from what appeared to be burns. One eye was completely covered, and I was careful not to be rude in my inspection. He and an attractive woman sitting on the other side of Evek were the two people who weren't familiar to me.

The surprise guest, Korbath Mondrig, sat between this woman and Hadar. Considering that Madred believed he was nothing more than a demagogue stirring up the service class with old resentments and divisive rhetoric, I wondered how this group planned to use Mondrig.

"Let us be clear about what unites us," Parn warned. "We have our differences. We've even had our troubles in the past," he said, looking directly at me. "But they can't be allowed to deter us from our main purpose."

"Which is?" I asked, returning his look.

"To crush any attempt by any group to espouse Federation ideals as we rebuild our society," he answered.

"Rebuild it to where it was before we doomed ourselves with that treaty," Evek added.

"And I believe that's why you've joined us today, Garak," Parn said, never taking his eyes off me.

"If I may," the woman next to Evek spoke up. I was grateful for her interruption; I needed more time to orient myself. She signaled to Madred for recognition; he appeared to be the moderator.

"Of course, Gul Ocett," he replied. So this was Malyn Ocett, I realized; the only resistance leader who had survived when the cells were betrayed by Gul

Revok. Her courage and resourceful tactics had not only inspired her followers, but her call to the military after the Lakarian City massacre was largely responsible for our soldiers turning against the Dominion at the crucial moment.

"I share Legate Parn's concern that the Federation wants to 'absorb us,'" she said. "All of us here know their strategy has never been a military one; it's political. At this point, we're weakened, vulnerable. The Federation recognizes that the current dislocation is the moment to inject us with their democratic ideas, because there are people like Natima Lang and Alon Ghemor who would gladly carry them to the rest of us." Natima Lang, Quark's old paramour, was obviously back on Cardassia along with every other political opportunist. "We're deeply wounded now, and if we're not careful we could end up with a political system that would not only place us firmly within Federation hegemony, but would destroy our identity."

Gul Ocett was persuasive in her quiet and reasoned strength. Indeed, the irony, Doctor, is that she was espousing the very argument I had made to you any number of times. Even now there was a part of me that accepted the logic of her argument, especially when coming from someone who was neither a fool nor an opportunist. Gul Madred saw his opening.

"I think this is the moment to let Korbath Mondrig speak and explain what we have in mind as a strategy." Madred nodded to Mondrig, a physically small man who had been listening very carefully.

"Thank you," Mondrig said with a smile his closely set eyes didn't share. "Unless, of course, others wish to express their views," he graciously offered. The only people who hadn't spoken were Nal Dejar and the disfigured man. Because of her training and naturally closed face, Dejar was hard to read. Not a flicker of recognition registered when she saw me. And the man's face was so damaged and his body so still, he had almost no presence. Both of them remained silent.

Mondrig nodded. "It is an honor to be among people I consider heroes of the Empire," he said.

"What little is left of it," Evek muttered. Hadar sighed again, and Evek gave him a hard look but held his tongue.

"Yes, unfortunately, as Gul Ocett has said, we have been deeply wounded." Mondrig's tone was deferential, almost obsequious, but there was a mannered quality I didn't trust. At that moment he looked right at me. "And I must confess that the presence of this gentleman surprises me as well. Forgive me," he nodded in my direction, "but in our Paldar Sector he is associated with Ghemor and Parmak. If I'm not mistaken, you even held a rally for their Unity Project at your . . . memorial?" It was phrased as a question, but the intent was clear. The attention of the others now shifted to me.

"Reunion Project," I corrected.

"Yes, of course," he accepted the correction.

"How chummy," Hadar commented.

"Yes, I hosted the rally," I admitted.

"Why?" Hadar asked.

"I admire Dr. Parmak. I'd been working with him on a med unit, and when he asked if he could use my home for a rally, I agreed."

"Why?" Hadar repeated with the satisfied look of a clever interrogator.

"Because I wanted to hear his point of view," I replied.

"You've lived on a Federation outpost for how many years?" Hadar asked pointedly.

"I also went to school with Alon Ghemor, and I've always found him to be an honorable man."

"A family of traitors!" Hadar concluded, looking at the others as if he'd made some damaging point about my character. I simply smiled at him, genuinely amused by his amateur attempts to discredit me. I was surprised by my responses. I was here to play the role of double agent, and I found that as the meeting went on I didn't have the energy for the requisite guile and misdirection.

"What are you telling us, Garak?" Parn challenged. I smiled at him. It was so transparent, what they were doing. So predictable. Each sector was planning to choose a leader. A council would then be formed from the "elected" leaders of each sector, which would lead the city and most likely a reorganized union. Public sentiment for this democratic process was too strong to oppose, especially when there was no longer an army to throw against the heretics. The Directorate wouldn't oppose the vote, but they would get around it by backing their candidate in each election, thus creating a council that would then become an instrument of their will.

"What are you telling us?" Parn repeated the challenge.

And then a strange sensation went through me, Doctor. I looked at the faces of these people. Here we are, I thought, sitting in the basement of a ruined civilization and conducting business as if nothing significant had changed. The enemies were still the same, somewhere "out there," plotting how to "destroy our character" and colonize us with their political system. And we were down in the basement with our own plots and shifting alliances, tenaciously holding on to the very ideas that had brought us here. But what ideas, Doctor? There's nothing left. Only fantasies of power. These faces with their masks. With the ironic exception of the disfigured face, the masks hadn't changed. They reflected the usual range of hidden agendas, each competing for dominance and ascendancy with an energy commensurate to the amount of fear and self-loathing that fueled and motivated that person. I started to laugh.

"Does my question amuse you, Garak?" Parn asked, his mask revealing the anger and the lust for power that fueled *his* agenda. He didn't even try to disguise his impatience with me. The ideology, the patchwork of old ideas and mythology was in place; the boundaries that determined what was sacred and received "truth" and what was heresy were set: all that remained was for him to arrange the power structure and assign each person his or her role in it. He was the deal maker, the broker—and he wanted to get on with the business of satisfying his lust.

I looked around the table, from face to face, mask to mask. Evek and Ocett were honorable soldiers who had dedicated themselves to the old ideals of Cardassian purity and superiority. But the failure of the system that had contained these ideals, and the ensuing devastation, had left them deeply troubled and confused. What was their responsibility in the breakdown? Who was this man Parn hastily reassembling these ideals into a system they both knew could never be the same? But their education, their conditioning, their having been bred to a society that answered all problems with a received set of answers enabled them to question only so far. Parn had skillfully used limits set long ago; beyond them was the demonized void dominated by Federation ideas waiting for the right moment to attack.

Unlike Evek and Ocett, Mondrig was a little man without a center, Parn's propagandist and puppet, whose job was to stand in front of the people with a mask that would mirror our beliefs, our prejudices, our hopes, and our fears. He was the consummate politician who would deliver the message in a way that would never threaten or challenge us. He desperately aspired to belong to this group, the repository of Cardassian power, and the group only wanted to use him for the demagoguery that would further entrench its power.

Hadar was a degenerate. His mask, like the features of his face, was without the definition of a life that was lived and thought and felt. He accepted his privilege without question or gratitude to those forebears who had passionately struggled for their beliefs. He believed in nothing but his appetites. The ultimate parasite.

Madred had the same forebears, but his mask was sharper than Hadar's because he still had the passion of his beliefs: he desired to maintain the old ways at all costs because anything else was inconceivable. He would even associate himself with Mondrig, a man he'd said he wouldn't let "clean his shoes," if it meant the old order could be restored. There was fear in his mask: the fear of change.

Nal Dejar's mask was closer to home; she reflected my own religious dedication to the "secrets of the state." We lived in the shadows, and our masks played with light and darkness, like the *regnar*'s skin. We passed through life like Tain's "night people," with no allegiances except to the secrets. And the more successful we were, the slighter and more invisible we became, until we easily occupied space the way a shadow falls across light.

And the disfigured mask, the most honest one in the room. . . . The one good eye, peering out at me from an interior prison of pain and bitter disillusionment, gave me permission to study his mask—and we made contact.

It *was* him, Doctor. It was Pythas.

"My friend," I whispered. I think only Madred and Nal Dejar heard me.

"Are you willing to help us?" Parn asked harshly, his attention still focused on my loyalty to his cause. I remembered my conversation with Tolan about the price of "status." "Or are you sympathetic with these people?"

"Yes," I replied, taking my eyes away from Pythas. "I am indeed." I rose from my chair. "I shouldn't be here. This is not my place. I apologize for the intrusion." I looked again at Pythas. I didn't know what to say to him. But even with his one good eye he could still communicate with depth and meaning. Not here, he told me. Not now. Madred also rose.

"Thank you, Gul Madred, but I can find my way out." I bowed to the company, and turned my back on them.

5

Entry:

Ever since the negotiations came to a conclusion, and with the transfer of Terok Nor to the Federation now imminent, I'd waited for some kind of communication concerning my status. Nothing but silence. Still, I was certain that my exile would end with the Occupation, and that soon we would all be on our way back to Cardassia Prime. This morning I decided to go about my routine even though I had no real work to speak of. After all, if the garrison and all Cardassian civilians are scheduled to depart today, why would any of them leave garments with me? However, I still had my own clothing designs to wrestle with.

When I came out onto the Promenade, I was stunned. It was like a holiday. The Bajoran population had obviously been celebrating all night. Groups of them were singing, dancing, holding each other up as they staggered and howled their delight. Debris was everywhere, as they tore down and scattered the remnants of the makeshift shelters they had lived in for so many years. I could hear the din from Quark's bar, which evidently was doing a booming business. I ducked back into the shop as several inebriated celebrants came careening my way. When they had passed, I stepped out to where I could see more clearly down the Promenade. There wasn't a Cardassian in sight. The only officials were Bajoran military and Federation people. The withdrawal had taken place during the night, and Terok Nor was now Deep Space 9.

I heard someone yell, "The tailor's still here." I hurried into my shop and locked the doors behind me. I stood in the darkness, trembling. Not a word. Nothing! They'd left me here. I wanted to contact someone. To protest. But ever since I had filed my last report about the negotiations, they had cut me off. I felt impotent. Ashamed. Elim Garak, a Cardassian tailor on a Federation outpost, cowering from drunken Bajorans.

There had to be a limit. My crime was a serious miscalculation, no doubt; I had ignored the warning, disobeyed my superior, and given in to the passion of my life. But I had dedicated myself to the state! This couldn't possibly be unpardonable . . . not when idiots and butchers are promoted and prosper every—

The door chime rang. I froze. I wondered about my status. Would I be allowed to remain in the shop and work? Did I want to? Did I have a choice? The chime rang again.

"Yes?" My attempt to sound normal was pathetic.

"Are my c-clothes ready?" It was Rom. I had forgotten that I was still working on the suit of clothes he had "bought" from his brother.

"Just a moment." I turned on the lights and took a moment to compose myself before I let him in.

Rom was apologetic. "I thought you were open, otherwise. . . ."

"Not to worry, of course I am," I brusquely assured him, as I fetched his tunic and trousers. "And I think you'll find everything fits quite well." I held the curtain to the changing room open for him, and he took the clothes and entered. I pulled the curtain closed and checked behind the counter to see if there was anything left in the *kanar* bottle. There wasn't even a bottle.

"How, uh, did you know I'd still be here, Rom?" A quaver undermined the attempted nonchalance.

"My brother said you would be, but I wasn't sure, and when I saw that the Cardassians had left during the night. . . ."

I could tell from his tone that he wondered why I hadn't left but was too shy to ask. Strange people, these Ferengi. Rom had a sensitivity, almost a delicacy that was totally lacking in his brother. Was there such a thing as a typical Ferengi? Most people judged him to be simple, as if simplicity was somehow a substandard quality. He came out of the changing room wearing his new garments. I had certainly dressed him like a Ferengi, and I could see that he was pleased.

"Tell me, Rom. Are they all gone? The Cardassians?" I stopped trying to disguise my concern. Rom looked at me with that fearful directness of his and nodded.

"Y-yes. Late last night. Gul Dukat passed the station over to the Federation and a Commander . . . Sisko and . . . they left." He still wanted to ask why I had stayed.

"Well, Rom, the trousers and tunic fit quite well, don't you think?" I pulled the tunic down at the back. "Don't wear it so far up on the neck; it ruins the line. And I'd be grateful if you'd tell any interested parties that indeed I'm still here and very much open for business."

"Oh, yes . . . yes! And I like. . . ." Rom made a broad, awkward gesture toward his new ensemble. I thanked him, and we walked out onto the Promenade, as if it were just another business day. We said goodbye, and I watched him march proudly through the ragged celebrants. I had a fondness for him. It was an odd relief, especially at this moment, to converse with someone who literally meant everything he said. My attention was drawn to a group of drunken Bajorans across the way who had interrupted their celebration to stare at me with hostile disbelief. They had the same question as Rom. I smiled graciously and went back into the shop.

I sat in the shop and tried to busy myself with a design

that had been eluding me. It was almost as if the suit was designing me, and I thought that somehow this was appropriate at this stage of my life. I had my back to the door, but I could hear a crowd gathering outside. Their sounds were low but threatening, and I knew that my presence was the focal point. Would rule of law prevail now that the Occupation was at an end and I was the only Cardassian left on the station?

Individual voices could be heard yelling from the crowd and urging that action be taken. I could sense the growing anger as their numbers increased. And they weren't complaining about their pants. The muscles of my neck and shoulders were tense as I sat hunched over the work table. I erased another design and started again, chasing the design that in turn was chasing me.

Someone broke away from the crowd and stormed into the shop. I braced myself, but I didn't turn to face her: a woman screaming at me in a peculiar Bajoran dialect that was totally incomprehensible. I continued to work, focused on a design that was now oddly coming to life. I could feel the heat of her rage, and believed that there was no way to confront it without making the situation worse. But more people had entered the shop, and suddenly I was grabbed from behind with great force and pulled to my feet. I stumbled against the table, quickly regained my balance, and turned to confront a Bajoran man who immediately realized that he needed the rest of the crowd to follow through with his intent. The others stood behind him and the moment was suspended. No one spoke, no one moved. We just looked at each other. Their hatred was a unified field that blurred all individual distinction. I realized in that moment the gravitational field of the station had been adjusted to a heavier setting, and the wave of hatred flowing from these people made it even more oppressive. I felt as if I were carrying twice my weight. I fully expected to be torn to pieces.

"That's enough!" a harsh voice commanded. The constable of the station, the shapeshifter Odo, was standing at the top of the outside steps. With his customary dignity he made his way through the crowd, which was now half in and half out of the shop.

"Clear this space," he told them. "Go on! Get about your business." Two of his Bajoran officers were directing people back onto the Promenade. Odo grabbed my attacker unceremoniously by his shabby tunic and turned him over to one of the officers.

"Put him in the holding cell," he instructed. As the man was escorted off, several parting curses and threats were hurled from the Promenade. "Are you harmed?" Odo asked me in his formal manner.

"No, not at all. Thank you for your concern . . . and your intervention," I replied. He stood for a moment, studying me, trying to divine why I had not been allowed to join the withdrawal. Unlike the others who assumed that because I was a Cardassian I had a choice, Odo knew that I'd been abandoned.

"Was there any damage or theft?" he asked.

"No," I answered. I knew little about Constable Odo, but I was confident that he would never ask me questions that went beyond his function as security chief. He kept his distance and carried himself like someone who understood exile.

"I will make sure that nothing like this happens again." Odo gave one last look around the shop, wondering, I'm certain, who was going to do business with a Cardassian tailor. He left with the same lack of ceremony with which he'd entered.

The room was suddenly empty. I studied my reflection in the full-length mirror. Changes were in order for my new life. For one thing, I thought, I'm too heavy for this gravitational field. I patted my stomach: silence, exile, cunning . . . and less spice pudding.

6

The Directorate wasted no time: a "Restoration Cadre" was established in each sector. Ostensibly its purpose was to maintain order while Cardassia recovered enough "strength of will" to restore its former governing structures. The Directorate presented itself as the legitimate agent of this restoration, and in each sector the Cadre supported the Directorate's choice of leader. In the Paldar Sector they had chosen Korbath Mondrig.

The reality, Doctor, is that the Cadre functions to intimidate the people of each sector into accepting this restoration and condemn the Reunion Project as a subtle Federation corruption. But instead of submitting to the Cadre's threat of violence, many people throughout the city—and indeed the planet—are resisting and organizing along the lines of the Project. For these people, a restoration means returning to the conditions that created the rubble and dust that now surround and choke us.

For the first time in our modern history, Doctor, we are faced with a choice between two distinct political and social philosophies. The crucial question is *how* we are going to make this choice. Is a consensus achieved by peaceful means? Or do we now go to war with each other?

I had anticipated the current stalemate. I had even anticipated what happened last night, when I was awakened from my usual fitful sleep by the sounds of falling debris. For a moment I thought we were still under Dominion attack. I jumped up and looked outside. Several men dressed in the makeshift Cadre uniform and led by someone I recognized as one of Mondrig's aides were pushing over the roughhewn memorials. I set off a loud alarm I had created for just this kind of event. After the rally for Alon Ghemor, the grounds had become a magnet for the Reunion. In an amazingly short period of time scores of my neighbors, including Parmak and Ghemor, had appeared. The outnumbered marauders, expecting a violent confrontation, prepared for battle. We had agreed beforehand, however, that violent resistance was pointless; all that would happen would be a further escalation of violence until one side dominated the other and we would be left with less than the nothing we now had.

It was an eerie scene, Doctor: mute witnesses, men and women, surrounding a phalanx of sweating belligerents prepared to fight to the death. Cardassian against Cardassian—a unique and disturbing sight. Some of the marauders were ex-soldiers following new masters, some were no more than orphaned children. Some probably were in the service of the restoration ideal of returning Cardassia to its former imperial glory. Most were just hungry and desperate. It was a dangerous tactic on our part, Doctor, and as the tense and silent standoff continued I could see certain faces on both sides giving in to the strain. It was only a matter of moments before something happened.

Suddenly one of the younger marauders broke ranks and attacked a man across from him. Several of the witnesses immediately reacted to defend the fallen man.

"Hold!" Ghemor commanded. They did. No one retaliated and the young marauder stood over the man with a confused look. He had hoped, I'm sure, that his action would have been absorbed by an ensuing battle; but now, being the focus of every eye, he had no choice but to accept sole responsibility for his act. When he received neither guidance nor approval from his superior, he found the attention unbearable and ran off. The standoff continued, but now the marauders became restless. The watchful stillness of the witnesses began to unnerve them. If they weren't going to fight . . . ?

"This is shit," an older soldier muttered in disgust. He looked around at his companions and at Mondrig's aide in contempt. "Shit!" he repeated with greater force. His hard face and warrior poise told me that he held no fear of battle. "Shall I fight women?" he asked the aide. To answer his own question he spat and walked off into the night. His uneven gait and low center of gravity reminded me of Calyx.

Mondrig's aide attempted to salvage the situation, and ordered the marauders to continue the destruction of the memorials, but the older men took the lead of the grizzled veteran and dispersed. The younger inexperienced men realized that they were no match against the organization of the witnesses. And it was this discipline that also reminded me of Calyx. Ghemor had not only learned how to "hold his place" in the Bamarren Pit, he was able to teach others as well.

After the remainder of the Restoration Cadre had made their careful retreat, the witnesses, without any perceivable instruction to do so, began to rebuild the toppled piles. When someone voiced the worry that he wasn't sure how the formation had looked before the damage, I assured him that it didn't matter. Dawn was breaking when we completed our repair work, and people began returning to their homes. Parmak, Ghemor, and I stood silently among the formations, inspecting the results of our work in the first light.

"I mean no disrespect, Elim," the Doctor said, "but the memorial looks even better." I nodded in agreement.

"Please, Doctor," I replied. " 'Restoration' is fine for artifacts and museum pieces. When it comes to building a new community, I think what we did tonight is more to the point."

"And we did it without murdering each other," Ghemor added.

"How un-Cardassian of us," I observed. But we knew this was only one skirmish that had been avoided. Although it had bolstered our spirits for the moment, we could only hope that it was an indication of the battle fatigue of our people, and not an aberration.

Shortly after the incident, Parmak came to Tolan's shed and informed me that Gul Madred had requested a meeting between the Directorate and the leaders of the Reunion Project. He asked if I would join them, and I demurred.

"Given the circumstances of my last meeting with them," I explained, "I think it would be best if you and Alon heard what they have to say." Parmak paused, turning a thought over in his mind.

"You know what they're going to say, don't you?" he asked.

"I do," I replied. "And so do you." Parmak paused again, the thought deepening as it turned.

"Certainly they'll offer us some kind of compromise," he began.

"A compromise that will prove fatal to your ideals, Doctor. And you know that, too," I said with certainty. "These people are holding on desperately to an idea of power that they refuse to admit no longer exists. They will offer you and Alon important places in *their* structure . . . but there will be no compromise."

"Only choice," he nodded. "Which is all there can be at this point."

"When you meet with them," I suggested, "just listen. Try to ascertain if they're willing to risk a civil war. They're desperate, but not all of them have been made stupid with a desire for power; some of them know how depleted we are. My guess is that the incident here the other night has them worried."

"Yes, I agree," the Doctor nodded. "I'd better go over our strategy with Alon. Thank you, Elim."

"If there's a man with a disfigured face at the meeting, try to make contact with him. Don't be put off by his remoteness."

"Who is he?" the Doctor asked.

"An old schoolmate of mine . . . and Alon's," I replied. "He's a good man."

"What's he doing with them?"

"I don't know, Doctor. That's one of the things I want to find out."

"And once I've made contact . . . ?"

"If it's possible, tell him I need to see him."

"I'll do my best, Elim." The Doctor hesitated.

"What is it?" I asked.

"A civil war would destroy us," he said.

"Indeed." I could see that he was feeling the weight of his mission.

"You know, Elim, I'm neither a soldier nor a politician. I'm a doctor."

"I do know that. I also know that we've been betrayed by our previous leaders. Our only hope is that men like yourself can offer an alternative."

"But you have the expertise that can. . . ."

"Doctor, I have the expertise that comes from survival and compromise. There's already plenty of that on the other side . . . and it's not an alternative that will create a new and lasting union."

"No, I suppose you're right," he conceded.

"You're a doctor, yes, and that's your strength. I've learned something about your profession over the past several years. Don't think like a politician. Think of the planet as a patient barely hanging on to life. Think like a doctor. How would you save this planet?" He considered what I'd said in his careful manner.

"Thank you, Elim. I'll keep you informed." He started to leave. A group of people were gathered at a nearby formation chanting names of the dead.

"Ah, Doctor," I stopped him. "You can't go to your meeting like that."

"Like what?" he asked with a puzzled look. Without explaining, I helped him out of his worn outer coat and showed him a ragged tear in the fabric. Despite his protests, I made him sit down and wait while I gathered my sewing kit and repaired the tear.

"Appearances are very important to these people. You can't let them think you're oblivious to details," I said, as I reunited the torn and separated threads.

My suspicions were correct: the more the Directorate pushed their aggressive agenda, the more their support eroded. The appetite for violent confrontation among the survivors simply wasn't sufficient; those few who wanted to enforce their will by any means found themselves surrounded and isolated by a vast majority who wanted nothing to do with them. In their meeting with Parmak and Ghemor, the Directorate had finally agreed to a "voting competition" between representatives of the Restoration and the Reunion Project in each sector. With few exceptions this modified but radical competition would take place throughout Cardassia on the day celebrating Tret Akleen's founding of the early Union. This satisfied both sides, since each claimed that the day supported and validated their legitimacy.

The actual procedure of the competition was both crude and complicated. Members of both sides would witness the actual voting at the designated voting areas, and archons would oversee the counting of the votes and adjudicate any disputes. To my surprise, the voting competition in the Paldar Sector would take place at my memorial. This last point was hotly disputed by Legate Parn, Gul Hadar, and Mondrig, but in the end they had to acquiesce because they couldn't come up with a reasonable alternative (and, ironically, they were outvoted by the others). The memorial had already been established as the only public area in the sector.

Parmak had been able to pass on my message to Pythas, who received it, according to the Doctor, without any response. Ghemor had received no recognition from Pythas, and I think he doubted my claim that this was his schoolmate Eight Lubak. Whatever had happened, his physical disfigurement was a mask that reflected a deeper change. As I worked with my colleagues preparing and setting up the memorial for the following day's voting competition, I wondered if I would ever see him again. The thought occurred to me that perhaps I should include him in a chant for the dead.

"I think we're ready," Parmak pronounced with satisfaction. We had arranged a path that people would follow to insure an orderly progression.

"How many people are we anticipating?" I asked. Parmak and Ghemor just looked at me, and I realized that there was no way of knowing. We didn't even know how many people were left in the sector.

"Hopefully, tomorrow's vote will give us an idea," Alon finally replied. "I think we should get some rest before the competition begins. We've done what we can." It was a wise suggestion, but each of us knew that we were taking a step into the unknown, and sleep at this point was not really a choice. We *had* done what we could, and probably it was best if each of us retired to the privacy of his own thoughts. We said our goodnights, and as I watched them leave I felt an enormous gratitude that I had been given the opportunity to work with these men. Once again in my life I felt that I had been resurrected from the dead.

I moved to the constructed formation that stood in the space formerly occupied by Tain's study and almost directly above where Mila's body had been sadly abandoned in the basement. When I was a boy, I had unending dreams that centered around the memorials of Tarlak. As I lay on my pallet in the basement of Tain's house, I would plan the scenario that would play out when Tolan took me with him to Tarlak. It would always involve me as the hero paying homage to a comrade fallen in a battle where we had both distinguished ourselves. I would tell the gathered assembly of notables every detail of the battle; people would weep, cheer, listen in stunned amazement as I explained how we had saved the Union from certain destruction. When I had finished, Mila and Tolan would escort me through the adoring crowd. What a terrible irony, Doctor, that those forbidding, impersonal memorials to the heroes of the Cardassian Union should ultimately become transformed into these ragged formations on the grounds of my childhood home . . . and that I would sit here, a middle-aged man, trying to mourn a fallen comrade who was still standing but barely recognizable. And yet, the irony of a Cardassia reborn with the help of a memorial built from the remains of Tain's home didn't escape me either.

"Elim." The voice was hoarse, strangled, but I knew it was him. He was the only person who could creep up on me like that. I turned, and he stood there—with the help of a walking stick. Behind him was the silent, impassive Nal Dejar. She was **obviously** his constant companion.

"Pythas." The same mocking smile.

"Get too lost in your thoughts, people can surprise you," he rasped.

"Or ghosts from the past."

"I came close."

"I was beginning to think I had imagined you at Madred's."

"Not very pretty, is it?"

"What happened?" I asked. He shook his head, his mocking smile tinged with bitterness.

"Nothing that hasn't happened to millions of others. I was one of the lucky ones." I didn't press him for details; there was another question I wanted to ask.

"I was surprised to see you at Madred's."

"I could tell," he replied. Pythas looked at me with his one good eye, amused, I'm sure, by my barely contained curiosity.

"Are you a member of the Directorate?" I asked.

"I was." I waited for him to explain, but I had forgotten that maddening habit he had of leaving questions half answered and hanging. This time I was going to press him.

"What changed your mind?"

"Your friends, Elim. Very impressive people . . . and persuasive."

"What had you expected?" I asked.

"The usual amateurs who never understood what was at stake . . . the hard choices that had to be made," he explained. "To be honest, I had thought your attachment to this Reunion Project was. . . ."

"Sentimental," I finished. He smiled knowingly at the reference.

"But when I heard Ghemor—someone I have always respected—and especially this Dr. Parmak speak, it became clear to me that we were fighting a rearguard action and calling it leadership. Parn and Hadar tried to dismiss what he said as Federation propaganda, but Evek and Ocett were also affected." With the help of his stick he lowered himself carefully to a sitting position. "As I listened to him speak of the responsibility that we had as survivors to the life that remained, I also realized how bitter and hardened I had become." He stopped and looked back to Nal Dejar, as if he were making sure she was still there. She met his eyes with a communication I couldn't decipher, and he nodded. "Nal nursed me back to where I could function . . . part of me wished she hadn't. Until your doctor spoke about healing . . . on every level. It's what the body wants, he told us . . . unless we choose otherwise." Pythas sat with his head bowed for a long moment. "I'd become very bitter, Elim." I sat on a rock across from him and gently put my hand on his. What was it about this place, I wondered. And I remembered Parmak saying that if we couldn't mourn, we couldn't move ahead.

"Healing on every level," I repeated. After another long moment Pythas turned and nodded again to Nal Dejar who stepped forward.

"I'll be back tomorrow," he said.

"To vote?"

"Whatever you call it," he replied. Dejar helped him up. I began to understand how difficult movement was for him. Judging from his hands and the way he moved, his entire body was certainly covered with terrible burns.

"You were in the grounds that night, weren't you?" I asked.

"Yes," he replied. "I wanted to warn you."

"But Tain wouldn't let you."

"Does it matter, Elim?" Pythas's voice was less hoarse and more like his own.

"Do you know where Palandine is?" I asked. He just looked at me. "Is she still alive?"

In the darkness, it was difficult to read the expression in his one good eye. The silence that followed my question was broken only by his rasping breath. Behind her mask of disinterest Nal Dejar was studying me carefully. Even when she was a probe I was impressed by the strength of her focus. Pythas was fortunate to have her care and devotion.

"The group you took her to. . . ." Pythas cleared his throat. "The Oralian Way. Look there." Slowly they made their way back through the shadowy memorials. Movement was not only difficult for Pythas, it was painful. Had he followed me there as well? Had Tain assigned my friend to be my shadow all these years? And does it matter now?

"Thank you, Pythas," I called after their retreating outlines. Without turning, he partially raised his free left arm in farewell.

I looked up. The Prime Taluvian Constellation and the Blind Moon were barely visible. It was unusual to see any light beyond the dust clouds that still hovered over the planet. I remembered that evening in the Bamarren Grounds. Just enough light, I thought. Just enough light for lovers. I squinted to make out the faint pulse of the Constellation. I tried to measure its rhythm, to decipher the hidden code. Following a sudden thought I put my hand over my heart . . . and the two pulses began to synchronize. As they came together as one, I felt like the child who made no distinction between his dreams and his waking life. For those brief, eternal pulses. . . .

Cracks of early dawn opened throughout the darkness, and the Constellation and the Blind Moon were absorbed into the growing light. I heard voices, and when I looked in their direction I could see people beginning to gather at the edge of the memorials.

Just enough light to begin, I thought.

EPILOGUE

". . . it's just Garak. Plain, simple Garak."

My dear Doctor:

Again, forgive my further tardiness in sending this—I don't even know what to call it. Memoirs of a Cardassian tailor? I suppose that's as accurate a description as any. You see, Doctor, I seriously debated whether or not I should send this to you. As I went over it I wondered who this mawkish and self-serving person was. Grow up! I wanted to tell him. Get on with your life.

Well, I am; and sending this to you is going to further that cause. As I said, I'm an unfinished man reassembling the pieces of a broken world, and I have asked you to be a witness because you would never judge me as harshly as I judge myself. You would never deny me the opportunity of a second chance.

Someone once said that democracy was the flawed solution to a perfect mess . . . and I absolutely agree. The Reunion Project won a majority in four of the six sectors, and instead of being able to impose their will on the political situation, everything is discussed endlessly . . . and then put to yet another vote! Is this your vaunted democracy, Doctor? To be subjected to the opinion of any person who has the breath to utter one? How does anything get accomplished? If this is—as some fervently believe—a Federation plot to diminish Cardassian involvement in the quadrant, then it has succeeded ingeniously. We're much too involved in discussions over power grids and waste disposal to care about anything else.

But I am getting on with my life. And oddly enough

my home is somehow emblematic of my progress. It ends up being a true memorial to Mila and Tain and Tolan, but the paradox is that I have never felt so free of their influence. Wherever I am along my fateline, Doctor, I no longer feel that my life is a reaction to the choices other people have made for me.

I live with my orchids, which have unified and softened the increasingly popular grounds of my home. Their beguiling blooms, and the presence of children who come to play among the structures (as I did in Tarlak), help to dispel the somber mood that initially hung like those clouds of dust over our world. The sounds of their voices as they play function as a music that never fails to lighten my work. The children call it the "tailor's grounds," and the name has caught on. Yes, Doctor, I continue to work at my "new" profession. As you can imagine, there's a good deal of mending to be done.

And what of Paladine? I went to the Oralian Way in a state of anxious expectation. As we filed into the makeshift meeting room, I tried to be discreet as I searched for her face. The ceremony began and a young woman, whose eyes and strong features looked disconcertingly familiar to me, stepped onto the dais and began to read form the Hebitian Records. It was her voice, Doctor. It wasn't Palandine, but it was *her voice*. And then I realized—it was Kel. She had grown into a powerful young woman with a sturdy beauty that was a harmonious blend of both parents. I was totally disoriented, and when the meeting was over I didn't know what to do. It was clear from her behavior and conversations with the other people that she was deeply involved with both the Oralian Way and the rebuilding process. I wanted to introduce myself and ask her about Paladine—

but I didn't dare. I was afraid that if she knew the truth, she'd only be able to see me as the man who killed her father and destroyed her family.

I'm sure it doesn't come as a big surprise, Doctor, when I tell you that I attend the Oralian Way meetings on a regular basis. Now that the group is no longer outlawed, the meetings have become quite popular with the people curious to learn about the Hebitians and their culture. Kel has become one of the Guide's assistants, and her work with the recitation mask is deeply moving. Palandine, however, is nowhere to be seen, and all my attempts to gather information about her are fruitless. Kel would be my only source, but there's a distance between us I don't know if we'll ever be able to bridge.

So, for the moment, I am satisfied to witness her spiritual growth . . . and to hear the echo of a lilting voice that long ago drew me out of my pain and self-pity in the Bamarren training area.

I have expanded my shed in the never-ending quest to find my place. I feel that I'm getting closer, Doctor, especially as I continue to refine the structures. One, which began as a memorial to Tolan, has a crude but effective representation of the winged creature from the Hebitian sun disc—turned toward the radiating sun, reaching, striving, while the sun-fed filaments stream down from the body and connect with the bodies of people standing on a globe and looking up to the creature for this divine connection. . . . I've attached the recitation mask he gave me to the creature's face, and somehow it has become my personal totem. I hope that someday you'll have the opportunity to see it. Nothing would please me more. You're always welcome, Doctor.

Prologue quote from "The Wire." Written by Robert Hewitt Wolfe.

Part I quote from "In Purgatory's Shadow." Written by Robert Hewitt Wolfe & Ira Steven Behr.

Part II quote from "Cardassians." Story by Gene Wolande & John Wright. Teleplay by James Crocker.

Part III quote from "In the Pale Moonlight." Story by Peter Allan Fields. Teleplay by Michael Taylor.

Epilogue quote from "Past Prologue." Written by Kathryn Powers.

ACKNOWLEDGMENTS

Gratitude begins with Rick Berman and Ira Steven Behr, who hired the actor who didn't know a Cardassian from the man in the moon: Thank you for your trust and support.

Thanks also to Peter Allan Fields, who created the character, and to the writing staff (especially Robert Hewitt Wolfe) who nurtured and guided Garak's progress, under Ira's sharp and unerring eye. If it ain't on the page. . . .

Thanks to Denise and Michael Okuda, whose *Star Trek Encyclopedia* was my constant companion; to Matthew Lesher, my hard-working and enthusiastic manager; to Lolita Fatjo and the Stillwells, Eric and Debra, for *Trek* guidance and wisdom; to Armin Shimerman and David George not only for encouraging me but for leading the way; to John Ordover of Pocket Books, who first said yes; to Gayle Stever for her Herculean efforts on behalf of fandom and our chosen charity, Save the Children; to the amazing cast, crew, and staff of *Star Trek: Deep Space Nine,* a show that dared to walk on the wild side; and to the fans, without whom there would be no *Trek.*

ACKNOWLEDGMENTS

Thanks, finally, to Margaret Clark, my intrepid and thoroughly informed editor who not only gave me the kind of creative guidance that helped me find the book's spine, but who knew that *hasperat* was a Bajoran not a Cardassian dish—thereby saving me from eternal *Trek* infamy.

OUR FIRST SERIAL NOVEL!

Presenting, one chapter
per month . . .

The very beginning of the
Starfleet Adventure . . .

**STAR TREK®
STARFLEET: YEAR ONE**

A novel in Twelve Parts®

by
Michael Jan Friedman

Chapter Ten

Hiro Matsura had retrieved his pod and was about to break orbit when his navigator notified him that the *Maverick* was in the vicinity.

Matsura hadn't expected any company at Oreias Seven. "On screen," he said, settling back into his center seat.

A moment later, Connor Dane's face filled the forward viewscreen. He didn't seem pleased.

"Tell me you had better luck than we did," said Dane.

Matsura shook his head. "My team didn't find anything of significance."

Dane scowled. "Maybe we'll figure something out when we compare notes with Shumar and Cobaryn."

Matsura couldn't keep from smiling a little. "You really think so?"

Dane looked at him. "Don't you?"

"With all due respect," Matsura told him, "I think we can sit and compare notes until the last days of the universe, and we'll still just be groping in the dark."

Dane's eyes narrowed. "And you've got a better way to dope out what happened?"

"I think Captain Stiles had the right idea," said Matsura. "The only way we're going to find the aliens is by going out and looking for them."

"It's not that big a system," Dane responded. "We don't *all* have to be looking for them."

"It would speed things up," Matsura noted.

"Or slow them down," said Dane, "by putting all our eggs in the wrong basket. Depends on how you look at it."

Matsura was surprised at the man's attitude. "I didn't know you had such deep respect for research scientists."

Dane's mouth twisted at the other man's tone. "You mean butterfly catchers, don't you?"

Matsura found himself turning red. "I don't use that terminology."

"But your buddies do," the other man observed. "And don't insult my intelligence by claiming otherwise."

"All right," said Matsura, "I won't."

That seemed to pacify Dane a bit. "At least you're honest," he conceded.

"Thanks. Now, I'm sorry you took the trouble to fly all the way over here, but I'm leaving to try to hook up with Stiles and Hagedorn. You're welcome to join me if you'd like."

Dane snorted. "I'll put my money on Shumar and Cobaryn."

"Suit yourself," said Matsura. "I'll—"

Suddenly, his navigator interrupted him. "Sir," said Williams, her face drawn with concern as she consulted her monitor, "we're picking up a number of unidentified vessels."

The captain saw Dane turn away from the viewscreen and spit a command at one of his officers. He didn't look happy.

For that matter, Matsura wasn't very happy either. "Give me visual," he told Williams.

A moment later, Dane's image vanished from the viewscreen, to be replaced by that of three small, triangular vessels. They were gleaming in the glare of Oreias as they approached.

The aggressors, Matsura thought. It had to be.

"Raise shields," he announced. "Power to all batteries."

"Raising shields," Williams confirmed.

"Power to lasers and launchers," said his weapons officer.

"You still there?" asked Matsura over their comm link.

"Yeah, I'm here," came Dane's response. "But I've got to tell you, I'm not much of a team player."

No big surprise there, Matsura told himself. "I'll try to work with you anyway. Leave your comm link open. If I see an alien on your tail, I can give you a holler."

"Acknowledged," said Dane.

Then the enemy was on top of them. Or rather, the triangular vessels were plunging past them—so intent on the colony, it seemed, that they were ignoring the *Christophers* above it.

Matsura took the slight personally. "Lock lasers on the nearest ship," he told his weapons officer.

"Targeting," said Wickersham, a fair-haired man with a narrow face and deep-set eyes.

"Fire!" the captain commanded.

Their electric-blue beams reached out and skewered the enemy vessel—failing to disable it, but getting its attention. It came about like an angry bee and returned fire, sending out a string of scarlet fireballs.

"Evade!" Matsura called out.

But they weren't fast enough. The energy clusters plowed into the *Yellowjacket*, sending a bone-rattling jolt through the deckplates.

The aliens packed a punch, the captain realized. He had made the mistake of judging their firepower by their size.

"Another one on our port beam!" said Williams.

"Split the difference!" Matsura ordered.

At the helm console, McCallum worked feverishly. What's more, his efforts paid off. The *Yellowjacket* sliced between the two triangular ships, preventing them from firing for the moment.

Suddenly, the third vessel loomed on Matsura's viewscreen, its underbelly exposed, filling the entire frame with its unexpected proximity. He had never had such an easy target and he might never have one again.

"Target lasers and fire!" he commanded.

At close range, their beams seemed to do a good deal more damage. The enemy staggered under the impact.

"Their shields are at twenty-eight percent," Williams reported.

A barrage of atomics might take the alien out of the fight, the captain noted. But before he could launch one, the enemy was bludgeoned with blasts of white fury.

Dane, Matsura thought.

"Their tactical systems are offline," his navigator told him.

The captain could have finished off the alien then and there. However, the vessel wasn't in a position to hurt the colony anymore, and he still had two other marauders to worry about.

"Where are the others?" he asked Williams.

She worked at her console. "Right here, sir."

A moment later, he saw the two still-capable triangles on his viewscreen. They were going after the *Maverick* with their energy weapons blazing, trying to catch her in a deadly crossfire.

Unlike Matsura, Dane didn't make an attempt to dart between his adversaries. He headed straight for one of them, exposing his starboard flank to the other.

It was a maneuver that depended on the enemy's being caught by surprise and veering off. But if that didn't happen, it was suicide.

Had Matsura been fighting both the aliens on his own, he might have made an effort to do something similar. As it was, he found the move reckless to the point of insanity.

You idiot, he thought—and not just because Dane had endangered his own ship. By placing himself in jeopardy, he had made it necessary for the *Yellowjacket* to expose herself as well.

Matsura frowned. "Pursue the vessel to port, Mr. Weeks! Target lasers and fire!"

Weeks managed to nail the enemy from behind with both blue beams. He hit the triangle hard enough to keep it from striking the *Maverick* with an energy volley, but—unfortunately—not hard enough to cripple it.

As they dogged the alien ship, trying to lock on for another shot, the captain saw the other triangle peel off to avoid the *Maverick*—just as Dane had gambled it would.

But as surely as the *Maverick* had climbed out of the fire, the *Yellowjacket* was falling into it. As Weeks released another laser barrage, the enemy to port looped around with amazing dexterity. Then it came for Matsura and his crew, its weapons belching bundle after bundle of crimson brilliance.

"Hard to starboard!" the captain called out, hoping to pull his ship out of harm's way.

But it was no use. The alien's energy clusters dazzled his screen and rammed the *Yellowjacket* with explosive force—once, twice, and again, finally wrenching Matsura out of his captain's chair and pitching him sideways across the deck.

Behind him, a control console erupted in a shower of sparks. Black smoke collected above it like a bad omen. There were cries of pain and dismay, punctuated by frantic status reports.

"Shields are down!"

"Hull breaches on decks five and six!"

"Lasers and atomics are inoperable!"

Dazed, Matsura watched someone grab a fire extinguisher from the rack on the wall. Ignoring a stinging wetness over his right eye, he dragged himself to his feet and made his way back to his center seat.

On the static-riddled viewscreen, the battle had advanced while Matsura was pulling himself together. Somehow, Dane had incapacitated another of the enemy's vessels because only the *Maverick* and one of the aliens were still exchanging fire.

Abruptly, the commander of the triangle decided to change tactics. The ship broke off the engagement and went hurtling out into the void. And just as abruptly, its sister ships departed in its wake.

Matsura's first instinct was to follow them. Then he remembered that the *Yellowjacket* was in no shape to pursue *anyone*.

Without shields and weapons, she was all but helpless. The captain looked around at his bridge officers. They looked relieved that the battle was over, especially the ones who had sustained injuries.

"Casualties?" Matsura asked, not looking forward to the response he might get.

Williams, who looked shaken but not hurt, consulted her monitor. "Sickbay has three reports, sir, but more are expected. No fatalities as far as the doctor can tell."

The captain frowned. "Dispatch a couple of engineering teams to see to those hull breaches."

Williams nodded. "Aye, sir."

Matsura turned to Weeks, who was holding a damaged left arm and grimacing. "Tacticals are a mess, sir," he got out. "I'll see to bringing them back online, but it's going to take a while."

"First," the captain said, "you'll get yourself to sickbay."

"But, sir," Weeks protested, looking even more pained than before, "we're in need of—"

"Repairs? Yes, we are," Matsura told him. "But they can be carried out without you."

The weapons officer looked like he was going to put up a fight. Then he said, "Aye, sir," and made his way to the lift.

Matsura was about to check on his propulsion system when Williams spoke up. "Sir, Captain Dane is asking to speak with you."

His jaw clenching, the captain nodded. "Link him in."

A moment later, Dane appeared on the viewscreen. "You look like you took a beating," he observed. "What's your situation?"

"The situation," said the captain, doing his best to keep his voice free of anger, "is I've lost my lasers, my atomics, and my shield generators. And that's just a superficial assessment."

Dane grunted. "Tough luck. We suffered a little damage ourselves." He began tapping a command into his armrest. "I'll contact the others and let them know what happened here."

Matsura's mouth fell open. That was it? he wondered. No thanks? No recognition that he had put his ship and crew on the line to bail out a reckless fool of a comrade?

If this had been an Earth Command mission, Matsura's wing-mates would have been quick to acknowledge what he had done. But this wasn't Earth Command, he reminded himself bitterly. It was something completely different.

And Connor Dane was still a Cochrane jockey at heart, taking low-percentage chances as if his life were the only one at stake.

Matsura was tempted to lash out at the man, to tell him how he felt; but he wouldn't do that with two complements of bridge officers privy to the conversation. He would arrange a better time.

"You do that," Matsura said. "And when you're done, I'd like to speak with you. In private."

For the first time, it seemed to dawn on the other man that his colleague might not be entirely happy with him. "No problem," Dane answered casually. "I'll tell my transporter operator to expect you."

"*Yellowjacket* out," said Matsura—and terminated the link.

A moment later, Dane's face vanished from the screen, replaced with a view of his *Christopher.* Matsura studied it for a moment, his resentment building inside him.

Then he got up from his center seat. "You've got the conn," he told Lieutenant Williams and headed for the *Yellowjacket*'s transporter room.

As far as he knew, *that* system was still working.

"I'd ask you to pardon the mess," Dane said, "but I might as well tell you, it's like this all the time."

Matsura didn't say anything in response. He just frowned disapprovingly, looked around Dane's cluttered anteroom and found an empty seat.

Obviously, Matsura wasn't pleased with him. And just as obviously, Dane was about to hear why. Removing yesterday's uniform from his workstation chair, Dane tossed it into a pile in the corner of the room and sat down.

"All right," he told his fellow captain. "There's something you want to get off your chest, right? So go ahead."

Matsura glared at him. "Fine. If you want me to be blunt, I'll be blunt. What you did out there a minute ago was foolish and ir-responsible. Leaving your flank exposed, forcing me to go in and protect it . . . you're lucky you didn't get us all killed."

Dane looked at him. "Is that so?"

"You're damned right," Matsura shot back. "No Earth Command captain would ever have taken a chance like that."

Dane shrugged. "Then maybe they should consider it."

"Are you out of your mind?" asked Matsura, turning dark with anger. "You're going to defend that gambit—after it crippled my ship and injured seventeen of my crewmen?"

Dane smiled a thin smile. "Given a million chances, I'd do it a million times . . . hands down, no contest."

Matsura was speechless.

"Of course," Dane went on, "I'm not one of the noble black and gold, so none of my skill or experience means a flipping thing. But I'll tell you what . . . I've met a few Romulans in my day too. In fact, I was blasting them out of space long before you ever warmed your butt in a center seat."

Matsura's eyes narrowed. "There's a difference between expe-rience and luck," he pointed out.

"Men make their own luck," Dane told him. "I make mine by pushing the envelope—by doing what they least expect. Come to think of it, you might want to think about pushing the envelope a little yourself."

"Me . . . ?" Matsura asked.

"That's right. Dare to be different. Or do you want to spend the rest of your life living in your flyboy buddies' shadow?"

Matsura's jaw clenched. "I don't live in anyone's shadow—not Hagedorn's or Stiles's or anyone else's. What I do is carry out my mission within the parameters of good sense."

Dane grunted. "Right."

"You think otherwise?"

Dane shrugged. "I think good sense is what people hide behind when they can't do any better."

"Says the man who hasn't got any."

"Says the man who accomplished his mission," Dane noted.

Matsura flushed and got to his feet. "Obviously, I'm wasting my time talking to you. You know everything."

"Funny," said Dane, keeping his voice nice and even. "I was just about to tell you the same thing."

Matsura's mouth twisted.

"And just for the record," said Dane, "I didn't expect you to protect my flank. As I said, I'm not much of a team player."

The other man didn't respond to that one. He just turned his back on Dane, tapped the door control and left.

The captain shook his head. Matsura had potential—anyone with an eye in his head could see that. But the way things were going, it didn't look like he was going to realize it.

Not that that's any of *my* headache, Dane told himself, leaning back in his chair and closing his eyes.

Matsura was still boiling over Dane's remarks as he left the *Yellowjacket*'s transporter room . . . and on an impulse, headed for a part of his vessel he hadn't had occasion to visit lately.

Men make their own luck, Dane had told him.

But Matsura had done that, hadn't he? During the war, he had been as effective a weapon as Earth Command could have asked for. He had risen to every challenge thrown his way.

But Dane wasn't talking about efficiency or determination. He was talking about thinking outside the box. He was talking about a willingness to try something different.

You might want to think about pushing the envelope . . .

And, damn it, Matsura would do just that. He would show Dane that he could take the direction least expected of him—and do more with it than the butterfly catchers themselves.

Neither Shumar, Cobaryn, nor Dane had discovered anything of value with all their meticulous site scanning. But with the help of his research team, Matsura would turn up something. He would find a way to beat the aliens that his colleagues had overlooked.

Or do you want to spend the rest of your life living in your flyboy buddies' shadow?

Matsura swore beneath his breath. Dane was wrong about him—dead wrong—and he was going to make the arrogant sonuvagun see that.

The captain had barely completed the thought when he realized that his destination was looming just ahead of him. Arriving at the appropriate set of doors, he tapped the control pad on the bulkhead and watched the titanium panels slide aside.

Once, this relatively large compartment on Deck Eight had been a supply bay. It had been converted by Starfleet into a research laboratory, equipped with three state-of-the-art computer workstations and a stationary scanner that was three times as sensitive as the portable version.

It was all Clarisse Dumont's doing. If the fleet was going to conduct research in space, she had argued, it might as well enjoy the finest instruments available.

Matsura hadn't been especially inclined to make use of them before; he had left that to those members of his crew with a more scientific bent. But he would certainly make use of them now.

"Mr. Siefried," he said, addressing one of the three crewmen who had beamed down to the colony to collect data.

Siefried, a lanky mineralogist with sharp features and close-cropped hair, evinced surprise as he swiveled in his seat. After all, it wasn't every day that Matsura made an appearance there.

"Sir?" said Siefried.

"What have we got?" asked the captain, trying his best to keep his anger at Dane under wraps.

The mineralogist shrugged his bony shoulders. "Not much more than we had before, I'm afraid. At least, nothing that would explain why the aliens attacked the colony."

Matsura turned to Arquette, a compact man with startling blue eyes. "Anything to add to that?" he asked.

Arquette, an exobiologist, shook his head. "Nothing, sir. Just the same materials we saw before. But I'm still working on it."

"Perhaps if we had a context," said Smithson, a buxom physicist who specialized in energy emissions, "some kind of backdrop against which we could interpret the data."

"That would be helpful, all right," Matsura agreed. "Then again, if we knew something about these aliens, we probably wouldn't have needed to do site research in the first place."

The scan team looked disheartened by his remark. Realizing what he had done, the captain held his hand up in a plea for understanding. "Sorry. I didn't mean that the way it came out."

"It's all right, sir," said Smithson, in an almost motherly tone of voice. "It's been a frustrating time for all of us."

Matsura nodded. "To say the least."

But he wasn't going to accept defeat so easily. Not when Dane's smugness was still so vivid in his memory.

"Do you mind if I take a look?" he asked Smithson.

"Not at all," said the physicist, getting up from her seat to give the captain access to her monitor.

Depositing himself behind the workstation, Matsura took a

look at the screen, on which the Oreias Seven colony was mapped out in bright blue lines on a black field. He hadn't actually seen the site in person, so he took a moment to study it.

Immediately, a question came to mind.

"Why does the perimeter of the colony follow these curves?" he asked, pointing to a couple of scalloped areas near the top of the plan.

"There are hills there," said Siefried, who had come over to stand behind him. "Not steep ones, mind you, but steep enough to keep the colonists from erecting their domes."

Makes sense, the captain thought. Why build on a slope when you can build on a flat?

Then again, why build near hills at all? Matsura presented the question to his mineralogist.

"Actually," Siefried noted, "it would have been difficult to do otherwise. All the regions suitable for farming have hilly features. The area the colonists picked is the flattest on the planet."

"I see," said the captain.

He studied the layout of the colony some more, looking for any other detail that might trigger an insight. Nothing seemed to do that, however. Without anything else to attract Matsura's eye, it was eventually drawn back to the two scalloped areas.

"What is it, sir?" asked Arquette, who had come to stand behind the captain as well.

Matsura shook his head, trying to figure out what it was about those two half-circles that intrigued him. "Nothing, really. Or maybe . . ." He heaved a sigh. "I don't know."

But it seemed that a visit to the colony was in order. And this time, he was going to go down there *personally.*

As Bryce Shumar materialized on the *Horatio*'s transporter pad, he saw Cobaryn standing alongside the ship's transporter technician. Obviously, the Rigelian had decided to wait there for him.

That came as no surprise to Shumar. What surprised him was that Connor Dane was waiting there too.

"Welcome to the *Horatio,* sir," said the transporter operator.

Shumar nodded to the man. "Thanks, Lieutenant."

"About time you got here," the Cochrane jockey added. "Hagedorn and Stiles have probably finished all the hors d'oeuvres."

The remark was unexpected—even more so than Dane's presence there in the first place. Shumar couldn't help smiling a little. "I didn't know you were a comedian," he said.

"Who's joking?" Dane returned.

"I hate to interrupt," Cobaryn told them, "but now that Captain Shumar is here, we should get up to Captain Hagedorn's quarters as quickly as possible. I wish to be present when the decisions are made."

Shumar agreed. Together, the three of them exited the transporter room and made their way to the nearest turbolift, which carried them to the appropriate deck. From there, it was a short walk to the captain's door.

They knew that because the ships they commanded were exact replicas of the *Horatio*, designed to be identical down to the last airflow vent and intercom panel. Anyway, that had been the intent.

As the doors to Hagedorn's quarters whispered open, Shumar saw that there were at least a few details there that diverged from the standard. More to the point, Hagedorn's anteroom wasn't anything like Shumar's.

It had been furnished economically but impeccably, the walls decorated with a series of small, ancient-looking iron artifacts, the clunky, standard-issue Earth Command table and chairs replaced with a simpler and earthier-looking version in a tawny, unfinished wood.

Interestingly, there weren't any of the *customary* personal effects to be seen. Not a medal—though Hagedorn must have won lots of them. Not an exotic liquor bottle, a musical instrument, an alien statuette, or an unusual mineral specimen. Not a hat, a globe, or a 3-D chessboard.

Not even a picture of a loved one.

Shumar found the place a little off-putting in its spartan outlook, in its minimalism. However, it looked considerably bigger than Shumar's own anteroom. So much so, in fact, that he didn't feel cramped sharing the space with his five colleagues.

Then it occurred to Shumar that only *four* of his colleagues were present. Matsura was conspicuous by his absence.

"Come on in," said Hagedorn, his manner cordial if a bit too crisp for Shumar's taste. "Can I get you anything?"

Shumar noticed that neither Hagedorn nor Stiles had a drink in his hand. "Nothing, thanks. Where's Captain Matsura?"

Stiles frowned. "He'll be a few minutes late. He wanted to check out the Oreias Seven colony himself."

"Didn't he do that already?" asked Shumar.

"Apparently not," Hagedorn replied, obviously unperturbed by his colleague's oversight.

"You forget," said Stiles, "some of us aren't scientists."

Shumar hadn't forgotten. He just couldn't believe his fellow captains hadn't seen a value in examining the colonies firsthand.

"Why don't we get down to business?" asked Dane. "We can bring Matsura up to speed when he gets here."

Shumar had never heard Dane take such a purposeful tack before. Was this the same man who had lingered over his tequila while everyone around him was scrambling to fight the Romulans?

It seemed Connor Dane was *full* of surprises today.

Stiles glanced at Hagedorn. "I agree. It's not as if we don't know where Matsura will come down in this matter."

Hagedorn must have been reasonably sure of Matsura as well because he went ahead with the meeting. "All right, then," he said. "We're all aware of the facts. We've scanned all four colonies in this system, including the two the aliens have already attacked, and we haven't discovered anything to explain their aggressive behavior."

"Fortunately, we've shown we can track them down," said Stiles, picking up where his comrade left off. "But we can't match their firepower or their maneuverability unless we come at them with everything we've got."

"Even with the *Yellowjacket* damaged," Hagedorn noted, "we've still got five battleworthy ships left. I propose we deploy them as a group in order to find the aliens and defuse the threat."

"It's the only viable course of action open to us," Stiles maintained. "Anything less and we'll be lucky to fight them to a draw again."

Silence reigned in the room as they considered the man's advice. Then Hagedorn said, "What do the rest of you think?"

In other words, thought Shumar, you three butterfly catchers.

Cobaryn was the first to speak up. "I agree with Captain Stiles's assessment," he responded.

Shumar was surprised at how easily his friend had been swayed. It must have shown on his face because the Rigelian turned to him with a hint of an apology in his eyes.

"Believe me," said Cobaryn, "I wish we could have come up with another solution to the problem. However, I do not see one presenting itself, and the colonists are depending on us to protect them."

It was hard to argue with such logic. Even Shumar had to admit that.

Dane was frowning deeply, looking uncharacteristically thoughtful.

"You seem hesitant," Stiles observed, an undercurrent of mockery in his voice. "I hope you're not thinking of hanging back while the rest of us go into battle."

Obviously, thought Shumar, some bone of contention existed between Stiles and Dane. In fact, now that Shumar had occasion to think about it, he was reminded of an exchange of remarks between the two at the captains' first briefing back on Earth.

In response to Stiles's taunt, the Cochrane jockey smiled jauntily. "What?" he asked, his voice as sharp-edged as the other man's. "And let you have all the fun?"

Ever the cool head, Hagedorn interceded. "This is a serious situation, gentlemen. There's no place at this meeting for personalities."

"You're right," said Stiles. "I was out of line." But neither his expression nor his tone suggested repentance.

Hagedorn turned to Shumar. His demeanor was that of one reasonable man speaking to another.

"And you, Captain?" he asked.

As his colleagues looked on, Shumar mulled over the proposition before him. Part of him was tempted to do what Cobaryn was doing, if only for the sake of the colonists' continued well-being.

Then there was the other part of him.

Shumar shook his head. "Unfortunately, I'm going to have to break with the party line. I'll be beaming down to Oreias Seven in order to continue my investigation."

"Are you sure you want to do that?" asked Hagedorn.

Shumar nodded. "Quite sure."

"What about your ship?" Stiles inquired.

Shumar understood the question. Stiles wanted the *Peregrine* to go with the rest of the fleet to increase their chances of a victory. What's more, Shumar didn't blame him.

"My ship will go with you," he assured Stiles.

"Under whose command?" Stiles pressed.

"That of my first officer, Stephen Mullen. From what I've seen of him, he's more than qualified to command the *Peregrine*. In fact, considering all the military experience he's got under his belt, you'll probably feel more comfortable with *him* than you do with *me*."

But that didn't seem to be good enough for Stiles, who shot a glance at Hagedorn. "As it happens," he argued, "we've got an experienced commanding officer without a viable vessel. Why not put Captain Matsura in the center seat of the *Peregrine?*"

Shumar didn't like the idea. After all, Mullen had demonstrated an ability to work smoothly with the *Peregrine*'s crew. Besides, he wasn't going to let Stiles or anyone else decide whom to put in charge of his vessel.

But before he could say anything, the doors to Hagedorn's anteroom slid aside again and Matsura joined them, his forehead slick with perspiration. "Sorry I'm late," he said.

"It's all right," Stiles assured him. In a matter of moments, he brought his Earth Command comrade up to date. "So, since Captain Shumar has decided to stay here, we're talking about putting you in command of his ship."

"Which isn't going to happen," Shumar interjected matter-of-factly. "Captain Stiles may have missed it, but I've already decided who's going to command the *Peregrine*."

Stiles's look turned disparaging. "With all due respect, Captain—"

Matsura held up his hand, stopping Stiles in mid-objection. "There's no need to argue about it," he said. "As it happens, I'd prefer to stay here with Captain Shumar."

Stiles looked at Matsura as if he were crazy. "What the devil for?"

Shumar wanted to know the answer to that question himself.

Look for STAR TREK fiction from Pocket Books

Star Trek®: The Original Series

Star Trek: The Next Generation®

Star Trek: Voyager®

Star Trek®: New Frontier

New Frontier #1-4 Collector's Edition • Peter David
#1 • *House of Cards* • Peter David
#2 • *Into the Void* • Peter David
#3 • *The Two-Front War* • Peter David
#4 • *End Game* • Peter David
#5 • *Martyr* • Peter David
#6 • *Fire on High* • Peter David
The Captain's Table #5 • *Once Burned* • Peter David
Double Helix #5 • *Double or Nothing* • Peter David
#7 • *The Quiet Place* • Peter David
#8 • *Dark Allies* • Peter David

Star Trek®: Invasion!

#1 • *First Strike* • Diane Carey
#2 • *The Soldiers of Fear* • Dean Wesley Smith & Kristine Kathryn Rusch
#3 • *Time's Enemy* • L.A. Graf
#4 • *Final Fury* • Dafydd ab Hugh
Invasion! Omnibus • various

Star Trek®: Day of Honor

#1 • *Ancient Blood* • Diane Carey
#2 • *Armageddon Sky* • L.A. Graf
#3 • *Her Klingon Soul* • Michael Jan Friedman
#4 • *Treaty's Law* • Dean Wesley Smith & Kristine Kathryn Rusch
The Television Episode • Michael Jan Friedman
Day of Honor Omnibus • various

Star Trek®: The Captain's Table

#1 • *War Dragons* • L.A. Graf
#2 • *Dujonian's Hoard* • Michael Jan Friedman
#3 • *The Mist* • Dean Wesley Smith & Kristine Kathryn Rusch
#4 • *Fire Ship* • Diane Carey
#5 • *Once Burned* • Peter David
#6 • *Where Sea Meets Sky* • Jerry Oltion
The Captain's Table Omnibus • various

Star Trek®: The Dominion War

Star Trek®: The Badlands

Star Trek® Books available in Trade Paperback

ANALOG

SCIENCE FICTION AND FACT

Hours of thought-provoking fiction in every issue!

Explore the frontiers of scientific research and imagination. *Analog Science Fiction and Fact* magazine delivers an intellectual blend of stimulating stories, provocative editorials, and fascinating scientific fact articles from today's top writers.

**Kristine Kathryn Rusch • Jerry Oltion
Vonda N. McIntyre • Catherine Asaro • Kevin J. Anderson**

CALL TOLL-FREE TO SUBSCRIBE
1-800-333-4561

Outside the USA: 303-678-8747

Mail to: Analog • P.O. Box 54027 • Boulder, CO 80322-4027

☑ **YES!** Send me a free trial issue of *Analog* and bill me. If I'm not completely delighted, I'll write "Cancel" on the invoice and return it with no further obligation. Either way, the first issue is mine to keep. **(9 issues, just $19.97)**

Name _____

Address _____

City _____

State _____ ZIP _____

❏ Payment enclosed   ❏ Bill me

Send for your FREE trial issue of Analog today!

We publish a double issue in July/August, which counts as two issues towards your subscription. Please allow 6-8 weeks for delivery of first issue. For delivery outside U.S.A., pay $27.97 (U.S. funds) for 9 issues. Includes GST. Foreign orders must be prepaid or charged to VISA/MasterCard. Please include account number, card type, expiration date and signature. Billing option not available outside U.S.A.   5T91

STAR TREK
THE EXPERIENCE
LAS VEGAS HILTON

Be a part of the most exciting deep space adventure in the galaxy as you beam aboard the U.S.S. Enterprise. Explore the evolution of Star Trek® from television to movies in the "History of the Future Museum," the planet's largest collection of authentic Star Trek memorabilia. Then, visit distant galaxies on the "Voyage Through Space." This 22-minute action packed adventure will capture your senses with the latest in motion simulator technology. After your mission, shop in the Deep Space Nine Promenade and enjoy 24th Century cuisine in Quark's Bar & Restaurant.

Save up to $30

Present this coupon at the STAR TREK: The Experience ticket office at the Las Vegas Hilton and save $6 off each attraction admission (limit 5).

Not valid in conjunction with any other offer or promotional discount. Management reserves all rights. No cash value.
For more information, call 1-888-GOBOLDLY
or visit **www.startrekexp.com**.
Private Parties Available.

CODE:1007a   EXPIRES 12/31/00